GOLDY'S NUTHOUSE COOKIES

1½ cups blanched, slivered almonds,
toasted and cooled

½ teaspoon baking soda

½ teaspoon salt

1¼ cups (4½ ounces) cake flour

1 cup (4½ ounces) all-purpose flour

½ pound (2 sticks) unsalted butter,
softened to room temperature

2⅔ cups (10 ounces) sifted confectioners' sugar

1 large egg

1 teaspoon vanilla extract . . .

(MIXING AND BAKING DIRECTIONS CONTINUED ON PAGES 376-377)

"The queen of culinary mystery writers."
Charleston Post & Courier

"[Davidson] gives us, in Goldy,
an amateur detective who lives in a world
we understand, who interacts with people
we recognize, and who finds herself
in situations that seem entirely plausible."
Richmond Times Dispatch

"Fans of the chatty, hardworking Goldy
will be pleasantly energized."
People

"The recipes that Davidson includes
at story's end . . . leave hungry readers
with a mystery of their own: Which would
be more satisfying, settling in
for a long read or taking a kitchen break
to whip up something wonderful?"
St. Louis Post-Dispatch

"[*Double Shot*] is—forgive me, but I can't resist—
scrumptious."
Green Bay Press-Gazette

Books by Diane Mott Davidson

Double Shot
Chopping Spree
Sticks & Scones
Tough Cookie
Prime Cut
The Grilling Season
The Main Corpse
Killer Pancake
The Last Suppers
The Cereal Murders
Dying for Chocolate
Catering to Nobody

DIANE MOTT DAVIDSON

DOUBLE SHOT

HarperTorch

An Imprint of HarperCollins*Publishers*

This is a work of fiction. Names, characters, places, and incidents are products of the author's imagination or are used fictitiously and are not to be construed as real. Any resemblance to actual events, locales, organizations, or persons, living or dead, is entirely coincidental.

HARPERTORCH
An Imprint of HarperCollins*Publishers*
10 East 53rd Street
New York, New York 10022-5299

Copyright © 2004 by Diane Mott Davidson
ISBN-13: 978-0-06-052730-3
ISBN-10: 0-06-052730-7

First HarperTorch paperback printing: September 2005
First William Morrow hardcover printing: November 2004

HarperCollins®, HarperTorch™, and ❦™ are trademarks of Harper-Collins Publishers Inc.

Printed in the United States of America

Visit HarperTorch on the World Wide Web at www.harpercollins.com

10 9 8 7 6 5 4 3 2 1

To Jasmine Cresswell
A brilliant writer and unfailing friend

But if any one has caused pain, he has caused it not to me, but in some measure ... to you all.

—*II Corinthians 2:5, RSV*

If you sit by the river long enough, the bodies of all your enemies will float by.

—*Chinese proverb*

Prologue

You think you know people.

You see a snapshot from the old days—from fifteen, sixteen years ago. The memories swim up. You think, *Ah yes, those people from long ago.* There were folks who were kind. Some who weren't. And then there were some you barely knew. You stare at the photograph. *Do I really remember these people?*

Define *remember.*

Then you hear about a sacrificial gift, a private kindness pitched your way. Oddly, the gift was given so you'd be kept in the dark. Is it always helpful to be the recipient of good deeds?

Define *good.*

Say the snapshot does not reveal another reality—a hidden darkness, a nefariousness. A *sin,* as we Sunday-school teachers say. At the time of the photograph, a bullet was fired from far away. Not a real bullet, mind you, but a metaphorical one. An evil was done; a cruelty committed; a line crossed over. But it was hushed up. Denied. Forgotten.

Define *forgotten.*

Because, see, some people never forget.

They're called *victims.*

Celebration of the Life of Albert Kerr, M.D.

**THE ROUNDHOUSE
TUESDAY, JUNE THE 7TH
TWELVE O'CLOCK NOON**

*Chilled Asparagus Soup
Radiatore Pasta Salad
Arugula, Watercress, and Hearts of Palm Salad,
Champagne Vinaigrette*

*Herb-Crusted Grilled and Chilled Salmon
Potatoes Anna
Spinach Soufflé
Mini-baguettes*

*Tennessee Chess Tartlets
Fresh Peach Pies
Homemade Vanilla Bean Ice Cream*

Chapter 1

It's a funny thing about being hit in the head. Afterward, you're never quite sure what happened. You only know that something did.

At five in the morning on June the seventh, I was pushing my dessert-laden old pie wagon up the walk to the Roundhouse, a failed restaurant I'd leased and was converting into a catering-events center.

At half-past five, I was lying in the grass, wondering what I was doing there and why I was in so much pain.

Reconstruct, I ordered myself, as I wiped gravel from my mouth. I hadn't fainted. But I *had* been knocked out. My head throbbed, my knees stung, and the back of my neck felt as if it had been guillotined with a dull blade. I groaned, tried to move my legs, and was rewarded with a wave of nausea. I rubbed my eyes and tried to think, but the memory remained out of reach.

My husband, a cop, often tells witnesses to begin their story at daybreak on the day they see a crime. This gives folks a chance to talk about how normal everything was before events went haywire.

So that's what I did.

I closed my eyes and recalled rising at four, when mountain chickadees, Steller's jays, and all manner of avian creatures begin their summer-in-the-Rockies concert. I showered, did my yoga, and kissed Tom, to whom I'd been married for two years, good-bye. He mumbled that he'd be in his office at the sheriff's department later in the day.

When I checked on my son, Arch, he was slumbering deeply inside his cocoon of dark blue sheets. I knew Arch would wait until the last possible moment before getting dressed to assist with that day's catered event. But at least he was helping out, which was more than most fifteen-year-olds would be willing to do at the start of summer vacation. I loaded the last of the event's foodstuffs into my catering van, made the short drive up Aspen Meadow's Main Street, and rounded the lake. A quarter mile along Upper Cottonwood Creek Drive, I turned into the paved Roundhouse lot, where I'd parked and unloaded.

So far so good. I remembered merrily wheeling my cart up the gravel path toward the back door of my newly remodeled commercial kitchen. Peach pie slices glistened between lattices of flaky crust. A hundred smooth, golden, Tennessee chess tartlets bobbled in their packing. Threads of early morning sunlight shimmered on the surface of Aspen Meadow Lake, two hundred yards away. In the distance, a flock of ducks took off from the lake, quacking, flapping their wings, and ruffling the water.

Recalling all this made the area behind my eyes sting. But when I tried to turn over, pain ran up my side and I gasped. The desserts, the lake, the ducks. Then what?

As I'd steered the wagon toward the ramp to the back

entry, I'd noticed something odd about the Round-house kitchen door. It was slightly ajar.

A thread of fear had raced up my neck. My body turned cold and I stopped the cart, whose creaky wheels had been filling the morning silence. A thump echoed from out of the kitchen. Then a *crack.* As I reeled back on the path, someone leaped out of the kitchen door.

A man? A woman? Whoever it was wore a black top, black pants, and a ski mask. The intruder lunged down the ramp. Wrenching the pie wagon backward, I teetered, then backpedaled furiously. He—was it a man?—shoved the cart out of the way. It toppled over. Pastries spewed onto the grass. The prowler loomed, then hand-chopped the back of my neck. The force of the blow made me cry out.

With silver spots clouding my eyes, I'd registered crumpling, then falling. I'd bitten my tongue and tasted blood. Then there had been the terrible pain, and the darkness.

Okay, so that was what had happened. But why had someone wearing a mask been in my kitchen in the first place? I did not know. What I *did* know was that lumps of granite and sharp blades of drought-ravaged scrub grass were piercing my chest. Again I tried to lift myself, but a current of pain ran down my body. When I thought, *You have an event to cater in six hours,* tears popped out of my eyes. Who could have done this to me? Why *today,* of all days? My business, Goldilocks' Catering, Where Everything Is Just Right!, was set to put on only our second event since I'd leased the Roundhouse. It was a big lunch following a funeral—a funeral that might as well have been mine.

Water burbled nearby: Cottonwood Creek, a foot be-low its normal flow. A car rumbled past—the beginning of the morning commuter traffic from the stone and stucco mini-mansions that ranged along the upper part of the creek. Positioned as I was on the far side of the Roundhouse, it was unlikely that any of the lawyers, accountants, or doctors making their way down to Denver would see me and call for help. With enormous effort, I pushed up to my elbows, fought queasiness, and got to my feet. The overturned pie cart lay a few feet away. Crusts and fruit slices littered the sparse grass. Tartlet filling oozed into the dust.

I almost thought, *Peachy!*, but stopped myself.

I limped to the van and climbed inside. Then I locked the doors, opened the glove compartment, and pulled out the thirty-eight I'd started keeping in there since the twenty-second of April. That was when my ex-husband, Dr. John Richard Korman, had had his prison sentence commuted by the governor of Colorado.

He had been serving four years for aggravated assault and probation violation. Although he'd beaten me up plenty of times before I'd kicked him out seven years ago, the assault he'd been convicted for—finally—had been his attack on a subsequent girlfriend. Unfortunately, he'd been behind bars for less than a year.

I sighed and peered through the windshield, alert to any movement that might indicate a prowler. Could John Richard Korman have done this? For the Jerk, which was what his other ex-wife and I called him, nothing was impossible. Still, this attack was a departure from his usual MO, which meant letting you know in no uncertain terms that *he* was the one with the power. Besides, he was coming to the funeral, since he'd worked with the doctor who'd passed away. The doc's widow had apologetically asked if that was all right. I'd said yes. In front of others, the Jerk was unfailingly charming. It was when he got you alone that you had to worry.

With the ominous gray weapon lying on the dashboard, I assessed myself. In the physical department, it no longer hurt to breathe. My neck ached, my knees were bleeding, and my support hose—I called them "the caterer's friend"—were ruined. Still, I no longer felt dizzy or disoriented, and my Med Wives 101 knowledge assured me I hadn't had a concussion. I opened my trusty first-aid kit with one hand and pressed the automatic dial for Tom's cell with the other. He must have been out of range, so I left him a message. I then pressed the numbers of the sheriff's department.

Tom wasn't at his desk yet, either. I gave another brief account to his voice mail, then toggled over to the department's operator and explained what had happened. Yes, I needed a patrol car to come up. No, I did not feel I was in any immediate danger. No, I did not think anyone was still in the Roundhouse, and no, I did not know what this attacker was doing in the kitchen or if my business had sustained any damage. Did I have any idea who this prowler was? she asked.

"Not really," I answered truthfully. "You've got files on my ex-husband. But he's never gone to the trouble of wearing a mask. I have competitors, but most of them are in Denver." I took a deep breath, eager to be off the phone.

The operator assured me an officer would be up within forty-five minutes. Was that all right? she wanted to know. I told her the sooner the better. I had work to do.

I opened a bottle of water, took four ibuprofen, and had the comforting thought that my body did not hurt as much as it would in a few hours. I wrenched off the torn stockings, dabbed blood from my knees, and smeared on antiseptic. Once I'd smoothed a pair of large bandages into place, I winced as I slipped on a new pair of hose. Then I changed into a clean catering uniform—black pants, white shirt—and checked my watch. Just past six. Time to hustle.

First things first. I'd done the right thing by calling the cops. But I was determined to follow through with the funeral lunch. Nevertheless, with the tartlets and pies ruined, we would need a new dessert.

I put away the first-aid kit and punched in more numbers, this time for Marla Korman, the Jerk's other ex-wife and my best friend. I was still keeping a close eye on the Roundhouse—in case anyone was lurking about or my prowler decided to return.

Marla's phone rang ten times before I got her machine. I tried two more times and again was connected to her recorded voice. I knew she was home. She just wasn't picking up, which figured at six o'clock in the morning. Resigned, I kept calling until the phone was whacked off its cradle and I heard distant groaning.

"This better be good," Marla announced, her voice even huskier than usual.

"It's me. I need you to come to the Roundhouse. Please."

"It's not even . . . the Roundhouse? Goldy? They don't even serve coffee!" She yawned. "Oh, yeah, you took over there. Hold on." Shuffling noises engulfed the receiver, and I could imagine ultrawealthy Marla re-arranging her Delft-blue chintz-covered comforter and mound of feather pillows on her cherry four-poster bed.

"I'm sorry to call so early." Tears again slid out of my eyes, but I whacked them away. "I . . . can't reach Tom. Something bad has happened."

"What's the matter?" Marla's suddenly sharp voice demanded.

"I've been hit. Attacked. I didn't see who it was."

"You have to call 911."

"I did. A sheriff's car is en route. Tom's not at his desk, and whoever did this is gone. Could you please come over here, Marla? And I'd appreciate it if you could bring those cakes I made for your garden-club splinter-group bake sale. My dessert for the Kerr reception was wrecked."

"You've been beaten up and you want me to bring you some *cakes,* for God's sake?"

"Yes, please."

Marla cursed, said she'd be right over, and hung up.

Runners and walkers were beginning their morning circuit of the lake. On the far side of the water, a few kids with rods and reels had started casting for lake trout and tiger muskies. It had been almost an hour since I'd been knocked out, and there'd been no sign of the marauder coming back to finish me off.

Only slightly reassured, I hobbled from the van back to where I'd been hit. Unfortunately, there were no telltale shoe prints or conveniently dropped clues as to the identity of my attacker. I glanced at the broken back door. There was no way I was going inside without Marla. Still, I had sixty guests arriving in just five and a half hours, and the mess outside had to be cleaned up. Moving cautiously, I set the cart upright, loaded it with broken crusts and pieces of peach, and transported the debris to the Dumpster at the edge of the lot.

Fifteen minutes later, horn blaring, auxiliary lights

flashing, Marla roared into the parking lot. Hefting a large canvas bag, she lunged from her new gold Mercedes sedan.

"You know he did this," she cried when she caught up with me.

"Let's talk in the van."

She flung her sack onto the passenger-side floor, then climbed in beside me. Voluptuously pretty, she wore a hot-pink silk caftan shot through with gold. Gleaming barrettes of pink diamonds and tiny cultured pearls held her brown curls in place. She looked like a sunrise.

I said, "You didn't put any of my chocolate cakes in that bag, did you?"

"Don't start. They're in my trunk." Marla dug into the bag. "Here, have this." She handed me one of her special drinks, a Mason jar filled with ice cubes, espresso, and whipping cream. I thought of it as "Heart Attack on the Rocks," but took it gratefully.

Marla snarled, "I'm sure this was the work of el Jerk-o. The governor might as well have said, 'Get out of jail free! Go be naughty, we don't care.'"

"I don't know who it was, I just know that I hurt." I sipped the luscious, creamy drink. "This is from heaven, though. Thanks."

"I'd still like to know where our ex was this morning."

I was back to peering out the windshield. "How about, rolling around in bed with Sandee Blue?"

"Girlfriend almost half his age," Marla shot back. "It's a wonder *he* didn't have a heart attack, instead of me. Actually, that's not a bad idea. I can see Cecelia's headline now: 'What Prominent Local Doctor, a Convicted Felon, Died of Coronary Arrest While Bonking His Fifty-fourth Conquest?'"

I smiled. Cecelia Brisbane was our town's ruthless gossip columnist. In Aspen Meadow, Cecelia's weekly feature in the *Mountain Journal* was more feared, and more quickly devoured, than any national tabloid.

"Wait a minute," Marla said. "How about 'Fart's Heart Departs'?"

"Too obscure. And what makes you so sure Sandee was his fifty-fourth?" Marla's hobby of obsessively tracking John Richard's girlfriends, finances, and legal troubles gave her life meaning.

"Put it this way, I'm fairly certain Sandee's fifty-four. Courtney MacEwan was fifty-three. Ruby Drake was fifty-two. And then there was Val," she mused, "fifty-one. You don't suppose one of his old flames could have attacked you, do you?"

I shrugged. "A slightly plump, mid-thirties ex-wife, with a fifteen-year-old son and a husband who's a cop? Doesn't sound like a target to me."

"Maybe, maybe not. But there's something else I'd like to know. Now that the Jerk is out of jail, where do you think he's getting his money? You can't keep a young girlfriend and rent a house in the country club area on your good looks." She eyed me. "Speaking of appearance, *you* look like hell. No doubt about it, Goldy needs a chocolate-filled croissant." She burrowed back in her bag.

I declined the croissant and slugged down the last of the latte. "Listen, could you help me set up? I don't want to be alone in the Roundhouse."

"Absolutely. But bring the gun." She pushed open the passenger door and yelled, "If you're in Goldy's kitchen, she'll shoot you in the nuts!"

"I don't *want* to bring the gun."

She gave me a wicked look. "If the Jerk's in there, you could pop him off."

"Not funny."

"Then give the gun to me. *I'll* protect us."

"Forget it."

"Goldy, if you don't take that weapon, and then the cops arrive, they'll say, 'What the hell were you doing going into that place unarmed?'"

I sighed, handed Marla the entrance key—I thought the cops might want to photograph the kitchen door—and got out of the van. Then I snagged the thirty-eight and pointed it down, safety on, as we approached the Roundhouse's French doors. But another nasty surprise awaited us.

"Oh my God!" Marla cried after she'd pulled the key out of the lock and opened the doors.

My heart plummeted as I reeled back.

The smell of spoiled food was horrific. I thought, *I'm doomed.*

Chapter 2

"It's a *body*," Marla whispered. "The killer hit you so you couldn't witness anything."

"It's spoiled *food*," I corrected her. I limped inside, still aiming the gun at the floor. The putrid stench turned my stomach. Not meaning to, I took a deep breath. The smell filled my nostrils and I coughed. I panted—anything to avoid using the olfactory gland.

Delicately holding her nose, Marla followed me into the Roundhouse dining room. The place had never served as an actual train roundhouse, but was merely a fifty-year-old hexagonal building constructed of dark-stained pine logs. With a massive stone fireplace at its center, the dining room resembled a giant wooden teepee. The irony was that I'd been looking forward to the Roundhouse's early morning aroma, where smoke from thousands of barbecued steaks still lingered in the log walls.

"What do you want to do?" Marla asked, her voice nasal.

"Check everything in the kitchen," I replied. "Trash—every container. Refrigerators."

I chewed the inside of my cheek. "With a simple assault and vandalism, there's no way the cops will do prints and all that. Let's go around to the side. Whoever attacked me came out that way, and probably broke in there, too."

"Just make sure you've got hold of that gun," Marla ordered.

"That's the last thing we're going to need." My mind seized on the funeral lunch. "What we're going to *need* is more food. And *quick.*"

Our footsteps echoed on the wooden deck as we made our slow way around to the side of the old restaurant. My back still ached and my knees hurt. The sight of the wooden ramp that my attacker had raced down gave me gooseflesh.

A hundred yards away, the sun had risen higher, and Aspen Meadow Lake was a field of sparkles. When I'd signed the lease on the Roundhouse at the end of April, the large deck and magnificent view of the water had been selling points. In Colorado, people want to hold events both inside and outside, and any catering center that doesn't offer both is sunk. I shook my head, remembering my early enthusiasm for the Roundhouse. While reconfiguring the place for catered affairs, I'd come to wish the lake was full of cold cash instead of chilly snowmelt. But it was still a nice view. Calming. And calm was what I needed at the moment.

When we arrived at the back door, the reek was even more intense. I peered at the spot where the lock had been forced. Splinters littered the deck and the kitchen floor. Yellow wood showed where the hinge had been torn off from the paneling around it. Carefully, Marla and I tiptoed inside. She flipped on the lights—no power outage, anyway—and the spacious, newly painted kitchen popped into view. To my surprise, the place was completely clean.

"Stop. Take the safety off," Marla whispered. "I hear something."

Oh, man, I knew we should have waited in the car. Marla pointed to a paper grocery bag on the far side of the floor. With its flap rolled tight, the contents lay shrouded in darkness. But was it . . . *moving*?

"Stay put," I ordered, then advanced, thirty-eight raised, across the kitchen.

Without warning, the bag shuddered open and a dozen mice raced out. Startled, I accidentally shot off the damn gun.

Marla shrieked and ran outside. The rodents scattered. I cursed, eased the safety back on the thirty-eight, and placed it on the counter. Now the place *really* stank, with gunsmoke in addition to the stench of garbage. And probably a neighbor would call the cops. Maybe that would get them up here quicker, I thought as I pulled over some folding chairs to prop open the wrecked door. If my attacker had planted more mice, we needed to provide an easy exit for the furry little creatures. Plus, I was desperate to air out the place.

"Stop that!" Marla snapped from the deck. "You need to get the cops to get clues from the door."

"They won't have time for that, trust me."

The ibuprofen was kicking in and I could move a bit more easily as I limped back over to the bag, now empty. I didn't want to ponder how much a fumigator was going to cost. Oh, *hell,* I thought as I looked ruefully at the bullet hole in my new kitchen floor. Add on to that the price of oak-floor repair.

I took what they call in yoga a cleansing breath. If

you're smelling something putrid, does the breath still cleanse? I didn't think so. *Focus,* I told myself. Marla, whom I always depended on to be brave and helpful, was blubbering on the deck.

First I had to find the spoiled food. I began to check the trash containers. Every one of them was empty.

"Why didn't you shoot them?" Marla wailed. "You had the gun, for God's sake, why didn't you keep firing? Oh my God, mice! Maybe they were rats," and so on.

I stared at the two commercial refrigerators I'd installed in the kitchen. They were walk-ins I'd bought at a restaurant auction. The previous evening, I'd placed eleven hundred dollars' worth of grilled and chilled herb-crusted salmon, potatoes Anna, radiatore pasta salad, and spinach soufflé mixture into them. The food cart had contained the now-wrecked desserts. When Julian Teller, my longtime assistant, drove over from Boulder, he was bringing a vat of his luscious cream of asparagus soup. Liz Fury, a forty-two-year-old single mom who was my other helper, was visiting an early-bird farmers' market to pick up fresh arugula and watercress for the salad. These she would toss with delicately marinated hearts of palm and her own champagne vinaigrette.

Slowly, I opened first one, then the other refrigerator door.

I lurched away from the blast of hot, putrid air. A second later I was taking shallow breaths through my mouth and peering inside.

The refrigerator interiors were warm and dark. They stank of rotten food. I knew the math of spoilage; every caterer did. For every hour foods with mayonnaise and other perishable substances are at a temperature above sixty-five degrees, the toxins multiply exponentially.

My attacker couldn't just have shown up this morning and wrecked this food. So what was going on?

I moved outside as quickly as my battered body would allow. Marla was still sniveling on the deck. I checked the compressors. Someone had thrown the safety switches on both of them. I howled and pushed them into place, then hobbled back inside.

The refrigerators had hummed to life. I pulled open the doors, then stared inside. I couldn't comprehend what I was seeing.

The bowls, vats, and trays of salmon, potatoes, pasta, and spinach reeked of putrescence. So the guy, or whoever it was, had thrown the compressors last night, to guarantee that the food would be wrecked? And then he'd broken in this morning to plant some mice? Had he done anything else?

I saw the answer in a line of small, dead trout strung across the shelves of one refrigerator. On the base of the other walk-in, another paper bag seemed to be wriggling . . . oh God.

About six mice—fewer than in the other bag, anyway—scampered out. I jumped from one foot to the other, which made my body scream with pain.

"More mice coming!" I hollered at Marla.

"Will you shoot that damn gun?" she shrieked from the far side of the deck.

"Not again," I called back. I limped back to my van and stowed the thirty-eight in my glove compartment.

This was not, as it turned out, one of my better ideas.

Within ten minutes, I'd rustled up both Liz and Julian on their cells. I said I needed a ton of d-Con, at least a dozen mousetraps, and a carload of air fresheners.

"Okay, boss," Julian agreed. The kid was calmer

than any twenty-one-year-old I'd ever known. "But what're you going to do for food?"

"*Assiettes de charcuterie,*" I said decisively. "Plates of chilled imported salami, Westphalian ham, and Port Salut cheese. And some lovely fresh rolls. Can you find an open delicatessen in Boulder? And a bakery?"

"No prob."

"Plus, I'll need a load of unsalted butter and . . . jars of gherkins, if you can manage it. With your soup, Liz's salad, and the garden-club cakes, we ought to be in good shape."

"The *garden-club* cakes?"

"Flourless chocolate. Marla ordered them to sell for her splinter group's bake sale. But they're not going to get them."

"Goldy, what're you going to do if Roger Mannis shows up?"

"Oh, God help us."

Roger Mannis was the new district health inspector, assigned to make life difficult for yours truly and other caterers in our part of the county. The guy was a nightmare, Uriah Heep meets Jack the Ripper, with a Ph.D. in biology, to boot. He'd shown up—unannounced, as was his prerogative—at our very first event in the Roundhouse. I'd been serving tea, sandwiches, petits fours, and sliced fruit out on the deck. Unfortunately, the garden-club ladies had been acting anything but ladylike in their fight over a town tree-planting campaign. Roger Mannis—thirtyish, tall, and dark-haired, with deep-set eyes and a chin that could have sliced a pork loin—had started writing up every infraction he could find. He shook his head at the landscaping over my new plumbing lines. He stuck his little thermometer into the fruit salad and found it insufficiently chilled. He claimed to have detected insect remains on the floor of the deck. Julian and I knew to beg pardon and act obsequious, especially since we needed to calm the enemy armies of the garden club, who'd been on the verge of a fruit fight.

My dear Liz Fury, however, had been a bit more flippant. Tossing her silver-white hair and thrusting a long finger in Roger Mannis's face, she'd told him that the staff of Goldilocks' Catering abided by all hygiene rules. She announced, moreover, that Roger was being an *ass*. Distracted, the garden-club ladies had begun to titter. Liz hollered that Roger could get that ass, *his* ass, away from the Roundhouse immediately. Otherwise, she'd call his supervisor, her uncle Ozzie, who also happened to be the Furman County Health Inspector, and have him canned. "So to speak!" cried one of the women, and the entire garden club had snickered.

Roger Mannis had responded by narrowing his pupils, bottomless dark caverns that made most caterers' innards quake. His sharp chin had quivered as he'd stepped toward me and hovered ominously, clutching his clipboard. He'd been so close I could smell his aftershave. I'd actually cowered. Then Roger Mannis had turned on his heel and left.

Unfortunately, someone had been sitting right next to where I was standing during the whole interchange with Mannis. The wrong someone, as it turned out: Cecelia Brisbane, that most ruthless of gossip columnists, had been peering through her thick, cloudy glasses as she tried to cover the garden-club meeting. I heard later that she'd been hoping for hot items on the tree-planting conflict. Instead, Cecelia had mercilessly skewered me, the event, and the district health inspector. *During what recent get-together was a county offi-*

cial with a chainsaw chin, muskrat eyes, and clothes resembling a nuclear-bomb inspector told off by our town's caterer?

There was no point calling the *Mountain Journal* office and complaining. I'd tried that once and it hadn't worked. I just didn't want to think about it.

So . . . now, in answer to Julian's question: What was I going to do if Roger Mannis made an unexpected visit to this catered event . . . and saw all this spoiled food? I didn't want to contemplate that, either.

"Goldy, are you all right?" Julian asked, startling me.

"Sure. Thanks for reminding me about the dear inspector," I replied into the phone. "Let me see if Marla can waylay him."

While Marla and I dumped the vats of slimy pasta, stinking salmon, and putrid spinach into plastic bags, I tried to think of a way to bring up the Mannis predicament. The apparent disappearance of the mice had soothed Marla's nerves somewhat. Plus, she'd been eager to speculate about who could have done all this damage— although her considerable moneybags were still placed on the Jerk.

"He threatened you from prison," she asserted as she lugged a trash bag to the Dumpster. "To your face and behind your back. To Arch, to his lawyer, to anyone who would listen. He read the *Denver Post* and the *Rocky Mountain News* every day, and when some guy got off for beating or killing his wife, he *mailed* the article to you, Goldy. For God's sake!" She paused at the far end of the parking lot. "I suppose he's making an appearance at the lunch?"

"Holly Kerr invited him," I replied. "You remember Holly, don't you? Albert's wife, now widow? She wanted to include all the old gang from Southwest

Hospital." I grunted as I heaved my bag over the lip of the Dumpster.

Marla groaned and clumsily tipped in her sack. I frowned. Her beautiful pink-and-gold silk dress was stained with sweat and spotted with spoiled food. Dear Marla. And here I was going to ask something else of her.

"Uh, girlfriend?"

Marla lifted her chin and shot me a wary look. Her brown curls had come askew from the sparkling barrettes, and perspiration streaked her face.

"Now what?"

"I'm sorry, but when the cops arrive, I need you to do one more thing."

"It can't be worse than this."

"Would you be willing to go home," I asked quickly, "take a nice shower, put on something really sexy, and find a county employee named Roger Mannis? I'll give you his work number and address. Then distract him, seduce him, or do *something* to keep him occupied over the next few hours."

"You mean Roger Mannis, the health inspector who hassled you at the garden-club lunch? The subject of Cecelia's column, he of the muskrat eyes? One and the same?"

"Does that mean you'll do it?" I asked as a sheriff's-department vehicle finally, *finally* drove into the lot.

"You know what, Goldy?" Marla wiped her brow, glanced at the cop car, then put her hands on her hips. "If you weren't my friend, I would have *no* excitement in my life."

Chapter 3

She drove off, as they say in this part of the world, in a cloud of dust. The cop, a brawny blond fellow named Sawyer, had me repeat what had happened and show him the scene of the crime. He frowned at the place where I'd fallen, probed the splintered door frame with his finger, and narrowed his eyes at the bullet hole in the floor. He also told me I should see a doctor. I promised I would when the dust settled.

"Still, Mrs. Schulz, I'm going to stay here with you until your help arrives."

"Feel like carrying some trash?"

His grin was expansive. "Sure."

With Sawyer at my side, I hobbled back to the kitchen. The two of us grabbed the last of the trash bags—Sawyer insisted on taking three, so I had only one—traversed the lot, and heaved them into the Dumpster.

"I need you to show me the gun you used in the kitchen," Officer Sawyer said mildly as we made our way back to the Roundhouse.

I veered toward the van, unlocked it, and flipped open the glove compartment. Then I unloaded the gun and handed it to him. He looked at it briefly before giving it back. His expression was inscrutable.

I put the thirty-eight into the glove compartment and slammed it shut. "My permit's in the kitchen, in my purse."

"That's all right." He waited for me to close the van door, then walked beside me back to the Roundhouse.

The breeze that had been ruffling the lake's surface died down. Half a mile away, the lake house was deserted. Paddleboat and skiff rental did not begin until ten, and even the walkers and runners had hightailed away to their daily pursuits. The small commuter rush had abated, and Upper Cottonwood Creek Road was quiet.

I walked slowly. My shoulders ached. My back throbbed. Our footsteps on the gravel were the only sounds. Things seemed, as they also say in this part of the world, *too quiet.*

"Officer Sawyer?" I said suddenly. "Have you had this kind of attack around here lately? Somebody in a ski mask, vandalizing commercial establishments?"

Sawyer shook his head. "There's always a first time. I wish you'd go see a doctor."

I thought, *Sure, right after I find some electric fans, get the bleach, clean out the walk-ins, and start setting up. . . .*

"I know that we are all thankful for the life of Albert Kerr," Dr. Ted Vikarios announced, his voice as authoritative as that of Moses descending from Sinai. Dr. V., as we'd always called him, towered over the microphone, his six and a half feet not even slightly reduced by having reached his early sixties. His long, large-featured face was as imposing as ever, although I was pretty sure he was now dyeing his jet-black hair. He still wore it swooped up in front, like a wave cresting toward shore. "We rejoice in spite of our pain!" his voice boomed, and the mourners jumped in their seats.

Tell me about pain, I thought. My back, neck, and knees were still in a world of hurt. I shifted from foot to foot and glanced out at the people gathered for the memorial lunch. Most of the sixty guests had served in Southwest's ob-gyn department sixteen years ago, during the time that Drs. Kerr and Vikarios had been co-department heads of ob-gyn. And maybe they wished they hadn't, because Dr. V. had already been preaching to them for twenty-five minutes.

John Richard Korman, looking breezy, nonchalant, and as devastatingly handsome as ever, sat by the French doors. He wore a pink oxford-cloth shirt, patterned gold-and-green silk tie, and khaki pants. Did he look freshly showered? I mean, you would have to fix yourself up if you'd taken time out that morning to attack your ex-wife. At the very least, your naturally blond hair would get messed up underneath that ski mask. *Stop it,* I ordered myself. *You're not at all sure that John Richard was the culprit.*

I returned my attention to the lunch. The only way I was going to get through this event was not to care that he was present. Make that *not to care insofar as possible,* since I had already noticed how he was charming the women at his table with sly grins, winks, and an occasional backward flip of his careful-to-look-casual bangs. It did seem that he was studiously ignoring me. Not that I gave a slice of salami about that, either . . . at least until I could prove or disprove that he was the one who'd attacked me.

Anyway, I certainly wasn't going to confront him. Not here. Not now.

"We need to focus on gratitude!" Dr. V. shouted. He opened his long, thin arms to their full width, like one of those hang gliders you're always seeing taking off from Colorado peaks.

Okay, I could focus on gratitude. Clutching a glass of water, I backed into one of the Roundhouse's dark corners and swallowed four more ibuprofen. I believed that *I* was more thankful than Ted Vikarios. If I hadn't been choking on the pills, I would have been giving fervent praise to the Almighty that Julian, Liz, and I had somehow, *somehow,* pulled this lunch together after all.

"We miss Albert!" Dr. V. moaned, and the mourners groaned in response.

I swallowed hard and wondered if I missed Albert Kerr. Before Albert's wife, Holly, had returned to Aspen Meadow with Albert's ashes the previous month, I hadn't seen either one of them for over fourteen years. But they had doted on Arch when he was a newborn. It hurt not to see someone for a long time. I had liked the Kerrs, and had felt a pang to hear Albert had died of cancer while serving as the priest for a small Anglican congregation in Qatar, of all places. Still, Albert's lovely wife—widow—Holly had called me to do this event.

We had been close to both the Kerrs and Vikarioses when Albert, Ted, and the Jerk had worked together, Holly had reminded me.

I had gritted my teeth and promised Holly we would have a lovely lunch. And whether we had an anonymous attacker, a herd of mice, or a four-figure cost overrun, I was going to finish this luncheon, by golly. I took a deep breath, which was not a good idea.

Had anyone else noticed that the Roundhouse smelled like a pine forest? I stepped out from the corner and tried to avoid looking at the Jerk, who had put his arm around his new girlfriend. Girlfriend, schmirlfriend, my main question was whether anyone was sniffing the air and making faces. The scent, Organic Pine, could have been called The Woods You'll Never Get Out Of. It certainly smelled like a denser forest than anything Hansel and Gretel had dealt with. Okay, Liz and Arch had gone too wild with their enthusiastic spraying. They'd coated the kitchen with the stuff, emptied a can each into the refrigerators, and squirted the fragrance into every corner of the old restaurant.

I blinked at Cecelia Brisbane, who was seated close by. Her wide body spilled over the chair seat as she hunched over the table, her thick glasses perched on the edge of her bulbous nose. She was taking notes, for God's sake! If she made fun of the Roundhouse's pine odor in her next column, I'd tell her to be grateful the folks hadn't inhaled what had preceded it.

I focused on the rest of the guests. Gray-haired, squirrel-faced Nan Watkins, a longtime ob-gyn nurse at Southwest Hospital, nodded to me and gave a thumbs-up. I was doing her retirement party this week, so it was a good thing *she* was enjoying the lunch. In fact, *all* of the guests looked satisfied—at least with the food, if not with Ted Vikarios's droning on. I'd been gratified by the way they'd slurped down Julian's herb-topped chilled asparagus soup. After that, the mourners had dug into our quickly assembled *assiettes de charcuterie*. Amazing how a long church service can stimulate the appetite.

And speaking of church, God, and things we were thankful for, I'd also been grateful to the Almighty that

Liz had been able to muster Arch out earlier than I'd requested. Looking over at Arch, now quietly filling water glasses at a far table, I was filled with pride. At fifteen, my son was finally getting taller. His shoulders were broadening, he'd cut his toast-brown hair short, and he'd traded in his thick tortoiseshell glasses for thin wire-rimmed specs.

But there was another change in Arch. Toward the end of the school year, I'd finally had enough of my son's self-centeredness and obsession with having *stuff*. I'd barely been able to deal with a stream of demands for an electric guitar, a high-tech cell phone, a new computer, and other paraphernalia. Worse, his annoying behavior was increasingly expressing itself as verbal abuse directed at yours truly. I'd lived in denial for all those years with the Jerk, I said to myself one particularly sleepless night, was I going to do the same with Arch?

I was not. No matter whose "fault" his behavior was—I blamed the brats at Elk Park Preparatory School, Arch blamed me—I decided to pull him out of EPP. Unfortunately, there was no Episcopal high school in the Denver area. So I told Arch he could go away to military school (I was bluffing) or he could attend the Christian Brothers Catholic High School, not far from the Furman County Sheriff's Department. After much yelling and door slamming, he chose the Brothers.

Once Arch had been admitted, the school had phoned and invited him on a class retreat. Arch had had a fantastic time. He had made a slew of new friends who now invited him to skate, play guitar, or just hang out, something he had never, ever been asked to do by any student at Elk Park Prep.

And then my son had started required community work in a Catholic Workers' soup kitchen. Chopping fifteen pounds of onions on Saturday mornings to go into stew he then helped serve to two-hundred-plus homeless people—*this* had changed his materialism, *but quick*. Now he put away half his allowance for the Catholic Workers and begged me for paid work so he could help more people eat.

Well, I was all for helping people eat. I mean, just look at this lunch! It might be costing me a mint, but it was *happening*. Right from the start, Liz and Julian had commandeered Arch into an assembly line that would have left Henry Ford in the dust. They'd zipped around the kitchen prep table, placing slabs of creamy Port Salut cheese beside delicate rosettes of spicy imported salami. Because I was hurting, they'd given me the meager job of rolling the delicately smoked Westphalian ham into thin cylinders. They'd placed these next to slices of a heavenly homemade goat cheese Liz had nabbed at the farmers' market. We'd all pitched in to pile Liz's salad— crisp, tender field greens mixed with crunchy slices of hearts of palm and coated with her scrumptious vinaigrette—into pyramids in the middle of each *assiette* just as the first cars wheeled into the gravel driveway. Right before the lunch had commenced, when we'd been finishing the last of the plates, Dr. Ted Vikarios had burst into the kitchen. Apparently, Arch wasn't the only one with matters religious on his mind.

"Jesus God Almighty!" Ted Vikarios yelled.

The four of us had jumped. After recovering, I'd reminded him of who I was. *Goldy, from the old days, remember?* Limping along, I'd led him back out to the dining room and asked him what I could do to help him. When he'd mumbled *microphone* and *podium*, I'd carefully shown him where he'd be giving his speech after the meal. Seeming preoccupied, he'd wandered off.

After that inauspicious kickoff, however, the lunch itself had been stupendous. The guests had devoured every morsel of food, right down to the baguettes, the butter—even the gherkins. Moving through the tables, I'd noticed a few members of the crowd making sandwiches from leftovers and tucking them into purses and sacks—a sure sign of success, if not good manners.

And now the guests were devouring the swoon-inducing slices of the flourless chocolate cakes I'd made for Marla. We'd topped them with Häagen-Dazs vanilla ice cream, quickly purchased by Julian, as our homemade batch had melted when the compressors were shut off. Julian had handed the portable mike—at least I'd set *that* up the previous day—to Albert's widow, Holly. Short, gray-haired, as vibrant and energetic at fifty-five as she had been at forty, she'd given an enthusiastic thanks to everyone who'd come. She'd added that there would be one tribute only, from Albert's old friend Ted Vikarios.

As Ted now proclaimed into the microphone, his wife, Ginger Vikarios, smiled nervously at the crowd. Like her husband, Ginger, slender and overly made up, had taken unsuccessful steps to look as if she had not aged. She'd dyed her hair orange, the lipstick on her downturned mouth was orange, and she had bright spots of orange blush on each cheek. She looked fragile and unhappy, like a sad clown. I certainly hoped Ginger had not heard the insensitive comments on the way her curly orange hair matched her unfashionable orange taffeta dress. Whatever had happened to people wearing black to funerals? they wanted to know. I hadn't the foggiest.

John Richard Korman's late arrival with his blond, nubile new girlfriend, Sandee Blue, had caused a ripple in the crowd. Sandee, her platinum curls swept forward in a sexy do, ignored Ted Vikarios as she giggled and nuzzled John Richard's ear. Smiling, John Richard pulled away, ran his fingers through his long hair, and winked knowingly at Sandee. I wondered if he was technically old enough to be her father.

Marla and I had met Sandee two weeks before, when we'd delivered Arch to John Richard's house prior to a golf lesson. Clad in a bikini (to the best of my knowledge, the Jerk had not installed an indoor pool in his country-club rental house), she'd opened the heavy door, looked us up and down, and introduced herself.

"I'm Sandee Blue. That's Sandee with two *e*s."

Arch had done his best not to gawk. I'd shuddered and, for once, been tongue-tied.

Confused, Sandee had asked, "Are you here with money?"

Without missing a beat, Marla had said, "No, but we'd be blue, too, if we didn't have any." Sandee had retreated, looking even more perplexed. Then we'd heard the Jerk yelling at her from inside the house, and finally he'd appeared and wordlessly taken Arch. What was that French saying—*plus ça change?* Well, anyway, stuff doesn't change and neither do jerks.

According to Marla, Sandee worked in the country-club golf shop, and that was where John Richard had decided he had to have her. Also according to Marla, once John Richard met Sandee, he'd dumped his willowy, wealthy, gorgeous, brunette girlfriend, Courtney MacEwan. Courtney was a highly competitive tennis-playing socialite. She was known for throwing her racket *and* her fluorescent pink tennis balls at opponents who beat her—and hitting them. This was not the kind of woman I'd want to have as an enemy, but John Richard was an expert in—Marla's term—the Art of Bedding Dangerously.

Now, watching John Richard lean over and whisper in Sandee's ear, my gaze traveled over to lovely, brown-haired Courtney MacEwan, standing on the far side of the French doors. Unlike Ginger Vikarios's orange gown, Courtney's dress *was* black, but it was so low cut and tight—showing muscles I wasn't even sure I *had*—that it made Ginger's pouffery look tame. I racked my gray cells to figure out why Courtney was here, and then remembered that her former husband— he had died of a heart attack when Courtney had surprised him in bed with a flight attendant—had been a top executive at Southwest Hospital.

Courtney had been John Richard's squeeze in— what, April, the beginning of May? Then the Jerk had moved on to the greener Sandee pasture, and they'd split. Now Courtney stared in his direction. The bitterness of her expression shrieked, *If I can't have this man, no one will!* I wondered if her copious Louis Vuitton bag held a couple of tennis balls.

The crowd scooped up the last of their cake and ice cream, glanced at their watches, and rustled in their seats. Oblivious, Ted Vikarios rumbled on about the good deeds Albert Kerr had done. Albert had sold his possessions and taken Holly to England, where he'd gone to seminary. He'd accepted a call to a small Christian mission in Qatar—he *really* hadn't liked the cold English weather—and served there for twelve years. He'd fought valiantly against the disease that had finally claimed him, etc., etc.

Again waves of fatigue and pain washed over me.

The places where my attacker had hit were killing me. When I'd signaled to Julian and Liz to stop clearing, I'd had no idea Ted Vikarios would talk until mold grew on cheese. On and on he went, about how the Lord had done this in Albert's life and the Lord had done that. The agnostics among the country-club set were stirring in their seats. To them, a *conversion experience* was changing dollars into euros.

When a couple of people scraped back their chairs and got up to leave, Dr. V. cleared his throat into the mike. It came out like a thunderclap, and a spontaneous titter swept through the Roundhouse dining room. More people began to stand up and move about. I glanced at Holly Kerr. She kept her chin up and her back straight as she spoke to well-wishers.

If I could just finish the cleaning without losing my temper with the Jerk and accusing him of beating me up, I could count this event as a salvaged success. I scanned the crowd again. Ted Vikarios was still talking. I had to clear away the dirty dishes, whether it made noise or not.

Holly Kerr caught my eye, nodded, and smiled. Then she handed an envelope to a young man and indicated that he was to give it to me. My eyes snagged on Courtney MacEwan, whose rage-filled stare at John Richard—who was again cozying up to Sandee—had not quit. Courtney folded her arms, which made a whole bunch more muscles pop out. Now John Richard and Sandee-with-two-*e*s were exchanging a not-so-surreptitious kiss. I turned quickly, picked up a tray of dirty glasses beside one of the tables, and only vaguely registered footsteps clicking up to my side.

"Ever noticed," Courtney MacEwan hissed in my ear, "how people can't *wait* to have sex after funerals?"

I lost my grip on the tray. Unbalanced, one of the glasses popped upward and spiraled toward the floor. An alert guest, a bodybuilder-type guy with thick, dry blond-brown hair that resembled a lion's mane, dove for it with an outfielder's extended reach. Grinning hugely, he held it high. The guests at the table applauded.

"Courtney," I said through clenched teeth—and a false smile—"get into the kitchen if you want to talk about sex."

Courtney fluttered sparkly eyelids and mauve-toned fingernails and slithered ahead of me. It was a good thing, too, because the crowd parted like the Red Sea for that low-cut dress.

"And dearest, loveliest Holly," Ted droned on.

"Was that a trick play with the glass?" an older woman asked me. Her broad face lit up with an admiring smile. "If you toss two glasses into the air, Dannyboy here will be able to catch both of those, too." The table giggled and leaned forward. I noticed several bottles of wine between the plates, *not* served by yours truly. In fact, I was willing to bet that the folks at this table had never worked at Southwest Hospital. There were two guys (including Dannyboy, he of the lion mane) who looked like thugs, and three women, two pretty younger ones and the one who'd first spoken to me. Her thick makeup and dyed black hair screamed Aging Hooker. Still, she looked familiar. But I was distracted from trying to place her by Dannyboy, whose drunk, raised voice announced: "If you toss *three* glasses in the air, I can juggle those, too!"

"And dearest, loveliest *Holly*," Ted Vikarios shouted into the microphone, "was a nurturing presence all along." Registering the disturbance—Dannyboy, the joker who wouldn't let me pass—Ted glared in our direction. "She even nursed Albert, whom we are re-membering today, whom we are *trying* to remember today"—more glaring—"beginning when he was sick and missed school as a teenager . . ."

"So did John Richard cheat on you, too?" Courtney stage-whispered over her shoulder. "And what did you do to his girlfriends?" I kept a white-knuckled grip on the tray and refused to answer.

"Hey, caterer," Dannyboy was saying as he tugged on my apron. Behind him, his table laughed wildly. "C'mon, let's have some fun. With the glasses, I mean."

I tore myself away and limped painfully toward the kitchen. When I finally made it, I placed the tray next to the sink, then walked over and carefully closed the door to the dining room. I took a deep breath before facing Courtney, who had almost screwed up this *already*-almost-screwed-up event.

"Doggone it, Courtney, what is the matter with you? I've been divorced from John Richard for over a de-cade! Of *course* he cheated on me. I didn't do anything to any girlfriends of his except feel sorry for her, who-ever she was. And as to the sex-after-funerals question, how should I know? When I'm catering a funeral lunch, what I do afterward is *dishes*."

She looked over at me, then pressed her lips together. But it was no-go. Tears slid down her cheeks. In an ef-fort to look stronger than she apparently was feeling, she rolled her shoulders and flexed those arm muscles.

"God*damn* him," she said. "He *owes* me." She slapped tears away. I plucked a clean tissue from my apron pocket and handed it to her. "I just hate him so much now." She honked into the tissue. "We were go-ing to get *married*. We'd been together for less than a month, and he sent back my stuff from his house in boxes from the *golf shop,* for crying out loud. Why the golf shop?"

She started to cry. I rinsed dishes, wondering how long this would last. *The golf shop,* she kept repeating. *Why the golf shop?*

"Maybe Sandee gave him the boxes," I offered. "I mean, she's some kind of golf expert, isn't she?"

To my great surprise, Courtney burst out laughing. "Oh, yeah, Sandee's a golf expert, all right! Puts the ball right in the hole!"

Her facial muscles jumped and twitched. Oh boy, she had it bad. This was unfortunate. John Richard never went back to a woman he'd abandoned.

"What is going on in here?" Marla demanded as she banged through the kitchen door. She was holding an envelope, which she handed to me. "This is from Holly Kerr. Some guy was waiting to give it to you, but was afraid to come into the kitchen because the door was closed. Ooh, yummy, leftover cake." She daintily helped herself to a corner of chocolate, then noticed Courtney MacEwan. "For crying out loud, Courtney, what are you so bent out of shape about? I mean, besides being dumped for a twenty-one-year-old?"

Courtney glared at Marla, who shook her head at Courtney's décolleté dress.

"Very sexy, C. You ought to be able to pick up somebody new, right here at this funeral."

Courtney lifted her chin and appraised Marla's black linen dress. "You look pretty inviting yourself, Marla. Did you have a hot date before the funeral?"

"Oh, darling, did I!" Marla replied, rolling her eyes.

"But what *are* you doing here?" I asked Marla, once I'd stashed Holly's payment, which I intended to refund to her since we'd never had the poached salmon.

Marla turned her attention to me. "You are *so* ungrateful."

"But what about you-know-who?" I whispered as Courtney cracked open the kitchen door to check on the whereabouts of John Richard. I didn't know if she was listening to Marla and me or not, but you couldn't be too careful with Courtney. I was pretty sure she still blamed me for being hostile to her relationship with John Richard. I had been nothing of the kind, of course; this had been John Richard's excuse to Courtney for why they had to break up. ("'Goldy is such a jealous ex-wife,'" Marla said the Jerk had claimed to Courtney. "'If she finds out you're staying here at the house, she'll go back to family court and try to have my visitations with Arch reduced!'")

"At this very moment," Marla said as she picked up a corner of cake and checked her new diamond Rolex, "my lawyer is in the office of your favorite district food inspector, claiming he's going to sue him and his entire staff on behalf of his client who has food poisoning."

"You're *so* bad—" I began.

Courtney let out a gargled noise and reeled back. None other than the Jerk himself popped his head into the kitchen. He looked all around, then grinned widely.

"Oops!" he said with mock surprise. "Three old girlfriends. What're you doing, plotting? Goldy, I need to see you. Now."

"I'm not going *anywhere* with you."

He stepped all the way into the kitchen, put his hands on his hips, and announced in a low, threatening voice, "I. Need. You. Now."

Before I could say "Tough tacks," Courtney

shrieked, "You bastard! I ought to—" She strode toward him. John Richard rolled his shoulders and got ready to fight. With sudden deftness, Marla picked up a crystal platter of leftover cake, stepped in front of Courtney, and used the platter as a shield. Most of the chocolate landed on the ample tops of Courtney's breasts.

"You bitch!" Courtney cried as my platter fell to the floor and broke to smithereens.

John Richard pointed at me and said, "Parking lot." Then he slithered away.

Courtney refocused her energy on the Jerk. She stalked out of the kitchen, chocolate coating and all.

Julian, dark-haired and efficient, pushed into the kitchen with a tray of dirty dishes. He glanced at the floor with its shards of crystal. "What happened here?"

"I'll explain later. Listen, I don't want to face the Jerk alone. The cop's left. Would the two of you come with me?" I begged Julian and Marla in a low voice.

"Of course," the two of them said in unison. Liz came into the kitchen and announced that Arch had left with his friend and his friend's mom, and that I had said it was all right. I nodded, although with all the events of the morning, I had no idea what I had promised Arch. Liz said she would press on with the cleanup. Marla and Julian nipped along ahead of me, out the trashed back door and down the gravel path. Halfway down, we came to an abrupt halt.

Ted Vikarios, evidently having finished his eulogy for Albert, had planted himself in the Jerk's path and was shaking his finger in my ex-husband's face. John Richard, unusually for him, was speaking in a low, reconciling tone. Ted turned red, bared his teeth, and kept ranting. I could only make out a couple of his phrases:

asking an important question and *should be ashamed of yourself*.

"We ought to go back," I murmured to Marla and Julian.

"Forget it," Marla replied. She put her hand on my arm and edged closer to the two men. "We're *just* out of earshot. Maybe super-Christian Ted is upset by the Jerk serving time as a convicted felon."

John Richard, retreating to his usual gracelessness, told Ted to *go home* and *stop acting like an old man*. Leaving Ted dumbfounded, John Richard trotted out to the parking lot. After a few moments, he revved his new Audi TT, circled the lot in a spray of gravel, and pulled up near the path. In the front seat, Sandee was checking her lipstick in the visor mirror. Julian, Marla, and I gave a fuming Dr. V. a wide berth and stopped short a safe three yards from the roaring Audi.

"I need you to bring Arch over in three hours," John Richard yelled at me. "I got my tee time changed."

Even if John Richard had shoved me and whacked my neck and screwed up the lunch food, I did not *also* need him to holler orders in front of the Roundhouse windows. Julian and Marla edged closer to the Audi. They crossed their arms and stood their ground in front of me.

"John Richard, did you have anything to do with a break-in here at the Roundhouse?" Marla called merrily. "Spoiled food? Mice?" Her voice turned sharp. "Did you beat Goldy up, you son of a bitch?"

"Goldy!" John Richard ignored Marla and raised his voice a notch. "Four o'clock! Got it?"

My ears burned. I tried not to think about how everyone in the dining room, everyone within a half-mile radius, could hear John Richard yelling at me. Could someone be so brazen as to assault his ex-wife in the morning and then demand she bring over their son in the afternoon?

"I'm busy," I called. "So is Arch—"

Moving quickly, John Richard jumped out of his car, slammed the door, and strode around Marla and Julian to tower over me. "Let's get this straight," he announced. "I don't care about *you*! I don't care about how supposedly *busy* you are! I don't care about your little *schedule*! I don't care, do you understand?"

Julian darted around me with sudden quickness, planting himself face-to-face with John Richard and folding his arms. Although the Jerk was a couple of inches taller than Julian, the Jerk's prison-induced softness was no match for Julian's compact, muscled, twenty-one-year-old body. John Richard backed up to the Audi.

I felt the old panic well up. A lump the size of Pikes Peak formed in my throat. When I glanced over my shoulder, it was as I expected. More than a dozen faces peered at us from the Roundhouse windows.

"Get out!" Julian yelled. "Drive away now, or we'll call the cops for the second time today!"

John Richard stood staring at us for a long moment, then got into his car. He strapped himself into the TT beside Sandee with two *e*s and roared off. He didn't look back.

Chapter 4

"Whoa!" Marla patted Julian on the back. "Good work, kiddo!" Julian beamed, nodded, and walked wordlessly in the direction of the kitchen. Marla asked me, "So are you going to take Arch over?"

"I have to. At this very moment, John Richard is probably calling his lawyer on his cell. He'll complain about Julian and about how uncooperative I am."

"Want company on the drop-off?" Marla wanted to know. "I could duck out of PosteriTREE's bake sale. By the way, you're going to bring me something to make up for my loss of cakes, aren't you?"

"Sure, sure. I've got brownies in the freezer. And I'll be fine dropping off Arch, thanks." I stared at the dust settling in the parking lot after the Audi's departure. "Arch might have other plans. Do you think that ever occurred to el Jerk-o? This is so typical of him, I can't believe it."

"Believe it."

In back of Marla, people streamed from the Roundhouse. I hugged my friend, thanked her, and limped back to the kitchen. From the dining room, the scrape of chairs, shuffle of footsteps, and gurgle of relieved voices announced the end of an event. Was I imagining it, or were people calling to each other in exultation: *Ted Vikarios has left the podium, at last, at last!* I glanced around for Ted and Ginger Vikarios, eager to find out what had precipitated Ted's fury. But the Vikarioses had already left.

In the kitchen, Julian and Liz were loading the commercial dishwashers. What would I do without my two masterly assistants?

Julian stopped loading. "You okay, boss?"

"No, but never mind."

"We heard John Richard yelling." Liz's large eyes were filled with sympathy. "Sorry he's back to ruin your life."

"Yeah, well."

"Boss?" Julian again. "You're going to have a problem, I think. When Arch left with the Druckmans, he said he wasn't sure if you knew his schedule. He said he'd write you a note when he got home." I groaned. *Great.* "Look," Julian went on, "why don't you let Liz and me finish up here? It's no big deal. We can board up the back door, too. We've already figured out how to do it."

"First I need to know how much the two of you spent on cheeses, meats, and salad ingredients. This function never would have happened without you. I'm not leaving until I get your receipts."

Before they could reply, my cell phone rang again. Oh, great, a call from John Richard's lawyer, already. *Mrs. Schulz, you promised to accommodate your ex-husband with requested visitations . . .*

It was not a lawyer. It was Tom. Finally.

"I've been in a meeting with the sheriff and just got

your message," he said, his voice subdued. "Are you all right?"

At the sound of Tom's voice, something twisted inside my chest. No, I was not even close to *all right*. I wanted Tom here with me, wanted his handsome face, his green eyes the color of the ocean, his big body surrounding mine.

"Um—" I said, faltering.

"Goldy? Why did you call me?" The distant tone that I'd come to know in the past month crept into his voice. In May, Tom had lost a case, and a guilty defendant had gone free. The shock felt in the department had been profound. Tom had gone into such a deep depression that he seemed to be a new man, not the jovial, affectionate one I'd married.

"I had a problem here at the center." The places where I'd been hit ached deeply. Somehow, though, I didn't feel able just then to tell Tom what had happened.

"I'm reading a report here of shots fired. Down near you, about eight this morning?"

"That was me. I fired my gun." I wanted to elaborate, but somehow felt unable to. Ordinarily, he *was* able to return my calls right away, sheriff or no sheriff. And he usually greeted me so enthusiastically, *Miss G., what are you up to now? Miss Goldy, everything all right?* As silence lengthened between us, I had to remind myself again that his behavior was not owing to anything I had done. Tom had turned all his anger at losing that case inward, and I was going to have to gut it out.

Finally Tom said, "You want to tell me what's going on?"

"Oh, Tom. Somebody broke into the Roundhouse. I surprised him when he was still here. He . . . shoved me out of the way and whacked the back of my neck so hard that I passed out—"

"Wait, wait. Do you need me to come up there? Are you all right?"

"I'm fine. Really. I called the department and they sent a patrolman who took a report. You should know, though, the prowler had sabotaged me. He must have thrown the switches on the fridge and freezer compressors last night, so all the food was spoiled. Then this morning, he broke down the back door and left a string of trout in the refrigerator and bags of mice on the floor. I didn't see a face."

"But you tried to shoot the guy?"

"No. I was so startled by the mice that I shot the gun by accident. I made a hole in the floor, but—"

"Goldy. Who do you think could have done this?"

"John Richard? Some enemy I don't know about? I can't imagine. Listen, I'll be okay. Julian and Liz have offered to clean up. And get this, John Richard was at the Kerr lunch. Demanding loudly that I bring Arch over at four to play golf."

"Let me meet you at his house. Please?"

"Marla's already offered. I turned her down. I promise, Tom, I'm staying in the van while Arch hauls his clubs to the Jerk's door."

He sighed and said he'd see me that night. I clapped the phone shut and consulted my watch: 1:15. My aching body pined for a shower and a nap. Unfortunately, I had miles to go before I slept . . . not to mention returning home to a husband who was on an entirely different emotional path from mine.

I wrote checks to Liz and Julian. A short while later, my van pulled out of the Roundhouse parking lot. When I opened the windows, the hot scent of dry pines gusted inside. Had my assailant been watching for me very early this morning, perhaps from the trees on the far side of the creek? Who would want to ruin a caterer's food? And most problematic: Would this person strike—and strike *me*—again?

I piloted the van around the lake and down Main Street. The severe drought and ensuing watering restrictions had given Aspen Meadow the dusty look of an Old West village. Still, the merchants had bravely put out a profusion of artificial flowers. Fake geraniums poked from window boxes outside Aspen Meadow Jewelry. Plastic ivy twined around lampposts the length of Main Street, from the Grizzly Bear Saloon to Darlene's Antiques and Collectibles. Local kids and tourists vied for the best viewing spot in front of Town Taffy's big window, where mechanized silver arms pulled and stretched shiny ribbons of candy. Aspen Meadow depended on tourists and locals alike to spend large amounts of money during the summer months, and the store owners were determined to don their usual festive look. I'd even heard that members of our Chamber of Commerce had pestered CNN to quit reporting on Colorado forest fires. Those newscasts were ruining business!

When I pulled up in front of our own drying, dying lawn, I tried to ignore it, along with the flowers, now struggling, that Tom had so lovingly nurtured through the last two summers. The Alpine rosebushes, chokecherries, and lilacs, even the aspens and pines, all drooped with thirst. But I was powerless to help them, as exterior watering had been banned.

Inside, Jake the bloodhound bounded up and covered my face with kisses. Scout, our long-haired brown-and-white cat, watched reproachfully from the top of the stairs. The feline would never lower himself to ask for affection. In the way of cats everywhere, he would wait until people needed *him*.

After feeding and watering the animals, I checked the phone messages. There was always the possibility that Arch had called to say something helpful, like that he'd be back by three. No luck.

Out of habit, I booted up my computer to check upcoming events. Alas, nothing magical had appeared on the culinary horizon, as gigs had dried up along with the mountain grasses. This week held only two other assignments. Day after tomorrow, I was doing breakfast at the Aspen Meadow Country Club for Marla's garden-club splinter group, PosteriTREE. Presumably, they'd be discussing how much money they'd made on today's bake sale. That same afternoon, Julian, Liz, and I were doing a picnic under a rented tent, paid for by the Southwest Hospital Women's Auxiliary. They were hosting a retirement party for Nan Watkins, who'd been a long-time nurse at the facility. At least the free day before the picnic would give me time to have the Roundhouse back door replaced, install some kind of fence around the compressors, and bring in a class-A fumigator. . . .

There was a scribbled message from Arch on the counter:

> *I forgot some stuff. It was just hockey gear (that's why I'm home writing you this). Todd's mom is taking us down to the rink in Lakewood to play with some other kids from Christian Brothers. We'll call her when we're done, so don't worry. I thought your lunch thing was good. Hope it's okay that I didn't stay to help with the dishes. I'll do them next time. A.K.*

It was a nice note. Lakewood, just west of Denver, was forty-five minutes away. But I had to convince Arch to leave, get him cleaned up and golf-ready, and probably take Todd home, too. How was I going to deliver Arch to the Jerk's by four, given that it was now one-thirty? And how come my ex-husband was always able to screw up my life?

I dug around in my freezer, snagged four bags of frozen brownies, and walked back to the van as quickly as my bruised knees would allow. As I zipped down the interstate, I called Eileen Druckman and asked her if I could pick up the boys. She said yes, thank goodness. When I pulled up in front of the Summit Rink forty minutes later, even the van was panting.

Once inside the rink area—I never could imagine how much it cost to keep this place so freezing cold—I found it hard to make out Arch and Todd. The kids playing a makeshift hockey game were wearing masks and a ton of padding. Of course, I knew better than to call out my introvert son's name—oh, did I ever. When he was nine, Arch hadn't spoken to me for a week after I'd had him paged in a grocery store.

Finally I picked out a possible candidate and watched him carefully. Yes, that had to be Arch. I signaled to him three times until finally he got the message and wearily skated over to the gate.

"Mom! What's going on?" He lifted his mask, revealing a flushed face streaming with sweat. Another teenager skated up and tilted back his face gear: Todd, his face as red and wet as Arch's.

"I've got to take you to play golf with your father."

"Oh, Mom. Not now. Please!" Arch pulled down his mask and pushed off from the gate. I was impressed by how well he was learning to skate backward, anyway.

"When does Dad want me?" he demanded through the mask.

"ASAP. Sorry."

Arch's shoulders slumped. "We're in the middle of a scrimmage."

Todd called, "Aw, c'mon, Arch. Play golf with your dad. He just got out of jail."

At these words, a few players hockey-stopped nearby. *Somebody's dad was in jail? His kid might be a really good hockey player!* The opposing team used the sudden break to send the puck whizzing into the goal, and the eavesdroppers squawked. If I could have disappeared, I would have.

Meanwhile, Arch was skating back to the gate. I was thankful. In the Elk Park Prep days, we would have had a long argument—which I would have lost.

"Just pretend the golf ball's a hockey puck and really slam it," Todd called to him. "That's what the pros do."

Arch, the mask again tilted on his brow, shook his head. But at least both boys tramped off the ice.

My guilt at pulling them from the scrimmage prompted me to buy a king's ransom of soft drinks, chips, and candy bars, for which they were noisily thankful. The van chugged back up the mountain to the sound of ripping wrappers and breaking chips. By three o'clock, I had gotten Arch home and convinced him to take a very quick shower, while Todd played video games. After some searching, I laid my hands on a passably clean polo shirt and a pair of khakis. When I hauled out the golf clubs John Richard had bought for Arch, I marveled that *they* were immaculate, anyway, without a speck of mud or grass on them. By three-fifteen, we were off.

I dropped Todd at his house and thanked him for his patience. At half-past three, Arch and I toted the bags of almost-thawed brownies through the service entrance of the Aspen Meadow Country Club. Or as Marla and I referred to it, the so-called country club. If Aspen Meadow didn't have inbred high society, and it didn't, it also had nothing to rival the magnificent colonial clubs of the East. But AMCC's big motel-like main building had just undergone an expensive remodeling, with new locker rooms, golf and tennis shops, a weight room, and a meeting room, where Posteri-TREE, as the garden-club splinter group called itself, was having its bake sale from three to five.

Marla stood with some pals behind one of the three buffet tables girdling the crowded room. She bustled toward me. She was wearing her third lovely outfit of the day, this one a casual suit in a printed jungle-motif fabric.

"Cecelia is here," she muttered, and I felt my eyes drawn to the *Mountain Journal*'s gossip columnist. Cecelia, her large pear shape not enhanced by a shapeless white man's shirt and baggy black pants, was thrusting her bespectacled, shovel-shaped face into the middle of a conversation between Ginger Vikarios and Courtney MacEwan. Ginger immediately put her head down, turned on her heel, and walked away, while tall, gorgeous Courtney looked down her nose at Cecelia and said nothing.

"Oops, maybe Cecelia just insulted Ginger," Marla said mildly. "Wouldn't be the first time."

"Look, here are your brownies," I said quickly. Arch had handed me the bags and scuttled off. He was in the process of admiring the cakes, cookies, and muffins being proffered by the women. If I didn't get him out of there, he was sure to drop dollops of lemon curd onto his golf shirt.

But I was prevented from leaving by Cecelia Brisbane, who sidled up and pinched my elbow. Her bulging eyes were greatly magnified by her glasses' thick lenses.

She said, "I hear your ex is up to his old tricks."

Marla cleared her throat. I gazed innocently at Cecelia's wide, wrinkled face and unruly gray hair, which was the color and consistency of steel wool. I said, "Oh, really? Where'd you hear that?"

Cecelia was genetically incapable of grinning. Her uneven, greasy gray bangs fell across her forehead and over the tops of her glasses. She pulled her lips into a serious scowl. "I heard you had a bit of an incident at the Roundhouse this morning."

I smiled. "Define 'bit of an incident.' "

"Who do you think hit you?" she pressed.

"Hey!" Marla exclaimed. "How do you know what happened—"

I held up a hand to quiet Marla. "Actually, Cecelia," I replied, "you probably have a better idea than I do."

"I have complaints about your ex on file," Cecelia persisted.

"So do the cops, Cecelia."

"Not the same kind of files, I bet."

I tilted my head at her, curious. "You want to explain yourself?"

Cecelia straightened her glasses and squinted at me. She replied in a deadpan voice, "Not here. But I can, if you want. Especially if you can tell me what I want to know."

Arch bounced up, chewing on a brownie. "Mom! I thought we were in some kind of hurry to get to Dad's."

"We are," I told him. I bade Cecelia a polite good-bye, then hustled Arch out the service exit. Backing the van out of its narrow parking space, I came very close to whacking Cecelia's battered old station wagon. I hit the brakes and did some maneuvering to wiggle the van clear, without incident. Cecelia wasn't the kind of person you wanted to have as an enemy.

Zooming past the club's mini-mansions in the direction of John Richard's rental, I wondered what in the hell Cecelia had been talking about. There was Marla's question: *Now that the Jerk is out of jail, where's he getting his money?* He had no job that I knew of, or, more important, that *Marla* knew of. My best friend had also calculated that John Richard's highly publicized sponsoring of a local golfing event—twenty-five thousand bucks—plus purchasing the Audi—another forty thou—plus rent *must* have been subsidized by Courtney, the newly wealthy widow. Lots of her money, apparently, had been lavished on the Jerk.

But John Richard had dumped Courtney, and according to Marla, he was renting in the club area while he looked for a big house to *buy.* In this, Marla had joyfully concluded, he would not be successful. While our ex was incarcerated and deprived of the *Mountain Journal,* he probably hadn't heard that home sales in Aspen Meadow had virtually stopped. Fire insurers had refused to write new homeowner policies. This did not bring down the general anxiety level in the town. Was John Richard's search for a house what Cecelia wanted to know about? Maybe. But I doubted it.

I whizzed into an area of extra-large houses: here a huge colonial, there a rambling contemporary, around the corner a Swiss-style chalet. Every few houses, there was the type favored by John Richard: a mock

Tudor, with lots of plaster and crisscrossed exterior woodwork. One thing the houses in the club did have in common: They all boasted *very* green lawns. In town, rumors of how country-club residents managed illegal watering were rife. Some said hoses whistled across lawns at midnight. Others claimed that underground sprinkler systems hissed to life at three in the morning. Like the communists, residents were supposed to report infractions by neighbors. But in that department too, there were reports of deals—*I won't tell if you won't.* So much for community spirit.

When I piloted the van into the dead end that contained the Jerk's current mock-Tudor domicile, another car was parked out front. I sighed and prayed that this was not a new girlfriend. Maybe that was why John Richard favored the architecture he did: He fancied himself a contemporary Henry the Eighth. Lotta wives, lotta girlfriends.

I parked the van behind the car, an older blue Chevy sedan that looked as if someone was in it.

"Okay, hon," I said to Arch. He looked passably clean. He'd neatly parted and combed his wet hair after the shower, and he'd managed to lick all the chocolate away from around his mouth. "Just take your clubs and go to the door, do you mind? I'll wait here until you're inside."

Arch pushed his glasses up his nose. "Okay, Mom. Sorry you had to go to so much trouble."

"Don't worry about it. Just hurry." It was exactly ten to four, which meant Arch and his father didn't have a whole lot of time to get down to the club for their tee time.

Arch let out a long, exasperated breath, hopped out of the van, and heaved the strap of his golf bag over his shoulder. Then he trudged up the driveway, turning left to go up the steps to the house.

A sudden rapping on my hood startled me. An older man, maybe in his mid-fifties, with a receding hairline, gray hair combed straight back, and one of those thin-skinned, skeletal faces, wanted to talk to me. I caught my breath and looked out the windshield. He'd left the door to the Chevy sedan open.

"Mrs. Korman?" he called.

I lowered the window. "Excuse me?"

"Dad!" Arch was calling. "Dad! Open the door!"

"Mrs. Korman, do you have my money?" the man demanded. He wore a plaid cotton shirt, brown poly-ester pants, and worn, mud-colored leather shoes. Def-initely not a country-club type.

"I'm sorry, I—" I began.

"Please tell me you have my money, Mrs. Kor-man," the man pleaded. "I was here when I was sup-posed to be."

The van's side door slid open. The clubs clanked fe-rociously as Arch threw them in the back. He banged the door closed, then opened the passenger door and hopped back into the front seat.

"Dad left without me! Let's go!"

"Look," I said to the man, "who are you? What money? Why do you think *I'm* supposed to give *you* money?"

But Skeleton Face had had enough. He was trotting back to the sedan.

"Colorado GPG 521, blue Chevy Nova," I said un-der my breath. Then I dug into my purse, nabbed a ballpoint and an index card, and wrote it down. Had John Richard gotten himself into debt? Was this guy a creditor?

"Mom, he's not here. I knocked and knocked. Come on, let's split."

I squinted up at the Tudor. I reached for the cell and punched in the numbers for Dr. Hiding-in-the-House. No response, but I didn't expect there to be, since my caller ID came up as restricted. I left a message, saying that if John Richard wanted to see his son, he'd better get his butt out here. Nothing happened.

As a breeze swirled the dust in the street, I wondered what to do. Go home, and risk an angry call from the Jerk's lawyer? Or bang on the door myself and run the hazard of a very unpleasant encounter, possibly as bad as, or worse than, the attack that morning?

I glanced at the glove compartment, but just as quickly dismissed the idea of brandishing a firearm. What if he startled me and the thirty-eight again went off accidentally?

I said, "Get your clubs, Arch. Let's try one more time."

As Arch trudged around to get his golf bag, I reached under the van seat and took out the Swiss Army knife I kept under there. I opened it, slipped it into the pocket of the caterer's apron I was still wearing, and climbed up the front steps with Arch. We knocked and yelled for John Richard. I didn't doubt that he was watching to see if his creditor was truly gone, and not returning.

"Wait here," I said. "I'll check the garage and see if the Audi's inside." I gripped the knife and hobbled back down the steps. John Richard's geraniums and delphiniums were lush and full, I noted, no doubt from illegal watering. Still limping slightly, I rounded the house to the three-car garage.

Two bays were closed; the third, nearest to the back

door, was partially open. Still holding the knife handle, I ducked down to peer into the open space. I saw myself staring at my reflection in the TT's chrome. So he *was* home, the bastard.

My aching back and legs made it difficult to tuck myself underneath the garage door. Plus, I had to come up with a plan. My cell phone was in my other apron pocket, in case I needed it.

The garage smelled of grease, exhaust, and something else. . . . What? My footsteps gritted over the concrete as I eased around the back of the Audi. As soon as I got to the inside door to the house, I vowed, I'd call Marla. I wouldn't go in, but I'd tell her I *did* need her to meet me over here and force the Jerk to open up, just in case he decided to—

I stopped and stared in disbelief. I couldn't move, couldn't process what I was seeing. And yet there it was. There *he* was. John Richard, with his head skewed at a crazy angle, his body sprawled across the front seat of his car. His chest was covered with blood. He was a mess. And he was dead.

Chapter 5

I had loved him. I had hated him. He had stood beside me, grinning, when Arch was born. Many nights, he had thrust out his chest and thrashed me, until welts rose on my arms and back. I'd been convinced he had a black heart. Now his chest cavity was a gory mass of skin, bone, and blood.

And his heart wasn't beating.

I couldn't look at him, or what was left of him. I knew that smell now: cordite, the gas produced when a gun fires. My clammy hand gripped my cell phone. I called 911 and shakily explained that my ex-husband, Dr. John Richard Korman, had been shot. Yes, I thought he was dead. They asked for my location and I blanked.

"Aspen Meadow Country Club." My voice cracked. "A rental. Tudor house, on a dead end. This is a new place, and he's lying in the garage. Wait. We're at 4402 Stoneberry. I can't remember—"

But there was something I did remember: Arch. Oh my God, *Arch.* He was at the front door, waiting. Waiting for his *father.* What if he came looking for me in the garage? I was not going to allow him to see this.

"Ma'am?" The emergency operator's voice spiraled into my ear. "What do you mean, a new place for him?"

"Look, I have to go. I'll be out front when the sheriff's department shows up. My van, Goldilocks' Catering, is parked there. Please, I *have to go*. My fifteen-year-old son is here. He doesn't know his father is dead."

The operator's voice droned on. I didn't know if I was hearing her words or just mentally substituting what I knew she would say. *Stay on the scene, stay calm, stay put, do not hang up.* I ducked beneath the half-open garage door and closed the cell phone.

A sudden wind whipped the aspens and pines around the houses of the cul-de-sac. A cloud of dust rose into the air and shimmered in the sunlight. Then it blasted against John Richard's house. I closed my eyes against the grit and fought dizziness.

For he himself knows whereof we are made; he remembers that we are but dust.

What was I going to say to Arch? I simply could not imagine how to announce, "Your father has been shot. He's dead."

Riffs of jazz guitar emanated from the van radio. Arch had gotten tired of waiting. The time was ticking down until I told him.

I was having trouble breathing. Inhale, I ordered myself. Exhale. I pulled out the cell and dialed Tom.

"Somebody's shot John Richard," I announced to his voice mail. "He's dead. Oh, Tom, please come up to his house." The wind rose again and showered me with dust. "We need you. *Please.*"

I closed the phone. I would have to get rid of the hysterical note in my voice before talking to Arch.

John Richard's chest had been blown wide open. The image of what I'd seen made me dizzy. John Richard's pink shirt had been drenched in blood. And his pants . . . khakis, had been covered with blood, too. Oh, God, I couldn't think about it.

I dialed Marla's cell.

"Get over to the Jerk's new house as quickly as you can," I said to her voice mail. "I think somebody's shot him. He's dead."

My knees buckled and I sat down in the driveway. The wind picked up another nimbus of shiny dust and whacked it onto the cul-de-sac. John Richard's lush grass bristled and flattened. The blue delphiniums rimming the house bent and swayed.

Our days are like the grass; we flourish like the flower of the field.

I prayed. *Help me.* Perhaps God was already sending these verses from the 103rd Psalm, one my Sunday-school class had memorized. We flourish like a flower in the field, and then?

When the wind goes over it, it is gone, and its place shall know it no more.

John Richard was no more. Was it possible, after all these years? Was he really gone, this man who had hurt so many people? I swallowed hard, stood, and steadied myself. It was time to go talk to Arch.

"Hon, something very bad has happened." I slipped into the van driver's seat and turned off the radio.

Arch furrowed his brow. "What? Is Dad okay?"

"Arch, I'm sorry, I'm *so* sorry, but your dad is not okay." Arch frowned, his eyes fixed on me. "It's very bad news, I'm afraid, so prepare yourself. Your dad is dead. I think he's been shot. The police will be here soon."

"What are you *saying,* Mom? Dad's been involved in a shooting? When? Where is he?"

"He's in the garage. Something went very wrong. That's why the sheriff's department is coming."

"Where's your cell?" Arch demanded, his voice loud. Denial, denial, of course. "Call an ambulance, they might be able to revive him!"

"Oh, Arch—"

Dust sprayed on the windshield. There was the distant sound of sirens. The sheriff's department must have had an officer patrolling Aspen Meadow. They'd have radioed and told him to hightail it over here.

"Mom!" Arch yelled, his eyes wild.

It had been a long time since Arch had let me hug him, but he did now. He was trembling violently.

"Mom—" His voice cracked. "Please!" He wrenched away. "What happened? Why won't you tell me?"

"I don't know what happened. If I did, I'd tell you."

Arch put his head in his hands. He began to sob, wrenching cries that felt as if they were ripping my chest open. After a while, I reached out for him, but his hands batted me away. The tear-stained face he turned to me was filled with rage.

"Tell me what happened, Mom! Who was that guy who was here? Did he shoot Dad?"

"I don't *know*! That's why the police are—" *Mrs. Korman, do you have my money?* What kind of money problem had John Richard gotten himself into? Had he plunged himself into a debt jam? One he couldn't climb out of? My mind wheeled and bumped over the possibilities as Arch continued to cry.

Without warning, the van's back door rumbled open, startling both of us. Arch used his shirt to wipe his face, then adjusted his glasses.

"It's me," Tom's deep, authoritative voice announced. He climbed in, sat heavily in the rear seat,

and wordlessly handed each of us a homemade quilt.
These thick handmade creations were for victims and
survivors of violent crime, stitched by volunteers in the
county. I wrapped myself in mine, a red-and-white
beauty with, ironically, a heart motif. Arch let his
black-and-gold-patterned one fall to the floor.

My cell phone chirped and I picked it up. The caller
ID indicated it was Marla. Tom gently removed the
phone from my hand and pressed Talk.

"Yeah, Marla. It's true. Goldy and Arch are right
here with me, in the van. Yeah, I sped up to Stoneberry.
No, don't come. I'm telling you, *stay away*. Keep your
cell next to you and we'll call you back. Yeah, *soon*."
Then he pressed End.

A sudden rapping on the side window made me
jump. It was the same sound the skeleton-faced fellow
had made when he'd asked for his money. I wanted to
tell Tom about that, but I didn't want to upset Arch
more than he already was.

My son's face was very pale. He was shivering and
biting his bottom lip. I picked up the quilt and tucked it
behind his shoulders.

"Schulz," said a uniformed cop. "They're asking for
you up on the driveway. They want to know your relationship with all this."

Tom climbed from the van. I watched his commanding swagger as he accompanied the cop up the driveway. Three police cars now ringed the dead end. I
turned to my son, who had pulled around the edge of
the quilt to cover his face.

"Arch, honey," I said gently, "what can I do for you?
Do you want me to call Todd? See if he can come over
here? The cops are going to want to talk to me . . . because I found your dad. They'll probably talk to you,

too. Then I'll have to go down to the department. When I do, would you like to go over to the Druck-mans'? Or do you want to stay with me?" I paused. "I'm willing to have you with me every minute."

Arch hesitated, then poked his head out of the quilt. He was scowling, trying to keep a lid on his feelings. "I don't know. All right, I'll be with Todd." He raised his eyes to mine. "What about you, Mom?"

"I'll be fine," I said, with more calm than I felt.

I called the Druckmans' house and told the machine that we'd had a family emergency. If Eileen could come to the Stoneberry cul-de-sac to wait for Arch, we would deeply appreciate it. I closed the cell phone, thinking I should call St. Luke's Episcopal Church, where John Richard was a sometime parishioner. But I couldn't face it. I stared out the windshield, unable to think. The sun's glare on the dust burned my eyes.

Cops swarmed all around us. Once again, Arch's breath began to come out as soblike gasps. I hugged him. Shoulders heaving, he accepted the embrace.

Tom startled us by opening the back door. He slid in again, his face grim. Still, he reached over and patted Arch on the back.

"Hey, buddy. I'm sorry. We're going to take care of you."

Arch cleared his throat once, twice. Then the three of us were silent. What if the cops insisted Arch go to the department with me? I couldn't contemplate it.

When Eileen Druckman's black BMW wagon roared up, I thanked God. Eileen leaped out of the car and trotted toward the van. She wore a gray sweatsuit. Her dark hair was wet, as if she'd just gotten out of the shower. Bless her for answering my desperate call so quickly.

I jumped out when Eileen was intercepted by a cop. He seemed to accept her explanation for why she was here, and let her go. As I walked over to meet her, I noted that what had to be my heightened adrenaline from finding John Richard had diminished the physical pain from that morning's assault. Once again, I shook my head at the irony.

"John Richard's been shot," I murmured. "He's dead."

Eileen's slim, pretty face twitched. "Good Lord."

With Tom helping him, Arch slowly descended from the van. He still had the black-and-gold quilt pulled tightly around his head and shoulders. On this breezy, dusty June afternoon, he needed the protection. Before my son was allowed to leave, though, the same policeman intercepted him.

"We need him to give a statement, ma'am," the cop informed me.

My shoulders slumped. "Can't it possibly wait?"

He shook his head, but his tone softened. "The detectives aren't here yet. Tell you what, I'll take a preliminary report. You need to be here, though."

I nodded. Of course. I knew a parent had to be present when a minor was questioned. But I sure didn't look forward to it.

We walked to his car, which smelled of tuna sandwiches and old vinyl. In a halting voice, Arch told the patrolman everything he'd seen, from the old man in the blue sedan (he'd been up knocking on the door when the guy asked for his money), to there being no answer at his father's house. When we got to the part about how I'd told him to wait while I went to the garage, the patrolman flicked me a look. Still numb, I pressed my lips together and shrugged. When Arch broke down and started crying, the cop told him he could leave.

Eileen walked over and held Arch. "Todd's waiting for you. Oh, you dear boy, I'm so sorry."

"Arch!" Tom called after him. "I'll come over to the Druckmans' house as soon as I finish here with your mom. All right?"

Arch looked back and nodded, his face a pale sliver inside the dark quilt.

When Eileen's wagon had belched smoke and taken off down Stoneberry, Tom muttered to me that he'd return in a few minutes. He strode back up the driveway. I couldn't think of what I was supposed to do. The policeman said I needed to wait for the detectives, so I climbed back into the van's driver's seat. There were now six Furman County Sheriff's Department cars parked at various angles in the cul-de-sac.

It was going to be a long afternoon.

Cops came and went. One unrolled yellow crime-scene tape around John Richard's rental property. The coroner arrived.

I had no idea how much time had passed. Finally, *finally,* Tom came walking back down the driveway. When he climbed into the passenger seat, his ordinarily rosy face was drained of color.

I said, "Now what's—"

He held up his hand. Then he reached forward and opened my glove compartment. My glove compartment that I usually kept *locked.*

It was empty. I stared at the vacant space, not comprehending.

"Dammit!" Tom whacked the compartment closed. This unusually violent act unnerved me. My ears began to ring.

"Tom. Don't tell me they found *my* gun in the garage."

He shook his head. "You know they're not going to let me be part of this investigation. But . . . I happened to see the thirty-eight beside the driveway, like someone had tossed it there. I just didn't want to believe it."

"I did *not* shoot him. I swear."

He reached out for my hands and held them. "I know." He paused. "After you accidentally fired at the mice this morning, you didn't lock your thirty-eight back in your glove compartment, did you?"

I thought back, now wholly confused. I must have locked the compartment. I'd unlocked it when I'd shown my gun to the officer investigating the attack. He'd left when Julian and Liz arrived. Then we'd been in such a hurry to get new food, my body had hurt so much from being hit, and I'd been so worried about Roger Mannis showing up . . . no, I remembered replacing the gun, but not relocking the compartment. But aside from that cop, Marla, and Tom, who knew I kept a gun in the van? And Marla would never have done this. She was working at the bake sale, and she would have joked that that was *much* more important than shooting the Jerk.

Tom reached for my cell phone and pressed the buttons for Marla's cell. She must have answered right away, because Tom began talking almost immediately.

"Trouble here, Marla. We need you to find a criminal attorney for Goldy and have him meet her down at the department ASAP." Tom paused. "What do you mean, why? Of course she didn't do it. But things aren't going too well. We'll tell you more later." Then he pressed End. I could just imagine Marla hurling her cell phone against whatever wall was convenient. She *hated* people hanging up on her.

Tom handed me my phone. "Put this in your pocket. We're going to have to talk quickly because—"

"Oh, Lord, Tom, I'm going to be sick."

"Listen to me. Look at me."

I focused on those green eyes, usually liquid with love. Now they were stern, commanding. My stomach tightened even more. "Say as little as possible, understand? Don't worry that it makes you look guilty." He touched my cheek, as if to soften his words. "Do not talk about being attacked this morning. Do not tell them the gun went off in your hand. *Do not even tell them you have a gun.* Give as brief a statement as possible. Then when you get down to the department, demand to confer with your lawyer." His eyes turned gentle. "You have to trust me on this."

"I trust you on everything," I said weakly.

Two detectives were sauntering down the driveway. I knew they were detectives because they wore dark suits and sober ties. One held a clipboard. The other signaled to Tom that they wanted to talk to me. Panic rose in my throat, as it had so many nights when John Richard had been raging, hollering, and throwing things. The memory of that fear immobilized me.

I wanted to bolt.

My mind, so blank a while ago, was now whirling. This morning I'd been beaten up and sabotaged. Of course I'd *suspected* the Jerk. I'd taken my thirty-eight into the Roundhouse and been so startled by rodents, I'd accidentally fired at the floor. *And now I had gunshot residue on my hands.* John Richard had been shot with *my* gun, stolen from *my* glove compartment that I'd stupidly forgotten to lock. He'd been killed sometime in the three hours between when I'd last seen him at the Roundhouse and four o'clock. And *when* I'd last seen him at the Roundhouse, sixty-plus people had witnessed the two of us locked in a shouting match.

"Mrs. Korman? I mean, Mrs. Schulz?" said the first detective, a young, red-haired fellow with a name tag that said "Reilly." His clipboard, I noticed, was filled with bright white paper. Behind him was someone else I didn't recognize, a taller, older man with black hair, a ruddy complexion, and "Blackridge" on his name tag. "Could you get out of your vehicle and talk to us for a few minutes?"

I obeyed him. Tom had put his career on the line by checking my glove compartment, to see if the weapon they'd found was mine. My dear husband. How different he was from the one who now lay dead up in the garage.

Everything will be all right, I told myself. But it sure didn't feel that way.

Chapter 6

"Will you give us permission to search your vehicle?" Reilly asked in the same formal tone.

"Yes, yes, of course," I said automatically. And then I had a horrible thought: What if the killer who'd taken my gun had planted something in my car? The detectives had already nodded at two crime-scene guys; one of them clambered into the car. Tom looked at me and gave a thumbs-up. I wanted to feel confident, but I didn't.

I took a deep breath and followed the detectives halfway around the cul-de-sac, until we arrived at a department car.

"When did you get here, Mrs. Schulz?" Reilly asked, his blue eyes flat.

"Just before four. Maybe five, ten of."

He scribbled. "And why were you here?"

"John Richard Korman, the man who was . . . shot, is, was my ex-husband. This morning, well, actually, this afternoon, he . . ." Suddenly I couldn't stand it. Literally. "I need to sit down."

They opened the doors of the department car, and the three of us slid in. Blackridge sat in the driver's seat. Reilly, beside me in the back, told me to keep on with my story.

"He, John Richard, said he had a late tee time for playing golf with Arch. Arch is our fifteen-year-old son who just left." Neither detective spoke. Reilly motioned for me to go on. "John Richard said for me to bring Arch over at four, which I did."

When Reilly wrote, his short, pale, freckled fingers moved very fast. Blackridge's face, meanwhile, was impassive. When a groan escaped me, the detectives exchanged a glance.

"When you got here," Blackridge asked, "was anyone else here?"

"Yes, someone was." I described the down-at-the-heels fellow with the skeletal face. Blackridge wanted to know about the man's car, and seemed surprised that I'd written down the license number. Reilly retrieved the piece of paper I offered from my pocket and took more notes.

"What made you do that?" Blackridge again. "Take down this man's license number, I mean."

"He called me 'Mrs. Korman.' I guess he assumed I was John Richard's wife because Arch was up at the door yelling, 'Dad! Dad! Open the door!' Anyway, the man wanted to know if I had his money."

"'His money,'" Blackridge repeated. "What money?"

"Well," I said, "obviously, money the Jer—uh, John Richard owed him!" As Arch would say, *Duh.* Through all this, Reilly wrote.

"Then what did you do?" Blackridge demanded.

"Nothing. The guy seemed to get nervous. He left. Then I went up to the door with Arch. We both banged on it and rang the bell."

"You *banged* on the door?" Blackridge's dark brown eyes pierced me. "Why?"

I sighed. "Because I was *sure* John Richard was in there." I ordered myself to get the anger out of my voice before saying any more. In a calmer tone, I went on: "You have to understand. John Richard had been *very* insistent that I bring Arch over *promptly* at four. I was convinced he was hiding out from this fellow, one of his creditors, who wanted his money. But I figured that since the guy had driven off, John Richard just wasn't aware that the coast was clear. So when he still didn't answer the door, I said to Arch, 'Let's try one more time.'" I stopped talking, trying to recall what had happened next. What had happened *exactly*.

"Then what?" Blackridge prompted me after a few moments.

"I walked around to the garage."

"Where was your son?"

"I told him to wait at the front door."

"You said, '*Let's* try one more time.' Why didn't you have your son go with you?"

"I don't know." Why did the truth have to look so bad? *Just wait here, honey, while I go pretend to discover Dad, dead.* Heat rose to my cheeks. I added, "I told my son I was just checking to see if the Audi was there."

The detectives traded another look.

Blackridge said, "Go on."

"The garage door was half open, which was bizarre, or at least unusual for John Richard."

"Why's that?"

"Because John Richard loved that car, that new Audi. He was manic about his *stuff*. He'd never risk someone being able to break in through the garage." Blackridge nodded for me to continue. "I ducked down. I could see that the Audi was still there. So I scooted under the garage door—"

"Why not call Arch over at that point?" Blackridge wanted to know. "You'd been at the front door together, trying to summon his father."

I let out a deep breath. "I *don't know.*" This seemed to be my refrain for the day. "Anyway," I went on quickly, eager for this to be over, since I knew I was going to have to repeat the whole thing down at the department. "I went in, walked across the garage, and then . . ." I paused, remembering the horrid sight of John Richard's twisted body. "Then I saw him. In his car. I saw he'd been shot and that he was dead. So I called Tom and got his voice mail. I left a message about what I'd seen, and I asked him to come up here. Then I called you all."

"Did you touch anything in the garage? Move anything? Take anything?"

"No, no, no, of course not."

Reilly tapped the clipboard with his pen. "We'll be analyzing the tape of your call to 911," he put in.

"Go ahead," I retorted, feeling fury flare. So what if I'd hung up on the 911 operator? I'd been worried about Arch, still out front. I hadn't wanted him to make an appearance in the garage and see his father, so grotesque in death.

Blackridge lifted a warning eyebrow at Reilly. "And next, Mrs. Schulz?" he asked gently.

I bit the inside of my cheek. In a homicide case, the cops traced all the calls you made, so omitting the call to Marla was a bad idea. "I called my best friend, Marla Korman. She's John Richard's other ex-wife. I got her voice mail, too." I took a deep breath.

"And why did you call the other ex-wife of the man you'd just found dead?"

"I don't know. I didn't think. Because she's my friend, I suppose. I left her a message saying John Richard was dead. Then I went to tell my son there had been a terrible accident. That his father was dead. I knew he'd need me. Then the two of us waited for you all to show up."

Blackridge had hooked his meaty arm over the front seat so he could turn and look at me. "Do you have any idea who could have done this, Mrs. Schulz? Did Dr. Korman have enemies? Say, particular people who didn't like him?"

I thought of Courtney MacEwan's cold eyes and hardened visage this morning. *He owes me.* But she was only one of many women—present company included—whom John Richard had made love to passionately for a while before moving on to someone else.

"He had ex-girlfriends," I said lamely. "Lots of them. Fifty-some."

"*Fifty*-some? Can you give us names of the most recent ones?"

I felt horrid pointing the finger at Courtney, but I was being truthful here, right? "I'm pretty sure the most recent ex-girlfriend is named Courtney MacEwan."

"Spell her name, please." Reilly's thin voice startled me. Feeling like a total heel, I spelled Courtney's name.

"Anyone else?" Blackridge asked.

"His current girlfriend is named Sandee Blue. I think she works at the country-club golf shop."

"Anyone else?"

"Wait. He had an argument at the funeral lunch with a man named Ted Vikarios. I don't know where Ted lives or even if the argument is significant." I spelled

Ted's name for them. Did I know any other possible enemies of John Richard? they asked. I said, "Apart from the man wanting his money, I don't know who John Richard's current acquaintances are. Were." I did not add my usual comment, *I try to stay as far away from him as possible.*

"Okay, Mrs. Schulz," Blackridge said. Finally. "You know the drill here. You're the primary witness, and we need to take you down to the department to make a taped statement." Reilly flipped over the pages of notes he'd taken and tucked the clipboard beside him. Blackridge turned the key in the ignition, and we started out for the Furman County Sheriff's Department. There, I knew, everything would be different.

My new criminal lawyer would be waiting. This would make me look even more guilty, but tough tacks. And the taped interrogation would not be, as they say, a piece of cake.

Brewster Motley had wide shoulders, a mop of long, sun-bleached blond curls, and a tanned, boyish face complete with impish grin. He looked like a surfer who'd accidentally gotten tucked into an expensive gray Italian suit and dark gray leather loafers. Unfortunately, I'd had to deal with a few criminal lawyers. When you're telling them what actually happened, they smirk at you. And then when the two of you are with the cops, your lawyer commands you to shut up, even when you have a perfectly good explanation for how things went so wrong. In any event, I took to happy-go-lucky-looking Brewster Motley. He'd believe I was innocent, wouldn't he?

Tom had told me to demand to see my lawyer *immediately.* So when we reached the department parking lot, I astonished Reilly and Blackridge by announcing that my attorney should have arrived by now. I said I wanted to confer with him before any taping began. When Blackridge glanced in the rearview mirror to check my expression, I just closed my eyes.

After about ten minutes of bureaucratic wrangling and trying to find the person Mrs. Schulz was asking for, I was ushered into a room where Brewster Motley was waiting, grinning from ear to ear. *Surf's up!*

"I think I'm in trouble," I began, once the door was closed. Brewster suppressed his grin and nodded sympathetically.

"Tell me about it." His voice was as warm and comforting as custard sauce. "Let's sit." He snapped open a luxurious leather briefcase and pulled out a notepad. "Relax."

I did as told. No wonder they call them *Counselor.*

"First of all, Mr. Motley, I did not shoot my ex-husband."

"Call me Brewster. And by the way, I'm aware of the few times you've helped the cops with cases. I read about them in the paper."

"Super. But I have to tell you, Brewster, there are a lot of circumstances that are going to make this look really bad." I gave a very abbreviated account of the terrible history between John Richard and me. John Richard, I went on, was an unreformed batterer who'd beaten one girlfriend almost to death, an act that had finally landed him in prison for aggravated assault. He'd gotten out six weeks ago, on April the twenty-second, and had already dumped one girlfriend who was now furious with him. Brewster asked for her name and I spelled out *Courtney MacEwan* for the second time that day. I told him about the Jerk's brief argument with Ted Vikarios, and again spelled out that name. Plus, John Richard seemed to be in trouble with creditors. He was living a country-club lifestyle with no visible means of support. I believed he was borrowing large amounts of money, secured by who-knows-what. That could be the only explanation for his sudden ability to sponsor a golf tournament, afford the rent on a Tudor McMansion, and buy, not lease, a new Audi. John Richard had been trying to embrace the high-flying rich-doctor lifestyle he used to have. Except that he wasn't practicing medicine. His license had been suspended when he went to jail.

"How do you know he bought the Audi?"

"His other ex-wife, Marla Korman, and I are best friends. She told me."

"Yes. That's the Mrs. Marla Korman who hired me."

"Right. Marla loves to track the . . . John Richard, his love life and financial dealings. And she passes on all she learns to me." I felt my cheeks coloring. "We do gossip about him. Did."

Brewster tapped his pen on the desk. "Did you and Dr. Korman have any children?"

I told him about Arch, that my son had been with me when I'd discovered John Richard's body. Well, not *exactly* with me, and that was part of the problem.

Brewster held up a hand and gave me another charming grin. "Let's not get ahead of ourselves. Did Dr. Korman keep up with child support while he was in prison?"

"Yes," I admitted. "His lawyer arranged for the sale of the Jer—uh, John Richard's house, and supposedly the child support came out of that."

"What do you mean, *supposedly*? Did you ask Korman's lawyer where the money came from?"

"You bet I did. And he rudely informed me that as long as I got the money, where it came from was none of my beeswax. He also told me that Marla's snooping wasn't going to get her anywhere."

There was a knock on the door. Brewster Motley jumped from his chair to answer it. He spoke in a low but confident voice.

"No," he said finally, "my client and I will tell you when *we're* ready." Without waiting for a reply, he shut the door.

"Maybe we should move along to today," Brewster said lightly once he was seated again. "Tell me everything you think is pertinent."

I described showing up to prep a funeral lunch, being shoved aside by an unknown assailant and then chopped in the neck. No, I didn't know who the guy in the mask was. Yes, I suspected the Jerk. That was what Marla and I had begun calling John Richard at least ten years ago. It was based on his initials, I explained, and it suited his personality, too. Brewster shook his head, a grim smile on his face.

I summarized the rest of it—Marla coming, our discovery of the break-in, the mice, my firing the thirty-eight. Brewster wrinkled his tanned face.

"Where'd you get the gun?"

"I've been keeping the thirty-eight in my glove compartment ever since John Richard had his sentence commuted."

Brewster's blond curlicues of hair trembled. My heart plummeted.

"Why was his sentence commuted?"

I sighed. "A prison guard was having a heart attack. John Richard gave him CPR and saved his life. There were witnesses. The guard, his cardiologist, and everyone in the guard's family wrote to the governor begging him to let John Richard out."

Brewster frowned. "And nobody's tried to hit or ambush you until today?"

"No."

"And you fired the gun today."

"Right. You should know that my husband of the past two years is Tom Schulz, a sheriff's-department investigator," I added quickly. "He thought my having the thirty-eight was a good idea, as long as I kept the glove compartment locked, which I'm sorry to say I appear not to have done, um, after I accidentally fired at the mice." Brewster stopped writing and gave me a confused look. "A cop came and took a report. I showed him the gun, then put it back into the glove compartment. But I forgot to lock it."

"How do you know you forgot to lock it, Mrs. Schulz?"

"Because somebody stole my gun."

His expression was studiously flat. "Keep giving me an exact summary of events, please."

"My assistants and I were able to put together another meal, a cold plate. But after the lunch, John Richard started screaming at me, outside the Roundhouse. He wanted me to bring Arch over to his house at four so they could play golf. It wasn't a pretty exchange. Even worse, lots of the guests still at the lunch—"

Wait a minute. By the time John Richard and I were arguing, people had begun to leave. There'd been folks milling around in the parking lot, getting into their cars and taking off. One of them had gone into my van and stolen my gun. But why? And who? Usually people sneaked into my van to steal food. So the culprit hadn't found any food, had stolen my gun, and then had killed John Richard with it, just for good measure?

"Lots of the guests still at lunch," Brewster prompted me.

"And folks in the parking lot, too. They all witnessed this argument. Anyway, I rustled up Arch, who was with a pal at an ice rink down in Lakewood. I brought them to our house, got Arch cleaned up, delivered some brownies to a bake sale, dropped Arch's friend at his house and arrived at John Richard's just before four."

"Please give me the times, exactly."

I did. I also repeated the scenario of the fellow asking for money, then driving off, and how I'd discovered the body—by myself. Brewster nodded and kept writing.

"But you haven't heard the worst part, Mr. Mot—Brewster."

"He was shot with your gun?"

"My gun was at the scene. How'd you know?"

"More important, how do *you* know, Mrs. Schulz?"

I let out a breath. How could I say this without it sounding as if I was somehow collaborating with my cop husband? "Even though he's not on the case, my husband had been up at the garage with the team. When he came out, he spotted my thirty-eight lying beside the driveway. He came back to my van and opened the glove compartment. When there was nothing there, I knew my gun had to be up near John Richard."

There was another rap at the door. Brewster put the notepad back in his leather briefcase and stood up.

He said, "Every time they ask you a question, look at me before you say a single word." He hesitated, then gave me his beach-boy grin, as if he were actually looking forward to the interrogation. Still smiling, he said, "Let's boogie."

I followed Brewster down the hall until the cop who'd knocked on the door ushered us into an interrogation room. Two more cops were there, along with Blackridge and Reilly. The cops shocked me when they stepped forward and placed brown paper bags over my hands, then taped the bags closed. Meanwhile, Blackridge was talking.

"Mrs. Schulz, you have the right to remain silent. You have the right to an attorney. If you cannot afford an attorney . . ."

Aw jeez, Miranda? And they were checking for gunshot residue *already*? There was *no way* they could have run the serial numbers on my thirty-eight that quickly.

"I strongly object to the placement of bags on my client's hands." Brewster's voice was suddenly authoritative, cold with rage. "She is here as a witness, not a suspect. Either arrest her or take the bags off."

"Sit down, Counselor," ordered Blackridge. "She's a suspect." He motioned me to a chair, too. I stared up at the blank mirrored wall, behind which, I knew, a video camera was rolling. Probably the chief of detectives was back there, too, observing this little drama along with a prosecutor. Oh, joy. "While the two of you were having your conference," Blackridge went on, "we had a chance to check our files. There are quite a few reports in there from you, Mrs. Schulz." He raised those same questioning dark eyes and black eyebrows at me. "Your ex-husband perpetrated violence on you? Did you finally see your chance to get even?"

"We resent the question," Brewster quickly announced. "My client will not answer. And if you checked those files thoroughly, you saw that Mrs. Schulz has helped your department with several homicide investigations."

Reilly snorted.

Unmoved, Blackridge went on, "We also had the chance to talk to a few guests at the lunch you catered today. They said that when folks were beginning to leave, you and your ex-husband had a screaming match outside."

Brewster piped up, "Dr. Korman yelled at my client. He demanded she bring their son over at four o'clock today, which was not a prearranged visitation. As you saw from your files, he was a violent, dangerous man, given to fits of temper. His demand was extremely inconvenient for my client, and she said so. If you check your witnesses, you'll see it was Dr. Korman raising his voice. Not my client."

I sighed and put my bagged hands up on the table. This was a mistake.

"How'd you get those marks on your arms?" Blackridge demanded.

Puzzled, I looked down. The places my arms had hit when I'd landed on the ground this morning had had time to swell and turn red. In some places, they were already shading to purple.

"My client refuses to answer questions on her appearance," Brewster said, indignant.

Blackridge ignored him. "Can you account for your movements, Mrs. Schulz, between the time of your argument with Dr. Korman and your finding his body?"

I glanced at Brewster, who nodded. In as few words as possible, and looking straight at the video camera, I recounted the chronology.

"And you told us earlier there was a man there?" Blackridge prompted.

Brewster indicated that I could answer, so I again summed up the story about the down-at-the-heels gent wanting his money.

Blackridge leaned into my face. "Do you own a gun, Mrs. Schulz?"

"I'm advising my client not to answer," Brewster interjected. "And I want you to take the bags off."

"Look, Counselor, either you let us swab her hands or we'll get a fast court order to do it."

"You *will* find GSR on my client's hands," Brewster announced, his voice matter-of-fact. "The explanation is simple."

"I'll *bet* it is," Blackridge muttered.

"There was a rodent infestation at her place of business this morning. She was carrying a firearm to protect herself and accidentally fired when surprised by the rodents. Not only do we have a witness to this shooting, but a Furman County patrolman, called to the scene, saw the bullet hole in the Roundhouse kitchen floor. He also saw her weapon in her van's glove compartment."

"Right," said Blackridge. Then he turned to me and glowered. "So you *do* have a gun. Your ex beat you up today, didn't he? Or maybe he did it last night. So you planned today out. You put mice in your restaurant, got a friend to meet you there, and then you shot at the little furry creatures. That way, you'd have a good explanation for the GSR. You knew you'd see Dr. Korman at the event you were catering, and that he'd want something right away. He always wanted something, didn't he? You'd have to do something for him, take something over to his house. Or maybe you made up an excuse to go over there."

"No—" I protested.

"You saw your chance and you took it, didn't you, Mrs. Schulz?"

"No!" I yelled. My voice was loud and vehement, but I didn't care. "I'd have everything to lose and nothing to gain by doing such a thing!" Under the table, one of Brewster's loafers nudged my left sneaker. I pressed my lips together.

"Again, Mrs. Schulz, for the record, do you know who else disliked Dr. Korman as much as you did?"

"My client refuses to answer unless you reword the question." For a surfer dude, Brewster Motley sure seemed to know his stuff.

"Calm down, Counselor, we're not in court yet." Blackridge tilted his wide, meaty face at me. "Do you have any idea who Dr. Korman's enemies were, Mrs. Schulz?"

For the third time that day, I found myself spelling *MacEwan* and, even more reluctantly, *Vikarios*. I said John Richard had no job, and appeared to be living on what I surmised was borrowed money. Beyond that, I did not know.

"What about the other ex-wife? Marla Korman? Any enmity between her and Dr. Korman?"

Brewster shook his head and said, "My client refuses to answer any questions about Dr. Korman's other ex-wife. You'll have to interrogate Marla Korman yourselves."

Well, I certainly didn't like the idea of *that*. But Brewster had not given me permission to speak.

"Where is your gun now, Mrs. Schulz?" Blackridge asked.

"My client refuses to answer." Brewster had allowed a weary note to creep into his voice. "Okay, boys, do the GSR test, and then we're done here, unless you intend to arrest my client."

Blackridge made a face, but glanced over at the cops who'd bagged my hands and gave a single nod. They brought in the distilled water and Q-tips, removed the bags, and swabbed first the top and inside of my index fingers, then the web of my hands going to my thumbs, and finally the top and inside of my thumbs. Checking for antimonium barium, otherwise known as gunshot residue. Which they were going to find, all because I'd been startled by mice.

The cops left the room with the swabs. The detectives exchanged some prearranged facial signal and told us to wait. When they banged out the door, it shook on its hinges.

I covered my mouth and leaned over to Brewster. "What are they doing now? Where'd they go?"

Brewster, with a palm over his own mouth, whispered, "They're consulting with whoever was behind the mirror. They're trying to decide if they have enough evidence to go to a prosecutor now. They're also trying to decide if you're a flight risk. My guess is that they'll answer no to both questions, and let you go."

What seemed an eternity later, but was probably only ten minutes, Reilly reentered the room. I thought of Arch. My stomach cramped. *Please, God, let me not be sent to jail.*

"Mrs. Schulz?" His tone was solemn. "You may go for now. Please do not leave Furman County. Do you understand?"

Did I understand? How dumb did he think I was?

My voice was weak and my body was unsteady. But I said, "Sure," scraped back my chair, and followed Brewster Motley out of the interrogation room.

Chapter 7

As we walked down the department's echoing metal steps, dizziness assaulted me. I grabbed the metal railing, which was shockingly cold. Or was it really hot? Hard to tell.

I told myself that grabbing something hot should remind me of . . . a delectable dish, something hot from the oven, its crumbly crust steaming, its fruit filling sizzling. . . . I stopped and closed my eyes.

The last time I'd burned my fingers had been when a pot holder had slipped, and I'd inadvertently grabbed the copper side of a hot tarte tatin mold. Straight from the oven, the tarte's luscious, bronzed apple slices had bubbled and popped around the edges of a circle of buttery, impossibly flaky pastry. To compound the injury to my burned finger, a few drops of scalding caramelized juice had oozed out of the pan onto my palm and I'd yelped. To comfort myself, I'd wrapped my hand in an ice pack; with my free hand, I'd scooped out a large helping of the tarte and heaped it with frosty globes of cinnamon ice cream. . . .

"Goldy?"

I opened my eyes and stared up at the wavy-glassed

four-story bank of windows. The glass caught and magnified the sunlight. I blinked in the glare.

What had I been thinking about? Oh, yes, caramelized apples. . . .

Brewster, seeing that I was no longer descending, turned and gave me a questioning look. "Need help?" he asked.

"Thanks, I'm fine," I replied, and started back down the ringing metal steps. Then I stopped again. I had no way to get home. The detectives had brought me down in a department car. Tom was either at the Druckmans' house or at home—in either case, he was with Arch and I didn't want to bother him.

"Actually, there is something you can do for me, Brewster. If you wouldn't mind." I told him I needed a ride back to my van, which was at the scene of the crime. If the crime-scene guys had finished with it, then I'd be able to pick it up and drive home.

"That's absolutely no problem," he replied cheerily. "I have a few more questions for you, anyway. Might save you an office visit."

Oh great, I thought dully as Brewster disappeared outside to retrieve his car. More questions. I'd already had what, three hours of interrogation at John Richard's house and here at the department? I just couldn't wait.

When Brewster pulled up in his gold Mercedes—a sleek, shiny sedan not unlike Marla's— I smiled at the unlawyerlike stickers on his rear window. On the right was "Burton," a brand of snowboard; on the left, bless my intuition, "Hobie Surfboards." I didn't care what kind of dude he was as long as he was a good attorney. And so far, he'd seemed more than competent.

The bright light and dusty wind momentarily

blinded me as I made my way to the passenger door. Once I was settled into the plush leather seat, though, Brewster smoothly maneuvered the Benz out of the parking lot. No question: This was not like driving with Marla. There, every item of conversation was punctuated with my friend either braking, accelerating, or cursing.

"By the way," Brewster began, as if reading my mind, "your pal Marla is paying for all my time. So don't worry about costs, and don't hesitate to call with questions."

"That's super. She's great." Then I tensed. "That's not a conflict of interest for you, is it? I mean, those detectives were acting as if she was a suspect, too."

"If Marla needs a lawyer, she can get her own. You're my client." Brewster whizzed onto the interstate. "Goldy," he said, "could you give me a quick history of your marriage to, and divorce from, Dr. Korman?"

And so I did. There was this glamorous, charismatic medical student, the story always began, and yours truly, spellbound at nineteen, hadn't been a very good judge of character. Yes, I said bitterly, the sheriff's department still had my complaints on file. Not that my pleas for help had done any good, since in those days a spouse had to agree to press charges, something I was reluctant to do. Even after we were divorced, John Richard had continued his brash and brutal ways with women, until he'd finally been thrown in jail. A prison sentence actually, that he'd been serving in the Furman County Jail because the penitentiary at Cañon City was overcrowded. But being incarcerated hadn't ended his ability to attract women.

"How long has he known Courtney MacEwan?"

"He's probably *known* her for eight or nine years.

The way I heard it, as soon as he got out, he called her to go out for coffee, which became lunch, which became a tennis game, which became a whirlwind affair."

Brewster nodded. "I know the firm that handled her husband's will. She got about twenty million."

"And don't think John Richard wasn't aware of *that.*" I recounted all I'd learned from Marla, how John Richard had promised Courtney they'd get married as soon as possible. But then he'd balked—because of *Arch,* he claimed. How Marla and I suspected, but weren't sure, that Courtney had been bankrolling John Richard's reentry into society. Until he dumped her, that is. Then we thought he might have started borrowing money. And Courtney had been *pissed.*

"I read about it in Cecelia Brisbane's gossip column in the *Journal,*" Brewster mused.

I groaned. As soon as I'd seen Cecelia's cruel column from Friday, the fifth of May, I'd snatched the newspaper and stuffed it in the garbage before Arch could see it. The column had read, "What cute doctor is back out on the golf course, wearing plus fours over his prison suit? And what well-moneyed tennis-playing widow is getting to know him (in the biblical sense, dear readers!) when the two of them leave the club and zip over to their love nest?"

How could people get away with this kind of stuff? I'd wondered. And is this what Cecelia had meant today, when she'd said John Richard was up to his old tricks? I did not know. Arch, studying for his final exams, had either not seen the "cute doctor" column or not cared. I doubted the latter.

"So when did he break up with Courtney?" Brewster asked.

"Arch called one Saturday and asked me to come get

him at John Richard's house. His dad was busy packing boxes, he said. The next thing I knew, Courtney was out and a new girlfriend had been installed."

"His new girlfriend? You mentioned her to the cops."

"Sandee with two *e*s, as she calls herself. Her last name is Blue. Supposedly, John Richard met her in the country-club golf shop, but she doesn't look like any lady golfer I've ever seen." Brewster gave me a questioning look. "They're usually svelte and trim. Long and lean. Sandee's short and buxom, and dresses, if you could call it that, to show off her figure. She doesn't look a day over twenty-five."

Brewster grunted. "And then Courtney showed up at the lunch today. And John Richard was there. With Sandee?"

"Yup."

"Any chance that John Richard could have just dumped Sandee? Or that Sandee might have another boyfriend?"

"Very unlikely that he just dumped her. I don't know if Sandee has any other love interest. But I do know this: John Richard and Sandee were smooching and snuggling very openly at the funeral lunch, all under the jealous eye of Courtney." Had I seen anyone *else* eyeing them? I wasn't sure. Had anyone been taking photographs at the lunch? I thought I remembered a flashbulb or two, but couldn't recall who'd been taking pictures, or when. But I did remember something else. "Brewster, when Courtney came into the kitchen, she said, 'He owes me.' I thought she meant in a general sense, but maybe that means Marla is right, and she was bankrolling him."

Brewster nodded. We crested the apex of the interstate and shot beneath the Ooh-Ah Bridge, so named because of its panoramic view of the Continental Divide. In this year of drought, only tiny snowcaps clung to the dull brown peaks. Possible good news, weather wise, was rising from the west: A steep bank of clouds moving our way might bring real rain, and not the dreaded virga. Virga, as the meteorologists were always telling us, was distinguishable as a dark, vertical band descending from storm clouds, but not reaching the ground. The rain fell, but evaporated in midair.

"Okay," Brewster said. "Now just a couple of quick questions. Who's this Vikarios fellow?"

I told him about Ted Vikarios, former co–department head at Southwest Hospital. He and his peer, Albert Kerr, had both left doctoring to pursue a calling to be . . . well, what would you call it? "More religious," I said finally. "Albert became a priest, and Ted made tapes."

"*Victory over Sin?*" Brewster asked. "I remember those. He was down in Colorado Springs, wasn't he? I heard he made a mint, then lost it all because of some scandal."

"That he did. But John Richard only went to the Springs on rare occasions, and as far as I know, they hadn't seen each other in thirteen, fourteen years."

Brewster nodded. "They'll be looking at all of Korman's known associates, including the guys he hung out with at the jail. Okay. So what's this about there being a problem that Arch wasn't with you when you discovered Dr. Korman's body?"

I explained my inadvertent use of the word *let's,* as in, "Let's try one more time." Then I'd impulsively told Arch to wait while I went to check the garage. I'd related all this to the detectives, back at John Richard's house. Now they were acting as if I'd killed my ex-husband and realized I had to spare my son the sight of his dead father.

Brewster grinned again but kept his eyes on the road. "Speaking of names. You and Marla need to quit using that moniker, *the Jerk*. Try to stop even thinking it, 'cuz you really don't want it to slip out inadvertently."

I sighed. "What happens next?"

Brewster chewed his bottom lip. "Do you have any ideas who might have attacked you this morning? Besides your ex-husband. Did he have enemies in jail? Or friends?"

"I don't know. He pretty much defined me as his main enemy, the one who'd ruined his life. He . . . threatened to try to get full custody of Arch, but he always did that. He just didn't like to pay child support. I've come to think he just liked to argue."

"Did he fight with everybody?"

"Eventually."

"This morning . . . when you made your report to the police? After the attack?" When I nodded, Brewster went on: "How about this. Someone wants to frame you for Korman's death. So they attack you and sabotage your food. You're going to think it's Korman, and be furious and suspicious. He's going to be as mean as he usually is, so when the two of you see each other at the lunch, there are more than the predictable fireworks. And then the killer somehow manages to get your gun and shoots Korman, knowing that you'll be bringing Arch over. The person who finds the body usually is the prime suspect."

"I know, I know." I looked out the window and thought. "What happens when they trace the gun to me?"

"They might come up to your house, bully you,

threaten you some more. Before you say a word, call me. Then wait for me to show up." A blast of dust hit the Mercedes. "You know, they're going to be doing ballistics tests on the bullets they take out of your ex-husband. They'll also be checking with Dr. Korman's neighbors about shots being fired. What did they see and hear, and when? And don't forget the fellow who wanted his money. They need to check on everything to build any kind of case, trust me."

"All right."

Brewster concentrated on the road for a bit, then asked, "Is there anyone who can vouch for your being at the Summit rink in Lakewood at two o'clock?"

"Arch's friend Todd Druckman. We took him home. A lot of folks must have seen me, in the parking lot, or buying candy from the vending machines." I chewed the inside of my cheek. "You know, getting back to the assault. Cecelia Brisbane knew about it soon after it happened. She confronted me at the bake sale."

Brewster nodded knowingly. "Don't get paranoid, but she may have rigged up a way to listen in on your phone conversations. It might be good not to talk about this case on the phone, just until I can get your lines checked by our security guy."

"Oh, great. What if Marla calls me with all the latest gossip?"

"Tell her you'll call her right back. Then use a pay phone. Just tonight." Brewster gave me his patented grin. "Goldy, this is a big case. The cops are going to put a lot of people on it, and so will the papers, especially since you've been involved with homicide investigations already. It's important that you watch your step."

"Okay." I took a calming breath. "Anything else?"

Brewster shook his head. Another gust of wind rained dust on the interstate. The big SUVs in the neighboring lanes rocked precipitously, but Brewster and his Benz were unfazed. When we zoomed down the exit for Aspen Meadow Parkway, he asked me where exactly my van, and John Richard's house, were located.

"Stoneberry, number 4402, I'll direct you once we get past the entrance to the country-club area."

"When we get there," Brewster advised, "the cops will be everywhere on the property. Somebody should tell you it's all right to take your vehicle. Or they won't, and I'll take you home. Just don't get into a conversation and don't linger. Once you get the okay, hop into your vehicle and take off. Got it?"

"Yes, fine, sure." I felt unbelievably weary. Every part of my body ached, and the swollen bruises throbbed. My legs tingled, as they always did in the aftermath of a demanding event. Even my brain felt as if it was closing down from overuse. I wanted to be home. Tears bit the back of my eyes. I couldn't hold them in, but at least I didn't sob. I bent over to my purse, fished around for a tissue, and carefully wiped my face. Brewster pretended not to notice.

At John Richard's house, the wind was blowing dust everywhere: into the driveway, onto the crime-scene tape, onto all the cops and investigators moving to and fro. In a couple of places, the tape had broken free of its moorings and fluttered in the breeze like bright party ribbons. I was about to leap from Brewster's Benz when he turned to me.

"Our security guy will check your phones, then I'll call you if there are any developments. You have to promise me you'll phone me if you hear anything."

I did. I also thanked him. A cop called out that they were done with my van and I could take it. Within moments I was back in the driver's seat, revving the engine and chugging away from John Richard's house. I didn't look back.

Tom's Chrysler, covered with grit, sat in the driveway. That was a relief. On the street, there was another vehicle I recognized, but couldn't quite place. It sported a bumper sticker that read: "The Episcopal Church Welcomes You." Somebody was here from St. Luke's. For this, too, I was thankful.

When I came through the door, Tom was right there. He folded me into a long, comforting hug.

"Where's Arch?" I asked, my voice muffled.

"Upstairs with Father Pete. I called the church from Eileen's. He was here when we arrived." I burrowed into Tom's shoulder, unable to think. "What do you want to do now?" Tom murmured. "Are you hungry? I barbecued some steaks for Arch and Father Pete. I made one for you, too, and saved it. It's good cold."

"Did Arch eat anything?"

"Not much. A few bites. And you've already got women phoning from the church. I'm sure you're not in any mood to return calls."

"You've got that right." I pulled away from him. "You know what I really want to do? Cook. More than anything, that'll soothe my nerves."

"No way." Tom assessed my bruised arms and legs. "You've got to be in pain."

"I promise to move slowly."

I washed my hands and put on an apron. I didn't have the apples to make tarte tatin, so I just took out unsalted butter, eggs, and slivered almonds. I placed them on the counter and stared at them. I felt a stab of worry for Arch. I grabbed the counter to steady myself, then tiptoed out of the kitchen and glanced up the stairs. With Arch's door closed, I could barely hear Father Pete's deep voice. I couldn't make out Arch's voice at all.

Back in the kitchen, I washed my hands again and told Tom to relax. He settled at our oak kitchen table and kept a watchful, dubious eye on me. Moving slowly, I gathered up flour, sugar, vanilla, and other ingredients I thought would make a delicate, crunchy cookie. As I toasted the almonds, I gave Tom a report of all that had taken place at the department and with my new lawyer. He rolled his eyes and shook his head. His only comment was that, as he'd suspected, they'd taken him off the case. Formally, he was out of the loop. Sergeant Boyd, an old friend of his, had promised to keep him informed of anything he could pick up.

I smiled as I measured flour. I could just imagine Sergeant Boyd, his dark hair clipped in an unfashionable crew cut, his barrel-shaped body, his short, carrot-like fingers. Like Tom, he was no-nonsense when it came to police work. If there was anyone who could bully information out of someone on the investigative team, it was Boyd.

I went back to stirring the warming almonds until they gave off an intoxicating, nutty scent, then I dumped them out to cool on paper towels. As I sifted the flour, checked the softening butter, and measured a judicious amount of sparkling sugar, I wondered what I would call this creation. How about Goldy's Nuthouse Cookies? I beat the butter until it was creamy, then blended in the sugar until the mélange looked like spun gold. After stirring in the other ingredients, I rolled the mixture into logs and set them in the freezer.

I couldn't stand it any longer: I had to see how Arch was. I crept up the stairs and listened outside the door of his bedroom, the room he had shared with Julian before Julian left for college. Arch's strained, occasionally sobbing voice alternated with Father Pete's low rumble. Probably not the best moment to interrupt, I decided, and tiptoed back down the stairs.

Tom and I cleaned the kitchen. Then I asked Tom to sit down with me. He took a moment to retrieve my new quilt. Then he wrapped me up in it and scooted his chair beside mine. He put his arms around me and pulled me close.

He murmured, "Maybe you shouldn't try to talk."

"I have to." My voice caught. In spite of the quilt, I was shaking violently. Then the words rushed out of me. "Tell me. Tell me who you think killed John Richard."

Tom sighed. "Goldy, don't."

"Please. They suspect me. And I'm very worried about how Arch will react to that." To my embarrassment, my stomach growled with hunger. My early-morning latte and toast was a distant memory.

Tom let go of me and walked over to the refrigerator. "I want the guys to look closely at that assault on you. I also want them to investigate the folks attending that funeral lunch. Somebody didn't want the event to be a success, and might even have been setting you up . . . although how or why isn't clear." He pulled out a covered plate, unwrapped it, and sliced off a corner of grilled steak. He stabbed this with a fork and held it up to my mouth. He said, "You need to eat."

I obeyed. The grill-flavored meat was succulent and

tender. "Thanks." I finished my morsel and crossed my arms. "Why look at people from the lunch? Because somebody whacked me and sabotaged my food? Because my gun was stolen there?"

"Yes and yes. I wish you wouldn't start probing this just yet. You're not only in pain, you're exhausted." I shrugged. Tom went on, "Then again, maybe someone was waiting here at the house for you. At some point, our perp searched your van for *something*. Maybe he or she was looking for that same money that the skeleton-faced man wanted, and found your gun instead. If the gun was stolen while your van was here at the house, that wouldn't have given the killer a *whole* lot of time to haul over to John Richard's house and kill him. But it might have been enough." He sliced off another piece of steak. Like an obedient baby bird, I gobbled it down. "That theory wouldn't quite fit with the half-open garage door and your ex in his Audi."

I swallowed. "Why not?"

"John Richard had to be just coming in or just going out, right? And the killer trapped him in his garage." I gave Tom a confused look. "It's a matter of trying to figure out a chronology. The department will know more when they get the autopsy report. Plus, the neighbors might have seen or heard something. Hopefully, our guys will be able to pin down the time of death as just when you arrived at the rink in Lakewood."

I undid myself from the quilt and retrieved the first almost-frozen cookie roll. "I hope Boyd can find out a *lot*."

While the oven heated, we worked together slicing the silky dough. As soon as a sheet went into the oven, the phone rang. The caller ID indicated that it was Marla.

"Uh-oh," said Tom. "You were supposed to call her the minute you walked in the door. Better answer it. I don't want her to bite my head off."

Now *there* was something. I'd never seen Tom afraid of anyone. I languidly picked up the phone and cried, "Girlfriend!"

"Dammit, Goldy," Marla's husky voice gasped, as if she'd walked up several flights of stairs. "I *just* talked to Brewster, and he said he dropped you off an hour ago! I want to hear *all* about it, plus I have stuff to tell you—"

Don't talk about the case on the phone. It was probably best to follow Brewster's expensive advice.

"Marla, I've gotta go! The timer's going off and a whole batch of cookies is about to come out of the oven!"

"Baloney! That never stopped you before. Just take them out of the oven! Now listen, John Richard and—"

"Omigod! Smoke!" I squealed. "The cookies are burning! Quick, Tom, get the fire extinguisher!"

In reality, I pulled a perfect batch of fragrant, golden cookies from the oven. Confused but prepared, Tom huddled next to me with the fire extinguisher poised to blast the cookies. I put the sheet down on the cooling rack and covered the phone with one hand.

"Don't you *dare*," I whispered.

"What's going on?" he whispered back.

"Goldy!" Marla screamed from the receiver.

"I'll call you back in ten minutes, Marla. Promise."

As I was putting the phone back in its holder, I heard Marla's diminished voice say, "If my phone still *had* a cord, I would use it to wring your neck! Don't hang up on me—"

Ah, silence. I eased the cookies off the sheet, nabbed

a piece of foil, and piled it with ten hot ones—they were small, I told myself—then invited Tom to have the rest.

"I'll finish the other rolls later," I said hastily as I grabbed my jacket.

"Goldy, for crying out loud! It's past eight o'clock. Where are you going?"

"To a pay phone to call Marla back." He began to pull on his "Furman County Sheriff's Department Softball" sweatshirt. I said, "No, please. Don't. Stay here with Arch. I won't be long."

"Forget it. You were assaulted this morning, and you're not going anywhere alone. Besides, what pay phone are you going to use?"

"The one at the Grizzly Bear Saloon." I eased the front door open.

"You're kidding!" he protested. He wrote a quick note to Arch, then hustled out behind me. "The Grizzly has at least one drunken brawl a night."

"Don't worry. The guys usually fight with each other, not some caterer who just wants to use the phone. At least, that's what I hope."

Chapter 8

As Tom and I made our way down the street, smoke suddenly filled our nostrils. I coughed, then took shallow breaths. This was no barbecue smoke. Moreover, the night was warm, the sun had just set, and I doubted anyone needed a fire for warmth. I hadn't heard a report of a wildfire, and neither had Tom. If there was any news, the Grizzly was sure to have it.

A sign hanging from the buckled eave read: "Never Out of Service Since 1870." Never redecorated, either, I thought as we pushed through arched, louvered half doors and shuffled across a genuine sawdust-covered floor. I registered the presence of at least six dozen bankers, electricians, lawyers, plus assorted ne'er-do-wells. Of course, they were all sporting cowboy hats, vests, and boots. That hadn't changed since 1870, either.

On the stage, a band was playing "Jailhouse Rock." A short but otherwise fairly convincing Elvis impersonator—upswept dark hair, skintight sequined suit, energetic hips—was bellowing, "Uh-uh-UH!" A glittery sign beside the band announced that they were "Nashville Bobby and the Boys," and they were going to be in Aspen Meadow for four more days. Then they moved on to Steamboat Springs, where they'd be playing at the Lonely Hearts Café for two days, before returning to Aspen Meadow the following week. They did seem to take themselves seriously. I took a deep breath and again started coughing.

"Does anybody know where that smoke smell is coming from?" Tom asked the crowd.

"New forest fire," a wiry fellow piped up. He wore fringed leather pants, a ten-gallon hat, and a shirt sewn with his name on it: "Tex." Tex took a long pull of beer. "Up in the preserve. Fifteen miles away. Thousand acres, sixty percent contained."

"Hey!" A very blond, very pudgy woman hipped me to one side, and I fell onto the back of a chair. Around us, everyone laughed.

"Do you mind?" I yelled at the woman, rubbing my ribs that were already bruised enough, thank you very much. Tom tried to hide his smile.

She was probably ten years my senior. She wore fringed beige leather that sparkled with . . . was there such a thing as fake rhinestones? I didn't have time to think about it, because I found myself staring at how the rhinestones were also scrolled into a name: "Blondie."

"Hey!" she yelled again, poking my chest with a long, scarlet fingernail. I stared at her. Her thick pancake makeup glittered under the saloon's electric-torch chandeliers. I stared at her scarlet-lipsticked mouth as it formed the words "Gitcher own boyfriend!" This time it was the stench of bourbon that made me reel back. Blondie thrust her double chin in my direction. "Ja hear me?" her drunken breath demanded. "Get lost. Tex is mine."

I teetered backward over two more chairs. "I've got a husband, thanks," I mumbled as more folks laughed.

Tex, immensely pleased to be apparently desired by two short, blond women, tipped his beer and gave me a sly look. I turned to Tom, who winked at me. Tex cleared his throat loudly.

"The fire should be out by mornin'," he said. Then he lifted his chin and raised one eyebrow. *I don't care about a husband! You interested in me?*

I shook my head in an emphatic negative. As I stumbled away, Nashville Bobby and the Boys started howling at the crowd about being nothing but a hound dog. I didn't care about Tex; I cared even less about Nashville Bobby and his boys. What *did* worry me was the new fire, since the Roundhouse was situated a mere eight miles from the preserve. How close was the nearest hydrant? If necessary, could the firemen pump water from the lake? *Thousand acres, sixty percent contained.* We'd become so accustomed to the wildfires that we just cited each one's statistics—where it was, how much under control, when the firefighters expected complete containment—and moved on with our lives. This was what I needed to do, I thought, then jumped as Nashville Bobby turned up the volume a notch.

Through the cigarette smoke, I could barely make out the stage. Colorado was most emphatically *not* California, so *everyone* smoked indoors, sometimes two cigarettes at a time. Nashville Bobby warbled, shook his hips, and finished his song with a bow. To raucous applause, Bobby then announced that the band was going to debut their new song, "Trash." Sad guitar-string plinking was followed by Bobby crooning:

> *"I'm just garbage under your sink,*
> *You threw me in here and didn't think!*

*Now I'm gettin' old, 'n startin' to stink
You don't check the bag; you don't even wink."*

Tom asked if I wanted anything, like a beer, but I said no. I pushed my way through the crowd until I finally arrived at the dimly lit phone, which was a grimy beige house phone with a stretched-out cord. It was perched at a slight angle between the heavy doors of the saloon's two restrooms. A stern admonition posted on the wall forbade long-distance calls and asked for coins to be left in a wooden honor box. I dropped in quarters, lifted the receiver, and pressed buttons. When Marla answered, our connection was rough and full of static.

"Marla? It's me. Marla?"

" *'Trash!'* " sang the band. " *'Trash! That's all I am.'* "

"Goldy?"

"Marla!"

" *'Trash!'* "

"Goldy, where the hell are you calling from?"

" *'Trash!'* "

"I can't talk about the case over my home phone!" I hollered. Three cowboys turned a baleful eye in my direction. Embarrassed, I turned toward the wall, where my nose scraped a map of the immense Aspen Meadow Wildfire Preserve. Raccoon Creek, Cherokee Pass, Cowboy Cliff: These were just a few of the landmarks connected by fire roads and hiking trails. Things could be worse, I realized. I could be out fighting that fire.

I realized I was still wearing my apron, the pocket of which bulged with still-warm cookies. Most of them had probably broken in my journey through the crowd. But at least I had an emergency sugar-carb supply.

"For crying out loud, Goldy!" Marla screeched.

"Tell me what happened at the sheriff's department! Do they know who killed the Jerk? Was it the same person who assaulted you?"

"I don't know anything—"

"You're holding out on me!"

I pulled the phone's cord so I could get the receiver inside the swinging wooden door to the ladies' room. A massive cement column separated the two stalls. The wood-paneled interior, dimly lit by a solitary hanging lightbulb, also revealed two stained sinks, a large cracked mirror, and an enormous black garbage can.

"Don't start, Marla!" I warned her. "This has been one of the worst days of my life!" I tried to get comfortable. This was difficult since I had to grip the phone while my knuckles were getting flayed on the rough paneling. I softened my tone. "Listen, thanks for sending Brewster. He was great."

"So *tell* me about it, would you? I'm dying over here without any information. Tom wouldn't breathe a word and neither would Brewster, damn him."

"Oh, Marla, I can't go into detail. The bottom line is that I don't know anything new. I can't talk because Arch is at home and he's a wreck." But she insisted, so I gave her the shortest possible précis of the day's events, including the cops finding my gun not far from John Richard's body. "At the lunch, you didn't happen to see any suspicious folks around my van, did you?"

"No," she said. "Sorry. But I *did* find out something that might be significant." My heart leaped. Or was it my stomach growling again? Hard to tell. Marla went on: "Sandee with two *e*s does *not* work at the golf shop. She never did. She's a stripper at the Rainbow Men's Club in Denver."

"*What?* How did John Richard meet her?"

"As they say, 'One can only presume.' But I didn't. Presume, that is. I asked Courtney. John Richard met Sandee *at* the Rainbow. *That* is how low the Jerk had sunk. Picking up girls at strip clubs!"

"You called Courtney? But she's . . ."

Words failed as my stomach howled again. I didn't care about Courtney; I didn't care if the Jerk had sunk to hell. Despite the bites of steak, I was ravenous. I groped in my apron pocket, pulled out a warm cookie, and popped it into my mouth. The crunch of toasted almonds and the pure, buttery flavor made my head spin. I stuffed in another two.

"Of course I called Courtney," Marla retorted. "And whatever you're eating, I want some as compensation for my legal bills. Goldy?"

"Mmf." My mouth was full. I didn't really feel guilty, but what was going on here? I'd been attacked; my food had been sabotaged; renegade rodents had caused me to fire my gun. I stuffed two more cookies into my mouth and didn't answer Marla. Our ex-husband had been murdered. At this point, I was the prime suspect in his murder. I shoved in a few more cookies and realized I was beginning to feel a bit better. Well! This was how low *I* had sunk: crammed into a stinking saloon toilet, I was discussing strippers on a grimy phone while stuffing myself with nut cookies. Close by, Bobby and his boys launched into "I'm Just Roadkill on the Highway of Love."

"The *main* reason I called Courtney," Marla went on, "was to tell her the Jerk was dead. Wanted to see what kind of reaction I'd get."

I finished the cookies. "Brewster says we can't call our ex the Jerk anymore. Even in death."

I guess I couldn't really blame Marla for rapping her

fancy phone against her tiled kitchen wall. But it did hurt my ear.

"Goldy? Brewster takes orders from me, not vice versa. And are you listening to my story here? Courtney was stunned to hear about the Jerk. It was either total disbelief or a great acting job. She exploded. We're talking nuclear. We're talking *nova.* She screamed that you'd prevented them from getting married, because of some custody problem. Plus, she'd loaned John Richard a hundred thousand dollars at the beginning of May, and two weeks later he dumped her for Sandee with two *e*s. How's she supposed to get her money back now? she screamed. So! The Jerk owed her money, the same way he owed the man at his house," Marla concluded triumphantly.

"Wait a minute. Courtney *loaned* him that much money? How stupid is she?"

"You got me."

"And the gent at John Richard's house didn't look as if *he* could have loaned John Richard anything—"

"Let's go down to the strip club tomorrow!" Marla squealed. "We can question Sandee, just the two of us."

I slumped against the rough wall. "I can't. I have your PosteriTREE meeting and Nan's retirement picnic to prep, and the cops and Brewster told me to stay away—"

She rapped the phone again. "Girlfriend! Tom is not working this case. Without him, the sheriff's department will *never* find out who shot the Jerk. They need *us!* So I'll pick you up at eleven. Then we—"

Without warning, pain racked my wrist as Blondie barged through the restroom door. The phone cord sprang away like a bowstring. I grabbed for it, but ended up seizing Blondie instead. Her warm, drunk breath said, "Erf?," while she struggled mightily for balance. I tried to hold her up, snag the phone, and reach for the swinging restroom door all at once. I failed on all counts.

Blondie had not been expecting a sudden embrace. Her high-heeled boots clattered backward. Her leather-fringed arms windmilled away from me as she tried to get her balance on the slick floor. The phone cord wrapped around the wire suspending the lightbulb and boomeranged in a high arc toward the ceiling. I gargled for help as Blondie's cowgirl-skirted butt crashed into the cement post separating the two stalls. Marla's distant voice shrieked, "Goldy?" Unfortunately, the laws of physics were already sending Blondie catapulting into the yawning trash can, where she promptly threw up. Following the same laws of physics, the returning restroom door smacked me in the face just as the phone cord finished its downward trajectory and Marla's screaming voice splashed into the toilet.

I grabbed my nose, sure that blood was streaming out of it. Black spots clouded my vision. I groped with my free hand in the direction of what I hoped was the saloon. I bumped into a body, a man's body, and prayed it was not a catering client.

"Sandee Blue is *my* girlfriend," the man's voice whispered in my ear as he swung me around and clutched my shoulders. "And don't you forget it."

"Okay, okay," I mumbled, suddenly fearful. Was this the person who'd beaten me up that morning? "Who are you?" I struggled against his viselike hold. "Could you please let go of me?"

"Go on, get out of here," he said, pushing me roughly away. I fell onto the filthy floor. By the time I could turn around, he was gone.

I blinked and steadied myself until I could see the red exit sign. Cursing under my breath, I lurched in the direction of Tom's table.

"Goldy!" It was Tom's calming voice. "Are you all right? What happened to your nose? There's blood everywhere." A rough paper napkin was pushed into my hand, and I pressed it to my nostrils. I gasped and begged Tom to take me out for air. Some tourists told the bartender to call a cab. He replied that there were no cab companies in Aspen Meadow.

With Tom holding me up, I finally, finally stumbled out the saloon doors. Behind us, Tex's voice announced: "You know, she didn't *seem* that drunk."

Chapter 9

"**M**y dear wife," Tom said gently as he guided me through our front door. "You don't look so hot."

"No kidding." I stepped carefully into the hallway. Assaulted by dizziness, I blinked at the sudden bright light. Tom's strong hands reached out to grab me. "Something happened there, Tom. At the Grizzly. Back by the phone, I bumped into a man who said that Sandee Blue was his girlfriend, and I shouldn't forget it."

"Any idea who he was? Maybe your early-morning attacker?"

"I can't say." I grasped Tom's hand.

"Well, what did he look like?"

"I don't know. He turned me around, then pushed me down. By the time I got up, he was gone."

Tom pulled me in for a hug and was silent.

I gently extracted myself and squinted at my husband's handsome face. "Tom?"

"Goldy, do you go looking for trouble? Or does it just find you?"

"Thanks. No more calls using the Grizzly phone. Promise."

"Did you ever get to talk to Marla?"

"Not really." I closed my eyes and rubbed my aching forehead. How late was it? I had no clue. And where was Arch? How was he doing? I mumbled, "Arch?"

Tom pulled me back into a hug. "Father Pete's car is still out front. I assume he's in there with him."

Upstairs, a quietly closing door was followed by shuffling. The stairs creaked as Father Pete Zoukaki's immense bulk began to descend. I did not know how Father Pete had come to be an Anglican, because he looked like central casting's idea of a priest from *The Godfather*. I held my breath as his small black shoes trundled into view, followed by short chopstick legs. These balanced slowly on each step, so that his black-swathed calzone of a body could lumber downward without toppling. At the landing, he turned slowly, like a jumbo jet moving into a gate.

"Arch is sleeping," he announced. His voice was low pitched and warm, perfect for pastoring. He maneuvered down the last three steps, mopped his brow, and gave us a solemn nod. His ultradark hair and beard were intensely curly. His skin was the color of olive oil. His espresso-black eyes filled with concern as he reached out for me. "Goldy." I let go of Tom and allowed Father Pete's sausage arms to pat my back. "This will all be over soon."

This will all be over soon? When was *soon,* exactly? When Father Pete had counseled Arch some more? When the sheriff's department found the killer? When the Jerk was deep in Aspen Meadow Cemetery? I swallowed and tried to get hold of myself.

"Thank you for coming," I said softly.

"No trouble," Father Pete's commanding voice assured me. He let go and assessed me with those dark eyes. "You don't look well. You should try to get to bed."

I clenched my teeth. "I'm *aware* that I don't look well." After an awkward moment, I asked, "What about the . . . uh . . . ?" I cleared my throat and smoothed my face into an attempt at composure. Tom gently took my hand and flicked me a questioning glance. He wanted to bail me out, but had no idea what I was asking.

"It's just that I'm worried about . . ." I tried again. Well, everything. Father Pete and Tom waited. My hit-with-the-restroom-door nose was throbbing. Father Pete pursed his thick lips, glanced at my bruised arms, and frowned.

"There's the matter of"—I cleared my throat—"a service."

Father Pete nodded. "Besides Arch, did Dr. Korman have next of kin?"

I shook my head.

"All right then," Father Pete said in that deep, comforting voice. "I'll call the coroner, see if they know who's been designated to make arrangements." When he furrowed his forehead, his bushy black eyebrows appeared truly ominous. "Someone from the church will call you with the details. It would be good for Arch—"

"We'll bring him," I said hastily.

Father Pete nodded again, gave Tom a grim *take care of her* look, and trundled out the front door.

"Would it be possible for you to put this whole rotten day out of your mind for a while?" Tom murmured in my ear.

"I wish."

"Try."

I tiptoed upstairs, peeled off my clothes, and took a

long, hot shower. When I emerged, the mirror revealed my very red nose and two purple bruises on my lower arms. My back sported a bright pink sore spot. I closed my eyes and gingerly put on a terry robe.

I slipped between the cool sheets and reached out for Tom's warm body. With a gentleness that brought tears to my eyes, he put his hands on my cheeks and whispered that I should tell him if anything hurt. I nodded. He wiped my tears away, pulled me closer, and gave me a long kiss. It was the kind of kiss that went on and on, passionate, insistent, tender beyond words. It was like drowning—and I wanted to drown. His large, muscled body enclosed mine. He touched me, gently sliding his large hands over my sore neck and bruised arms.

He said, "You are the most beautiful woman in the world. I love you now and forever and ever. I'm . . . sorry I haven't been a very good husband lately."

"*Shh*. You've been fine. The best."

"Well, I'm going to kill the bastard who hurt you."

"Great. When?"

"Now it's your turn to hush."

So. Afterward, Tom held me next to him, unwilling to let me go even in slumber. I listened to his soft snoring, to the beat of his heart inside his big chest. For the first time that day, I felt safe.

Courtney MacEwan had been right. People *do* have sex after funerals.

A thunderclap jolted me from a deep sleep. Fear gripped my chest as I sent the covers flying. My body's numerous aches screamed in protest.

Tom reached out for me. "*Rain*, Goldy. It's rain. I'll make sure Arch is all right." Tom slipped quietly away.

Arch was most emphatically *not* all right. He was

sobbing loudly, uncontrollably. Tom was murmuring, but I couldn't make out what he was saying. I slipped on my robe, crept down the hall, and peered into the room.

"Arch? Honey?" I tried. A sudden flash of lightning illuminated Arch's room. Julian's old twin bed stood flat and empty. Arch, covered by the black-and-gold quilt, lay facedown on his own bed. He was screaming and writhing, yelling something about *his fall, his fault* . . .

I called to him again. He did not respond to me.

Perched beside Arch, Tom kept his voice soothing. "Arch. You're going to be all right. This is the worst part. Arch, *nothing* was your fault."

But Arch was having none of it.

"It *is* my fault," my son's voice hollered. He pounded his bed, making it shudder. I moved hesitantly into the room. "I *never* should have gone down to play hockey. If we just could have been there *earlier,* this never would have happened! Oh, God! It *is* my fault! *Don't say it's not my fault when it is!*"

Tom motioned me over and mumbled that he was going to get our sleeping bags. I took his warm spot on the quilt and tried a few comforting words of my own. Arch's body writhed with his sobs.

"Honey, don't," I tried. "Please stop crying. You're going to make yourself sick." I kept my voice calm, kept repeating the same things, kept hoping Arch would calm down. "Please, Arch. Your dad's death had nothing to do with you, or when we got to his house. I promise."

I reached out to rub Arch's back, but he shrugged me away. Then he lowered one leg and kicked his foot against the floor. The bed wheels creaked and the bed rolled sideways. He didn't want to be comforted, and that was that.

While I was puzzling over this, a small stone pelted the dark window. My heart jumped into my throat. Soon, another tiny rocket popped against the glass. Then another and another. Handfuls of pebbles were being tossed at the window. I turned on the lamp by Arch's digital clock. Another flash of lightning brought the room and the pine trees outside into sudden focus. A pile of hail was accumulating on the windowsill. The thunder boomed again. So we were at the last of the Colorado seasons: blizzard, flood, fire, *hail. Great.*

Tom shuffled back in, clutching a pair of red sleeping bags. Their whispery nylon rustling, combined with the thunder and the drum of hail, startled Arch out of his crying jag. He rubbed his face and reached for his glasses, next to the lamp.

"What's going on?"

Tom stepped purposefully across the room. "Your mom and I are going to spend the rest of the night in here. It'll be better if we can all be together tonight. Your mom'll be over here on Julian's old bed." He hefted one of the slithery bags onto the empty mattress by the window. "I'll sleep on the floor. You need anything, look down and yell for it."

"Has anybody . . ." Arch's voice caught. "Has anybody called Julian? To tell him what happened?"

Above the patter of hail, I promised, "First thing in the morning."

I hunkered down into the flannel. Yes, we needed Julian. Since he'd helped with the funeral lunch, the cops had probably already talked to him about John Richard. Then again, maybe not. In addition to working for my business a couple of days a week, Julian held down a part-time job in a Boulder bistro. Plus, he was always taking at least one course at the University of Colorado, in pursuit of his degree. He wasn't the easiest person to find, as the cops would probably discover. Then again, those law-enforcement folks had proved that they could zero in on connections between the murder victim and just about anything they wanted.

The hail continued to hammer the roof. *Rat-a-tat-tat! Do you own a gun, Mrs. Schulz? Rat-a-tat-tat!*

Why did hail have to sound so much like a firing squad, anyway?

The phone started ringing at 6:22. The incessant, demanding ringing seemed to be coming from inside my head. I blinked at the red 6:22 on Arch's digital clock, and wished I had a baseball bat. The kind you break phones with.

My head ached; my body throbbed. I needed *quiet.* I needed *healing.* I scooted down into the flannel and pulled the sleeping bag over my static-charged hair. When the ringing stopped, I again poked out my head.

It was a typically chilly June morning in the mountains. Brilliant sunlight glistened through the windowsill's melting mounds of hail. Rainbows shimmered across the walls of Arch's room.

I assumed that the unmoving lump on the neighboring bed, still covered with the black-and-gold quilt, was Arch. Tom's sleeping bag lay flattened and empty. The phone started up again. *Who could possibly be calling at this hour?* Like a leaden cloak, the events of the previous day descended on my brain. Who could be wanting so desperately to talk? Let's see: *The cops. The local paper. My new criminal lawyer, who would have bad news.*

I sat up. Droplets of water gleamed on the pine branches brushing Arch's window. The previous day's fierce, dusty wind had indeed pushed in those storm clouds hovering over the Continental Divide. With any luck, the hail would have smothered the fire up in the preserve. At least *one* thing around here could be under control, and that would be a welcome change.

Tom appeared at the doorway and motioned for me. I shed the flannel-and-nylon cocoon, tiptoed out to the hallway, and followed him into our room. There, I tucked myself into a fresh sweatshirt and pants.

"Who keeps calling?" I asked.

"Tell you downstairs."

Our wooden steps creaked more loudly than usual as I headed for the kitchen. I listened for Arch, but heard nothing.

"It's the paper," Tom announced ruefully, once we were seated at our oak table and he was revving up the espresso machine. "First Frances Markasian, then somebody else from the *Mountain Journal*. They want to know how long they're going to have to wait until they can get a statement from you. Then Frances Markasian two more times."

I couldn't help myself; I cackled. Frances Markasian, a legend in her own mind, was a so-called investigative reporter at the *Mountain Journal*. Sometimes, when she wanted information, we were pals. Most of the time, we weren't.

Suddenly, it was all too much. I laughed as my arm made a sweeping gesture to indicate the entire outdoors. Dazzling remainders of hail sparkled on the aspens, the lodgepole pines, the blue spruce. Our dry grass was spotted with white. The tender shoots of our perennials glistened with unaccustomed wetness.

"Hell has frozen over," I announced. "But it doesn't matter. I'm not talking to the *Journal*."

Tom added water to the coffee machine. "You're sounding *slightly* bitter this morning. Here's some good news, though. The hail helped the firefighters get that blaze out in the preserve. Unfortunately, with more dry weather on the way, they're warning that the fire danger is still high. Okay, how many shots of espresso would you like?"

"I'll take a double, thanks." Ordinarily I would have had six, but in the last couple of months, I'd been trying to cut back.

Tom warmed a cup and pressed the machine's buttons. When he set the steaming dark drink on the table, he placed his hand on mine.

"We need to talk. As in, strategy."

The phone rang again, and I was tempted to throw my luscious cup of hot espresso at it. Reading my mind, Tom checked the caller ID.

"Priscilla Throckbottom?" Tom asked me.

I groaned. Priscilla Throckbottom, head of the St. Luke's Episcopal Church Women and several other local organizations, had booked me to do the breakfast for her PosteriTREE committee at the country club, to be held the following morning. Now either she wanted me to work with her to plan John Richard's funeral *or* she wanted to see if I was still doing her breakfast. Perhaps she wanted her own version of what had happened. Maybe she wanted all three. And at six forty-five in the morning, no less.

"Let's turn off all the ringers," I proposed. "I don't want them to wake Arch. The machine can take the messages. I'll call Julian at eight or so."

Tom nodded, fussed with the buttons on the kitchen

phone—our home line and my business number had separate ringers—then left to silence the receivers throughout the house. I sipped Tom's dark brew and felt a bit better, even though my body still ached from the previous morning's attack outside the Roundhouse. The question of who had sabotaged and hit me, and why, was like a puzzle locked inside a rock. Who hated me that much? Somebody trying to divert attention from himself as the Jerk's killer? A competitor? Who? The only other catering competition I'd ever had in Aspen Meadow had all switched over to being chefs of the personal (forty or so clients) or private (one big, demanding client) variety. As far as I could see, I posed no threat. Maybe Marla would have a lead on it this morning. You didn't make all that mess at the Roundhouse and not brag to *somebody*.

Recalling the detectives' interrogation, I wondered why they hadn't asked me if I'd set up a friend to assault me. They clearly thought I'd planned the accidental-shooting incident. Maybe they speculated that the bruises on my arms were self-inflicted. I should have given them a good look at my neck.

And of course, I wanted most of all to know who had killed my ex-husband. I had concern for myself, as a suspect. And perhaps I did, after all, have concern for him.

A sudden vision of John Richard's bloody body loomed. I resolutely put it out of my mind, but it popped up again. Something had been wrong . . . something apart from the fact that he'd been *dead,* of course. I swallowed more coffee, closed my eyes, and went over the mental image. The blood, his face, his hair . . . something had been off, or strange, or at the very least, out of place. I hadn't spotted my gun, so that wasn't it. Still, something had struck me as weird, and I was fairly sure this was *beside* the fact that John Richard had been shot. But the observation, or realization, or whatever it was, flashed just out of reach, like a silvery trout wriggling off a hook.

At least I could remember John Richard's body, or what I'd been able to see, given its skewed angle. Who could have done such a thing? Was it the same person who'd attacked me? And how was I going to find out these things?

I put my cup in the sink and did a few gentle yoga stretches. Blood flowed to my bruises like an anesthetic. If Yogi Berra was right, and 90 percent of baseball was half mental, then perhaps the same was true of pain. I took more cleansing breaths before stretching, breathing, and stretching some more. I had another double shot of espresso and felt restored. Ready to face the day, I booted up my computer.

Tom lumbered back into the kitchen, full of purpose and resolve. Overhead, the shower water began running.

He rubbed his hands together. "Miss G.? You seem to be feeling better."

I nodded. "So do you, Tom. Are you doing better?"

"Last night was great."

"Besides that."

His face darkened and he turned away. "Sometimes. It feels good to help you and Arch. I wish I could work on this case, but the department actually told me to take some time off, to help the two of you."

"Well. Thanks."

His smile was rueful. "All right, then. I still need to get Arch out of here. If people can't get you to answer the phone, they'll come to the door. Believe me, I know." He pulled out a kitchen chair and sat down. "I want to get him somewhere safe, as in emotionally safe. Do you have plans for today?" I told him about the two events I needed to finish prepping. Then Marla was taking me out to lunch. I omitted the strip-club part. "Let me tell you what I've been thinking," Tom went on. "Call Trudy next door, and ask her if she can take in cards, flowers, casseroles. Meanwhile, Arch and I are going out." He looked at the ceiling. "Maybe we'll play golf."

"*Golf?* The day after his father's been killed?"

"It was my idea. And he doesn't want to sit around." He stood, reached into a cupboard for a tray, and set it with a plate, napkin, and silverware. "The fresh air will do him good. Miss G., trust me—you don't want him *here* if reporters start swarming."

Tom poured a glass of juice for the tray. I smiled. He had called me Miss G. twice this morning. Maybe he *was* getting better.

"Since I don't belong to the country club," he went on, "I suggested the municipal course by the lake. It's not a bad course, and it's unlikely he'll see anybody he knows. No embarrassing questions that way."

I shook my head, dumbfounded. Whenever someone close to me had died—a grandparent, an uncle I hadn't seen in years—I'd felt numb. Even throwing myself back into whatever work needed doing had been an emotional chore. Then again, until the last two years, I hadn't had Tom to help me through a crisis. Maybe I would have been willing to go play golf with him, too.

Tom popped two slices of brioche into the toaster and gave me a sidelong glance. "Couple more things." He handed me a new cell phone and an index card. "Use this instead of your old one. Brewster Motley's guy brought it by this morning. Also, the home phones are secure." He smiled. "He also swept the place for bugs, if you can believe it. More important, I called a buddy of mine and ordered a chain-link fence and gates, complete with heavy-duty locks, to be put in around your compressors and switches outside the Roundhouse. Boyd will bring your new keys by later. He also promised to call either you or Marla, strictly on the q.t., if he heard any details about the investigation. Okeydoke?"

"Great. Thanks." I watched in puzzlement as Tom zapped thick-sliced bacon in the microwave, then buttered the brioche. Within moments he was layering sizzling bacon strips on the toasted bread. My mouth watered.

"Bacon sandwich," Tom offered. "I'm taking this up to Arch." He lifted the tray to his shoulder, waiter style. "We should be taking off within twenty minutes."

Upstairs, the water was still running. "Tom," I protested gently. "He's still in the shower. Why won't you just let him have his breakfast after he's dressed, in the kitchen the way he usually does? Please? I want to see him. Talk to him. Check on how he's doing."

Tom hesitated at the kitchen door, still gripping the tray. Finally, his green eyes met mine. "He's not quite ready to see you, Miss G."

"What?"

"Just . . . give him some time. All right?"

"What are you *talking* about?"

Tom hesitated, then put the tray down on the counter. He walked over, embraced me, and murmured in my ear, "Arch needs somebody to blame. Last night he blamed himself. This morning, it's you. He doesn't understand how you let your gun get stolen. He thinks you should have called paramedics once you found his dad in the garage." Tom sighed. "He's not doing well, Goldy. As soon as the department figures out what happened, he'll have the *right* person to blame. Just . . . don't overreact, okay?"

"But I didn't *do* anything," I protested. "Arch was less than thirty yards away from me when I found John Richard, who was already dead."

"I know that. On some level, he does, too. He's just real wound up now, and he's not being logical. He needs a friend, someone he can trust, to start his grieving with. I'm not talking about Todd. Right now, he feels okay with me. Let me go with it, will you?"

My face, my ears, every part of my body began to pulse with heat, not to mention embarrassment, shame, and worry. Somehow I had failed my son. I thought I was going to be sick. Trust *Tom*? I was beginning to feel I couldn't trust *anyone*. I couldn't even think. My ex-husband was dead, and my beloved son wouldn't even *talk* to me? What was going on here?

Tom picked up the tray and disappeared. I ran cold water from the kitchen faucet, splashed my face, then dried it with a rough paper towel. I swallowed back the rock in my throat, and tried *not* to picture Arch's freckled, innocent face, with his glasses riding down his nose. I tried to imagine him *not* being angry with me.

Cook, an inner voice advised. *It's better than just standing around feeling bad.*

My computer laid out the prep I still had to do. Regardless of whatever problems a dead ex-husband, an alienated son, nosy churchwomen, or bothersome journalists could pose, I *had* to work. Not only that, but I was determined to do a thorough check of my van to see if anything besides my thirty-eight had been ripped off. The cops wouldn't have been able to tell that, would they? I took a deep breath and tapped buttons. First I printed out the inventory sheets for my equipment boxes. Then I pulled up the menus for the two upcoming events.

I wondered uneasily if Priscilla Throckbottom had been calling to change the time or place for the committee breakfast. My computer reminded me that I'd already made and frozen her mini-brioches, but that I still had to make the Crustless Fontina and Gorgonzola Quiches. Very early the next morning, I would slice a mega-ton of fresh fruit. Ah, the caterer's life.

As I pulled out eggs, cheeses, cream, and butter, I worried that Priscilla might be immersed in one of her last-minute crises, where she insisted on adding or subtracting two, three, or six guests. Then again, maybe the death of John Richard had made Priscilla wonder if things were proceeding normally chez Goldilocks. Well, doggone it, they were. And if she wanted to add, subtract, or *cancel,* she'd be out of luck. More than one person in this world could be hard-nosed!

I pictured Priscilla's committee as I began crumbling pungent Gorgonzola. Ostensibly, the eight women of PosteriTREE, the ones who'd held the previous day's bake sale, were doing a town-beautification project. They were raising funds to buy and plant native trees around Aspen Meadow. But as usual with these types of groups, I suspected that the real *reason* for belonging to the committee was to be able to *say* that you were on it. I'd heard one woman brag that PosteriTREE members belonged to the crème de la crème of town society.

I set aside the Gorgonzola and started grating the fontina. The crème de la crème of town society? From a caterer's viewpoint, Aspen Meadow didn't *have* any society. At least, we didn't have anything as identifiable as what you'd see in a major metropolis. I'd worked for clients who'd hailed from the nation's capital: Two entire shelves in the library had been devoted to their collection of *The Green Book*, also known as *The Social List of Washington*. And Washington was not alone. Victorian London had had its Upper Ten Thousand; New York had its Dun and Bradstreet; even early twentieth-century Denver had had its Sacred Thirty-Six. But what did twenty-first-century Aspen Meadow, Colorado, have? A country club that looked like a Holiday Inn, a saloon featuring every band from Nashville Bobby and the Boys to Backhoe Dan and the Dumpsters, and oh, yes, a yearly cultural event that brought in folks from all over the country: the Aspen Meadow Rodeo. I rest my case.

I moved on to beating the eggs and mused about the fact that some folks do need to cling to the idea that by doing this or that they will prove that they are superior. Far be it from me to shatter their illusions. Folks in the catering profession nurture dreams of grandeur, right? It's our bread and butter.

I fixed myself another espresso and doused it with cream. I'd been intending to cut back on the dark stuff, but I rationalized my current overload by reminding myself that espresso contained much less caffeine than regular coffee. And, at the moment, I needed it for medicinal purposes.

I clicked to a new file in the computer. The next day's committee breakfast should be a no-brainer. I'd worked in the Aspen Meadow Country Club kitchen before, and the staff—unlike the members—were very friendly. But after the breakfast, I had a larger and more much challenging affair: the retirement picnic for Nurse Nan Watkins.

The Southwest Hospital Women's Auxiliary had commissioned the party, and I'd been glad to get the booking. Nan was Marla's and my old friend. Not only had she survived working for John Richard, she was able to do dead-on impersonations of him. Since Nan was five-two and weighed in at two hundred pounds, these were invariably hilarious. There was John Richard's frightening steely look, which Nan would imitate as she snapped her fingers in your face and shouted, "Did you hear me?" Sometimes we could convince her to do his seductive routine, which involved Nan running her plump fingers through her short gray hair, tossing her head as she thrust her hips to the side and growled, "You're new to this hospital, aren't you?" You couldn't help but love her.

Nan's retirement as a longtime ob-gyn nurse at Southwest Hospital promised to bring together many of the same people who'd been at Albert Kerr's funeral lunch. Nan herself had been at the lunch; she'd nodded to me and given me a thumbs-up. But we hadn't had time to visit.

I didn't know how I felt about Nan's picnic coming on the heels of John Richard's suddenly turning up dead. Everyone would be buzzing with questions, and I was in no mood to be thinking of answers.

What I *did* want to know the answer to, though, I reflected as I whisked cream into the beaten eggs, was what it was going to take to restore the relationship with my son. I set aside the silky egg mixture. My stomach protested, so I sliced myself a slab of the luscious fontina. It was heavenly.

Tom and Arch clomped down the stairs while I was chopping scallions. To my dismay, they departed by the front door without saying good-bye. I could just make out Arch saying that his clubs were still in my van from the day before, and would it be all right if he brought his hockey stuff, too? Tom murmured assent, and after some clanking and banging, they were off.

At ten after eight, I slid the first batch of garden-club-meeting quiches into the oven, closed the door, and dialed Julian. Yes, he whispered, he had heard about John Richard. Two investigators were sitting in his apartment. They had driven to Boulder that morning and knocked on his door at seven. They should be leaving soon, Julian said guardedly.

Julian said he was sorry this was happening to me. Was I okay? I told him I was coping, but Arch was not. He cursed under his breath. He'd committed to a full day and evening of work at the bistro. Could he come over first thing tomorrow morning? he asked. He wanted to be with us.

Absolutely, I replied, relieved. I was desperate to know if he'd seen anything at the lunch, anything at all suspicious. But that would have to wait until he didn't have a pair of Furman County's finest breathing down his neck. We signed off.

As the quiches baked, I got down to the serious work of prepping the pork chops for Nan's picnic. Back in the mists of time—that is, in my childhood—everyone's mother, including my own, had fried pork chops and served them for dinner. But since then pigs had been bred to be so lean that if you tried to fry one of their chops today, you'd end up with a piece of leather. Enter the brine, and as we sometimes say in the catering business, *it's a good thing.* Brine recipes had been passed from caterer to caterer like secret codes, and I'd finally found one I liked. The idea of chops rather than the usual hamburgers and hot dogs had intrigued the women's auxiliary, and we'd settled on them for Nan's meat main dish.

After the brine tenderized them, I would put them into a garlic-thyme-balsamic-vinegar marinade and cook them until they were golden. The worst part of this particular specialty of Goldilocks' Catering was getting all the pork chops into and out of the large quantity of brine. If I could manage all that without incident, it would be great. Another *good thing*.

I had finished mixing what felt like a hundred gallons of brine and was just easing the chops into the solution when the doorbell rang. I groaned: reporters? Irritated, I washed my hands and resolved that they were going to get nothing out of me by coming to the house.

At our front door, I peeked through our peephole.

It was not reporters. It was Marla, whose glare indicated she hadn't had any caffeine yet. I let her in.

"Is your house bugged?" she whispered.

"Not according to Brewster's security guy. Come on, I'll make you an iced espresso and cream."

She sighed and followed me. "I know I'm early." She squinted at the vats of pork chops. "But Brewster has been calling you and you're not answering your phone or listening to your machine."

My shoulders slumped. Why did being a suspect have to be so *exhausting?* "Tom turned off all the ringers. Look, don't say any more until I've fixed us both something to eat. I can't take any more bad news without some breakfast."

Marla groaned in agreement. She perked up ten minutes later when I handed her a quadruple iced espresso and cream and a plate of steaming-hot Julian-made chocolate-filled croissants.

"Thank God and thank *you*." She took a bite of

croissant and rolled her eyes. When my own teeth sank through the flaky pastry, warm chocolate spurted onto my tongue. I felt better already.

I said, "All right, now I can take some news."

"Brewster wants you to come up with a list of enemies you and John Richard had in common. He also wants you to try to write down the names of any folks who were just the Jerk's enemies."

"Is that all?"

"Very funny. Brewster also says you and Tom need to start working on your defense. As in *be prepared,* that kind of thing. He also wants to know if we can recall the history of the Jerk beating up other girlfriends."

"Does Brewster mean girlfriends who lived?"

"I think he means all of John Richard's lovers or women or whatever you want to call them," Marla replied. "I've got my list, and if you don't have time to do one, I'll just give him mine, which is probably more complete than any you could come up with. Do you know if the Jerk beat up Sandee? Not that that would be a good thing, but it might make things easier for you."

"Sorry, but I know next to nothing about his relationship with Sandee." I fortified myself with more chocolate croissant, then washed it down with a final espresso.

The doorbell rang just as the buzzer went off for the quiches. Marla held up a chocolate-smeared finger. "I'll get the door. You get the oven."

The quiches were puffed and golden brown. I laid them carefully on cooling racks and closed the oven door.

"It's Frances Markasian and another reporter from the *Mountain Journal,*" Marla announced. "They're even wearing press badges! I didn't let them in. What do you want me to do?"

"Tell them I have no comment, except that they should go away!" I threw the pot holders on the counter. The heat on my face wasn't coming from the oven. Reporters were showing up to question me, the prime suspect, at half-past eight in the morning? My criminal attorney wanted to start working on my *defense*? My own son wouldn't *talk* to me?

When Marla returned from tongue-lashing the press, I asked her to accompany me to our detached garage. Then I stuffed Brewster's business card, my new cell phone, and my newly printed inventory sheets into my canvas tote. After checking that there were no journalists out back, I sloshed furiously through the wet grass with Marla on my heels.

It was time to figure out why someone was trying to frame me.

Chapter 10

I flipped on the garage light. With Marla growling, we pulled out all the boxes from the back of the van. After we'd gone through two of them, I used my new cell to call Brewster's office.

"Aw, Goldy, you're not on your old cell phone, are you? Gossip columnists can be such a hassle!" Even when Brewster was irritated, he couldn't manage to sound upset. *Aw, man, you're not telling me you forgot the beer! Dude!* I could just picture him, leaning back in a sleek leather executive chair, his blond curls framed in a halo around his head, his eyes contemplating an oil painting of a snowboarder catching air.

"Don't get paranoid on me, Brewster. I'm using the new one." I creaked open the door to the garage and glanced all around. "Nobody's hearing this except Marla. My home phone line started ringing at oh-dark-thirty, and now there are reporters at my front door. I may not be a criminal, but I sure feel like one. So what do you need?"

"How about a self-defense angle?"

"Brewster, he was already dead when I got there."

"We're just talking theories, Goldy. I might need to

know how he beat you up, how you responded, and his history of assaulting other women."

Suddenly chilled, I wished I'd put on a jacket over the sweatshirt. "Tell you what. If the cops arrest me, you and I can talk. In the meantime, I'll keep running my business, and Marla will work on a list of John Richard's ex-girlfriends and what she knows he did to them. Will that work?"

Reluctantly, he agreed. We signed off.

I pulled out my inventory sheets from the previous day and squinted at them. As usual after washing and drying each piece of equipment, Julian and Liz had meticulously checked off every single knife, serving spoon, grater, and other kitchen doodad before stowing it in three cardboard boxes. Marla and I wrenched open all the boxes. The cops had gone through them, all right, but it looked as if they'd put everything back, even if in a somewhat jumbled fashion.

The previous afternoon, someone had gone into my van looking for *something*. Maybe they'd found what they were looking for, and also taken my gun, as a bonus.

I peered at the top of the inventory sheets, and began to rattle off items, which Marla then found and laid to one side. *Two butcher knives,* check. *Three paring knives,* check. *Two graters,* check. *Butane torch,* check . . .

Twenty minutes later, we found the answer, but I was even more perplexed than I had been when I'd begun. Finally, I called Julian at the bistro. The bangs and shouts of a restaurant kitchen echoed behind him as he assured me that yes, he'd put the item into the van. He remembered wiping them off and stowing them.

But what, I wondered, as I stared at my inventory sheet, would anyone hope to do with my *kitchen shears*? Had the killer wanted to use the scissors as a murder weapon, then found the gun and decided to use that instead? But just in case, he or she had stolen both?

As Marla nabbed her cell phone to make a call, I put all the equipment back in the boxes. Then, filled with resolve, I stashed the inventory papers in the canvas bag. The two of us traipsed back to the house, Marla still jabbering, me thinking about how to proceed.

Okay. After Marla and I hit the Rainbow Men's Club to question Sandee, I wanted to meet with my client of the previous day, Holly Kerr. I felt guilty, calling on a widow right after I'd catered the funeral lunch for her dead husband, but I wanted to refund her payment and needed the guest list from the Round-house event. If Holly did not have a printed list, I'd ask for her best memory of who had attended. Kleptomaniacs included.

"Listen up," Marla said as she clapped her phone shut. "I found out some good stuff from Frances and her sidekick. They wanted a 'Do you confirm or deny' statement. I promised that if she left, I'd call her back, which I just did. I traded a couple of tidbits about the Jerk's girlfriends for facts we couldn't have weaseled out of the cops." Marla paused for effect. "The reporters have already canvassed the neighbors. They didn't hear *anything*. No yelling or fighting, no shots. But someone saw a woman, or someone who looked like a woman, wearing heels, a black raincoat, and a black scarf. The neighbor noticed the rain gear because it was dusty and windy, which he thought was weird. Anyway, the Jerk roared up the driveway in the Audi, and then this woman raced up after him."

" 'This woman'? What woman?"

"Good question. Apparently, after the lunch, Sandee arrived with him at his house. She stayed in his car for a while—I think we can guess doing what—then got out and drove off in her VW. Not two minutes later, this other person ran across the cul-de-sac and up the driveway. The neighbor figured it was somebody who knew him, because she was carrying a shopping bag. As if she was going to give him a present or something."

"Yeah, slugs in the chest. But the neighbor didn't hear anything?"

"Nada. Someone shooting inside a garage, with a wind howling outside? Gunshots could easily get muffled."

I bit the inside of my lip. "So are all the reporters gone?"

"Nope. Three of 'em from the *Furman County Monthly* haven't had this hot a news item since they caught eight real estate agents having a sex orgy in an empty house."

I smiled. "I need to change into something respectable. Those nut cookies I made last night are in a tin on the counter."

Marla didn't need a second invitation.

Upstairs, I rummaged through my closet, crammed myself into a black skirt and top, and put in a call to Holly Kerr.

"I'm just on my way to water aerobics," she said, with what sounded like forced brightness. "Everyone tells me that . . . after the death of a loved one, it's important to keep the routine going."

I thought of Arch and Tom out on the golf course. "This will just take a moment," I promised. Marla called up that she'd eaten the cookies and I needed to haul out to her Mercedes with her! I closed my eyes. "Holly, I was wondering if you had a list of the people who were invited to the lunch yesterday."

"There wasn't a list. That's what I told the police." I stifled a gurgle of dismay. "Apparently there was some trouble afterward, they wouldn't tell me what. I told them that you don't invite guests to a funeral. You call people up, tell them about it, and guess how many will be there. Remember, I told you to make food for sixty? We had fewer than sixty, I think. I have the guest *book* here somewhere. A friend brought it over. I don't know if everyone signed it. As soon as I find it, I'm supposed to call the police so they can come get it."

"Besides the guest book, did the police ask you to make a list of the other people you remembered who were there?"

"Yes, but why are you asking me this? Do they want you to make a list, too?"

"Holly, John Richard was killed after the lunch."

She gasped.

"*I'm* the one they suspect—"

"You? But Goldy, why?"

"I don't know. I did not do it. So I'm begging you, please, give me a copy of the list of guests before you give one to the cops. I need it more than they do, trust me. Could you?"

She groaned. "Oh, of course. Lord! And he looked so happy with that girl! She *was* awfully young for him. Do you think it could have been a jealous husband?"

I swallowed and remembered the hot breath in my ear at the Grizzly Bear Saloon. *Sandee Blue is my girlfriend.* "I don't think so." How would Sandee's other boyfriend look in a black scarf, heels, and black raincoat?

"My dear, the aerobics class is going to start without me. The police are coming back this afternoon at four."

"I'll be there in the early afternoon," I promised, and signed off. I grabbed a pad of Arch's school paper and a pen, and headed down the stairs. On the way out, I pushed past three reporters, one of whom identified himself as being from the *Furman County Monthly*.

"Mrs. Schulz—"

"We've heard—"

"Do you have any—"

"Hurry up!" Marla cried, beeping her Mercedes horn. At least she didn't scream, *We don't want to be late for the strip show!* I trotted to the Benz and tucked myself inside. We peeled away from the curb with a squeal of tires and another long beep, for good measure.

Overhead, a thick cloud cover made the morning sky smooth and bright, as if someone had pulled luminous gauze across the heavens. A wire strung across the lake's waterfall provided a flock of newly arrived cormorants with a place to preen, flutter, and stretch their wide wings. Not a hundred yards from the lake house, a heron lifted himself up and up, while a crowd of birders pointed and focused their binoculars. Ahead of us, a small herd of elk seemed to be waiting to cross the street. Beside them, a boy who looked just like Arch was looking both ways, as if he intended to hold up traffic to allow the elk to pass.

"Hey!" I cried involuntarily. I pointed. "Arch told me he was going to play golf with Tom!" The elk chose that moment to make a mad dash across the street. The boy scampered across beside them.

"Where's Arch?" Marla cried as she hit the brakes. The Mercedes skidded sideways, into the oncoming lane. Two elk bolted across; three more balked and cantered back to where they'd come from. "Damn elk!" Marla shouted. She hit the gas a bit too hard, which made the Mercedes roar forward. The trio of elk that had made it back to their starting point gazed in surprise. Marla honked, buzzed down her window, and shouted at the elk, "Where are the hunters when you need them?" The elk lumbered back toward the water, while Marla, still furious, overcorrected her steering and sent the Mercedes careening toward the ditch on the right side of the road.

"Goldy, would you quit distracting me while I'm trying to drive?" Marla reprimanded me, once we were back in our lane. "I didn't see Arch."

"Okay," I said with as much calm as I could muster. "Where were we?"

"Looking at something that wasn't there. Before that, the Jerk's exploits. Don't worry, I already e-mailed Brewster my old catalog." She tilted her head and gunned the engine again. "What I still can't figure out is why someone would sabotage your food, whack you out of the way, and then steal your kitchen shears. Was our killer going to hack the Jerk to death after shooting him?"

"Who knows? And anyway, who could hate both John Richard and me?"

"I'm going to have to ask around about that one," Marla mused. "I don't suppose you have any theories."

"Holly Kerr wondered if Sandee might have a jealous significant other hanging around," I told Marla about the hostile fellow whispering in my ear while I was stumbling around the Grizzly. "Maybe he thought the Jerk and I were colluding to keep Sandee away from her boyfriend."

"Hmm. Need to check in with the gossip network on that one. Can you hand my cell over, please?"

I did so. Marla glanced at her phone, punched in some numbers, and nearly sideswiped a garbage truck—all in the space of fifteen seconds.

By the time we reached the Rainbow Men's Club in Denver, Marla had learned that Sandee had dumped her boyfriend, Bobby Calhoun—aka lead singer of Nashville Bobby and the Boys—in favor of the Jerk. Marla's sources asserted that Bobby's black pompadour was a wig. But the muscular body that he rubbed with Vaseline before unbuttoning his satin shirt at performance time was real. Reportedly, Bobby Calhoun loved three things: singing, firefighting, and Sandee. When he'd saved up enough money, he was going to pack up his sequined suit, steal Sandee away from the Rainbow, and head back to Tennessee.

"And where did John Richard figure in this little scenario?" I asked. "Or me?"

"Apparently, neither of you did. None of my people seems to have heard Bobby complain about the Jerk or you."

"But I'll bet anything he was the guy at the Grizzly who warned me away from Sandee."

Marla raised her eyebrows.

"Since John Richard was killed, our little Sandee has moved back into Bobby's condo, outside Aspen Meadow."

Marla stopped talking as she peered through the windshield at the club door. "Doesn't the Rainbow have valet?" When it was apparent that they didn't, Marla started backing the Benz into a metered parking space. She cursed as she hit the bumper of the pickup behind us, jumped her car forward into the rear lights of a Subaru wagon, and came to a halt a foot from the curb. "Think I should leave a twenty under the wiper, in case a cop comes?" she asked.

"It'll get stolen."

With immense relief, I got out of the car and glanced up and down the street. The previous night's hail had cut shallow gullies into the curb's detritus. Remnants of torn paper cups, newspapers, and pizza boxes lay in the mud. We were less than two miles from the glass atria, sidewalk cafés, and bustle of suits that characterized downtown Denver. But here, everything looked scruffy, from the black fronts of bars to the shifty-looking men and women prowling the sidewalks.

Marla had finished clinking coins into the meter and was already bustling through the Rainbow door. I followed as quickly as my still-sore legs and neck would allow, and tried not to think about what we were doing, where we were going, and what we hoped to accomplish.

The Rainbow entryway was darker than a cave, and I had the sudden paralyzing thought that my only experience with an abundance of naked women had been in gym locker rooms. For crying out loud, I was a *Sunday-school teacher*. What if Father Pete saw me? What if I saw Father Pete?

As Marla leaned over a dark glass counter, I blinked at the large display of signs telling what you could and could not do inside the Rainbow. One sign screamed that "Public Fighting Is Illegal in Denver." Thank God for *that!*

I gaped at the older woman who was manning the cash register. She was the same heavily made-up, raven-haired lady from the funeral lunch, the one who'd asked me if I'd played a trick with a glass, when I almost dropped one. And she *still* looked vaguely familiar, but I was trying to focus on her question and couldn't place her. She said, "You *know* this is a *men's* club, ladies?"

Marla retorted, "We're coming in anyway, because we both belong to ACLU, thank you very much. My pal here even caters for them sometimes. So! We'll take two all-you-can-eat buffet tickets, and before you say it, I can read that there's a two-drink minimum. Not to worry, we're going to need all the booze we can get. And before you ask, no, neither of us has video-recording equipment stuffed in our purses." Before I could say anything, Marla asked, "We want to see Sandee with two *es*. Where would she be?"

"The table closest to the buffet," the woman replied, smiling. She stashed a huge wad of cash in the register, looked up at us, and hesitated. "Don't either one of you remember me?"

"I do," I said suddenly as a memory flashed. The Jerk had treated her. "Sorry. Lana Della Robbia, right? You were one of John Richard's patients."

She nodded. "And Dr. Kerr's. Dr. Kerr delivered my babies. Fifteen years later, Dr. Korman removed a cancerous growth from my female plumbing. I owe him my life." She smiled. "I was at the service for Dr. Kerr yesterday," she went on, "and at the lunch you did."

At the Roundhouse, she'd been wearing a black designer suit; her hair had been swept up in a tight chignon. She'd been seated at the table with the jokesters who'd brought their own booze. Next to Lana had been that wide-shouldered, tan guy with the body-builder physique, the one who'd offered to juggle glasses. What had she called him? Dannyboy. I also re-

membered Dannyboy's long, brown-blond hair that
fanned out around his unattractively ruddy face and
gave him the look of a hungry lion. Lana, Dannyboy,
and the liquor drinkers had been only a few tables
away from John Richard and Sandee.

"It was a nice event," Lana said, but her voice was
hesitant.

"But?" I prompted. Behind me, a gaggle of guys was
protesting and telling me to hurry it up.

Lana glanced at the rowdy fellows and lowered her
voice. "I guess I was surprised to hear Ted Vikarios
give a speech, since he and Albert Kerr had that big
falling-out all those years ago."

" 'That big falling-out'?" I repeated, before the
crowd jostled one of the guys into my side.

"Come visit us at our table!" Marla offered, tugging
me into the club's interior.

"Why did you *do* that?" I shouted to Marla over the
pulse of rock music. "I was just about to find out
something!"

"You were just about to get trampled!" Marla replied
as she pulled me down a dark hallway past a cloakroom.

I said, "Lana must have thought highly of the Jerk if
she referred to him as Dr. Korman! Maybe she fixed
him up with Sandee."

Marla raised an eyebrow at me. "More likely our ex
came *here*. Water seeking its own level, that kind of
thing. Let's sit down at one of these little tables."

The club's spacious interior encompassed six black-
mirrored, raised hexagonal platforms. On top of each
mirrored surface, a naked-except-for-a-thong young
woman danced. Well, you couldn't really call it *dancing*. It was more like stepping-in-place-while-
wiggling-hips-and-boobs.

And what boobs they were. I wondered how they'd phrased their requests to their surgeons. Maybe using fruit analogies? I've got tangerines now, but could you give me oranges? Grapefruit? And melons! The dancers were shaking everything from cantaloupes to pumpkins. I would have sworn a red-haired woman in front of us had asked for honeydews. I didn't know if docs would ever be able to bestow watermelons, but science was always advancing.

Around each of the black-mirrored mini-stages, men sat watching the naked lady in front of them. Electrified chandeliers flashed red, blue, green, and yellow along with the beat of the music. There was a bar on the far side of the space, plus a sprinkling of small tables ringing the place. We sat at one of these. After watching the goings-on for a bit, I noticed that the men seated around the large mirrored tables were expected, at regular intervals, to put a greenback into each dancer's proffered thong. Then the dancer dropped the greenback into a small hole in the center of the black table.

"There was a young woman who graduated from Elk Park Prep a few years back," Marla leaned over to tell me. "Her parents were strict—fundamentalists, I think. The girl turned eighteen two days after graduation. She announced, 'Forget it, I'm not going to college, I'm gonna be a dancer.' She works here."

"These girls are all so young!" I exclaimed.

"What did you expect?" Marla asked. "Forty-year-olds?"

"I don't know what I expected," I said, suddenly dizzy.

I had not expected to see a group of young women—only a couple of whom looked a day over twenty-five—parading in front of men who appeared to be between forty-five and sixty, with the preponderance of them in their fifties. Uh-oh, now they were doing something new. When they weren't doing the half wiggle, the dancers leaned their ponderous breasts over first one, then another of the faces of the men sitting around the tables. The men were expected to come up with more bucks for the boobs-in-the-face routine. But how they could breathe in that narrow space, much less rummage for their wallets? It would be like trying to do a nighttime sail through the Strait of Magellan.

We looked for Sandee but couldn't spot her. At the nearest table, the red-haired woman-with-the-honeydews was dancing in a more animated way than the other strippers, who looked as if they might be on drugs. A ruby-red light focused on the redhead, revealing that she was a bit older than her compatriots. The light made her hair glow almost purple, and also highlighted what I thought was a desperate look in her eyes. Each bill she received made her gyrate even faster. When her shift was over, she stepped down and approached us.

"Uh, what's happening?" I asked Marla as Big Red made a beeline for our table.

"I don't know," Marla replied, "but I hope she puts on a bra before she gets here. This table won't support both of those."

Thankfully, the red-haired lady did put something on, a black wrap shift that she fluffed out and tied before arriving beside us.

"Ladies?" she said. "May I sit? I'm Ruby Drake. I think we have something in common." As I opened my mouth in protest, she said, "I knew your ex-husband, John Richard Korman."

"Ruby Drake," Marla repeated. She frowned, as if

trying to remember something. "You were his fifty-second girlfriend."

"I was never Korman's girlfriend," Ruby Drake replied, her tone icy. "Far from it. In fact—"

Before Ruby could finish, Lana sashayed over to our table and interrupted her. "Ruby, you've got some men asking for you on the far side of the room." Lana pointed a lacquered nail at one of the Rainbow's dark corners, and Ruby slunk away.

"Dammit to hell," I said under my breath. "We try to find stuff out here, and all we get is interrupted. Don't folks come here to relax?"

"I don't know," Marla replied as she waggled her fingers at one of the platforms. "But check it out. There's Sandee."

Sandee Blue was wriggling seductively at one of the far mirrored tables. Through the cloud of cigarette smoke, I could make out a substantial crowd of men gawking at her. And what was she covered with, shortening? Her skin had a bright sheen, and I wondered if she'd learned that trick from her Elvis-impersonating boyfriend. A neat trick, if it was true.

"Why would John Richard," I asked Marla, "who could have any wealthy tennis-playing socialite he wanted, go for a young stripper who has no money, no brains, and a pair of breasts that could be mistaken for Crenshaw melons?"

"The Crenshaws, silly."

"But look at those guys ogling her. Don't you suppose the Jerk got jealous of all the male attention Sandee received?"

"Nah," Marla muttered. "It probably turned him on. C'mon. While we're waiting, let's eat. Gotta warn you, though, I doubt people come here for the buffet."

"Sort of like buying porn magazines for the articles."

Ten minutes later, I was trying to cut a fatty piece of what had been labeled "Prime Rib au Jus." Marla had ordered us each two glasses of dry sherry, which the waitress had never heard of. Not wanting to cause a scene—for once—Marla settled for five-dollar soft drinks, which we sipped as we watched Sandee fling herself around. Finally, still wearing the high heels that were de rigueur for the dancers, she reached into the hole in the middle of the table, gathered up her cash, and stepped into a black shift similar to Ruby's. Sandee wobbled down a set of steps beside the hexagonal table, but was stopped at the bottom by a short, bald, acne-faced young man who whispered in her ear. Whatever he said to her, it made her giggle, which made all the other parts of her jiggle. The man whispered some more. Sandee acted attentive, then nodded. She finally saw us waving to her and took her leave of the bald fellow.

"Hi-yi," Sandee said when she arrived at our table. "I didn't expect to see you two here." She looked over her shoulder, scanning the club.

Marla said, "The golf shop sent us over. They said you found higher-paying work elsewhere."

Sandee flinched. "Well, uh, John Richard told me to *say* I worked there. You know, in case people asked? He thought it would look better, you know, with him sponsoring the golf tournament. Anyway, I hated that shop! Who would *buy* those sucky old-lady clothes?" She shuddered as her eyes flicked around the club again.

I put down my fork. Was she looking for someone? "Sit down, Sandee," I urged, and flashed Marla a warning look. "We just want to talk for a bit."

Marla, unheeding, plunged onward as soon as Sandee had snuggled her thinly clad rear end onto one of the chairs. "You know John Richard is dead? Shot and killed?"

Sandee's eyes immediately filled with tears. "I heard," she whispered. "Two detectives asked me a bunch of questions. They said they'd be coming back today." Again there was the scared glimpse in all directions.

"Any ideas about who could have killed John Richard?" Marla asked.

"No way," Sandee croaked. She reached for a paper napkin, then dabbed her eyes. She cried for a minute, making a sound that was halfway between a cat mewing and a human choking. Then she honked into the napkin. "The detectives wanted me to think some more about who John Richard's enemies were. You know, if anyone argued with him at the lunch? Stuff like that."

Marla gestured to me with a bejeweled hand. "Speaking of the lunch, Goldy's making a list of the guests. We know most of the people from Southwest Hospital, but there are some people"—she nodded in Lana's direction—"who we're not sure about."

Although I didn't put a whole lot of stock in Sandee's memory, I obligingly reached for the pad I'd stashed in my purse.

"Oh, I totally don't remember anybody." Sandee frowned at the empty pad. She made another furtive scan of the club interior. Could Marla not be noticing? Was Sandee not allowed to be talking to us? Was she looking for Ruby, Lana, the bald guy? "The only person I knew at the lunch was John Richard," Sandee said, her voice halting. "I mean, besides Lana, you know, and Dannyboy. You know, and some other Rainbow people."

"What did you do after you left the lunch?" I asked gently.

"We went back to his house and, you know, messed around in the car for a while. But not for long, I mean, I had to go back to work." She raised mournful eyes. "Later, you know? He was taking Arch to the club. The *golf* club." Her chin trembled, her eyes filled, and she again began mewing into the napkin. Marla rolled her eyes. I was thankful for the clink of glasses and pound of music around us.

"Sandee," I said, as calmly as I could over the cacophony, "what are you worried about? Lana told us it was okay to talk to you."

"She did?" Sandee seemed surprised, but looked around again, as if to confirm that Lana was not hovering.

"We just need to ask you about his money," I continued. "John Richard's money."

At that moment, we were interrupted *again*. This time it was the bald guy, who leaned his pimply-faced, hunchback-of-Notre-Dame body over the table, nuzzled in next to Sandee's neck, and whispered more words in her ear. Then he handed her some cash, which she thrust into an unseen pocket of the black dress. She smiled up at him, gently turned his wrist to see what time his watch said, then whispered something back.

Marla raised her voice. "Sandee!" The bald guy jumped, then trundled off. "Remember that day," Marla continued, "when we came over to John Richard's house and you asked us if we'd brought money? What was that about?"

"Uh, let's see." Sandee dabbed at her smeared mascara. "I asked *you* for money?"

"Yes, you did," Marla replied evenly. "And then

when Goldy showed up at John Richard's house yesterday, a tall guy driving a blue sedan was parked out front. He asked Goldy if *she* had *his* money. Now, John Richard had no job, but he was living a fancy lifestyle that included a house, an Audi, and a cute . . . how old are you?"

"Twenty-eight," Sandee replied, blushing.

"Twenty-eight-year-old," Marla continued, giving me a raised eyebrow. "He also forked over major bucks to sponsor a golf tournament. We are his ex-wives, Sandee. His *expensive* ex-wives. We know his money situation coming out of incarceration was *not good*."

"Incarceration?"

"Jail," we ex-wives said in unison.

"You were living there, Sandee," Marla went on. "How did he have an income? Was he borrowing money? Were people demanding that he repay it? Do you think that's why he got killed?"

"I don't *know*," Sandee insisted. She crumpled the napkin with fingernails painted a glittery green. "You know, his *cash*? He just had lots of it. That's all." Her tone turned morose. She glanced in the direction of the front door. "Know what? I don't care what Lana told you. Club policy is, I can only stay at one table for two minutes. Besides, I gotta go fix my makeup." With that, she took a deep breath, pushed out her chair, and clattered away.

"Let's get out of here," Marla said abruptly. She looked down with distaste at our barely touched plates. "We can stop for sandwiches and ice cream on the way home. Think, prosciutto and arugula. Think, butter-roasted pecan ice cream. Think, no one making a declarative statement and posing it as a question. Think, fudge sauce."

But for once I wasn't pondering food. I was mentally totting up the lies I was sure Sandee had told: She was closer to twenty-one than twenty-eight, and she *had* asked Marla for money. Did this prevarication mean that Sandee knew more than she was letting on? Or was she just a flake who lied about her age and couldn't remember anything? And where had Ruby Drake disappeared to?

The sudden appearance of Lana Della Robbia distracted me from these questions.

"Lana!" I said. I could see now that she, too, was wearing the clingy black signature dress of the women who worked at the Rainbow. "Tell us more about the Kerr-Vikarios conflict."

"It was a long time ago, after I had my babies. I heard they had some kind of falling-out, right around the time Dr. Kerr and Holly left for England. I don't know what it was about," Lana concluded dramatically.

Marla and I exchanged a glance.

"That's interesting, Lana, really," Marla said. "Just out of curiosity," she plowed on, "how did John Richard come to get hooked up with Sandee? He came over to receive your thanks for saving him? Then he picked a nubile filly from your little stable? I mean, she did have a gun-toting boyfriend, right? The singer? Am I wrong?"

"Dr. Korman was a good customer," replied Lana, her tone diffident. And yet now it was her turn to scan the club, looking nervous. "Anyway, that's not why I came over to your table."

A young woman running the cash register called to Lana for help. Lana, who was clearly the boss, turned and beckoned with that formidable-looking, scarlet-painted acrylic nail for us to follow. Did everybody in this place have killer nails?

Marla sighed audibly, but we obliged. Once she was at the front counter, Lana dealt with the crisis—a group of twenty handsomely dressed guys in their forties were arriving for a late lunch. The adding machine had frozen up and Lana needed to count the cash and hand the guys their tickets.

"They look like lawyers," Marla said in disbelief, eyeing the suits.

"They *are* lawyers," Lana muttered under her breath, frantically counting bills.

"So what happened to American Express?" Marla asked. "Visa?"

"We take 'em," the young woman who'd called Lana over said mournfully. "But the guys don't want their wives checking the statements. I mean, how would you feel if your husband ate lunch at a strip club?"

"Our ex-husband did," Marla and I said in unison. The young woman shrugged, as if to say, *See?*

"Goldy and Marla," Lana said softly, rubber-banding the bills. "Do you know when Dr. Korman's funeral will be?"

"Not yet," Marla replied. "Probably sometime this week. You can call St. Luke's Episcopal Church in Aspen Meadow for more info." And with that, Marla hustled me out the exit.

"Are you out of your mind?" I shrieked at Marla once we were striding along the gritty sidewalk.

"No, I'm *hungry,*" she said. "By the way, did you notice that Lana never asked who we thought killed the Jer . . . Oh Christ," she said, when she spotted her car. She grabbed my arm.

I thought she must have gotten a parking ticket, or been sideswiped by a garbage truck, maybe retaliating for that morning. At the very least, the Mercedes must have a flat.

But no. The unattractive bald man, Sandee-the-stripper's admirer, lay sprawled across the hood of Marla's Mercedes. Ringing started up in my ears. I trotted across the gritty sidewalk, feeling in my pocket for my new cell phone. As I got closer, I could see blood streaming out of the man's nose and mouth.

He wasn't moving.

Chapter 11

Before I'd pressed the 9 in 911, Marla wrenched the phone from me.

"What the hell do you think you're doing?" she demanded.

"This guy is bleeding—"

"Forget it. You can't see that because *you're not here.*" She closed my phone and handed it to me, nabbed her own cell from her big Vuitton bag, and punched buttons. As she did so, she leaned down over the injured man and shook his back. He groaned. Marla then held up a warning finger while informing Denver emergency response that a man had been beaten and left on the hood of her car. Yes, he was conscious. Yes, there was blood, lots of it, all over the place. No, it didn't look like a gunshot or a stab wound . . . well, a wicked bloody nose, not something you could do to yourself. Marla gave an approximation of our street address, then closed the phone while the operator squawked, "*Please don't hang up, ma'am, we need to know your name and the man's identity if you happen to know—*"

The bald man moaned again and struggled to turn his head. I scrambled over to him.

"Don't move!" I barked while assessing his bloodshot eyes. I tried to make my voice reassuring. "Help is on the way." The man moaned more loudly.

"Hey!" Marla hollered, her head next to mine. "Who hit you, guy?" When the man didn't answer, Marla raised her voice. "Whoever beat the crap out of you left you on *my* car!"

With great effort, the bald, bloodied man focused on us. He blinked. He burbled something. Marla and I edged closer and said, *"What?"*

The man wheezed. He announced, a tad louder, "Elvis."

Marla and I looked at each other.

Marla said, "Goldy, you need to scram. Let Denver PD handle this. If the Furman County detectives get wind of what's happened here, and that you were involved, they could haul down the mountain and demand to know why *you* were here questioning Sandee. As for Sandee, she knows more than she's letting on. Looks to me as if her jealous boyfriend Bobby could be snagged for assault, end up doing the jailhouse rock."

"Sandee was checking around that club like a parakeet looking for the house cat. She and Lana both. I should have known something was up."

"Something's *always* up at a strip club," Marla commented somberly.

"We shouldn't joke," I said. "This poor guy"—I gestured at the fellow groaning on the hood of her SL—"probably got beaten up for paying attention to Sandee with two *e*s. Think our ex got whacked for the same reason?"

Marla shrugged. I slumped against our parking meter and tried to think. Why would Nashville Bobby have stolen my kitchen shears? Had he beaten me up prior to killing John Richard, just for good measure? Or was my being assaulted incidental to the theft of my kitchen shears and my thirty-eight? The theory of Bobby-Elvis as the killer was intriguing, if mystifying. Then again, we didn't yet have the autopsy results. Maybe Marla was right, and John Richard had been shot and then stabbed with the shears. I shuddered.

Worry for Arch solidified into a hard pain in my chest. How was he doing? Shouldn't I be trying to comfort him over the death of his father instead of racing around Denver trying to figure out who had *killed* his father?

I tried to stand up straight, felt dizzy again, and grabbed the meter. Arch was blaming me this morning. For not locking up my gun. For not calling paramedics. And yet this was the same Arch who saved half his allowance for a soup kitchen. *He's not himself, Goldy,* Tom had said. And then instead of feeling dizzy or worried, I realized I was experiencing something else: a rising panic, a raw fear that *only* figuring out who had murdered John Richard would restore my relationship with Arch.

"Damn the Jerk!" I jumped away from the parking meter and started kicking it. "Damn him!" The meter clanked more loudly inside its concrete hole each time my foot whacked it.

"*Now* what?" Marla cried.

"I hate him! He wrecked my life while he was alive. And now he's screwing it up from the grave!"

"Take it easy, will you?" Marla cried, inserting her large body between me and the meter. "There's a fine for destroying Denver city property, you know." She seized my shoulders. "When the Jerk is actually *in* the grave, you and I can go dance on top of it. In the meantime, go stand there by the bald guy. Kick my tires if you want."

I stalked over to the Mercedes, crossed my arms, and fumed. I hated John Richard Korman more than ever, with his schemes, his libido, his lying, and all his excuses and justifications for bad behavior. Now he was dead, and I was the prime suspect in his murder.

When was all this going to end? But I knew the answer to that: when the cops, or I, or *someone* figured out who had killed John Richard. And why. Oh, yes, and then there was that dancing-on-the-grave bit.

"I just called you a limo," Marla announced as she snapped her cell phone shut. "They're right around the corner, and I ordered you an express. In a few minutes, you'll get transported back to the mountains in style." She frowned. "You look awful."

"I don't care." I stared at the Mercedes hood and the poor bloodied bald fellow, who was still moaning. "Look, I don't need a limo. I'll take an express bus to Aspen Meadow and walk the twenty minutes to my house."

"The hell you will," Marla retorted. "There's no way I'm letting you brave those reporters camped on your porch. The driver's going to escort you right to your door. And *I* am going to stay here and deal with the Denver police. Not to mention whatever city agency oversees parking-meter destruction."

I frowned at the meter, now listing toward the street. And then, for the second time in two days, sirens wailed in the distance, and they were coming toward a crime scene that involved yours truly. I kicked the parking meter again.

"Will you *stop*?" Marla hollered. "Pay attention. I

need you to tell me what to say to the cops. Quickly. Should I tell them about this bald guy"—she pointed at the man on her hood—"and his connection to Sandee's boyfriend, Nashville-Bobby-the-Elvis-impersonator, and Sandee's connection to the Jerk?"

"You already said you didn't want Denver PD to connect this to Furman County. So *don't* mention Sandee Blue or Bobby Calhoun."

The guy on her hood moaned. "It was *Elvis.*"

"Why not?" Marla demanded. "It wouldn't involve you."

"Look. If you say *anything* about this guy somehow being connected to John Richard's murder, Denver PD *will* call the Furman County detectives, who will roar down here and demand to know what *your* connection is to the Jerk and his death. And by the way, they'll ask, 'What were you doing here, Mrs. Korman? Who was with you?' Then they'll talk to everybody in the Rainbow, demanding to know how long you were in there and if you were alone, on and on until we're all hauled in for questioning again. This would not make Brewster-the-criminal-lawyer happy. Marla, please. I'm thankful you got me a limo. Trust me with the cop stuff."

"But—"

"Listen. Let Denver PD do a simple assault report. Tell them this fellow who got beaten up said the guy who hit him looked like Elvis. Then say vaguely that you think the Elvis impersonator hangs out around here, and if the Denver cops go into the Rainbow, they might be able to get the name of the assailant. The end."

A silver stretch limo rounded the corner and flashed its lights.

"But how will they ever connect the beating of the bald guy with the Jerk's murder?" Marla protested.

"Anonymous tip. As in, you call Furman County later and leave one."

Marla rolled her eyes, then bustled me and my cell phone, purse, and sore kicking foot in the direction of the limo. A tall, smiling driver held the door open. The limo's plush red interior was frigid from air-conditioning. I shuddered and stared out the darkened windows that filtered what was now murderously brilliant sunshine. Without warning, the limo floated away from the curb. Twenty yards from the Rainbow Men's Club, we sailed past two shrieking black-and-whites and an ambulance.

There was chaos on the street. I closed my eyes. Again anxiety gripped me. There was chaos in my soul, no question. My life had turned into one big chaos soup, and I was not happy about it.

As we headed west, I tried to think. Form a plan, I told myself. Luckily, I still had Holly Kerr's phone number and address, off Upper Cottonwood Creek Drive, entered in my Palm. Sometimes I was grateful I'd entered the Age of Technology, I thought as I retrieved my new cell and punched in Holly's numbers. Yes, her voice crackled, she was back from her class, and she'd be happy to see me now. When I asked for directions, the driver interrupted to say he had an onboard navigation system. I whispered for him to wait as I tapped directions into the Palm—five dirt roads and a curvy mountain turnaround. I closed the cell and informed the driver that the Age of Technology did *not* extend to finding remote areas and landmarks of Aspen Meadow, Colorado. We'd had whole passels of bewildered tourists toting their handheld Global Positioning Systems as they searched for abandoned gold mines and cowboy hideaways. They invariably became lost. Just last week, the forest service had helicoptered out six rock-climbing orthodontists from New Jersey, and told them never to come back.

Forty minutes later, the driver was cursing under his breath as the limo bounced along a cratered single-lane dirt road that meandered off Upper Cottonwood Creek Drive. Melting hail had rendered the byway an obstacle course of stone-washed gullies, soft dirt, and mud-filled holes. Rocks and gravel scratched mercilessly against the sides and underbelly of the sleek silver vehicle as we splashed through the puddles. I wondered how much paint had been scraped away, and if they'd charge Marla for it. Finally, we ran aground in front of a dirt driveway that climbed upward at a forty-five-degree angle.

The limo guy eyed the steep driveway and shook his head. "Lady, it's not happening."

"I can walk." We both disembarked. The driver squinted in all directions, at aspens, pines, and rocks. There wasn't another house in sight. "An hour or so, okay?" I asked.

"It's your dime. Where are we, Wyoming?" He rubbed the toe of one of his formerly shiny black shoes to get off the dust. "There's something else," he added.

"Go ahead," I said, trying not to sound impatient.

"It's just that I've got a job tonight, and I wasn't figuring on driving all the way up here, and . . . well . . . if the lady you're visiting is passing out extra sandwiches—"

My own stomach was growling, so I understood. "If she doesn't give me something for you, I'll fix you an Italian sub at my place."

He nodded shyly. I began hoofing my way up the driveway, a mile-long affair that led to Holly Kerr's fabulous home, a manse of the genus *Mountain Contemporary.* Cantilevered out over granite outcroppings, the wood-and-glass home possessed an unparalleled vista of Upper Cottonwood Creek, the Aspen Meadow Wildlife Preserve, and the plum-shadowed peaks of the Continental Divide. All this made me even more grateful that Holly had decided to have Albert's memorial lunch at the Roundhouse. Getting supplies up this driveway would have been as the driver said: not happening.

I'd visited Holly at the beginning of May. That was when she'd first moved here, bringing Albert's ashes with her from Qatar. While we were working on the lunch menu, she told me she'd been able to snag the house in less than a week after her arrival. Word was, the country-music singer living in the big place had just been dumped by his label. It seemed strange that the childless widow of a missionary would want to settle so far west of town, where the snow fell to greater depths and the plows rarely visited. But Holly told me that her one criterion for a retirement home was that she would never again have to live anywhere near the equator. To each her own.

I'd submitted to her enthusiastic tour of all seven thousand square feet of glass, wood, and stone. I'd oohed and aahed over the high ceilings pierced by skylights, the ten fireplaces, the twelve bedrooms. With her photo and Christmas card collections, her Save the Rainforest work (another oddity for someone who'd been living in Qatar), and her many weaving, jewelry-making, and craft projects, Holly had filled up the place with . . . well, with stuff. *Lots* of stuff.

Later, Marla had told me that Holly had inherited enormous parcels of land in Nebraska and Colorado. For decades, her parents had owned a chain of feed-and-farm-equipment stores. With the profits, they'd quietly bought up defunct farms in both states, and held on to them. When they'd died two years ago, the sale of the land had netted Holly eight million dollars. Not only that, Marla had reported, but Holly had bought the country-music star's house right after the season's first forest fire had come raging down from the wildlife preserve. The star had told his real estate agent to make any deal he could. Without irony, Marla said that Holly had gotten the place for a song.

I began huffing and puffing up the driveway again. Unlike most wannabe buyers, Marla had said, Holly had not been spooked by the fire. Still, worry that the whole town would be engulfed in an even bigger conflagration had translated into a flood of homes for sale and a panic within the insurance industry. Within two weeks, companies had stopped writing policies for fire insurance. Holly, Marla repeated, had been lucky.

At the top of the driveway, I gulped air, wiped sweat off my face, and looked longingly down at Cottonwood Creek. Truth to tell, I would have preferred to be *in* the creek.

"You made it!" Holly cried when she swung open the massive front door. I trudged inside, barely able to murmur thanks. I was immediately greeted by the scent of baking bread threaded with a hint of citrus. My stomach howled, and I worried for my poor limo driver.

"I made brioche yesterday and was just heating some up," Holly said, her friendly, sun-aged face smiling. Her petite frame was clad in a gray sweatsuit that matched her short, bouncy gray hair. "Are you hungry? I never eat before class and am always famished afterward. I was just making a late lunch."

"Sounds divine."

I followed Holly as her tiny gym shoes bounced forward over plush, burgundy-patterned wool rugs. She and Albert had "picked some up in Saudi Arabia," she'd told me offhandedly the last time I'd visited. After the inheritance came through, it seemed Albert and Holly had made numerous jaunts throughout the Middle East, picking up "stuff," as Holly called it. The "stuff" had been in boxes when I'd visited before, but now it was everywhere. And I do mean *everywhere*.

Tapestries and artwork bedecked the wood-and-rock walls. Holly had arrayed ivory and wooden knickknacks over a dizzying number of wooden shelves. Afghans and coverlets spilled off leather couches, leather chairs, even leather ottomans that traversed the huge living room like a line of tugboats. The artwork, I noticed as Holly began banging around in the kitchen, consisted mainly of nineteenth-century prints, hammered gold-and-pearl jewelry, and antique china plates. Holly had shown me one of her own craft pieces on my first visit, an intricate weaving involving silk knots, pearls, and gold beads. I'd never seen anything like it in any macramé class, that was certain. Now there were at least a dozen of these bejeweled masterpieces hanging on the walls. Holly had told me that without kids or work, she'd had lots of time for craft work. No kidding.

After a mile hike on an empty stomach, I didn't want to look at artwork. I joined Holly in her pale yellow kitchen, where high walls, maple cabinets, and gold-streaked granite counters were mercifully free of ornament. While Holly prepared plates of warmed brioche rolls, shrimp salad, and tomatoes vinaigrette—ah, how I loved it when somebody else prepared food for me!—I washed my hands.

"Marla hired a driver to bring me up here," I said, accepting a towel from Holly. "Any chance I could take him some food?"

"Of course."

"And something else," I said as I placed an envelope on her counter. "Here's your check back from yesterday. I'm not cashing it, since we didn't have the menu you ordered."

"Don't be ridiculous!" Holly exclaimed. "Now eat your salad!"

I shrugged and dug into the salad she placed in front of me. It featured fat, succulent shrimp combined with fresh dill, diced celery, scallions, and artichoke hearts, all wrapped in a velvety homemade mayonnaise, salmonella be damned. The light, feathery brioche rolls, their centers folded around a smear of orange marmalade, were a perfect accompaniment. After I'd polished off a second helping of salad, two more rolls, and several glasses of iced tea with embarrassing quickness, Holly cleared our plates and waved away my thanks. She disappeared from the kitchen, then returned with a clipped packet of papers, which she handed to me.

"Here are copies of the guest-book pages. Most of the people I invited were folks from Albert's doctoring days, when he and Ted Vikarios were co–department heads at Southwest Hospital. I was surprised by how many people came, really."

I nodded. How could I ask her about a long-ago falling-out between Albert and Ted without seeming rude? "You were able to get in touch with a lot of people," I commented.

Holly smiled. "When you have *nothing* to do in a hot Arab country where you can't even go *out,* you do tend to write a lot of letters. You remember the old hierarchy in teaching hospitals, Goldy. Department heads, attending physicians, fellows, residents, interns. And of course there were the charge nurses, any students I had addresses for, plus some of Albert's patients who've kept in touch over the years. I invited them all."

I frowned at the sheets. There were Lana Della Robbia, Courtney MacEwan, Ted and Ginger Vikarios. Nan Watkins, R.N., Dr. John Richard Korman, Marla Korman. No Bobby Calhoun. Had I registered an Elvis impersonator lurking at the edges of the lunch? I didn't remember.

I riffled through the pages. If the key to who had killed John Richard was there, it was not readily apparent. I folded the papers, tucked them into my bag, and resolved to look at them when my head was clear.

"Before you leave, Goldy, I want to show you something. You're doing Nan Watkins's retirement picnic tomorrow afternoon, right?"

If I can manage, I thought, but said only, "Yes. You're coming, aren't you?"

"Nan was always a great help to Albert. I found an album you might like to borrow. It has some photos you might enjoy. Med wives never throw anything away, right?" She disappeared for a moment, then returned with a thick volume sporting a faded, hand-quilted cover. "Have a look."

I flipped open to an early page. "You weren't just a med wife, were you? In his eulogy, Ted mentioned that you were a nurse."

She stopped beside one of the tables and gave me a bright smile. "Not a real nurse. Albert was an only child. His parents were disappointed, since they'd wanted lots of kids to help with the farm. They were also Christian Scientists. Remember what John Richard used to say?" Holly managed a tight smile. "Christian Science was neither Christian nor scientific."

I closed my eyes. The Jerk and his insults. *May he not rest in peace.*

"And so you nursed him?" I asked.

"You could say that." Holly opened a cupboard and pulled out a plate containing, to my surprise, half of one of the flourless chocolate cakes from the previous day's funeral lunch. "According to your friend Julian, this was all that was left after the guests departed. Care for a piece?" I again thought guiltily of my driver. "Don't worry," Holly said brightly, "I'll pack some for your driver."

"Great. Thanks."

She cut each of us slices, then sat back down. "The Kerrs didn't get immunizations, wouldn't see a doctor. One time when they came into town for supplies, they caught a harsh influenza virus. Albert's parents were both dead within a month."

"That's terrible." I flicked a glance around the kitchen, hoping for a coffee machine. "How old was he?"

Holly turned to a page of photos. "Thirteen. Here he is when he came to live with our family." I looked at a tall, earnest-looking boy clad in farm clothes. "He had to come to school with me, and he immediately got sick." She pointed to another picture, this one of Albert sitting up in bed, smiling, with spots covering his face.

"He got chicken pox and roseola," Holly said. "Measles. Mumps. He would have died, he used to say, if I hadn't taken care of him. It was a story he loved to tell," Holly said, a quiver in her voice.

"You probably saved his life."

She lifted her chin. "I brought him homework and homemade chicken soup and we fell in love along the way. He had money from the sale of his farm, plus loans and scholarships, to get him through college and medical school." She closed the book. "Payback to his parents, I guess you'd say. Albert became a medical doctor and an Episcopalian, and got a flu shot every year."

I tried to reach for a cliché about things coming full circle, or something along those lines, but what I really wanted was to delve into the conflict between her and her husband and the Vikarioses. Could the food sabotage and resulting assault on me have been a product of that feud? I had gotten in the way, and so, somehow, John Richard had, too? I wondered. I was worried about my limo driver, but I needed, somehow, to keep Holly talking. I said, "I didn't know him, Albert, too well when he turned to religion."

"You were busy with Arch. He was just a newborn, and John Richard was at the hospital all the time, along with Albert and . . . and Ted." Her voice caught. "Oh, Goldy!" Pressing her lips together, she turned away. I moved quickly to her side and folded her in a hug. Maybe it had been a bad idea to come over here for something as trivial as a guest list. And there was no way I'd hear about any conflict between Albert and Ted Vikarios now, with Holly getting upset so easily. I felt like a complete heel.

"I'm sorry," I soothed. "I apologize for coming over, truly. Dear Holly."

"No, it's all right." She cleared her throat. "Going

through the photographs for Nan's retirement brought it all back." Her blue eyes were full of tenderness. "Imagine Ginger's and my surprise to see Arch all grown up! And so handsome, just like his fa— Oh God." Her voice cracked, but she held on. "He must need, you must need . . ."

"I'm fine, Holly, really." *Ginger's* and my surprise? So whatever conflict they'd had had been patched up, and now they were pals, talking about Arch and the old times? I hesitated. "Do you want me to call someone from the church to come over here to be with you?"

"No, thanks. I'm all right. You're very dear to stay with me for a bit and share a meal." She rubbed her eyes with her fingertips. "I suppose I'm just not looking forward to talking to the detectives."

That made two of us. If the cops saw me, they'd want to know the reason for my visit. Still, I was reluctant to leave Holly when she was not doing well emotionally.

"Let me fix that food for your driver," she said, suddenly decisive. Clearly, she didn't want me to feel sorry for her. She organized plastic containers and filled them. "Be sure to check the photos in there from Southwest Hospital. There are some from when Arch was born. Don't you remember, when John Richard passed out bubblegum cigars? You were both *so* happy."

"I'll . . . look at them." I struggled for more words, but couldn't find any.

Within five minutes, I was toting a bag bulging with containers of shrimp salad, rolls, and cake. I thanked Holly and promised we'd chat more at Nan's picnic. I did not add, *If I'm not arrested first.* She reminded me that she'd be seeing me at the tree-planting fund-raising breakfast the next morning. The committee had surprised her with an invitation to join! She seemed happy about this, and didn't seem to realize that fund-raising groups almost always beg wealthy folks to be a part of their efforts. Still, mention of the committee breakfast only reminded me of how much work I still had to do. I forced a smile to match hers and hightailed it out of there.

The chauffeur was puffing on a cigarette, stomping from foot to foot, and hollering into a cell phone that it was *three hours past his lunch break and he was out in the middle of the wilderness and he was so starved he was ready to shoot an elk and eat it raw!* At that very moment, apparently, his connection was lost, and he hurled the phone into the forest. Fortunately, there were no elk passing by that he could have hit. I sidled up to him and handed him the food. Then I settled myself in the backseat while he dug in, grunted, chewed, and moaned until he'd polished off the whole thing.

Within moments, the limo was banging and shuddering back down the dirt road. I felt a sudden wave of exhaustion. I remembered being on the Jersey shore as a kid, when the occasional huge breaker would knock me over and grind my face in the sand. I blinked at my watch: Could it really be 1:30? I had two events to prep, a list of funeral guests to investigate, and a body still aching from the assault. I closed my eyes. But not for long.

My fingers were inexorably drawn to Holly's photo album. I had to see the pictures. I had to face those memories before going through them with Arch.

I came to a page labeled "Arrival of Archibald Korman!" Eight photos were arranged on facing pages. There was John Richard, as handsome as ever, and youthful looking, too, without the strain that had crept into his face over the years. And me! Had I ever been that young? My face did look weary, but my hair fifteen years ago had been quite a bit bouncier and, alas, blonder. Arch, a tiny bundle, was being held up to the camera by a pretty, uniformed girl, who was also beaming. Was she a candy striper? Oh yes, wait. She was Talitha Vikarios, daughter of Ted and Ginger. I barely remembered her.

John Richard, clutching a fistful of blue bubblegum cigars, wore a T-shirt given to him by Drs. Kerr and Vikarios. In capital letters, the T-shirt screamed "PROUD PAPA." Albert Kerr and Ted Vikarios, beaming in the background, looked as happy as if they, too had just had little boys.

Arch, with his little wizened face and tiny wrapped body, seemed to be giving a puzzled look to the camera. I held the photo closer. Pretty Talitha Vikarios, her candy-stripe uniform setting off her rosy cheeks, clutched the sides of Arch's baby blanket. I opened my eyes and took in John Richard's tanned face and arms, how they contrasted with the white T-shirt. I looked closely at Arch. His eyes had been blue then, of course, before they'd turned brown and needed glasses. Was I just reading a look of intense worry on my son's infant face, or had he seen disaster coming?

I shifted on the leather seat, trying to get comfortable. Spending an hour with Holly Kerr had been too much. The bumps in the road, the shrimp salad and cake, the bleeding bald guy outside the strip club, the strip club itself; they had all been *too much.* And now these photos. *Our beautiful family.* Right.

I looked at the last snapshot. Arch, John Richard, yours truly.

What's wrong with this picture?

I closed the photo album. I shut my eyes, lay my head back on the seat, and let the tears slide down.

Chapter 12

Half an hour later, the long silver car slid slowly down Main Street. I looked out the window and tried to pull myself together. The plastic flowers in their hanging baskets shook in the fresh, dusty breeze. Tourists bunched and drifted along the sidewalks. They licked ice-cream cones, chewed taffy, and munched on popcorn from paper bags. Out of nostalgic habit, I glanced at Town Taffy, where Arch had pressed his nose against the glass on many a summer afternoon. The subject of his fascination had been the taffy machine's arms as they stretched and pulled impossibly long strands of bright pink, green, blue, and white candy.

And there he was. Arch was once again standing in front of Town Taffy, his eyes fixed on the mechanical arms moving around and around with their thick ribbons of candy.

What was the matter with me? How bad a bump on the head had I gotten at the Roundhouse?

"Mister!" I called to my driver, regretting that I didn't know his name. "Do you see a kid, there, a kid!" Unable to describe what I was sure was a phantom, I pressed down the window button. "Hey, Arch!" I screamed. "Arch, over here, in the limo!"

"Lady, do you want me to pull over?"

I watched as the kid, Arch, or whoever he was, moseyed off down the sidewalk, where he met up with an older, dark-haired man whom I could see only from the back. They were absorbed into a group of tourists who were heading up toward the lake.

"No, that's okay," I told the driver. "I was mistaken. It's been a long day."

"And it's not even over," the driver muttered.

He piloted the limo off Main Street and up our road. My eyes searched hungrily for our brown-shingled house. I finally picked out our newly painted white shutters and trim shimmering in the bright June light.

"Mrs. Schulz?" asked the limo driver. "Is this home?"

My mind again blanked as I looked out at the reporters and photographers crowding our small lawn. Was this a vision, too, only a bad one?

"Mrs. Schulz? Do you want me to help you to your front door?"

When he braked, the tires squealed. A sea of hungry journalists surged toward the curb.

"Keep going!" I cried. A wave of eager faces called to me. "Hit the gas!" I hollered.

As we screeched up the street, I tried to think. My reflection in the rearview mirror did not look good. Holly's dirt driveway and my unwanted tears had left my cheeks a dusty gray. The last thing my business needed—besides my being convicted of murder, of course—was a photograph of my smudged and soiled self sprinting toward our door.

"Turn left and see if you can circle the block," I said.

"There's an alley that cuts behind our house." I couldn't go to Marla's or anywhere else, because hiding out was not on the agenda. With any luck, the journalists wouldn't have thought I could sneak in the back without them seeing me. But I had to get into my kitchen. In the Life Goes On department, I was a caterer until further notice.

"Okay, just a quick left," I told the driver once we'd reached the alley. Even with the drought, profusely blooming branches of Alpine roses arched over the alleyway and almost concealed our brown-shingled garage. Thorny branches scratched the windshield and sides of the formerly pristine limo. "Once we get there, could you run me to the back door?"

The driver nodded assent, then eased in behind our garage. I readied my keys and grabbed my bag. Once we were out of the car, the driver took my elbow and we quickstepped toward the house's rear door. We were halfway through Tom's back garden when the shout went up.

"She's coming in around back!"

Dammit.

"Mrs. Korman, did you kill your husband?"

"What are those papers sticking out of your bag, Mrs. Korman? Do they have something to do with the case?"

Ignoring the shouted questions, I repeated the mantra, "Coffee, coffee, coffee, coffee," the last few steps to the back door, until I had it unlocked and the security code entered.

"Thanks," I told the limo driver, and meant it. I suddenly realized I had no money for a tip. I imagined the headline: "Caterer Refuses Fellow Service Person Gratuity."

He read my mind. "Don't worry, a twenty percent tip's included."

From behind him, a third reporter shouted, "Did you kill your ex-husband, Mrs. Schulz?"

I ignored him and turned to go in the house. The limo driver gently caught my arm.

His low voice murmured, "If *coffee* is the password to your security system, you better not be saying it so loudly. People could break into your house."

"It's okay," I whispered, and patted his arm. "Thanks for everything. You've been great."

I slammed through the door. Once inside, I raced through each ground-floor room, pulling down shades, curtains, and blinds. Then I took a few deep breaths, fixed myself a double shot of espresso, and used it to down four ibuprofen.

Wherever Tom and Arch were, playing golf or touring Main Street, they were still out. I sloshed a medicinal amount of whipping cream into a second *doppio* and booted up my computer. Within moments I had opened a document and was assiduously typing the names of all the funeral-lunch guests from Holly Kerr's photocopied guest list. I didn't want to call the document "Jerk Death," in the remote event that Arch went trolling through my database. I finally just gave it the initials "JRK." Because I had learned a thing or two from Tom, I also typed in every conversation I'd had with anybody—right from the beginning of the previous morning. The memory is a slippery thing, Tom often said. We tend to reshape dialogue after the fact, and details slide away. I was under suspicion for my ex-husband's murder and I was estranged from my son. I couldn't afford to let *anything* slip.

I sat back, reread what I'd written, and tried to come

up with some ideas, or at least a strategy, as I'd promised Brewster I'd do. How could I get the cops to investigate Bobby Calhoun? And more pressingly, what intersection of my life and John Richard's had precipitated the attack at the Roundhouse, and perhaps also John Richard's death? I returned to the computer and typed in those questions. I noticed one thing: In the department of the Jerk's mistresses, my memory had not only slipped, it had deleted all those names except the most recent. I didn't know if that was good or bad.

The fact that I had food to prepare weighed heavily on my mind. I also felt like absolute hell—from my aching body to my throbbing head. But I reminded myself that Furman County investigators were out there gathering evidence, trying to decide whether to arrest me. Maybe they were merely waiting for the firearms report and GSR results. Oh, joy.

I checked my answering machine—the only message was from Trudy, next door. A flower arrangement had arrived. She thought the presence of reporters had driven more well-wishers away. We were welcome to eat at their house, if we wanted. Otherwise, she'd bring some goodies over when the coast was clear.

More troubling, though, was the fact that there was no message from Brewster Motley. What was the point of Marla's paying him so much money if his investigators couldn't come up with information to exonerate me? Just how good a criminal defense attorney *was* he?

I opened another computer document. I had the names and conversations; now I had to type up everything that had *happened* so far. I figured if the cops wanted an exact chronology, I should have one, too. I began in late April, when John Richard had reentered our lives as a free man.

On April the twenty-second, the day John Richard had walked out of jail, I'd been catering another lunch, a bittersweet remembrance requisitioned by Cecelia Brisbane. She'd invited the entire *Mountain Journal* staff to her house for what would have been the sixtieth birthday of Walter Brisbane, her dead husband. Three years before, while Cecelia was at a Women in the Media convention in Las Vegas, Walter Brisbane, the ultracharming publisher of the *Journal,* had killed himself with one of his own firearms.

According to the *Journal,* the police had confirmed an accidental suicide. Only one bullet had been missing from Walter's twenty-two, the one that had entered his skull. There had been gunshot residue on Walter's hands, the twenty-two had been at an odd angle, not entirely consistent with intentional suicide. A neighbor had heard the single shot and called the police. There had been no sign of forced entry. Walter had apparently been alone, and he had not left a note. According to Cecelia, he had been *happy,* their family had been *happy*; everyone at the *Mountain Journal* had been happy, happy, happy!

Yeah, right, I had told Tom while he helped me put salmon on the grill for this year's posthumous Brisbane birthday. Still, no other story had surfaced. Tom had shared the tantalizing fact that Walter had had a phone call from a Denver pay phone not twenty minutes before he died. But without more, Tom said, we'd never know what had really happened.

The Brisbanes' daughter, Alex, short for Alexandra, was serving on a nuclear submarine deployed in the Mediterranean. A navy chaplain had called Cecelia and relayed the message that Alex could not be notified of her father's death for at least a month, and thus would miss the funeral. At this April's birthday lunch, I'd seen a photograph of a solemn-looking Alex on Cecelia's coffee table. The brown-haired young woman, wearing a navy pea coat and sailor cap, standing at some distance from the camera, had been pointing at a Greek temple. Recently, when the Aspen Meadow library had opened a photo exhibit featuring "Local Men and Women in the Armed Services," Cecelia had had the photo blown up for the display. It was now pinned next to a picture of the Vikarioses' son, George, who was serving in the army in Germany. I'd never met George Vikarios, and I supposed the army kept him busy. But I did wonder about the navy being so demanding of Alex that they would never allow her home for the yearly posthumous birthday parties Cecelia insisted on having for her dead husband. Then again, there were many reasons for family members not appearing at anniversary functions. Moreover, family absences at parties was such a sore subject, most caterers wouldn't touch it with a pole the length of the Alaska pipeline.

In any event, the whole Walter Brisbane thing was weird, Tom had said. In addition to the mysterious phone call, Walter Brisbane had been very careful with his guns; he'd been a seasoned hunter. And there had been no witnesses to the shooting. *That's* why we'll never know what happened, Tom had told me, as he magnanimously flipped the salmon.

I'd hated doing that lunch, as much as I'd hated doing that birthday celebration every year since I'd been in business. I'd hated parking beside Cecelia Brisbane's dumpy old wood-sided station wagon that she refused to get rid of. I'd hated seeing Cecelia Brisbane's bespectacled, shovel-shaped face crumple in grief, as it did every year when we sang "Happy Birthday." Most of all, I'd hated Marla bursting into Cecelia's pine-paneled kitchen, ashen-faced, her voice cracking.

"Goldy. The Jerk's out. Forever. The governor commuted his sentence."

Yes. I'd hated that most of all.

Marla had peppered me with questions for which I'd had no answers. No, I didn't know if he'd be settling down alone. No, I didn't know where he was going to live. And no, I didn't know what he was going to do for money. But we should have guessed.

He'd found a woman, of course. Courtney MacEwan had become his girlfriend almost immediately. Where did he find such willing females? Unlike Val, a vampy former girlfriend who'd been charged with murder herself, Courtney belonged to the country club and had a tennis figure to die for. I hadn't seen any pictures of Courtney in Holly Kerr's album, but back in our married days, John Richard and I had known Courtney and her hospital-CEO husband well enough to make small talk. Last year, the sudden death of Courtney's husband had netted her those big bucks, and John Richard had begun to salivate.

I reached for a couple of cookies to go with the last of my coffee. The buttery crunch of nut cookies helped jog my memory of the events of May.

On Saturday, May the seventh, Arch had called me from John Richard's house and asked me to come get him, since his father was "busy with a move." When Marla had accompanied me to take Arch over for a golf lesson the next week, Sandee with two *e*s had answered the door. Would Marla know the exact timing and rationale for the swap of one girlfriend for another? I made myself a note to ask. In any event, after the girlfriend switch, things had been fairly calm with John Richard, at least by Jerk standards, except for this obsession with teaching Arch to play golf, Tuesdays and Thursdays, one o'clock on the dot or risk being yelled at. Except for yesterday, when he'd wanted me to bring Arch at four because of the lunch screwing up the timing.

And then there had been the funeral lunch the previous day, where all hell had broken loose. Actually, Hades had erupted before the lunch had even begun. Someone had thrown the switches on my compressors Monday night, the sixth of June. Why? By Tuesday morning, my food had spoiled. Why go to such trouble? Did someone really hate Albert Kerr and want his memorial lunch wrecked? Or did someone want me embarrassed, not to mention shoved out of the way and chopped on the neck?

My mind kept circling around the same question: What could be the reason for that attack? John Richard hadn't had any *current* conflicts with me that would have led him to bust me up, had he? Then again, when had I ever been able to figure out the Jerk? Maybe he'd been ticked off over something I didn't even know about. This would have been typical. Still, he'd usually let me know *exactly* what transgression brought on a beating. I shuddered, remembering, and touched the thumb he'd broken in three places with a hammer. The only thing I could figure was that these days he *knew* I'd report him, and that he'd face jail time again. That might have made him keep his assault "anonymous."

I chewed on an ice cube and recalled the theory put forward by the detectives, that John Richard had beaten me up Tuesday morning, and I'd gone over to his house and shot him for revenge. That was ridiculous, of course . . . but say someone was carefully setting up this crime, and framing me. *You beat up Goldy, steal her gun* . . . Had the person who burgled my van been looking for the kitchen shears or the gun? If that person wanted the gun, he or she would have to know I kept it in the glove compartment. I had to face the fact that my best friend was the most notorious gossip in town. Could Marla have "let it slip" that I kept a thirty-eight in the van glove compartment?

I closed my eyes and rubbed them. Yes, of course she could.

And then there was Brewster's question: Who would have been mad at both of you? Under this theory, whoever had sabotaged my food and hit me had then gone on to shoot the Jerk. I wracked my poor little brain until it hurt. The *only* person I knew of who held a grudge against both the Jerk and me was Courtney MacEwan. According to Marla, Courtney claimed that I had ruined her chances with the Jerk. But that was ancient history, wasn't it? And would gorgeous Courtney know about freezer compressors and the math of spoilage? Would she be brave enough to handle bags of mice? I thought not. Talk about grasping at straws.

I stared at my blinking computer screen. Back to the chronology. At the memorial lunch itself, I typed, Courtney MacEwan had been upset, Ginger Vikarios had seemed tense and unhappy, and Ted Vikarios had been talkative, then angry with John Richard. What had that been about? Unfortunately, after *that* conflict, the Jerk and I had had a very public argument about a new tee time for Arch—with the funeral guests looking on. I'd gone home, driven to Lakewood to pick up

Arch, and taken him over to John Richard's rented house in the country-club area.

Wait. First I had stopped by the clubhouse to leave brownies for the PosteriTREE bake sale. And Cecelia Brisbane had sought me out. All right, then, while I was in the straw-grasping business, what was it Cecelia had been referring to regarding files on John Richard? I was willing to believe that she was paying someone to listen in on cell phones or calls to the sheriff's department, so that she'd heard about the Roundhouse break-in, and surmised that the Jerk was the culprit. But what had she meant when she'd said she had different files from the police?

I put in a call to the *Mountain Journal*. Cecelia Brisbane was not at her desk. I left a message for her to call me, but didn't hold out much hope for that happening. Belatedly, I thought to dangle the idea of a hot piece of gossip for her column, but the receptionist had already hung up.

I needed to cook, and I still hadn't finished writing up the events of the previous day. My fingers paused over the incident with the skeleton-faced man waiting in the cul-de-sac. *Mrs. Korman, do you have my money?* I'd written down that guy's license-plate number. Surely *someone* at the sheriff's department had tracked down the plate by now. Even better, maybe that someone would know what funds the guy had been after.

Who at the sheriff's department could help me with the license plate? I called Sergeant Boyd, but he was not available. I cursed voice mail silently and left a purposefully vague message for Boyd to please, please, call me back *ASAP.*

I took a break and tiptoed onto our back deck to feed

Scout the cat and Jake, our bloodhound. The chatty reporters had reconvened on our front porch. Both animals seemed to know something was up, and I murmured to them to be quiet. Scout ignored his food and rolled on his back, demanding that his stomach be rubbed. Sometimes I thought that cat could read my mind. My own need for comfort, he seemed to be saying, could be assuaged by comforting *him*. Jake, meanwhile, gobbled his food, stepped on the cat to get to me, and whined as his tongue slobbered kisses on both of my cheeks. I told him, "Okay, boy, okay," and turned my face away. He whimpered and started licking my hands and arms. Well, my animals loved me. When you're a suspect in a murder case, you'll take affection wherever you can get it.

I went back inside, took a shower, and changed into clean clothes. Reentering the kitchen, I resolved to put the life and untimely death of John Richard Korman out of my mind—for a few hours, anyway. I needed and wanted to prepare food for others. My eyes caught on two things I had not noticed that had fallen out of my bag, along with the guest list: the envelope with Holly Kerr's check to me, and a recipe. Holly had written:

> Thought you might enjoy this. It's the recipe for the brioche! And thanks again for a lovely lunch in remembrance of my dear Albert. Goldy, I am sure all will be well soon.
>
> *Holly*

That was nice. I glanced over the recipe, which seemed straightforward enough, and would give me the opportunity to work with my hands, as in pretending I was wringing the neck of . . . whoops! Wasn't going to think that way for a while. From our walk-in refrigerator, I took out yeast, eggs, milk, and unsalted butter, then searched the cabinets for bread flour, sugar and salt, lemons and oranges, extracts, and a jar of glistening honey from a local producer.

Soon the yeast was proofing and I was creaming the butter, honey, and eggs into a fluffy, fragrant mixture—the beginning of the journey into making bread. I kneaded in the flour, and didn't pretend it was anybody. I allowed myself to float into the meditative, repetitive movements that cause bread making to be so therapeutic. Soon the dough beneath my wrists was a lovely, silky, smooth texture. It took me several moments to realize the phone was ringing. Marla must have turned on one of my ringers.

"Uh, Goldilocks' Catering?" My hands, covered with flour and bits of dough, inadvertently let the receiver slip away. I fumbled it as I tried to wipe one hand clean on my apron. The phone banged hard on the floor.

"Goldy!" came Sergeant Boyd's curt voice from far away. "What's going on over there? Are you all right?"

"I'm fine!" I called. No question, I was having trouble with phones these days. I picked up the receiver, clutched it to my ear, and made my tone as normal as possible. "Thanks for calling back. Did you find out anything?"

"You never heard any of this from me."

"Sergeant Who?"

"All right. Looks like your ex was in the money-laundering business."

"*What?*"

Boyd blew out air. "We don't know for whom, and

we don't know how much cash we're talking about, because we only caught that one Smurf."

"That one—?" Balancing the portable phone against my ear, I moved the dough into a buttered bowl, placed a cloth on top, and transported the whole thing out to the dining room.

"That's what we call them. Smurfs, like the toys. You met one at Dr. Korman's house right before you found the body. The Smurfs deposit chunks of cash their captain gives them. Korman was captain of we don't know how many Smurfs, and we don't know who he was working for. That's the whole point of hiring these Smurfs to work for you. You keep them out of the loop."

I looked out the window over the sink, the only one that had no shade or curtain. Had I detected a movement in the lilac bushes outside? I'd cracked the window before starting to knead the bread. This was summer, after all, and the kitchen was hot. The hail had evaporated, and our dry, dusty, fire-feeding weather had returned.

"Wait a sec," I warned Boyd. I tiptoed into the first-floor bathroom, where the window was shut and covered by a curtain. "Okay, now I can talk. You mean, my ex-husband was running a money-laundering business out of his country-club home? Did he set up this business while he was incarcerated? Was it drug money? Proceeds from illegal gambling? Could a Smurf have shot and killed John Richard?"

"Hold on, hold on. We don't know anything. That Smurf you met doesn't know anything, either. He was supposed to pick up his usual forty-five hundred dollars, and that didn't happen. The investigators are looking at all of Dr. Korman's known associates, the guys he hung out with in jail, that kind of thing. Someone had a *lot* of cash that they didn't want to pay taxes on, that's for sure."

Hold on. I gripped the towel bar. *Duh.* I'd seen lots and lots of cash, you bet I had, all over the place, *because businessmen didn't want their wives seeing these bills on their credit cards.* And yes, John Richard had had some known associates in that business, the business where women didn't wear clothes. Was this grasping at straws, too? Or could it be true?

"Listen," I said, "this is a stretch. A big stretch. But John Richard's girlfriend, Sandee, works for the Rainbow Men's Club. It's a Denver strip joint run by a woman named Lana Della Robbia, a former patient of John Richard. Her sidekick is a mean-looking, muscle-bound guy named Dannyboy. Anyway, Lana worshiped the ground John Richard walked on. *And* the Rainbow was swimming in cash when I visited today."

There was a pause. "This is when I'm supposed to ask you what you were doing at the Rainbow strip club where Dr. Korman's girlfriend works. What you were doing there *today.*"

"Watching the show," I said innocently. "Look, I've got a lot of cooking to do."

"You've always got a lot of cooking to do when I start asking *you* questions."

"Could you get back to me when they have the autopsy and ballistics results?"

"Oh! She wants autopsy and ballistics results! Why, yes, ma'am." But there was affection in his voice. When he signed off, I knew his only challenge would be figuring out a way to say that someone had tipped him off to the remote possibility that the Rainbow

Men's Club was laundering cash through Dr. John Richard Korman, deceased.

Even I thought it sounded a bit ridiculous. Still, Lana Della Robbia had been rolling, drowning, really, in currency. Also, Marla should have called in her anonymous tip by now, so Furman County investigators might even be on their way to the Rainbow at this very minute, to search for an Elvis impersonator. Did possible money laundering plus a possibly jealous boyfriend add up to homicide? I had no idea.

I put in another call, this one to the Rainbow. After asking my name and putting me on hold for five minutes, the woman who answered said Lana Della Robbia was unavailable. When I told this gal I didn't believe her, she hung up. Not to be outdone, I slammed my phone down, too. What had clammed Lana up? Was she getting nervous about the case? Had the cops been asking her too many probing questions? And more important, how could I find out if the Jerk had been killed for his part in a money-laundering scheme? Would Sandee be willing to tell me anything? Sandee Blue was most emphatically not the brightest bulb in the box, but maybe she'd know enough to share information. I left a message for Marla—did *anyone* answer their phone these days?—asking her to find Sandee and offer to take her to John Richard's funeral service, whenever that was. I'd be coming, too, I added, then pressed End.

Time to concentrate on food.

I tiptoed out of the bathroom—just in case the reporters had their ears pressed to the walls to see where I was—replaced the phone, and started on the pies for Nan Watkins's retirement picnic. I'd been experimenting with crusts this summer, and for this event I'd concocted a crunchy mixture of butter, toasted filberts, confectioners' sugar, and flour. I'd already made these crusts and frozen them. I set them aside to thaw while I whipped cream into soft, velvety clouds. Then I beat cream cheese with vanilla and a bit more powdered sugar into a thick, smooth mélange, folded the cream into the cream-cheese mixture, and carefully spooned this luscious-looking concoction into the crusts. Wrapping the pies to chill overnight, I checked that I had plenty of irresistibly fat, fresh strawberries that would be cooked into a topping for the pies. I did. In fact, I washed one strawberry and popped it into my mouth. My excuse? Caterers need to test everything.

Without warning, John Richard's face loomed in my mind. All my aches and pains began hurting at the same time, while rage and anxiety again reared their noxious heads. What was going to happen to me? To Arch? Gooseflesh ran up my arms. I pulled the phone off its cradle and tried to reach Tom on his cell. Hearing his voice would help. But as with everyone else, there was no answer. I slammed the phone down without leaving a message. The municipal golf course was in cell phone range. Where was he?

Once again, I saw movement and heard rustling in the lilac bushes outside our kitchen window. I cranked the window open even wider.

"Hey!" I yelled. "Beat it! I'm married to a cop! He eats reporters for lunch!"

The lilac bushes were still.

I crossed my arms and stared out the window. Should I call 911? No; whoever it was would make a fast retreat as soon as the police showed up. Unfortunately, those detectives still had my thirty-eight . . . and I really wasn't sure I wanted to go find one of Tom's guns so I could shoot into the bushes. What if the movement was from a fox or a family of birds? Then I'd feel terrible. How would I feel if I shot a reporter?

Hmm.

In any event, I kept a sharp eye out the window. I was *not* going to be intimidated anymore, doggone it.

I returned to picnic prep. The pork chops were brining. The dough was rising. Whoever-it-was-in-the-bushes had been yelled at. I made the cooked strawberry topping for the pies and set it aside to cool. Was I done? Alas, no. I remembered that I had one more dish to think up for the committee breakfast.

I washed my hands and reflected on the inherent problem in serving food to any group of women: One has to deal with dieters and non-dieters. The dieter demands low-cal food; the non-dieter feels deprived if she isn't served a three-course meal complete with guacamole, béarnaise sauce, and crème anglaise. Complicating matters was the current popularity of high-protein diets. Any caterer worth her sea salt had to provide a protein source that could be lifted or scraped from its carbohydrate base. I had promised the head of the committee, Priscilla Throckbottom, that I could provide three such dishes. The entrées would appeal to dieter and non-dieter alike. I had two kinds of quiche. Now I just had to come up with one more recipe.

At first I had thought I would fry bacon and alternate it with strips of cheese on top of the split mini-croissants I had ordered. But the funeral lunch debacle had left me with numerous packages of untouched Gruyère and Parmesan cheese. Another rule of catering: Waste not.

I preheated the oven and split a croissant. After some thought, I sliced some juicy, fresh scallions Liz had brought from the farmers' market. Checking the walk-in, I realized I had many cans of luscious pasteurized crabmeat and, oh joy, jars of marinated artichoke hearts. I chopped the artichokes, flaked the crab, and grated the cheeses. Then I bound those ingredients with mayonnaise and spread it on the croissants. For a finishing touch, I crushed a garlic clove and gently sautéed it in butter along with fresh bread crumbs, then added judicious amounts of chopped parsley and dried herbs. I sprinkled this crumb topping over the crab-slathered croissant, and slid the pastry into the oven. I kept checking on my creation until the cheese was melted and bubbling, and the croissant looked crisp and brown around the edges. Even the scent was enticing. How long had it been since my lunch at Holly's? I couldn't remember.

Someone started banging on the front door. *Now* what? I groaned, slipped the croissant onto a cooling rack, and trotted down the hall. One check of my peephole revealed a gaggle of six stubborn reporters still hanging out on our front porch. Frances Markasian was back, and was acting as spokesperson.

"What is it?" I yelled.

"Look, Goldy," Frances pleaded, "we're *starving.* We've been here for *hours,* and we can smell something *wonderful* in there. Our editors won't let us leave until you at least say, 'No comment.' Can we make a deal here? Little snack, 'No comment,' and we leave? *Please?*"

I suppressed a giggle. "All right, I suppose. Just give me a minute to do a taste test!"

I raced back to the kitchen and sank my teeth into the pastry. It was heavenly: The rich crab, creamy mayonnaise, and tang of cheese melded perfectly with the

crispy croissant and crunchy herbed crumb topping. I
swooned, composed myself, and began carefully splitting croissants and slathering them with the crab mixture. Funny how the little crescents, when you put them
next to each other, resembled a tool from law enforcement. Oh, dear. Maybe I wasn't repressing things as
well as I'd hoped.

The croissants looked just like handcuffs. Well, I had
a name for my recipe, anyway: Handcuff Croissants. It
had a ring to it, somehow. A metallic one.

Once I had the croissants baking, I took out one of
the cream pies. I'd made plenty of them, and I knew a
sweet treat should follow a savory one. These people
were reporters, after all, and even if they printed, "No
comment," they might preface it with "After Mrs.
Schulz generously served the press some delicious
snacks courtesy of Goldilocks' Catering . . ." *Yes!*

I spooned the strawberry topping onto the pie, then
pulled out the croissants. They emerged puffed, flaky,
and golden. I placed them next to the pie on a large
wooden tray, along with piles of plastic forks, paper
plates, and napkins, and headed for the porch.

"Oh my God!" Frances cried when I swung through
the front door.

"Will you look at this!" another one yelped.

"I could eat all of these myself!"

And so on. I placed the tray on the porch table and
glowed. Twenty-four mini-croissants disappeared
faster than the hail had melted. I worried that the journalists might get sick. But I didn't say anything; I just
beamed.

"Mrs. Schulz," said one, his mouth full, "do you
think the killer might be a former patient of your ex-
husband? Say there was someone with a medical gripe

who couldn't sue because of his HMO or something? Maybe she'd be waiting for him to get out of jail so she could kill him?"

My mouth fell open in surprise. Why hadn't I thought of that? All the reporters stopped chewing, waiting for me to reveal—

"Now, just a minute! Just a minute!" Someone was screaming, pushing through the lilac bushes at the side of our house, then crashing into the front yard. "Stop! Stop eating this second!" He was covered with leaves and tiny branches, which he was trying to brush off with his clipboard. Clipboard?

Oh holy God. Please, let it not be. But it was. Roger Mannis, the district health inspector, was making a surprise visit! To do a surprise inspection! *Surprise!*

He straightened his back and marched up the steps to the porch.

"I insist that you allow me to inspect that food that you are serving to the public!" he announced. His dark hair, usually slicked back, was mussed from his time in the lilacs. He wore shiny, silvery-gray polyester pants that were an inch too short, black socks and shoes, and a short-sleeved white shirt complete with plastic pocket-protector, all of which still had bits of twig, leaf, and lilac clinging to them. His bladelike chin trembled, a meat-slicer about to fall.

But I was *not* going to take this. Not here, not now. It couldn't be legal for this man to hide in the bushes beside our house and then just pop out when he wanted to. It was nuts. Maybe Roger Mannis wasn't just anal. Maybe he was insane.

"No," I said, keeping my tone quiet but firm. "You may not perform an inspection now. These people are my personal guests, and this is not a convenient time for me. I am not serving the public. I am serving friends."

The reporters gaped. I noticed a couple of them surreptitiously reaching for tape recorders and notepads.

Roger Mannis stepped toward me. He towered over me, his face twisted into an expression somewhere between disbelief and hatred. "*What* did you say to me? I can do an inspection *wherever, whenever* I want."

I held my ground and swallowed. "You can't do one here. Not now. It's not convenient."

Before I could think, Roger Mannis was right in front of me and grabbing my left arm. *Hard.* "Listen, girlie, don't you *dare* tell me what to do. Because I—"

Hit groin. Hit eyes. My self-defense course, which had deserted me at the Roundhouse, rushed back. But I couldn't manage to knee him between the legs. Nor could I free my left arm from his viselike grip. Without thinking, I reached sideways with my right hand. Then I picked up the strawberry-cream pie and smashed it full in his face—just in time to be caught by the photographers from three newspapers.

I don't remember much after that. Mannis scuttled away in the direction of his white Furman County van. Muttering curses and threats, he stopped on the sidewalk and bent over as he tried to wipe glop from his face. The reporters avoided my eyes as they picked up their recorders, camera equipment, notepads, pop cans, foam cups, and assorted detritus. I realized I never had said "No comment."

As I eyed the broken pie plate, bits of crust and filling, and berry topping now flung in all directions on the porch, I did hear another reporter chastise Frances Markasian.

"Dammit, Frances! Why couldn't you have grabbed

that pie before she got it? I really was looking forward to that!"

"He called her '*girlie,*' Jack."

"That's worth a *slice,* maybe," Jack replied stubbornly. "Not a whole *pie,* for Chrissakes."

Chapter 13

It didn't take me long to clean up. It never does when an idea has sprouted in my head. Marla, Brewster, and even the cops had been thinking about the Jerk being plagued by ex-girlfriends and a need for money. But he'd been a doctor, after all. Could an old patient with a grudge still be out there? I wondered if this, too, was grasping at straws. In any event, there was something I really *didn't* want to wonder about, and that was the story *and photograph* of me pie-slapping the district health inspector.

I checked my watch: 4:10. Shouldn't Arch and Tom be back by now? Perhaps they'd gone out for a snack. Even so, I still had dinner to make. And before I got to that point, a few odds and ends for the next day's catering remained. Still, I had promised to call Brewster if I heard anything.

My criminal lawyer was in a conference, so I left a message on his voice mail that I'd heard "from a cop friend"—no sense getting Boyd in trouble—that John Richard had been involved in a money-laundering operation. Remember the older man who'd asked if I had his money? He'd been waiting for forty-five hundred in cash from John Richard. So, I concluded, it was possible that whoever John Richard was laundering cash for had killed him. At least, I hoped the investigation was turning in that direction. And if it *wasn't* turning that way, maybe Brewster could *prod* it. Also, I added, Sandee Blue, late of John Richard's harem, had a jealous boyfriend named Bobby Calhoun. And Bobby was prone to violence, I concluded. Just ask Marla.

I punched down the bread dough, divided it, and formed it into rolls for the second rising. That done, I set a fine-mesh strainer over a bowl and carefully spooned a gallon of vanilla yogurt on top, to drain overnight. I would fold the resulting ultrathick, delicious mass into whipped cream to layer with fresh fruit for breakfast parfaits. The rest of the committeewomen's muffins and breads I had frozen, so with minimal preparation in the country-club kitchen the next morning, I was in good shape. Trudy, my next-door neighbor, brought over the arrangement, a beautiful bouquet of spring flowers sent by a group of moms from Arch's new Catholic high school. Trudy apologized for there being no casseroles, but she said everyone was afraid to cook for a professional caterer.

Let's see. For dinner, I could make a shellfish salad like the one I'd enjoyed at Holly's. I opened the walkin and saw something that Tom had made a few days ago, during one of his blue periods. The label read "Happy Days Mayonnaise." For some reason, this piqued my anger all over again.

I calmly walked over to a cabinet filled with jars to be recycled. I picked out two big ones and threw them onto the floor, where they broke with a satisfying crash. My sneakers crunched over the broken shards as

I reached up onto the shelf and nabbed two more jars. These I hurled at the back door.

"Happy? Yeah, I'm happy!" I yelled as I chucked another pair of jars onto the floor. They splintered into a million pieces. "I'm happy now!"

Jake the bloodhound was howling. Immediately remorseful that I'd scared him, I let both animals out through their enclosure door. No way I was letting them into the trashed kitchen. Jake slobbered all over me again, worried that the woman-who-brings-dog-food was losing her marbles.

I went back into the kitchen and sank into a chair, exhausted. "Happy Days Mayonnaise," indeed. *Happy,* what a word. I remembered how ecstatic I'd been when Arch had been born, how it had seemed that every day was as fizzy with delight as a flute of sparkling champagne. After I'd brought him home, I'd proudly shown him off at church, at the library, even at the grocery store. People would look at me and say, "You look so happy!" And I had been. I had thought, *This is happiness, the rest of my life will be just like this, this is the beginning of it all!*

Uh-huh. I surveyed the layer of broken glass that now covered the kitchen floor. Jake had put his paws up on the exterior windowsill and was staring in at me and the mess I'd made. I didn't care; I wanted to break some more glass. And then I wanted to drive down to the morgue and shake John Richard's dead body until it told me who had killed him.

Yeah, well. Then the reporters really would have a field day. And I still had to figure out the evening meal for our family. My tantrum had drained me of all cooking energy. All right, I reasoned as my sneakers again cracked over the shards, I could resort to that great salvation of the American housewife: the frozen casserole.

I pulled out a frosty glass pan covered with foil, labeled "Whole Enchilada Pie." In a remarkable bit of foresight, I'd doubled the recipe of this favorite of Arch's and frozen the extra one. The recipe itself had come about one night when Arch had wanted enchiladas and I hadn't had any tortillas. So I'd thrown together a ton of Mexican ingredients, improvised layers with corn chips, and told him the dish had everything, "The Whole Enchilada"! He'd loved it.

I put the pan into the microwave, set it to defrost, and grabbed my broom. Of course, I'd managed to make one unholy mess. I swept up shards and dumped them, swept and dumped, swept and dumped. Then I sprayed a disinfectant solution onto the floor and mopped up the tiniest bits of glass with paper towels. With every swipe of the floor, I muttered, "You *Jerk.* You *damn* Jerk," or some variation on that theme.

When I'd finished washing the floor, I leaned back on my aching knees and surveyed the glowing wood. My heart was still pounding. Echoes of the curses I'd been muttering rocketed around in my head. I knew I needed to move from rage to a more productive emotional state, one that would bring rational thought and action. Problem was, I couldn't because I didn't want to. Whatever happened to *anger, denial, bargaining, grief, acceptance*? Maybe Elisabeth Kübler-Ross hadn't analyzed the emotional aftermath of the death of a jerk. I sprayed additional disinfectant on the floor and began scrubbing even more energetically than before.

Eventually, clouds moving in from the west obscured the sun. A welcome breeze cooled the kitchen and brought in the scent of lilacs. With every muscle aching, I surveyed the spotless floor. It was almost six o'clock, and I was exhausted. I stood up slowly, washed my hands, and slid the defrosted casserole into the oven.

There was a knock at the back door. Again wary of reporters, I peeked through the shade, only to see one of Trudy's freckled kids holding a covered casserole dish and a plastic bag.

"My mom made this for you, Mrs. Schulz," the kid—ten-year-old Eddie—said. "She said it's called Mediterranean Chicken."

"Thanks for bringing it over, Eddie."

"Well, my mom said I had to. Oh yeah, she put your mail in this bag."

"Want to come in for some pie, Eddie?"

"No thanks. My mom says if I want to go fishing to-morrow, I've gotta clean up my room. All these jobs, it's worse than school! Sometimes I hate summer."

I thanked him again, but he was already trudging back toward his house. I stowed the chicken in the re-frigerator. Then I turned my attention to the mail.

It was the usual assortment of bills and ads. A manila envelope from the *Mountain Journal,* with my name and address hand-lettered, took me aback. It had been postmarked the previous day. But the contents provided a much greater surprise.

I pulled out two pieces of paper. One was a note with the printed superscription: "From the Desk of Cecelia Brisbane." The scribbled words were in the same hand-writing as was on the envelope:

> *Here's what I was talking about at the bake sale. Do you know if the authorities ever followed up on this? I got it a couple of years ago, but your*

ex was already incarcerated. With him getting out unexpectedly, I thought maybe it would bear looking into. Would you please call me? C.B.

Clipped to this was a piece of faded paper, frayed at the edges. A short, typed message, with no greeting, read as follows:

```
    Dr. John Richard Korman raped a
teenage girl when she was a patient at
Southwest Hospital. It was a long time
ago. Are you afraid to research this? Are
you afraid to write about it? You could
start by asking his ex-wife Goldy if he
did it to her, too. Once you get the
facts, it's your JOB to expose him. . . .
```

Whoa. I read the typed note two more times, then reread Cecelia's short message. She'd had this typed note for *two years* and hadn't done anything about it? That was not like Cecelia. On the other hand, this was an explosive allegation.

Cecelia certainly hadn't done what the writer recommended: *Start by asking his ex-wife Goldy . . .*

I reread the note. This was an allegation of something so awful that it was hard to process. *John Richard Korman raped a teenage girl when she was a patient at Southwest Hospital . . . a long time ago.* I closed my eyes.

Did I believe it was possible that John Richard had done such a thing? I did. He had forced himself on me more than once. But I'd never heard of him being interested in teenage girls.

And yet now this note, which alleged he had raped a

very young woman *a long time ago*, was surfacing. Why would this story emerge right after John Richard had been murdered? Why had Cecelia sent the note to me instead of to the cops?

I was skeptical about the whole thing. Someone was, or had been, trying to frame me. And now suddenly Cecelia Brisbane was throwing suspicion elsewhere.

In any event, this note cast no light on anything I knew about John Richard being killed. Yes, I was going to phone Cecelia.

But my first call went in to Detective Blackridge at the Furman County Sheriff's Department. He said he'd drive right up to get the note. And doggone it, he told me *not* to try to contact Cecelia Brisbane.

But he didn't order me not to call Marla. Using my new cell, I punched the buttons for her home phone. As usual, I got the machine, to which I posed the first questions I'd written down: Did she know the timing and rationale for John Richard's breakup with Courtney? What was the cause or even the correlation between the dumping of Courtney and the subsequent involvement with Sandee? And then I dropped the bombshell: Did her list of the Jerk's sexual conquests include a teenager whom he'd raped? She'd been a Southwest Hospital patient when it had supposedly happened.

If there was anyone who could dig up dirt on the Jerk, it was Marla.

I closed the phone, filled my deepest sink with hot suds, and carefully washed the bowls and beaters from the pie making. *Would anyone else know about this allegation against John Richard?* Other physicians, possibly, but they were notoriously closemouthed when it came to criticizing their own, even when a crime was involved. I read the typed note again.

A patient in *Southwest Hospital* would not necessarily have been a patient from the *Aspen Meadow practice*. The note written—pointedly, it seemed to me—hadn't said "while I was a patient of his." And even if the teenager had been one of John Richard's patients, I knew I'd never get any records out of the doc who'd bought the Jerk's practice. Nor was Southwest Hospital in the habit of being forthcoming about patient records. On the other hand, would a young woman who'd been raped *want* this kind of thing in her records?

I set the table and tried to think. Who else would have an inkling about this? John Richard had employed a number of nurses in the Aspen Meadow office he'd shared with his father, but none of them had stayed more than a year. Wait: the deliveries. There was one other person who'd known and worked with John Richard over the past decade and a half: the longtime head nurse of ob-gyn at Southwest Hospital. I was doing the retirement picnic for her the next day.

Would Nan Watkins remember the specifics of any wrongdoings on John Richard's part? If she did, would she tell me about them? Maybe the cops would have already questioned her. Somehow, I doubted it.

I placed the risen rolls for the committee breakfast into the oven. Then I picked up the phone and punched the buttons to reach Nan Watkins, R.N.

She was not home. Would she talk to me about this allegation at her retirement picnic? I would just have to find out.

I set about cleaning up the kitchen. My stomach growled, so I allowed myself a few bites of Trudy's Mediterranean Chicken. The meat was tender and juicy, the sauce a delectable mélange of garlic, onion, sherry, and tomato. Yum!

I stowed the chicken and took the hot, puffed citrus rolls out of the oven. They looked as light as clouds, and perfumed the kitchen with a heavenly scent. I turned on all the fans, which meant I almost didn't hear the doorbell when Detective Blackridge rang. I invited him in and offered him a therapeutically sized piece of cream pie. He declined. I might be able to snow reporters, but cops were another thing altogether.

"I'll just see the two notes, please."

I'd put them into two zipped plastic bags. He read them both, his face impassive.

"And you just happened to receive these today?"

I bristled. "Here's what they came in." I handed him the manila envelope.

He squinted at me. "So did he?"

"Did who?"

"Did your ex-husband ever force himself on you?"

I exhaled. "Yes. I always just . . . went along with it. I mean, we *were* married."

"It's all very convenient for you, isn't it?" Blackridge asked, a ghost of a smile curling his lips. "He's killed, then an allegation of rape magically surfaces, and so it looks as if—"

"Why don't you ask Cecelia Brisbane about it?" I retorted.

Detective Blackridge turned toward the door, clutching the plastic bags and the manila envelope. "We tried. She's not at her office and not at her house. That's convenient for you, too. Isn't it?"

He shot a questioning look back at me. I said nothing. But I resolved that I would be *damned* before I gave him any more information on this case.

* * *

After the detective drove away, I went out on our front porch. In the Rocky Mountain summer, the sun seems to hover over the western horizon for hours before setting. The only hint that evening is coming is the gradual cooling and sweetening of the air, as Alpine roses and chokecherry release their perfumes into the coming night. I breathed in, looking up and down the street. The good news was that the reporters seemed to have dispersed. The bad news was that Tom's sedan was nowhere in sight. Not only did I miss Tom and Arch, I was getting worried. And I needed to talk to Tom. The events and news of the day had been too complex for me to sort out on my own.

I returned to the kitchen, where the clock read 6:45. Could they possibly have decided to play an extra round of golf? Somehow, that did not seem likely. Then again, Arch had taken his hockey gear. If he'd wanted to skate the day after his father died, Tom probably would have indulged him. Although I wished they would let me know what was up, I resisted putting in a call to Tom's cell. I could just imagine Arch rolling his eyes when the phone beeped.

Must be Mom, checking up on us!

I shuddered, then jumped when our own phone rang. The caller ID said it was my old pal Frances Markasian, pie-deprived reporter of the *Mountain Journal*. She was calling from home. I had to hand it to the woman, she was persistent.

"No comment," I sang into the receiver.

"Very funny," she groused. "The whole press corps is blaming me for not grabbing that pie before you whacked Roger Mannis. The *Mountain Journal* is still working on the caption for the photo. I think they're going with 'Stressed-out Suspect Splats Inspector.' I preferred 'Caterer Creams Killjoy.'"

"Frances, you all aren't *really* going to run an article showing me hitting the district health inspector with strawberry-cream pie, are you?"

"Not if you can give me something more substantive."

I groaned. "Such as?"

"Such *as,* Goldy, what the cops have on you. Such *as,* if they have anything substantive, why aren't you under arrest? Such *as,* do you or Tom know if they have any other suspects besides . . ." She paused, doing her best imitation of being tantalizing.

"Yeah, *besides* who? Don't play games, Frances."

"How about this game? Quid pro quo."

"What's your quid?"

"Let's go with the quo first," she said innocently. "What do the cops have on you, Goldy?"

I could act innocent, too. And smooth! Oh, baby, I could be silkier than that cream pie Frances never tasted. I cleared my throat and tried to adopt an appropriately rueful tone.

"At the end of the memorial lunch for Albert Kerr, witnesses saw me arguing with John Richard outside the Roundhouse. John Richard was trying to set up an appointment for me to take Arch over, and it wasn't prearranged. When I finally agreed, he took off."

"That's no quo. It's old news, Goldy."

"When I took Arch over," I went on, ignoring her, "I found John Richard in his garage, in his car, dead. Arch was outside. I was alone, so it looks to the cops as if I set the whole thing up to protect my son." That was as far as I was willing to go. With the phrase *potential jury pool* rocketing around in my head, there was no way I was spilling my guts to any newspaper about my missing thirty-eight, the errant mice, or the GSR test.

"I heard there was a problem with a firearm," Frances said.

"Where'd you hear that?"

"Was it a gun of yours that killed John Richard?"

"Good question. Now what's your quid? I've got a lot of cooking to do." This woman was tiring me out.

"How well do you know Ted and Ginger Vikarios?" she asked.

The question took me off guard. "I haven't been in touch with them for a long time. Ted was—"

"Yeah, yeah. Co–department head of ob-gyn at Southwest with Kerr more than a decade and a half ago. Then the Kerrs and Vikarioses found religion at the same time and went their separate ways. The Kerrs sold their worldly goods and sailed for seminary in England. Ted Vikarios figured he didn't need further study or ordination. All he needed was his message of morality and that mesmerizing voice of his. So he set up shop in Colorado Springs, where he constructed a multimillion-dollar tape-and-CD empire, selling *Family Values* and *Victory over Sin* for fifteen ninety-five a boxed set. Their own family wasn't in such good shape, though. You know about this?"

"I know he went under, and that there was some kind of scandal. That's it."

"Okay, family values, right? Ted and Ginger insisted their family was a marvel, the gold standard. Their only daughter, Talitha, ostensibly virtuous, was off doing health-worker volunteer work in South America. Meanwhile, when the money began to roll in from the tapes empire, Ted and Ginger mortgaged themselves into the high life—four BMWs, a ranch, a ski condo. That was until *oops,* one of our competitors in the newspaper biz got hold of the story that their daughter's sole connection with *missionaries* was the missionary *position.*"

"Frances!" I remembered Talitha Vikarios's shining face and innocent smile. She'd been wearing her candy-stripe uniform proudly. She'd loved little infant Arch so much, she'd become weepy when she doted on him.

"Oh, so you were acquainted with Talitha?" Frances demanded.

"I was, but it's been a long time. Back when she was a candy striper, she helped out at Southwest Hospital. She was great when Arch was a newborn."

"Uh-huh. Fifteen years ago? Talitha was, oh, eighteen then? Well, by the time the tabloids unearthed Talitha at age twenty-two, she was living in a hippie commune in Utah. She had a boyfriend *and* a child without, shall we say, the benefit of marriage? Hello! For the oh-so-pompous Vikarioses, everything went south. They lost the tape empire, their loans were called in, they had to sell everything. We're talking broke, broke, and very broke."

"I don't see how this pertains to John Richard."

"Background, Goldy. Ted declared bankruptcy four years ago. He and Ginger had been living in a friend's guest room until ten months ago. Then, what do you know! Guess who gives them cash to buy a country-club condo in Aspen Meadow? Their old friend Holly Kerr, who inherited big bucks, as it turned out, and can't turn her back on her destitute friends. Christians sharing the wealth, you get the idea. Or is it?"

"Frances—"

"You heard about the Kerrs and Vikarioses having a falling-out, Goldy?"

"I have. I just don't know what it was about."

"Neither do I, because nobody from Southwest is talking. But my theory is that Holly is now making up for it with her land-sale money. Whatever it *was,* Ted and Ginger, according to one of their pals in the country club, are living on a small stipend from Holly. How did the falling-out get resolved, Goldy? Do you know?"

"I sure don't," I said. But I wish I did, I added mentally.

"Ted is too old to start a new practice," Frances went on. "But he *can* collect on an old debt. So when his former subordinate, Dr. John Richard Korman, gets out of jail, and suddenly gets his picture in the local paper as appearing to have enough dough to start a bakery, well! Let's say our Dr. Ted becomes curious. Here's this convicted-felon doctor sponsoring a local golf tournament and driving an Audi and living with a floozy in the country-club area. So! Let's also suppose Ted figures it's time to collect."

Outside, I heard Tom's Chrysler crunching along the gravel toward our detached garage. Impatience raced up my spine.

"Frances," I demanded, "what are you talking about?"

"Goldy," she cooed, "did you ever wonder where John Richard got the fifty-thousand-dollar down payment for your little house? The same house you got in the divorce settlement?"

My entire body went cold. "He told me his parents gave it to him for graduating from medical school."

"I don't *think* so," Frances replied. "They may have

given him a cash sum, but he squirreled it away some-where, or spent it on his girlfriends, or whatever. A lit-tle birdie told me that for the down payment on your house, Dr. John Richard Korman borrowed fifty Gs from his old friend Dr. Ted Vikarios."

"I don't believe it," I snapped. "Who's the little birdie?"

"Actually," she said with the tiniest shade of uncer-tainty, "that particular factoid came from an anony-mous tip on my voice mail."

"From a man or a woman?"

"Couldn't tell. So are you going to confirm or deny?"

"Deny. Emphatically." But still, I felt as if I'd been punched. *Fifty thousand dollars? John Richard might have incurred a debt I'd never even heard of? To some people who were now bankrupt? Was this before or af-ter he supposedly raped a teenager?* Outside, Tom and Arch called to each other and shuffled their equipment out of the car and toward the house. Another wave of chills enveloped my body. "Did Ted Vikarios keep some documentation of this loan?"

"Nope," Frances replied. "At least, not according to Holly Kerr."

"Did Holly Kerr confirm the fact of the loan, Frances?"

"Well, actually," Frances admitted, "she just said if there *was* a loan, it was a gentleman's agreement."

"You're telling me Holly Kerr agreed to be inter-viewed by you?"

"Not exactly. But my Jeep made mincemeat of that driveway of hers, and I can camp out on somebody else's porch as easily as I can camp out on yours." She chuckled.

I shook my head. If I hadn't been afraid it would get

into the papers, I would have said, *Frances, sometimes you can be a first-class bitch.*

"All right," Frances went on blithely, "think about this. The Vikarioses' financial woes began at about the same time that your ex-husband started downhill, moneywise. And then of course he had those bothersome trips to jail. But all of a sudden, his sentence was commuted. And he had a big argument with Ted Vikarios, or at least a heated discussion, right before you and Korman went at it. Sort of puts that last conflict with your ex into better perspective, doesn't it? Him flying off the handle at you all of a sudden . . . seems a bit odd, doesn't it?"

Tom and Arch were punching the numbers on the deck-door security box and peering in. "No, Frances," I replied. "It wasn't a bit odd. In fact, him flying off the handle at me all of a sudden was the entire problem of John Richard's and my relationship. In a nutshell."

"Of course," she said slyly, "maybe you did know about the loan and its lack of documentation. Then you'd have had even more reason to shoot—"

"Look, I need to go," I lied. "If I find out anything, I'll call you."

While she was still squawking, I hung up. Her quid, in addition to being unsettling, hadn't made much sense. Besides implying that I would have had further motive to kill John Richard, was she saying it was possible that Ted Vikarios, unable to extract fifty Gs on the spot from John Richard—after not seeing him for nigh on fifteen years—had driven over to his house and shot him? Whatever chance Ted Vikarios would have had of extracting cash from the Jerk would have been extinguished with those shots in the garage.

When Tom and Arch traipsed through the door, I immediately knew that something was wrong. Tom's look was hooded. Arch's hair was matted to his head; his face was flushed, streaked, and glossy with sweat.

Arch nodded and acknowledged me with a "Hi, Mom! How're you doing?" that was way, *way* too enthusiastic. "Check it out! Tom bought me a new hockey stick I've been wanting! And a jersey, too!" He bounced past, mumbling something about needing a shower.

Wait a minute. Stick? Jersey? I glanced after him, but he was gone.

"Couldn't get a tee time?" I said lightly to Tom, who was washing his hands at the sink.

"Oh, we got a tee time, all right," Tom replied.

"But the two of you changed your minds?"

As if thinking over his answer, Tom said nothing. He began calmly fitting candles into crystal candlesticks for the table. Eventually he lowered himself, somewhat wearily, into a kitchen chair. Finally he gave me the full benefit of his sea-green eyes.

"I have news for you. Arch cannot play golf. He doesn't even know how to hold a club."

"But that can't be," I protested. "He's been playing twice a week with John Richard for the last month. John Richard hired the *pro* to work with Arch—"

Tom's look was even and steady. "I don't *think* so. Your son didn't tell me what he and his father were doing those two afternoons a week. But I can tell you this. Arch has never played golf in his life."

My fragile relationship with Arch at that particular juncture, i.e., right after the violent death of his father, did not permit me to interrogate him on the subject of what, exactly, he and John Richard had been *doing* every Tuesday and Thursday afternoon for the last month. When we came together at the candlelit dinner table at half-past seven, I thought I'd wait until we were all eating before posing any questions.

A sudden wind brought the temperature down twenty-five degrees, perfect Mediterranean- and Mexican-food weather. When I placed Trudy's hot, juicy chicken platter next to the steaming enchilada pie, Arch and Tom dug in with enthusiasm. The chicken was succulent and not too spicy. The Mexican-pie mélange of beef, garlic, onions, refried beans, and hot sauces also featured corn chips and enough melted cheese to smother Pancho Villa's entire army. I'd set out a bowl of rice and dishes of sliced fresh tomatoes and avocados, chopped lettuce and scallions, and a mountain of snowy sour cream. If nothing else, ice hockey did have a way of cranking up the appetite.

"Arch," I began, "I was wondering—"

But Tom warned me off immediately with one of his *He'll talk when he's ready* looks. Arch gave me a studiously blank stare. If he wanted to discuss his father, the funeral, or anything else, he gave no indication. When the plates were empty, I asked if anyone wanted strawberry-cream pie. Both Tom and Arch groaned and said that they were too full. And then Arch scraped back his chair and asked to be excused. When I acquiesced, he mumbled, "Thanks, Mom," and took off for his room.

"I know he's trying to be polite," I commented to Tom as we cleared the table. "But not only is Arch withholding evidence, he's going back into the infamous adolescent shell."

Tom put down a pile of dishes and gathered me into a hug. "We talked a lot this afternoon. He's torn up, all right." He kissed my neck and held me tighter. "Miss G., I'm more worried about you. I pulled out the trash container, and saw it was filled with glass shards. What's that about?"

"Rage. I have a lot to tell you."

He let go of me. "Rage about what?"

I gave him the executive summary of the morning: the strip club, Lana, the bleeding bald man left on Marla's car. Then I told him about the afternoon: seeing Holly, encountering the reporters, pie-slapping Mannis. Afterward, I'd broken a few jars in anger, yes. And then I'd read the notes from Cecelia Brisbane. Tom had listened this far without comment, but he held up a hand.

"Stop. Do you have these notes now?"

"You'll be happy to know that I turned them over to Detective Blackridge. But I did make copies," I added. I pulled out the copies I'd made of the notes, and again was thankful that Tom had given me a small photocopying machine for my birthday.

"Oh, my Lord," Tom said, shaking his head. He put down the copies and gave me a hard look. "Do you think it's true?"

I sighed. "I don't know. Someone is or was trying to frame me for John Richard's death. And now, all of a sudden, stories about him start surfacing."

"Are there other stories?" Tom asked.

I told him that Frances Markasian might have unearthed an old debt, to the tune of fifty thou. According to an anonymous source who'd called Frances, Dr. Ted Vikarios had loaned the Jerk the down payment on this very house in which we now found ourselves. The same source said the Jerk had never paid it back. Ted and John Richard had argued outside the Roundhouse, Frances's theory went, because the Jerk refused to cough up the funds. The implication was that this debt had given Ted the motive to fire a couple of bullets into the Jerk.

To my surprise, Tom laughed, a wonderful long, rumbling guffaw that made the dishes on the counter shake.

"I'm *so* glad to provide humor for you so soon after my ex-husband has been shot to death."

Tom wiped his eyes. "Miss G., you're trying *too* hard to get into the head of too many suspects. That is a very dangerous place to be. Don't get into the mind of a killer, either. It'll make you crazy."

"I appreciate the pep talk, Hannibal. May I say good night to my son now?"

When I knocked on Arch's door, I couldn't tell if he was talking on the phone or if the radio was on. He called, "Just a minute," immediately ceased the conversation or broadcast, shuffled around a bit, and then invited me in.

He was sitting up in bed, knees to his bare chest, writing in his journal. The lamp on the desk beside his bed was switched on. His window was open, and a cool breeze filled the room. He glanced at me, then at the wall opposite his bed.

"Yes, Mom?"

"I just wanted to say good night."

"Okay. Good night."

"Sweetheart, please." I gripped the door. "You know the cops suspect that I had something to do with your father's death. But you were right there with me. You know I didn't shoot him. So . . . could you please tell me what you and your dad were doing two afternoons a week for the last month?"

He glanced at his desk. In the poker world, this is

known as a *tell*. He said, "Nothing. I mean, well, I can't."

I ignored the desk. "May I give you a quick hug, hon?"

After a moment, he pushed his glasses up his nose and gave me a long look. "Sure. Just, please, you know. Don't start crying."

I briskly crossed the room, awkwardly placed my arms around his neck, and hugged his head. I managed this without tears, for which I was thankful.

"See you in the morning." I released him before he could pull away.

He placed his glasses on his nightstand, closed his window, and snapped off his light. Then he scooted underneath his sheet. I didn't see what he'd done with the journal—I would never read it or go through his desk, I'd have gone to jail first—but I did notice that he still had the black-and-gold quilt. He pulled it up around his ears, then turned away from me.

"When you leave," his muffled voice said, "could you please close the door?"

Chapter 14

Thursday morning I awoke to birds squawking, chirping, and singing their way through their June mating ritual. The only thing that bothered me was that this louder-than-usual cacophony started soon after four A.M. I had dreamed of nothing, for which I was thankful. Tom's warm arms were still holding me. I didn't want to move, and yet the merry avian racket and chilly air sweeping through the room made additional slumber impossible.

I eased out of bed, tiptoed across the cold floor, and peered outside. The hail had finally coaxed out a spurt of late spring growth. Leaves clothing the aspens' bone-white branches had opened from tightly closed fists to a chartreuse cloud. Periwinkle columbines bobbed along our sidewalk. Pearl-white anemones floated above the mulch that Tom had lovingly patted into place in front of our house. Even the lush native chokecherries between the houses seemed to have doubled their blossoms. The profusion of tube-shaped blooms gave off a sweet, heady scent. A fat robin hopped along the curb where the reporters had beaten their retreat.

I moved through a slow yoga routine. Yes, my body still ached, but getting the circulation going would offer more healing than any visit to the doctor. After breathing and stretching, I showered and put on a cotton shirt, shorts, sweatpants, and zippered sweats jacket. The morning was very cool—right at fifty degrees, according to the outside thermometer—but food preparation would have me shedding layers before long. Still, who cared? Come to think of it, why was I in such a good mood all of a sudden?

I frowned. *Wait a minute: the windows.* The lovely breeze was flowing into our bedroom because Tom had left the window cracked. For the first time since I'd had the security system installed, *Tom had turned it off.* A lightness filled my head and a buzzing invaded my ears. With John Richard dead, would we really, truly not need the system anymore?

No, wait. We would need it, at least until my attacker and the Jerk's murderer were apprehended. Maybe Tom had thought we'd all be fine for one night, with him at home to protect us. Maybe he'd forgotten to set the system. I breathed in another lungful of fresh air and closed the window.

In the kitchen, I brought myself back to reality with a double espresso poured over steamed half-and-half. There was the troubling matter of figuring out who had sabotaged my food and attacked me outside the Roundhouse. When we figured out who had done that, maybe we'd be able to sleep with the *doors* open.

I booted up my computer and printed out the list of food preparation for that morning. First up was the PosteriTREE committee breakfast. After splitting from the garden club, I wondered why they didn't call themselves the Splinter Group.

I checked on the vanilla yogurt: It had drained and left behind a thick, smooth, custardlike mass. I whipped a mountain of cream, folded it into the yogurt, and set the soft mixture back in the refrigerator to chill. Then I trimmed and chopped peaches, nectarines, and strawberries to layer with the yogurt mixture in crystal parfait glasses when I arrived at the country club.

With the fruit chopped, wrapped, and chilling, I checked my watch: 5:50. Would Marla be awake yet? Probably not. I desperately wanted the chance to visit with her away from the ever-eavesdropping ladies of the tree-planting committee, but if I phoned too early, her wrath would outweigh her desire to share gossip. I sighed. Next on the agenda was the croissants, and I was debating whether to fix those at home or put them together in the country-club kitchen while the quiches were heating. I couldn't decide, so I switched computer files from "Committee Breakfast" to "JRK."

Quickly, I typed in my new questions: *Is independent confirmation available that JRK raped a teenage girl? If so, then who was the girl, and when did this happen? Did Ted Vikarios loan John Richard 50K for the down payment on this house, and never get it back? Are these two stories meant to throw the cops off the scent of the real killer?* And then there was: *What in the world was Arch doing with John Richard for the last month, when they were supposed to be playing golf?*

If it was too early to call Marla, it was certainly too early to call the Vikarioses. And besides, what would I say to them? Did my ex-husband betray you, too? And by the way, did you shoot him? I fixed myself another espresso and stared at the computer screen. Poor Holly

Kerr. Who knew how much she'd told Frances Markasian, just to get rid of her?

I switched back to the problem with the croissants. As all caterers knew, How does it look? is the number one issue in food service. How does it taste? is number three. With the croissants, I was face-to-face with number two, to wit: How does it hold up? This was a general problem with breakfast and brunch food, but since complaining and worrying only makes the caterer's job seem longer and more frustrating, I set to work chopping the scallions and artichoke hearts, slicing the croissants, whisking together the crab-mayonnaise mixture, and melting the butter for the delicate crumb-herb topping. If these delectable open-faced sandwiches couldn't be totally assembled in advance, I decided, then I'd just do the last-minute work in the club kitchen.

And speaking of assembling things, I wondered, just where were the cops in their investigation? The rule of thumb in law enforcement was that murders that were not solved within twenty-four hours generally went unsolved. And yet here we were, at thirty-six hours.

Neither detective had told me a thing. Blackridge had been downright hostile. Tom had announced that Sergeant Boyd would be meeting me at the Roundhouse, and then we would drive to the club together. Boyd would be staying with me through both catered events today. He even wanted to help with the catering! I heartily disliked the idea of a chaperone, but Tom had been insistent. The upside was that Boyd might have new information. The key word there was *might*.

Meanwhile, once Julian arrived, Tom's plan to keep Arch busy included picking up Todd Druckman and taking the three of them to one of Denver's giant public pools. I've always felt that those pools, which feature wave-making machines and gargantuan slides, are meant to make kids puke up their hot dogs, chips, and milk shakes. That way, parents are forced to buy twice the amount of overpriced food than they would have anyway. But Tom had ordered me to not worry about what I couldn't control. After the pool, Julian would come to help me with the picnic, while Tom saw what else Arch and Todd wanted to do. Bless Tom. What would we do without him?

My stomach growled. It was six-fifteen and I hadn't had anything but coffee. I couldn't look at the croissants and yogurt. Here again, though, I was saved by Tom.

"Oh, Miss G., do I have a surprise for you." He swaggered into the kitchen with a sudden confidence that I hadn't seen for a while. He wore a black polo shirt and khaki pants, and looked utterly spiffy. "I did a very, very big shopping yesterday. Please sit down."

This I did, while Tom pulled out—from one of the secret corners of the walk-in, where he kept goodies just for the family—thick-sliced applewood-smoked bacon, eggs, and cream. Then, after he perused a new cookbook, he brought the bacon to sizzling and made the lightest, flakiest biscuits imaginable. These reminded me of the biscuits served at the Southern boarding school I'd attended. For some reason, this brought tears to my eyes. I sure seemed to be doing a lot of crying these days.

Tom used his thumbs to wipe my tears away, then gently kissed my cheek and told me to eat while the food was hot. Then he put in a call to someone at the department. After a few "Uh-huhs," and several requests along the lines of "Well, could you put me through to her?," and then "Yeah, yeah, hmm," he signed off. Frowning, he washed his hands and sat down with his own plate of bacon, biscuits, and jam.

"Want to know what the department has so far?"

I almost choked on a biscuit. "Don't tell me you got through to the coroner."

"Yup, and not only her. It wasn't a busy week, and the autopsy's done. John Richard was killed between one and three P.M. He was shot two times at close range. In the chest and in the genitals."

The espresso, biscuit, and bacon made a sudden turn in my stomach.

"Strange thing is," Tom went on, "whoever killed him cut off a big chunk of his hair. Like a scalping."

"A *scalping*?"

Tom chewed thoughtfully. "Well, not exactly. More like, *I want a chunk of this blond hair as a souvenir.*"

Deep breaths, I told myself. I looked outside, where bright sunlight was coaxing dandelion pods to release their seeds. As if on cue, thousands of tiny white fluffs floated toward the sky. *They're like aliens,* Arch used to say when he was little, *all being launched at once.* Another time, he'd said, *It's snowing up.* But the tiny, featherlike seeds always eventually floated back down, a gentle precipitation that accumulated in roads, piled up in ditches, and rolled like dustballs down our dry hills.

"Miss G.?" Tom's voice seemed far away. "Do you not want me to talk about the autopsy anymore? I mean, not at breakfast?"

I met his green eyes. "I'm not sure. Thanks for the delicious food, though. It'll help me survive my events today."

"You know," Tom said as he rinsed the dishes and gave me sidelong glances, wanting to make sure I was all right, "they do have good people working on this case."

"Uh-huh."

"It's their job, Goldy. They're not in it for the right or wrong of it. The morality part. All they do is law enforcement. Catch a killer and preserve evidence so that justice can be done—that is, so that a conviction of murder will hold up."

"Yes, yes, I understand."

"Okay. That guy you and Marla discovered on her hood? He's fine. Had a bloody nose, a few bruises. They nabbed that guy Bobby Calhoun, and asked him a bunch of questions, but he denies everything. They can't make him get his Elvis getup on for a lineup."

"That figures."

Tom shrugged. "They had to let him go. He's a volunteer fireman, and the Aspen Meadow Fire Department is fighting a new fire in Black Mountain Canyon, right next to the preserve. They beeped him several times while he was being questioned. Meanwhile, the bald guy we think he beat up has been released from the hospital and is home with a big bandage on his nose."

"Thanks for the update. Do you know what they found out about Courtney MacEwan? Did she have an alibi for the time John Richard was shot?"

Tom tilted his head thoughtfully. "Supposedly, around one she was unloading cupcakes for that bake sale. She was in and out until three, according to the lady manning the cash box, who admitted she was too busy to be able to account for Courtney's every minute."

"Hmm. Think I could or should talk to her?"

"No, Goldy. I believe if you say a single word to

Courtney MacEwan, those hostile detectives will try to get the two of you on conspiracy to commit murder."

"Come on."

"Conspiracy after the fact, then."

"Oh, wonderful."

Tom finished the dishes in silence and announced that he was going up to get Arch moving. I nodded and brought up my "Nan Watkins Retirement Picnic Prep" file. First I put water on to boil for the pasta that would form the base for the picnic salad. The salad, light and delicate on the tongue, had to be freshly made. Next I hauled out a mountain of cherry tomatoes, rinsed and dried them, and began slicing them in half. When was the last time I'd had my knives sharpened? I tried to remember. *Careful,* I told myself, *be very careful.* It was important for caterers to keep all their knives extremely sharp. It was the dull ones that were dangerous.

Dull knives, sharp knives. Neither one had shorn John Richard's hair. But who had, and why?

The juicy, ripe tomatoes fell into neat halves as I sliced. I didn't know *who* or *why,* but I could guess as to *when.* Whoever had stolen the thirty-eight from my van had also nabbed the kitchen shears. Within the next couple of hours, the thief had shot John Richard in the heart and the groin and used my scissors to lop off a chunk of his blond hair. And of course, I'd seen something out of place on John Richard's scalp, I just had not registered it. Something had been strange about his dead body, and the butchered hair was it.

Cherry tomato, slice in half. Tomato, slice. Tomato, slice.

Okay, *why?* Why would a killer keep a chunk of hair as a souvenir? Had the FBI profiled hair-collecting killers? I knew fans and friends of Beethoven had surreptitiously lopped off chunks of his hair after he died. But presumably, that was because they *admired* him.

Upstairs, shower water began running. Would Arch find out this horrid detail? I certainly hoped not. I sighed and kept on working.

John Richard had always been very proud of his hair. In fact, the way he felt about his hair brought to mind that biblical term *vainglorious,* a particular favorite of my Sunday-school class. What did it mean to be *vainglorious* about your *hair*? Well, you could use it to great advantage when seducing members of the opposite sex. (Of course, I didn't talk to the Sunday-school class about *that.* But they'd guessed what Jezebel was up to.)

I wished Tom had told me exactly where on John Richard's head this chunk of hair had been cut. Maybe our killer just wanted him to look unattractive in death. Closed casket, that kind of thing.

I shook my head and finished the tomatoes. Then I rinsed the cilantro, patted it dry, and spread it out on the cutting board where it looked like green strands of . . .

John Richard had always demanded that his gorgeous blond hair be cut *just so:* He'd have the stylist snip and rework his bangs until they were perfectly cantilevered over his forehead. While leaning toward a woman to ask, "So are you new to this hospital?," or to offer some confidential endearment, he would run one or both hands through his blond hair. The women had swooned.

I *had* to stop thinking about this. My knife guillotined the cilantro. Soon I'd made a deliciously scented pile of teensy-weensy green bits. I drained the pasta and set it aside to cool, then chopped fragrant scallions and crunchy daikon. I popped one of the left-over cherry tomatoes into my mouth, and was rewarded with sweet juice, firm texture, and eye-rolling lusciousness. I whisked together fruity olive oil, tangy red-wine vinegar, and Dijon mustard, then set all the salad ingredients aside to wait for the pasta to cool.

I switched gears to the committee breakfast, and began packing up those boxes. Because Sergeant Boyd would be there to guard me as well as help, I had told Liz to take the morning off. Julian was going to be with Arch. My two staffers would be working the picnic, though, and for that I was grateful.

The pasta was finally cool, so I gently mixed the salad together and set the whole thing in the walk-in. It was almost seven o'clock. Time to pack up the van and get cracking. After I loaded the last box, I took four ibuprofen. Then I waved to Julian, who was chugging up our street in his inherited Range Rover. I was so glad he would be with Arch and Tom today. I revved the van and headed toward the lake, where I passed a trio of boys casting their lines into the sparkling water. I wished I was with them. In fact, I'd rather be anywhere than catering to the most forbidding group of women in Aspen Meadow.

A transformation had taken place at the Roundhouse. To my great surprise, a team of workers from Front Range Rental had already shown up, and was putting up the large tent that would be the site for Nan Watkins's retirement picnic. And I felt secure from early morning attackers, because Sergeant Boyd had already arrived, and he would stay with me to help as well as guard me. The enormous mirrored sidelights of Boyd's dark sedan shone like beacons in the early morning sunlight. Those lights, and the ominous low-slung sedan itself, seemed to holler *Back off! I'm an unmarked police car.* And as if that wasn't enough to deter any would-be assailant, a deputy in a sheriff's department black-and-white had pulled up next to Boyd, in that way cops do when they're having an important conference on the highway. Even *I* was intimidated, and I was just the caterer.

Boyd stopped conversing long enough to hand me the keys to my newly secured domain. I walked around to the side of the Roundhouse. The security cage Tom had had installed around the compressors was truly impressive: A cube of chain-link fencing, secured by a large padlock, gleamed in the sunshine. The awe-inspiring new back door, made of solid oak and sporting two locks, looked equally impregnable. My sore body, two days after the attack, was healing; my soul was thankful for such a great husband.

"See you, Boyd," called the deputy before he roared off.

"Let's rock!" I said to Boyd. And we took off for the club.

We parked near the service entry and hopped out of our vehicles. Not far away, the plonk-plonk of tennis balls had already started up. Ambitious Colorado players lost no time getting to outdoor courts, once the snow melted. I wondered if I would see Courtney.

To my dismay, a white Furman County van occupied a space near ours. Not Roger Mannis, I prayed. But I couldn't be too careful.

"Sergeant," I murmured to Boyd. "There's a certain man I'm trying to avoid . . ." I described Mannis and his secretive tactics, and how much I needed him not to be allowed into the committee meeting.

Ever amiable, Boyd used his carrotlike fingers to smooth the wrinkles out of his white polo shirt and black trousers. "I've got it covered, Goldy. Any guy tries to get into the women's meeting, I'll demand ID. I turn up a guy named Mannis, I'll pull rank on him and send him packing." He nodded emphatically, and I gave him a quick hug. Boyd looked and felt as if he'd gained about twenty pounds since the last time I'd seen him. As I flung open the van doors, I wondered if he could still pass the rigorous physical regimen that was part of the department's yearly accreditation program. Still, he looked extremely pleased with himself, weight gain or no.

"Tell me what you need me to do, Madame Caterer!"

I smiled and handed him a box. I automatically headed for the kitchen entry, with the sergeant at my heels. By seven-fifteen, and with no sign of Mannis, we had carried in all our boxes. The club didn't serve breakfast, so we had the kitchen to ourselves. In the wood-paneled private dining room, Boyd and I pushed together two tables to make one long one for twelve.

"Now," Boyd announced, "I have a couple of surprises for you from Tom."

"What?"

"This is why we're called undercover cops," Boyd announced as he pulled a wrapped package from beneath his shirt. No wonder he'd looked heavier, he'd been hiding a bulky something. . . . The bundle contained, joy of joys, a new white Battenberg lace tablecloth. We unfurled it across the dark tables. It looked stunning.

Without the hidden tablecloth to slow him down, a greatly slimmed Boyd could move much more quickly. He trotted to his sedan and returned, holding a breathtaking floral centerpiece. There was simply no way that the wealthy-but-penny-pinching ladies of the tree-planting committee had ordered this fanciful arrangement, an abundance of spring flowers ingeniously set into the length of an aspen log. This second gift from Tom, Boyd explained, was meant to add a thematic touch to the breakfast.

"He knew you had some flowers at the house, but he thought you needed another arrangement," Boyd commented in his usual laconic way as he carefully placed the flower-filled log in the center of the table. "Silverware next." He about-faced and headed for the kitchen. I stared at the table.

Tom. I pulled out a chair and sat down. Oh, God, *Tom.*

Back when John Richard and I were engaged, and my mother finally met the ultrahandsome, ultracharming doctor-to-be, she'd trembled with excitement. She'd asked, "What does *he* see in *you*?" I hadn't quite known how to respond to this query, so I hadn't. My mother had shaken her head, eyed John Richard, and cooed, "Ooh, Goldy! You are so lucky! You must have done something fabulous to deserve such a *wonderful* man."

Bulldozing all irony into one of AMCC's golf course sand traps, I now wondered, truly, what I'd ever done to deserve *Tom.* Maybe the Hindus were right, after all, and there was some kind of karmic balance to the universe, the good stuff following the bad. My understanding of this theory was that the worse the bad stuff was, the better your good stuff would be. This theory would be harshly criticized by the old guard at St. Luke's Episcopal Church, I reflected, as I quickstepped to the kitchen to finish setting up for the breakfast. I hesitated, glanced back at Tom's gorgeous tablecloth and flowers, and thought, To hell with the old guard.

An hour later, when the first ten members of the committee arrived and started berating me, I had to remind myself that I didn't care about the old guard. They were in fine fettle, I had to say. While I offered trays of mimosas and coffee, the women eyed each other's casual summer outfits—de rigueur silk and cotton suits—and jewelry—single gold strands, double rows of pearls, and a few tiny gems—and settled into earnest bickering.

They ranged in age from thirty to sixty. I knew most of them from catering events or committee work at St. Luke's. The church meetings had been much harder than the parties, as parish youth-group parents or Sunday-school teachers or even vestry members often ended up stalking off. Behind their backs, each set of enemies claimed their adversaries *weren't good Christians.*

I took a deep breath. It could be a long morning.

Marla, looking gorgeous in a turquoise wrinkled-silk pantsuit adorned with turquoise feathers, came bustling up to me. My friend glowed with good health; tiny turquoise barrettes glimmered in her hair as she bent close to my ear. "The Jerk raped a young girl? How long have you know about this?"

"Look, I don't know if it's true. Have you dug up anything? A name, a date?"

"No," Marla replied, "but I've got my spies trolling the hills. Okay, I do have news about Courtney Mac-Ewan. I just saw her downstairs, by the way. She's on her way up here for the meeting."

Oh, joy. I concentrated on making Marla an alcohol-free mimosa. "Can you come over to the Roundhouse with me when this is over?"

Marla chugged her drink. "Sure. I could even talk to you here when there's a break in the action. I'd rather turn my back on a firing squad than give these women the chance to talk about me when I'm not in the room."

I nodded and moved efficiently around the table distributing the parfaits. The glittering crystal glasses filled with alternating layers of the creamy yogurt mixture and the rainbow of juicy fresh fruit made the flower-bedecked, lace-covered table worthy of a *Bon Appétit* centerfold. When I was done, Marla held up her glass as if she needed a refill. I sidled up to her.

"What?" I said under my breath.

"You need to explain who Boyd is and why he's here. Somebody just said that as soon as Cecelia Brisbane got here, she was going to tell Ye Olde Gossip Columnist that you were having an affair with a guy who thinks a mimosa is a flower."

I blew out air and glanced around the room. Maybe I should have called in sick.

At ten to eight, the women decided not to wait for their three missing members. As they sat down to eat, I introduced Sergeant Boyd as one of my new helpers. The women squinted at him. Boyd and I set about serving coffee, iced tea, and juice, then began fielding demands for low-cal sweetener and skim milk, apple juice instead of orange, and no fresh fruit *in* the parfait, but *on the side*.

No question about it, Priscilla Throckbottom—actually one of my longtime catering clients—was in a bad mood. I knew from experience that she could be difficult without trying very hard. Plus, I had forgotten to call her back the previous day. When elegantly coiffed, white-haired Priscilla, dressed in an exquisite red linen suit with white piping, began to lay into Boyd about something, I quickly stepped in.

Priscilla was holding up her parfait glass by her fingertips, as if it were a dead snake. "Goldy! Please bring me some eggs and bacon."

Boyd, immobilized, gave me a blank look. We didn't have eggs and bacon. I tilted my head knowingly toward the kitchen; Boyd followed me. I told him we weren't a restaurant and not to worry about any off-the-wall demand. This kind of thing happened. You just nodded, ignored the request, and went on with the event. If possible, you also stopped serving booze to whoever was making demands.

Boyd smiled and saluted.

Within moments, Boyd and I were again circling the table, this time with platters of the hot slices of quiche and the crab-and-cheese croissants. All the food was a huge hit. Courtney still hadn't shown up, and I didn't care. But I did feel sorry for Cecelia Brisbane and Ginger Vikarios, the other two missing members of the committee. Cecelia came for the gossip—that was why she'd been at the bake sale—and the women were afraid of what would be printed about them if Cecelia *wasn't* included. Poor Ginger Vikarios was the one who'd asked Holly Kerr to join. Holly, dressed in a black suit and looking miserable, undoubtedly wondered how a group of women could be so famished that they wouldn't wait for all the guests to arrive before plunging into their food. And really, it should not have surprised me that these women did not wait before plunging into something *else*.

"Goldy!" called Priscilla when I appeared with a pitcher of iced tea for refills. "We have some questions for you!"

Winks raced around the table. Only Holly Kerr appeared perplexed. Marla opened her eyes wide in warning. Too late, I realized I should have sent Boyd out with the tea.

Priscilla adjusted her oversize eyeglasses to get a good look at me.

"Do the police know who killed your ex-husband?" she demanded.

"No."

"But surely your *new* husband, that . . . that *policeman*"—she waved a hand—"has told you *something*," Priscilla persisted. "Or at least has provided you with some theories. Some *ideas*."

The women waited, forks poised.

I stared at the pitcher in my right hand and the glass in my left. I resolutely poured in tea. "Ah, no. I wish it were so, but it is not."

"*I* heard John Richard Korman fathered half a dozen bastard children in several states," Priscilla hissed to her colleagues. "I also heard he owed over two million dollars to creditors, and that there was a malpractice suit pending against him."

Say nothing, I ordered myself. *Keep your eyes down.* Avoiding eye contact, I'd always noticed, was the best way to become invisible. Not only that, but a humble, servantlike pose was a good way to learn interesting facts. But were these stories fact or fiction? I hoped for the latter. Still, in matters pertaining to the Jerk, I'd learned to expect the worst.

Holly Kerr's face was drawn into a look of horror. Her hands had gone to her throat, as if she were choking on a chicken bone. I noiselessly walked over to her.

"Holly, are you all right?" I whispered.

"More tea, please?" she squeaked. I poured some into her almost-full glass.

"Now," Priscilla went on, "has anybody else heard about Dr. Korman's outstanding house loan—"

"Uh, ex-*cuse* me!" Marla's voice was shrill. "Whatever happened to our agenda? I thought we were here to discuss planting trees! How about a few aspens along that ugly concrete wall they've put up next to those new condos—"

"And that reminds me, *speaking* of bastards!" Priscilla interrupted. Her eyes widened behind the huge glasses. "Will someone please tell me *who* appointed Ginger Vi*kar*ios to this committee? I thought *I* was the chairwoman, and then Ginger showed up at the bake sale with baklava, and I didn't know what to do!"

Marla interjected, "Oh, Priscilla, for heaven's sake! Ginger is trying hard to reconnect with the community since Ted's empire went belly up. Let's not be uncharitable."

Since *being uncharitable* was just a stone's throw from being called *un-Christian,* the women frowned. They seemed deep in thought, pondering ways to gossip about Ginger while still appearing charitable.

Priscilla said, "In her column a few years back, Cecelia said Ginger Vikarios had a child out of wedlock."

"Goldy?" Holly Kerr squeaked from nearby. "Do you know where the ladies' room is?" I gestured, and she tip-tapped away.

Another woman announced, "*Ginger* didn't have a child out of wedlock. Her *daughter* did. Not many people in Aspen Meadow remember, although some of us think they should."

Marla, sensing approaching chaos, sighed and flicked a glance in my direction. I quickly busied myself with the rolls and butter.

"Hey, girls!" Courtney MacEwan called from the door. "Who said you could start without me?"

There was a collective intake of breath as the women gaped at Courtney, who looked sexy and chic in a black linen pantsuit with an embroidered bolero jacket. Her shiny brown hair was swept up in a French twist, and she was draped with more gold chains than a professional wrestler. After pausing a moment for effect, she strutted to an empty seat and glared at me. I gave a questioning look, as in, *What can I bring you?* In response, she held out a muscled arm and snapped her fingers at me.

"Get me a mimosa and black coffee. *Now.*"

I stared at her, immobilized. Back in my doctor's wife days, Courtney and I had played tennis together. We'd gone to hospital parties with our then-spouses. Even the day before yesterday, at the Roundhouse, she'd joked with me about having sex after funerals. And now she was giving me orders?

I said, "Whatever," then turned and walked toward the kitchen.

Priscilla Throckbottom began to hyperventilate. "Girls! Girls! Has anyone else heard this rumor about the Vikarioses—"

The kitchen doors swung closed. I turned on the fans—I was sure steam was coming out of my ears—and wondered if Boyd could finish the breakfast. No, I couldn't do that to him . . .

"You bitch!" Courtney hissed from behind me. "What do you mean, *whatever*?"

"Get out of this kitchen." I faced her and made my face impassive. "You're violating county health regulations."

Her cheeks flared. "You implicated me to the cops. Who do you think you are? I didn't kill John Richard!"

I picked up one of the cookie sheets we'd used for the croissants and checked it for crumbs. "Then you have nothing to worry about. Now *leave.*"

"*You're* the one who made his life miserable," Courtney insisted. She placed her hands on her hips. Clearly, she'd determined to have a fight and wasn't planning on going anywhere.

I said, "You shouldn't have believed his lies, Courtney. He made his own life whatever it became."

"That's not the way I heard it. I loved him. We were going to get married. Then you screwed it up with your threats to cut off his visitations with Arch."

"Is that why you sabotaged my food and attacked me?"

She turned scarlet. "You're crazy."

"How did you manage to steal stuff from my van?"

"I didn't take anything of yours and you know it."

"Right. But John Richard took something from you, didn't he? Marla thought it was a hundred thou, but she was going to ask Cecelia Brisbane if it might have been more—"

"Shut *up*!"

"And while we're at it, Courtney, where'd you go after the funeral lunch, exactly?"

That did it. In a cloud of bolero jacket and gold chains, Courtney wheeled around, whacked through the swinging doors, and was gone. By the time I'd picked up a crystal pitcher of iced tea and moved back into the dining room, Courtney had stalked out. The committeewomen snickered, exchanged murmurs, and gave me questioning looks.

Holly Kerr, looking only slightly revived, had returned to her seat. The women, unwilling to move to their agenda, tried to remember the last thing they were complaining about.

"I still haven't heard a satisfactory reason for Ginger

Vikarios to be invited on to this committee," Priscilla huffed.

Holly Kerr looked earnestly around the table. "How can you say such a thing? *She* asked *me* to join so we would have time to work together and raise money—"

"I should think Ginger Vikarios's time should be spent raising money for a better wardrobe," Priscilla interjected. "Did you see what she wore to your husband's memorial, Holly? She looked like an orange Popsicle!"

Holly Kerr gasped. I wasn't sure she was going to make it through this meeting.

Priscilla continued, "Denver has any number of dress boutiques—"

"God *dammit,* Priscilla—" Marla interrupted.

"Now regarding swear words," Priscilla threatened, "I announced at the beginning of our work together . . ."

I moved noiselessly around the table, serving seconds on rolls and butter, offering refills on coffee, sugar, cream, iced tea, and lemon. No more mimosas for *these* ladies.

Beads of perspiration were forming on Marla's forehead. She glanced longingly at the flip chart Aspen Meadow Nursery had set up at the far end of the private dining room. When I leaned in to fill her iced tea glass, she whispered, "Can't you do something to get these bitches onto their agenda?"

"Like what?" I whispered back.

"Announce that it's time! Don't you think this damn country club has a dinner bell somewhere?"

"Sorry. The only bell Coloradans use is for calling in cows."

Priscilla interrupted by asking Sergeant Boyd how

she was supposed to stir sugar into her iced tea if he didn't bring her an iced-tea spoon? He swallowed, his expression somewhere between bemusement and dismay, and asked what an iced-tea spoon was. I quickly murmured to Priscilla that I would get one from the kitchen.

"Whitewash," Priscilla was proclaiming when I returned. She waved with one hand and adjusted her glasses with the other. "We still don't know what really happened. And Cecelia really is *so* odd, isn't she? We invited her to this meeting, and yet she can't be bothered to come. Maybe Walter wanted a woman who would be more like a real wife, not a silly gossip columnist."

"Walter Brisbane was *such* a charmer," another woman commented. "It *must* have been over another woman, don't you think?"

"Maybe another man!" Priscilla squealed.

A sudden banging and rush of footsteps kept me from dumping the pitcher of iced tea on Priscilla's head. The discussion came to an abrupt halt. Ginger Vikarios, her orange-red hair disheveled, her stockings askew, her appearance incongruously froufrou—she was wearing the same orange taffeta dress and matching orange heels she'd worn to the memorial lunch— stepped timidly toward the table.

"I'm terribly sorry to be late." Her voice cracked as she eyed the leftover crumbs on the women's plates. "I hope . . . you haven't begun to discuss our work together. I've been looking forward to it—"

Priscilla Throckbottom fidgeted with her fork and knife. "Of course we've been *waiting* for you, Ginger." She eyed Ginger's outfit. "You know, my dear, I can take you to Denver—"

"Priscilla!" Marla shrieked. The women jumped in their chairs, startled. Priscilla drew her mouth into a moue of protest.

"I . . . thought the meeting was at eight-thirty." Ginger fidgeted with her too-large double strand of pearls and glanced apologetically around the table. "And then I looked at my calendar, and said to Ted, 'Oh, no . . . ' "

"We all make mistakes," said Priscilla, with a knowing glance around the table. "In fact, some of us have made *many* mistakes over the course of our lives."

Ginger blushed and slithered into a seat. Marla caught my eye, and in that awkward moment, hollered, "It's time to get to our agenda!"

I headed for the kitchen.

Okay, there *was* one good thing that had come out of my divorce and involuntary demotion from the country-club set to the servant sector.

I'd been able to quit every committee I'd been on.

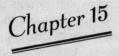

Chapter 15

I ignored the scathing looks I received when I brought Ginger Vikarios a fresh plate of parfait, quiche, croissants, and rolls. She was almost pathetically grateful. As Boyd and I began to clear the rest of the dishes, Priscilla Throckbottom grabbed my elbow and pulled me down next to her.

With her mouth next to my ear, she whispered, "Ginger arrived too *late* to be served breakfast."

Balancing two stacks of dishes, I tried in vain to release myself from her pincer grip on my arm and hot breath in my ear. It occurred to me that even though I'd quit my committees, and even though I'd learned to handle aggressive *men,* I was a tad behind the curve on handling aggressive *women.* I resolved to ask Tom about this.

My pal Marla, however, knew how to handle aggressive women because she *was* one. Sensing I was in trouble, she bustled around the table and grabbed Priscilla's forearm. The dirty dishes in my released hand made a precipitous slide toward another woman's frothy hairdo and pale pink suit.

Dear Lord, I prayed, *help me out of this.*

And He did, using my best friend as his instrument. Marla murmured a few choice words to Priscilla about exhibiting Pharisaic hypocrisy regarding feeding Ginger Vikarios. We didn't want that to get out, now *did we*? Especially since one of Marla's pals was the current editor of the St. Luke's newsletter. Of course, there was no way Father Pete would allow Marla or anyone else to put a bitchy tidbit into the church newsletter. But the women had all seen the power of *Cecelia's* gossip column, and Priscilla was properly intimidated, for once. She harrumphed and turned away. Boyd, again taken aback, cleared the rest of the dishes with miraculous swiftness.

But Marla was not finished with Priscilla, because she held on to her arm the way that Priscilla had held on to mine. She must have threatened something truly damaging, because Priscilla cleared her throat and stood up. Then she walked timidly in the direction of the flip chart.

For a moment, the women were stunned, as they seemed to think their leader was stalking out of the meeting. But Priscilla stopped abruptly, smiled nervously at her colleagues-in-gardening, and tapped the first illustration with her pointer.

"Root systems!" she gargled. The committeewomen frowned. Priscilla began lecturing apprehensively on the different trees' adaptability to rugged climate, sunshine, and shade. I tiptoed away with my last load and pushed into the kitchen. We would rinse the dishes as quietly as . . . no, I would *not* think of mice, not after what had happened on Tuesday. Boyd and I began scraping the plates and gently running water over them. I thanked him again for helping me out, and he waved this away.

"You can't imagine all I've learned today," he replied solemnly. "If I didn't before, I now have a genuine fear of, and respect for, the opposite sex."

"Right."

When Boyd and I had finished stacking the rinsed dishes and I was brewing a fresh carafe of coffee, Marla slid into the kitchen.

"From all committees, good Lord, deliver us," she announced, raising her hands in a gesture of prayer. All the feathers on her suit quivered. "Is there a back door out of here?"

"I thought you didn't want to turn your back on this committee." I finished drying the last cup. "You were afraid they'd talk about you during even the *teensiest* absence."

Marla exhaled. "I didn't bank on Priscilla doing a presentation on composting. Two of the women are asleep, and the rest are yawning. I figured it was safe to leave." She tilted her head coquettishly and batted her eyelashes at Boyd. "Why, Sergeant! You did an admirable job out there, and survived to tell the tale."

For the first time since I'd known him, I saw Sergeant Boyd blush. "Well, thank you, Mrs. Korman."

She poured two glasses of orange juice, handed me one, and held up her glass as a toast. "To Sergeant Boyd, for surviving his first women's committee meeting." We raised our glasses and sipped as Boyd's cheeks turned even darker. "Now, Sergeant Boyd," Marla went on, "one more thing. Could you keep an eye on the ladies out there, pretty please? I need to have a heart-to-heart with my girlfriend here, and we need to be warned if they start talking about us. Or if they want more food, God forbid."

Boyd nodded and mumbled that it would be no problem. Before he was even out the kitchen door, Marla started talking.

"What's this about the Vikarioses?" she demanded. "Mr. and Mrs. Family Values had a child out of wedlock?"

I shook my head. "That wasn't what I was hearing. Priscilla said the Vikarioses had a bastard *grand*child. But she also said John Richard owed a couple mil to creditors, so I don't know how reliable her sources are."

"Neither do I, but I'm going to start digging."

I sighed. "So, what were you able to find out about Courtney MacEwan?" Ever so quietly, I began to load the dirty plates into the club's commercial dishwasher.

"All right," Marla began. "The way Courtney tells it, she and John Richard were going to get married before the end of the year. He just needed some money. Also, he was starting a new business and was wondering if Courtney would be willing to 'help him out with it.' "

I groaned. "Why do I feel as if I know where this is going?"

Marla put her hand on her chest. "You haven't heard it all. Courtney was designing a big new house for the two of them in Flicker Ridge. She even promised to get new *boobs* for him."

"Marla, *don't.*"

Marla sipped her drink and rattled the ice cubes. "This is to let you know her motivation. She was so in love with him, not only was she ready to have surgery, but as we know, she also loaned him that hundred thousand bucks after they hooked up. She also rented him the Tudor house, ostensibly so that *you* wouldn't scream about him living with another woman when Arch came to visit. Really, of course . . ."

I said, "Yes, yes, she was naive."

"Courtney had given him a lot of money, which probably meant he saw her as getting controlling." Marla paused and raised her eyebrows. "And by the way, the Jerk said, he couldn't actually *marry* her anytime soon. Are we not surprised at this, either?"

"He wanted his freedom. He wanted to examine his options," I said dully. "See if he could trade up, so to speak."

"So to speak. Depends on how you look at a stripper who's ten years younger than Courtney." She did a little dance around the kitchen. "Okay. Remember the *Mountain Journal* of . . . of . . . Friday, the sixth of May?"

I slid in a dirty dish and paused. "Was that the one with the picture of John Richard sponsoring the golf tournament? Twenty-five thou to charity and you're suddenly back in the bosom of society?"

"Oh, darling, don't talk about the bosom of *society,* talk about Courtney and her upcoming boobs and her *money,* and Cecelia's column from that same issue, which precipitated the breakup. Do you *not* remember it? *What local tennis-playing merry widow is living with an ex-con? Could that be where the ex-con, an infamous local doctor, is getting the wherewithal to squeeze back into everyone's good graces and have them forget about the past? Are we as willing to forgive and forget a crime against a woman?* Courtney drenched herself in champagne cocktails and sobbed to me all about this at the club last night. She blames you *and* Cecelia for what happened to them. Although she ought to blame the Jerk, as usual," she muttered.

"I saw the column," I admitted. "I take it the Jerk objected to being gossiped about?"

"Courtney had been staying at the Tudor house, and only left when you brought Arch over. But the Jerk kicked her out the *morning* after the column was published," Marla said. "He said between dealing with you and the Arch-visitation issue, and facing negative publicity, they were through."

"Whoops." I wanted to feel sorry for Courtney, but couldn't. She had certainly proved to *me* that she was a bitch.

"Okay." Marla put down her iced tea and poured herself a cup of coffee from our drip machine on the counter. "What the Jerk said to Courtney was that they were officially broken up. Over. Kaput." Marla gestured with the coffee and slopped half of it onto the counter. "After the breakup, Courtney sobbed how *over* John Richard had said it should be. She should *not* call. *Not* write. No e-mail! And Courtney cried, oh, God, she *cried*." Marla blinked and drank a bit more coffee. "She demanded her hundred K back, but not that day. And guess what happened when Courtney went to her lawyer to get her money back?"

I said, "I can't imagine."

"The Jerk told *his* lawyer Courtney's cash wasn't a loan, it was a gift."

"Pretty big gift."

Marla smirked. "No kidding." My friend's tone turned serious. "Goldy, do you think Courtney could have shot him?"

I stopped loading the dishwasher and shook my head. "I don't know. When she came in here, she was furious. You have to suspect anyone with a temper like that." I remembered one of the places John Richard had been shot: the genitals. "I know Courtney's alibi is about as solid as carbon dioxide. In and out of a crowded bake sale five minutes away? But if she were ever caught, the negative publicity from Cecelia Brisbane would be *nothing* compared to being convicted of homicide."

"Let me ask you this, then." Marla picked up her purse. "Do you think Courtney would hire someone to kill the Jerk?"

"She's got the money, certainly."

"Yeah. And the motive."

Something in Marla's tone made my skin turn to gooseflesh. "Why? Do you know something? What have you heard?"

Marla chewed the inside of her cheek. "I haven't *heard* a word. But I did *see* something unusual when I arrived this morning. I walked around to the club service entrance, because I thought we could visit before the breakfast. You weren't there, but guess who was? That food inspector you hate so much—"

"Roger Mannis?" I interrupted, stunned. "A guy who looks like a weasel with an ax for a chin?"

"The same. And sitting in the passenger seat of the van, handing him an envelope, was Courtney MacEwan."

Marla said she hadn't seen anything else. She hugged me and took off, while I fought the knot in my stomach.

After checking that the committee meeting was finally on track, I asked Boyd back into the kitchen. I shared what I'd heard from Marla, and my questions. How much had Courtney resented me for supposedly breaking up her affair with John Richard? Could Mannis have been the one who'd attacked me outside the Roundhouse? He would certainly know about sabotage, or he could have tutored Courtney in what to do.

And then perhaps Roger, or Courtney, had driven over to John Richard's house and shot him.

"Could be," Boyd mused. "You always have to be open to theories."

"Do you think I should say anything to Reilly and Blackridge? They've been really hostile to me."

"Let me do it." Boyd nodded decisively. "They know I'm here guarding you, and I can say one of the women saw Ms. MacEwan give Mannis an envelope. Then it'll be up to them. You probably don't want them knowing you've got this information, anyway."

Plus, I thought, I sure didn't want Courtney Mac-Ewan to know I had even more reason to suspect her. That woman was dangerous.

An hour later, the committeewomen began to wrap up their meeting. Boyd and I were in the last stages of cleaning up from the breakfast. Priscilla Throckbottom did not give me an extra gratuity for Boyd, despite his hard work. I would do it myself, I resolved, when he departed from the Roundhouse this afternoon. And he was going to be there, he'd insisted. He'd informed me he was sticking with me until Julian and Liz arrived to help with the picnic. Ordinarily I would have bristled at being chaperoned, but I really did *not* want to go back into the Roundhouse alone, thank you very much.

At the end of the meeting, two things surprised me. First of all, the women actually did agree to *do* something. Lot purchases of trees were to be had at half price at Aspen Meadow Nursery, this week only. With their many donations and the success of the bake sale, PosteriTREE was buying sixteen dozen blue spruce, twenty dozen aspen trees, and fifty dozen lodgepole pines. They were going to organize volunteers to plant them in the burned areas of the Aspen Meadow

Wildlife Preserve. Since the canyon fire had just jumped over to the preserve, the women thought a re-planting scheme would be a worthy goal. I didn't know what volunteers would be willing to *work* for these women, but no one was asking me.

Tipping the emotional scales over to misery was the second surprise: the sight of Ginger Vikarios sobbing in her battered Taurus. The meeting had not yet ended when I'd finished cleaning and slipped out the service entrance with the trash. The food inspector's van was gone, of course, but I did spot a desolate Ginger when I rounded the corner to the club's Dumpster. Her fly-away orange hair was bent over the steering wheel; her body heaved with sobs. I tossed the trash into the Dumpster and headed in her direction to see what was wrong, to comfort her, *something*. But she heard my footsteps on the gravel and glanced up. Startled and gasping, she turned the key, pushed the old car into gear, and took off.

When Boyd and I finally finished, we were dismayed to see that two Cadillacs had been carelessly parked in such a way as to block the service lot exit. Cursing un-der my breath, I climbed into my van and revved the engine. With Boyd guiding me, I did a sixteen-point turn to get around the Caddies. Chuckling, Boyd hoisted himself into the passenger seat and we took off. As we drove up toward the tennis courts, we both saw Courtney MacEwan racing toward us. Oh, hell, I thought. Not again.

Courtney was wearing a skimpy white tennis dress that showed off her muscled arms and long legs. But she also had those strong arms raised, and each of her hands clutched her signature pink tennis balls. She did not look happy.

"You bitch!" she screamed at me. "You wrecked my life!" Before she could go on, she caught a glimpse of Boyd and clamped her mouth shut.

I gunned the engine to get up onto the club's main road. As we whizzed past Courtney, she gave me a hostile stare. I pressed the accelerator to go even faster. "That woman is a piece of work," Boyd commented, his voice amused.

Boyd reminded me not to speed, so I carefully slowed the van to make the turnoff to the lake. I needed to check on the tent setup, use my new keys to get through the Roundhouse's reinforced kitchen door, and generally make sure that everything was proceeding well for the next event. I certainly hoped Courtney MacEwan had not been invited to Nan Watkins's picnic.

After the mess at the club, the Roundhouse was a positively serene spot. The tent was up. Boyd gently took my new keys, opened the Roundhouse, and thoroughly checked the premises. He declared them clear.

We had just begun to haul out the boxes for the picnic event when my eyes caught on a sheriff's-department tow truck on the far side of the lake. It was the exact spot where I'd seen Trudy's son, Eddie, fishing with his pals earlier in the day. My heart turned over.

I remembered when Arch was nine and had come to the lake to fish by himself, because John Richard would never take him. I hadn't found him for hours and was sure he had drowned. I shook my head and walked even faster up the path to the kitchen door.

"Mr. . . . Sergeant . . ." I couldn't get the words out.

"What is it, Goldy?" Boyd asked calmly. He stopped unloading his box and came over to me. "Talk slowly." He nodded encouragingly. "Tell me."

"Lake," I said. "Here. Come!"

He accompanied me outside, and I pointed to the truck, which was now flashing its lights and backing up to the bank. With the truck reversing, I could now see two sheriff's-department vehicles and a state trooper's gray sedan near it.

"Oh, God!" I wailed.

"Goldy," Boyd said calmly. "Tell me what you think it is."

"Eddie!" I gasped. "Eddie from next door. Please. Call and find out."

Boyd told me to stay where I was, then unhooked his radio and walked ten paces away from me. His radio crackled as he talked into it.

I thought I was going to be ill. I was suddenly excruciatingly worried about Arch. About Eddie. About everything. I told Boyd I was going over to where the sheriff's-department cars were parked and see if Eddie was okay. Boyd relocked the Roundhouse and hustled along behind me. I pressed the buttons for Tom's cell phone and resumed trotting toward the far side of the lake.

Tom, happy to hear from me, said Arch had had one shaky period on the way to the giant pool. Tom had taken an exit off the interstate and found a church where he knew the pastor. The pastor had listened to and comforted Arch while Todd and Julian had waited patiently. The three boys had spent the morning riding man-made tsunamis in the wave pool. After that, they'd had banana splits, and then it had begun to rain, *hard*. Denver's weather could be entirely different from ours, no question. Anyway, Arch and Todd had decided to go back to the Druckmans', and Julian was on his way to the Roundhouse. I asked Tom if Arch had mentioned the non-golf lessons with John Richard.

"That's a negative, Miss G. My guess is that his guilt will catch up with him, and he'll offer the info to you. He . . . had a bit of a paranoia attack, too. He thought we were being followed. He said he thought somebody had followed him to the rink in Lakewood on Tuesday, too."

"Who could have been following him?" I glanced back at Boyd, who was talking into his radio.

"I don't know, but I made damn sure I watched for somebody once we got back on the interstate. There wasn't anyone."

"Tom, have you heard about a drowning at Aspen Meadow Lake?" I blurted out.

"No, I haven't. You want me to call in and find out? Is that where you are?"

"Yeah. Boyd's on the radio. I'm walking toward the recovery operation. Eddie from next door was going fishing today, and I'm so scared I'm sick."

"I understand. Boyd still checking?" Tom asked.

I glanced back and said he was. Talking, talking, talking. What was going on?

Tom said, "Tell me about your breakfast." I told him that Courtney MacEwan might be up to something with Roger Mannis. Tom chuckled. "Girls will be girls."

"I'm going to pretend I didn't hear that."

Boyd clicked off his radio and called for me to slow down. Meanwhile, two cops were lowering the truck's winch into the lake.

"I'll call you back, Tom."

"I'm on my way over there right now."

"Thanks."

"Eddie's okay," Boyd reassured me. "So are his friends." Relief washed over me. "They did find something over there, though."

The winch beeped and cranked. It was hauling a heavy load out of the water.

"It's a woman," Boyd told me grimly.

We were less than twenty yards from the sheriff's-department cars. A state patrolman signaled us to stay put. Meanwhile, the tow-truck engine growled as its tires bit into the dirt.

At the end of the winch, a car's grill glittered in the sunlight. I blinked in surprise. I knew that old station wagon. Water gushed out of the sides as more of it surfaced.

And then I saw her, her face pressed to the window. Even in death, I knew those thick glasses, that shovel-shaped face.

It was Cecelia Brisbane.

Chapter 16

Sirens wailed in the distance. On the far side of the tow truck, a small crowd had gathered behind orange cones I'd missed seeing before. The cops needed more cars, of course. The town gossip columnist would generate more gossip in death than she had in life.

Not long after more sheriff's-department cars had pulled alongside the tow truck, Tom's sedan swung onto the lakeside road. A more welcome sight, I could not imagine. I had checked that the tables were being set up inside the tent. But someone still needed to pick up the pork chops from our house. No matter what, I really, really wanted to see Tom.

As Boyd and I walked back to the Roundhouse, he asked me if I wanted him to stick around.

"Tom will want to guard you," Boyd said with a grin. "You don't need two cops to do that. Well, maybe *you* do."

"You've been great. Please let me pay you for this morning's work."

"Forget it. That was pure entertainment." He promised he'd wait for Julian and give him the keys to the Roundhouse. Tom saluted Boyd, who only smiled.

"Do you have any idea what's going on?" I asked Tom once he was sitting beside me in my van. "Did anyone know Cecelia was missing? How did she end up inside her car at the bottom of the lake?"

"Take it easy, Goldy. I only know what I've heard since I talked to you."

As he recited the facts, a sense of unreality crept over me. I had just seen Cecelia at the bake sale. Then I'd received a piece of mail from her. And now she was dead. I found this literally and figuratively hard to swallow.

About all law enforcement knew, Tom told me, was that Cecelia had been reported missing by her neighbor yesterday. Since Walter had committed suicide, this neighbor had vowed to check on Cecelia every single day, so she'd been sure, she told the sheriff's department, that something was wrong.

What did *I* know about Cecelia's history? Tom asked. Not much, I conceded, except that everyone in town feared being skewered in one of her columns. Of course, she'd hired me to do those posthumous birthday parties every year. And she seemed to pine for her daughter to come home, although she never said anything concrete to me.

Cecelia's neighbor, Tom said, was an elderly woman named Sherry Boone. Cecelia always told Sherry when she was going somewhere, as Sherry fed Cecelia's guinea pigs in her absence. When Cecelia hadn't answered her phone, Sherry had called the *Mountain Journal*, frantic. Not only was Cecelia not there, she hadn't phoned the paper that morning, as she usually did, to tell them when she'd be bringing in this week's column. Sherry Boone had finally convinced the sheriff's department to send a patrol car out to the Brisbanes' creek-side residence.

Nobody had been home. Cecelia's car was gone. In front of the deputies, Sherry retrieved Cecelia's spare key and went into the house. There was no sign of forced entry, no sign of a struggle, no note—only three hungry guinea pigs, which Sherry Boone immediately took into custody.

"Didn't anyone think Cecelia might have been so depressed she'd commit suicide?" I wondered aloud.

"Nobody knew her better than her own neighbor. And Mrs. Boone insisted Cecelia had been in a good mood on Tuesday afternoon." Tom's face was grim as he opened the passenger door to my van. "And then our guys got this call from Aspen Meadow Lake . . ." He got out of the van. "Anyway, they'll know more when they hear from the M.E."

I followed Tom's sedan home. When he saw I was shivering, he insisted I have a hot shower. He announced that *he* was going to do the final prep for Nan Watkins's picnic. When I protested, he reminded me that I always seemed to want to do an investigator's job, so wasn't it hypocritical to stop an *investigator* from doing *my* job? I smiled. Was he getting his old sense of humor back? Was the depression over that lost case finally lifting?

When I reentered the kitchen, showered and dressed in a clean caterer's outfit, the scent of warm rolls filled the air. I couldn't remember when I'd last eaten. It was just past noon; Julian was probably already at the tent, and Liz would be meeting us there at half-past one. There was a lot going on. Too much. In spite of the shower and Tom's help, I swayed on my feet.

"Sit down, wife," Tom ordered. "You haven't seen half of the stuff I got on my grocery-buying binge." He bustled me into a chair, then turned his attention back to his work. A copious white apron hugged his waist. He rinsed the brine from the chops, dried them, and set them aside. With studied purposefulness, he then washed his hands and proceeded to peel and halve an avocado. He filled both halves with chunks of cooked lobster. After drenching the whole thing with his homemade rémoulade sauce, he put two warm rolls next to his concoction, placed a fork, knife, and napkin on the table, and commanded me to eat.

He didn't have to tell me twice. Luxuriant lobster and creamy avocado robed in Tom's signature dressing made a perfect complement for the hot brioche rolls. For a few moments, I was able to forget that I had an event to cater that afternoon. Not only that, but it was the type of affair dreaded by all caterers—the outdoor picnic buffet. Why not just name the occasion Calling All Ants?

Tom stared into the refrigerator and read what I'd scribbled on the storage containers. "Pasta salad and these pies, plus greens for two salads?"

"Mmf," I said, my mouth full of avocado.

"I'll take that as a yes." Tom removed pans, bowls, and bags of ingredients, then set them on the counter and winked at me. "You don't mind if I pack the van, do you, Lobster Girl?"

"Mm—mmf."

He took that as a yes, too. Within half an hour, he had loaded everything, I had rinsed my plate, and we were almost ready to rock. While I printed out the sheets detailing the picnic prep schedule, Tom called Boyd, who was back at the department. On a whim, I ran up and grabbed Holly Kerr's old photo album, the one containing pictures of Arch as a baby. When I returned, Tom said Boyd didn't know any more about

Cecelia yet. But the Denver firearms examiner's report on my gun and the test for the bullets taken from John Richard was expected in a couple of hours. My heart plunged.

Tom thanked him and said that if the department needed him, he'd be with me. He'd drive his own sedan instead of accompanying me in the van, in case there was an emergency and he had to leave in a hurry.

"Which is unlikely," Tom commented when he'd hung up and we were heading to our vehicles. "The only departmental emergencies generated lately have *you* at the center of them. So I figure if I stick with my wife, I'll have a jump on everybody."

I shoved the photo album into the van and gave him a sour look. "Thanks a lot. You know how much I love being at the center of departmental emergencies." But he grinned widely, and again the jovial wisecracker I'd married seemed to be peeking out from the funk of the previous month.

Outside, the sunshine had completely dried all remnants of the hail. Spring—or the vestige of that season we see in the Rockies—had finally sprung. Our Alpine rosebushes' tight buds had opened into a cloud of creamy blossoms. Blue-button flax wavered on tall, sea-green stalks, and a profusion of chartreuse aspen leaves shone beside the jade green of new spruce growth. When a sudden breeze swished through the roses, a spill of petals floated downward, freckling the ground.

The *ground,* I thought miserably as Tom's sedan crunched through the gravel ravines made by the hail. The *ground* into which Cecelia Brisbane would soon be interred. And John Richard, too. I took a deep breath and made my way toward the van.

Driving up Main Street, I gripped the steering wheel so hard my hands became damp. With Tom, back at our house, I'd felt calm. Now my nerves were unraveling. I tried to distract myself by checking out the chattering tourists clogging the sidewalks. They ate taffy and popcorn, showed off their new Navajo turquoise jewelry, and asked for directions to the saloon, the sweatshirt store, and the art gallery. They were all oblivious to this morning's gruesome discovery. I stared ahead at Tom's sedan as we crested the road circling the lake.

A soft wind ruffled the water. On the far bank, six sheriff's-department cars were parked, lights flashing. Uniformed officers waved away the crowd of spectators as others combed the area where the tow truck had been.

My cell phone's *brat-brat* brought me back to life.

"Goldy?"

I did not immediately recognize the female voice, and hesitated a moment.

"Goldy? It's Holly Kerr."

I was so out of it that it took me a minute to realize that Holly, my catering client from Tuesday's lunch, was the same kind, wealthy woman I'd just visited yesterday and seen at that morning's committee breakfast. I said, "Yes?"

"I don't mean to bother you," she apologized, "but I have something to show you. Photographs from Albert's memorial luncheon. You said you were interested in seeing them."

"Of course, yes, please." I pulled the van into the Roundhouse parking lot. At the tent, Liz and Julian were directing volunteers setting up chairs. I couldn't see where Tom had gone.

"One of the guests took a whole roll," Holly went on, "then had the pictures developed overnight. I can bring them to the picnic, if you want."

"Oh please, yes. If you could come twenty minutes or so before the picnic begins . . ." I didn't finish my sentence. Where had Tom gotten to?

Holly murmured something about wanting to help and signed off. So now I was going to get some photos from Tuesday's lunch, and they might answer some questions, such as, who had sabotaged my food and attacked me that morning. Or if Bobby Calhoun, dressed as Elvis or as himself, had been present.

I finally saw Tom striding, head down, to the edge of the Roundhouse property. He put his hands in his pockets and gazed at the cops combing the scene where Cecelia's car had been recovered. I suddenly realized I had more to worry about than some pictures.

Tom's case that had been thrown out of court had been a drowning. Someone had intentionally, brutally held a young woman under water until she stopped struggling. Was Tom staring at the investigation on the far side of the lake and getting that distant look in his eyes—a look I'd seen far too much of lately—because he was reliving that final, astonishing day in court, when a witness had changed his testimony?

I wanted so much to take care of Tom, to reciprocate the affection and support that he'd lavished on Arch and me from the moment his big body and bigger spirit had swaggered into our lives. But would I really be able to help him? So far, I had no clue.

I threw the van's gear into Park and fought a wave of nausea. I did have a slew of my own problems. I didn't know how much time I had to try to figure out who had attacked me or killed John Richard. If the firearms examiner's report was due that afternoon, then the sheriff's department was bound to have obtained the results of the gunshot-residue test. Something congealed in my abdomen as I wondered how much trouble I was going to get into for not reporting the theft of my gun. And what if the bullets the coroner took from John Richard had come from my thirty-eight? I rubbed my eyes.

Too many questions, and no good answers. If all of the firearms tests pointed to my firing my own weapon into John Richard, then charges would probably be filed against me that afternoon. Suddenly the future looked darker and murkier than Aspen Meadow Lake.

Tom rapped on my window and I jumped. I hadn't even seen him come over.

"You all right?" he called through the glass.

"Fine," I replied. Then I stared into his eyes, searching. How about you? I wanted to ask him. Are *you* all right?

I rubbed my cheeks to try to get my circulation going. Then I jumped from the van and resolutely put my mind into catering gear. Work, action, moving forward: All these were the antidote for stress, depression, and a host of other ills, right? Tom and I both needed to get cracking.

The Southwest Hospital Women's Auxiliary and friends of Nurse Nan Watkins swarmed across the rutted parking lot and toward the bright white tent. They bore table linens, flower arrangements, baskets, bags, and boxes, all bulging with the flatware, china, glasses, and other odds and ends they'd insisted on providing. Two separate groups of volunteers were slowly hauling a pair of bulletin boards toward the speaker's podium.

I tried not to think that this might be my retirement party, too.

Soon I was loading Tom's outstretched arms with containers of pork chops. I balanced the containers of salad and followed him toward the Roundhouse kitchen. My eyes involuntarily wandered back to the sheriff's-department cars. Would they be done before the picnic started? I certainly hoped so.

Tom stopped short, and I almost crashed into him. "Tom." I rebalanced my load and moved to his side. "Tell me what's going on."

He lifted his chin. "Over there." His voice was matter-of-fact. "It's a possible crime scene. That's why they're taking their time." Of course, as much as I wanted to know what was going on *over there,* I wanted to know even more what was going on *over here,* with *him.* Oblivious, Tom mused: "Problem is, between fishermen and the joggers, any evidence of what happened is probably either contaminated or gone."

I shifted my grip on the pans. "Tom—"

His voice was deadpan, faraway. "Once they get the car down to the department, they'll extract the corpse before sending it to the M.E. The rest will go to the crime lab."

"Please—"

Tom shrugged, hoisted up his load, and resumed shuffling toward the kitchen. Without looking back, Tom said, "That's their job."

"Stop for a sec," I said, my voice low.

He turned and gave me a look of annoyance. "Didn't you tell me we had all kinds of work to do?"

Hearing our voices, Julian and Liz tumbled out of the kitchen. Julian, clad in a chic gray catering suit, wore a gray apron around his slim waist. A red neckerchief gave him the look of a real chef. Liz's spill of silver jewelry sparkled in the sunlight as she hurried toward me, a look of motherly concern on her slender face. The cops had come over to tell them they were closing down the lake's paddle- and sailboat rental, and cordoning off the lake path. Any curious picnickers from our event were to stay put. The cops had refused to tell Julian and Liz exactly what they were doing with their truck and personnel. Undaunted, Liz had called a friend of hers who lived by the lake and heard the whole story.

"Oh my God, Goldy," she began, "that poor woman. First her husband kills himself, and now this." She awkwardly tried to hug me around the pans I was carrying. The sharp smell of her cologne made me dizzy. Maybe I wasn't doing as well as I thought I was.

"It's gruesome," I agreed, and gently pulled away from her.

"Let Liz and me do the picnic," Julian offered. He scanned my face. "Go home, boss. You look exhausted. When Boyd gave me the keys, he told me the breakfast this morning was like a comedy made in hell. Tom," he began, looking for support. But one glance at the vacant look in Tom's eyes made him realize that my husband wasn't bucking up as I'd hoped.

"We're *fine*," I told them. "Stop fretting, will you? Now help us get this food going, okay?"

And so our team forged ahead. Julian and Liz tucked chilled foods into the walk-in and searched the cabinets for serving dishes. Tom preheated the ovens and clattered pans onto the stovetop. I pulled out my printed sheets and scanned the prep schedule. The first order of business was checking on the setup inside the tent.

There, all was activity. Volunteers worked feverishly, festooning the bulletin boards that they'd finally managed to set up beside the podium. Foil letters screaming "Happy Retirement!" and "We'll Miss You!" fluttered in the breeze. When I arrived beside the crookedly placed buffet tables, the auxiliary was pinning up photos and cards to commemorate Nan's twenty-five years at Southwest Hospital.

I requisitioned a volunteer to help me straighten the tables, and was unfurling a tablecloth when Holly Kerr arrived—early, as promised. After the horrid PosteriTREE meeting, she must have gone home, showered—to wash off the residue of the women's hostility—and changed her clothes. Now she was wearing a beige linen pantsuit accented with pearls, probably an outfit she'd worn often when Albert was a pastor and she was the dutiful pastor's wife. Oh well, you can take the girl out of the church, but you can't take the church out of the girl. Holly seemed as disappointed by all the women wearing jeans as she was sorry that I was too busy to visit with her just then. But the countdown to when we'd promised food service was fast approaching. I enthusiastically thanked her, slipped the envelope of photos from Tuesday's lunch into my apron pocket, and promised to chat with her about them later.

When I'd finished overseeing the setup in the tent, Marla's big Mercedes roared into the Roundhouse lot. I checked my watch, then slipped back inside and helped Liz unpack the strawberry pies. Within moments, Marla, who had changed into a spangled pantsuit, burst into the kitchen.

"Ooh, pie!" she cried. "Let's do that eat-dessert-first thing. Where are the plates and forks?" She began clattering through the cupboards until she found a plate and a fork. "Where's that damn pie server?" She looked at me expectantly, then lowered her voice. "I want to have a piece of pie while I tell you about the rumor I heard that Talitha Vikarios had an affair with Albert Kerr. I wish I had some idea of who this girl is—"

I said, "Some idea of . . . wait a minute." While Liz sliced a piece of pie for Marla, I ran out to my van and nabbed Holly's old album. When I returned, Marla was in the Roundhouse's empty dining room merrily digging into her jumbo slice of pie. I sat down beside her and opened the album.

"Remember this young woman?" I demanded, pointing to the photo of Talitha Vikarios in her candy-striper uniform.

She put down her plate and fork and stared at the picture. "Oh, right. *Her.* Sweet girl, Talitha. I *did* hear she slept with *Albert Kerr.* Apparently Holly was desperate to break up the affair, and that's why they left for England. I mean, we have seminaries here in the United States, don't we? Why go to England?"

"Albert Kerr, huh?" I examined the picture again: the buoyant young candy striper, baby Arch, John Richard, tall, Abraham Lincolnesque Ted Vikarios, and bald, grinning Albert Kerr. "I can't believe it."

Marla finished her pie and put down her fork. "I told you it was a *rumor.*"

"From your vast knowledge of John Richard's sexual conquests, do you know if Talitha might have been one of them?" I asked.

Marla said, "She's not in the data bank."

I snorted. "You and your data bank. Okay, now check these out with me." I put away Holly's album, pulled out the new batch she'd just given me, and laid them out on the adjoining table. "These are from Tuesday's funeral lunch. Anything jump out at you? My theory is that *somewhere* in here is the person who attacked me and killed our ex."

"So you don't like my Courtney MacEwan–Roger Mannis theory?"

"I like it. Just look at the pictures, will you?"

Marla sighed. But she was full of pie, so she didn't complain.

We pored over the glossy shots of Tuesday's event. There were Ted and Ginger Vikarios, Ted looking tipsy, Ginger forcing a smile. Holly Kerr appeared serene beside her church friends. Courtney, her figure shown off to advantage by her hands on her hips, stared in the direction of John Richard and Sandee. Her facial expression could have had the caption "Woman Chewing a Lemon." Lana Della Robbia and her sidekick Dannyboy laughed at somebody's joke.

"Hold on," I said, grabbing the photo with the laughing Lana and Dannyboy. Behind them, a man huddled beside the window.

"Who's he?" Marla asked.

"I think it's our Elvis impersonator! Bobby Calhoun, Sandee's boyfriend." Marla stared at the picture with me. "So," I went on, "he *was* there. I can't believe it! Maybe he's the one who trashed my food and chucked me into the ground."

"But why would he do that?"

I looked at her. "All right, think. If you're dying of jealousy, and you're going to kill the new boyfriend of your girlfriend, how do you set it up? Maybe you want to make it look as if it's the ex-wife of your girlfriend's new boyfriend."

"Hold on, I'm having a sugar rush." Marla closed her eyes, then opened them. "So you're saying Bobby trashed your place and chopped you in the neck so *you'd* have a motive to be pissed off with the Jerk?"

"Exactly."

"And why did he come to the lunch?"

I said, "My guess is that he followed Sandee everywhere. You remember how nervous she was at the strip club. And also, if Bobby's at the lunch, then he looks for an opportunity to go through my van, so he can steal something to drop at the scene. Imagine his delight when he found my gun."

"Uh-huh. And the reason he stole your kitchen shears?"

I tilted my head and blew air in the direction of the log ceiling. "Maybe he always wanted to be a barber."

"When all else fails, there's always wild speculation!" Marla said brightly. "Think we'll have this figured out by the time the picnic begins?"

"All right, I guess I should go work," I said, picking up the photos and the album. Marla snagged her dish and wiggled her hips as she sashayed out of the dining room ahead of me. The white spangles on her pantsuit glittered in the sunlight. Then she stopped abruptly and glanced back. "Goldy? Are you sure you're all right? You look bad."

"I'm fine," I lied, and followed her into the kitchen.

Marla left to see if she could find some old friends. I resolved to put the Jerk, Cecelia, and everything else associated with this frightful week out of my head. For the next half hour, Liz and I worked side by side, drizzling balsamic vinaigrette over the chops. The brining gave the pork its butterlike texture; the vinaigrette gave each bite a zingy taste of herbs. When we finished with the meat, I moved on to arranging the salad in lettuce-lined bowls while Liz whisked the dressing. After putting the last touches on the salad bowls, I washed my hands one last time. The thought of the medical examiner washing her hands before doing the autopsy on Cecelia Brisbane made me suddenly dizzy. What if Cecelia had been killed by John Richard's murderer, because of what she knew about the Jerk? I told myself to *stop thinking like this,* and picked up a carton of wine bottles. Then I turned to go back to the kitchen and ran right into Liz and her gallon of salad dressing. The resulting spew of oil, vinegar, herbs, and cuss words would have gotten me forever expelled from the Sunday School Teachers Association. Luckily, the vinaigrette missed my uniform. This was a good thing because I didn't have any more clean ones.

I helped Liz clean up and make a second gallon of dressing while Julian and Tom cooked the chops. Finally, it was time to haul the food out to the buffet. Taking care to give each other a wide berth, Liz, Julian, Tom, and I conveyed the chops, salads, and rolls to their long tables. I greeted old friends, answered questions about "dear Arch," and ducked queries regarding the sheriff's-department investigation into John Richard's death. Julian and Liz—sporting a clean pair of dressing-free pants from her car—guided the revelers down four lines for the buffet. The partygoers seemed both hungry and interested in the police work across the lake. But once they'd filled their plates with food and the speeches started, they focused on the matters at hand. Thank God.

Julian, Liz, and I were mercifully not expected to listen to the tributes. We moved between tables smoothly serving drinks and clearing plates, and eventually, serving thick wedges of strawberry pie topped with vanilla ice cream. To the unlucky few who were allergic to strawberries, we offered large bowls of ice cream.

When the last speech was done and the partygoers were heading toward their cars, Nan Watkins came over to thank me. Holly Kerr, patting her wiry gray hair, accompanied her. They were both beaming.

"That was splendid," Holly enthused. She'd clearly recovered from the committee breakfast, which relieved me. "How could you do three magnificent events in one week? You are a marvel."

"Really superb," Nan echoed. The dark eyes in her round chipmunk face had become brightened by several glasses of wine. "I'm going to be walking off this food for the rest of the summer. It was great."

"I'm glad you had fun," I replied.

Nan's voice cracked. "To see so many people, to have such lovely food, to have your staff serve so smoothly . . . it's just, well . . . how can I thank you?"

Lucky for me, I didn't believe in rhetorical questions. I said, "Well, would you look at something for me?"

Nan, taken aback, said that of course she would. I was not prepared, however, for Holly to follow her into the Roundhouse dining room. I made the split-second decision to open up the photo album anyway. It was Holly's album, in any event. The three of us walked to the wooden table holding the book of photos.

"See this picture of Talitha Vikarios?" I asked innocently. "From the old days?" With my free hand, I pointed to the candy striper holding Arch. "Did she have any dealings with John Richard?" I asked. "Did she have a negative encounter with my ex-husband?" If so, I was thinking, could *that* explain the fight that the Jerk and Ted had outside the Roundhouse Tuesday afternoon?

"Don't!" exclaimed Holly Kerr. To my surprise, she

whirled and walked away so quickly, I didn't have a chance to say anything. What was going on here? She was the one who'd *given* me these photos. Then again, maybe the rumor Marla had heard, about Talitha being involved with Albert Kerr, was true.

"What was that about?" I asked Nan as I watched Holly rush to her car. I turned back to Nan, whose face was studiously blank. "Nan? What is it?"

"I really shouldn't—"

Okay, now I was getting upset. "Can't you please help me figure out who killed John Richard? So I can get out of being a suspect?"

"Talitha Vikarios is dead." Nan's voice was matter-of-fact. "She was killed in a car accident in Utah last month." Nan clamped her chipmunk mouth shut; her eyes darted in all directions. She either wanted someone to rescue her, or she wanted to make sure no one was listening to us. She said, "The Vikarioses have suffered so much. Ginger still can't stop crying."

"I know. I saw her weeping in her car," I replied. "But I'm suffering, too. Did my ex-husband hurt this young woman? Did he have an affair with her and dump her?"

Nan's expression turned sad. "Oh, Goldy. I *don't* want to revisit the Talitha mess. I *don't* want Ginger and Ted to suffer."

"Nan," I said. "Could you just please tell me Talitha's history?"

Nan's small eyes got a faraway look. "Tal, that's what we called her. Rhymes with *Al*. She . . . left the hospital and virtually disappeared. Her parents said she was doing missionary work as a field nurse, but really, they had no idea where she'd gone. I used to correspond with her, in secret." Nan's small red tongue darted out to lick her lips. "Tal . . . was pregnant with Albert Kerr's child. The Kerrs had already left for England, and Tal had resolved not to make trouble for them." Nan sighed. "But when the Denver newspapers discovered Talitha and her son, she *did* tell her parents about Albert Kerr. Ginger and Ted contacted Albert and Holly, of course. A lot of people said they had a long-distance falling-out, but I don't know how true that is. And then Albert got cancer, so . . ."

"Did Albert admit fathering the child?"

Nan looked suddenly weary. "I don't know. But all of a sudden, Ted and Ginger Vikarios had money again. They moved from Colorado Springs back to Aspen Meadow this year. They bought a condo, they bought an SUV, they began eating out in new clothes, and they became members of the country club. And most weirdly, they were all reconciled. The Kerrs and Vikarioses became friends again."

"Friends? After the Vikarios *Victory over Sin* empire had been ruined?"

Nan shrugged her rounded shoulders. "If it looks like a payoff and smells like a payoff, maybe it *is* a payoff."

"A payoff—" I began, but was interrupted.

Liz and Julian had walked up to us and now stood side by side at one of the dining-room tables. They both looked extremely uncomfortable.

I turned my attention away from Nan. "What? The tent's coming loose from its moorings?"

Liz and Julian looked at each other, as if each was afraid to tell me the news. Liz pressed her lips together and stared at the ground. Julian blinked. Nan, suddenly curious, seemed to enjoy my being in suspense.

I flipped the photo album closed. Tears stung my

eyes as I faced Julian. "Something's happened to Arch?"

"No, boss," he replied, his voice quiet. "Just . . . don't worry about cleaning up from the picnic. Liz and I can do it." He cleared his throat. "The problem is that—"

But he was spared being the bearer of news. From the corner of my eye, I caught Detective Blackridge entering the dining room. My skin went colder than the inside of our freezer.

"What the hell—" I began.

"Mrs. Schulz?" asked Blackridge as he walked up. "You need to come with me."

Chapter 17

I glared at him. The detective didn't back down. I said,
"Forget it."

"Mrs. Schulz, please." Was that a hint of entreaty in
Blackridge's voice?

I turned to Julian. "Where's Tom?"

"We don't need Investigator Schulz," Blackridge interjected. "Just you."

I gave him as scathing a look as a woman scared out
of her wits could summon on short notice. Nan, meanwhile, scuttled off. I turned back to my assistants. To
Julian, I said in a low voice, "Could you please find
Tom and tell him I need him?"

Julian nodded and took off in the direction of the
kitchen. I addressed Liz. "Would you be willing to call
Brewster Motley? He's my attorney, and he's in the
phone book. If at all possible, I need him to meet me
down at the sheriff's department."

"I'm not taking you to the department." Blackridge
again.

"*You're* not taking me *anywhere*."

Liz took my cold hand in her warm one. "Goldy. He

says he's *not* here to arrest you. He just needs to talk to you."

Perspiration trickled inside my uniform. "I don't *think* so." Unfortunately, I knew all about how cops were allowed to deceive suspects to get the truth out of them. And of course I applauded the practice when law enforcement was dealing with a real criminal. But this was not one of those times.

"Let Julian and me clean up here. Please, Goldy, it's okay."

"Thanks, Liz, but it is *not* okay. Not two times in one week." I turned to Blackridge. "If you just want to have a conversation, what's wrong with the telephone?"

Blackridge closed his eyes. Then he rubbed his forehead and let out a huge sigh. *Women!* Finally he said, "Should we start over here?"

"Thank you, but I don't want to." If I was trying to teach Arch to be more polite, I needed to set the same standard for myself, right? And I recognized, belatedly, that I hadn't been exactly civil to this detective. On the other hand, we had a history, and not a happy one. "Sorry, but I need to finish up here, and I have my family to take care of."

Blackridge turned abruptly as Tom strode into the dining room. I could sense the difference in Blackridge immediately: a deferential attitude, and something like relief. And did I see in my husband's rapid walk, lifted chin, and commanding presence a hint of his old confident-investigator self? Relief surged through me, too.

"Schulz," Blackridge said under his breath. He moved off to confer with Tom, out of earshot.

My cell phone chirped. "Mom?" The connection was weak, and I could barely make out Arch's crackly voice. Even so, I was sure I detected a note of fear in his voice. "There are a couple of cops here at Todd's. They want me to . . ." His words dissolved in a storm of static.

"What? Arch? *Arch!*" The cell phone was silent.

Tom left Blackridge and approached me. "They need Arch's and your help." A note of authority underlay his soothing voice, and this made me uneasy. "You don't have to go with them, and neither does he. But I think it would be a good idea."

"They need our help for *what*, Tom?" My voice cracked.

My husband's handsome face softened. "First, you need to know that the firearms test came back. Korman wasn't killed with bullets from your thirty-eight. They're from a twenty-two-caliber Ruger."

"How comforting. So my gun was just dropped by his body?"

"Apparently."

"Then am I cleared?"

Tom's green eyes sifted through the gaggle of departing women outside. "Not totally."

"Tom!"

His mouth turned down at the edges as he returned my gaze. "The GSR test on your hands came back positive. Your weapon was found at the scene. They *can't* clear you yet."

"So their theory is that I used a twenty-two to kill him, but dropped my thirty-eight there because I'm terminally stupid?"

Blackridge coughed, as in *hurry up.*

Tom took my hand. "They're hoping you'll go with them to Korman's house now. If you want, you can give permission for Arch to be taken there—"

"John Richard's *house*?"

Tom paused. "Two men showed up at Korman's house a few hours ago. A neighbor thought they were investigators. But everyone over in the country-club area is so skittish now, the neighbor called the department to be sure. Our crime-scene guys pulled up stakes yesterday, so the department dispatched a car to investigate. By the time our deputies got there, the place had been ransacked. The pair of vandals making the mess had taken off." Tom sighed. "But they weren't just vandals. They were looking for something."

"Besides money-laundering, what was John Richard up to?" I shook my head. "I mean, it must have been something *big*."

"Our guys don't think the murder was a professional hit. Still, they have to try to figure out if the vandals took anything, and if they did, what it was."

"Tom, please! I haven't spent any *time* in that house."

"No, but Arch has." I snorted, but Tom went on: "Sandee the stripper can't leave the Rainbow now to help them out. This afternoon, she's dancing or whatever it is she does. So our guys are looking to Arch and you. And, since Arch is a minor, you have to be there."

Desperation rose in my throat. "I don't want Arch to have to look at his dead father's house, especially if it's been trashed. It could be too much trauma for him to absorb."

Tom put his arm around me. "Why don't we go outside?" He held up his hand to Blackridge, indicating that he didn't want us to be bothered.

Outside, I said, "I don't know, Tom."

He held me tight. "I understand. Whether you two do

this or not is up to you. I'm not going to pressure you, don't worry. You're the mom."

A sudden breeze washed down from the pines above the golf course, bringing the scent of smoke. Despite the recent hailstorm, the second forest fire the women had mentioned at that morning's breakfast seemed to be gaining. Fear lurched around in my chest: fear of fire, fear for Arch again being overwhelmed by grief. And something else: I was afraid to go into John Richard's rental house. Tom always said he could pick up the emotions of a homicide victim at the scene: the panic, the terror. I was worried for Arch, yes. I was also worried about myself.

"Tom, are you sure they don't suspect me of breaking in?"

"You're not two guys."

"Right." Still, I hesitated. My interrogation at the department had been no fun. The visit from Blackridge, when I'd given him the letter Cecelia had mailed me, had been very much less than delightful. "You're sure this isn't a trap? Blackridge trying to get me to say something incriminating? 'Whoops! There's my butcher knife I dropped here, too!'"

Tom shook his head. "He pulls that kind of stunt, he knows I'll make his life hell."

As if on cue, Blackridge approached us. "Mrs. Schulz, please," he begged. "Your ex-husband's place is a wreck. If we can develop leads from the scene, we'll have a much better chance of closing this case."

"I want to talk to my son first. This might be too hard for him. If he doesn't want to go into his father's house, I'm not going to make him." I softened my tone. "You do understand, don't you?"

Blackridge pursed his lips and nodded.

"And I want my lawyer there," I added.

"We already called him." Blackridge seemed eager to please, like a puppy dog that's pooped inside and now wants to be pals. "Motley's meeting us at Korman's house," he added.

"All right," I said. "Just a minute." I checked the tent. A few stragglers were disassembling the center-pieces and helping pick up trash. When I got back to the parking lot, I said, "I want to go over there in my own van. If I go in a police car, everyone will think I've been arrested."

"Suit yourself," Blackridge replied.

Tom promised to stay with Julian and Liz until the picnic detritus was cleared and Front Range Rentals had taken down the tent. I climbed into my van, followed Blackridge's sedan through the clot of departing cars, and gunned the accelerator toward Aspen Meadow Country Club.

Again the smoky wind whipped down from the mountains. Fluffs of dandelion and cottonwood scattered from the road and rolled into a ditch. Dust slammed my windshield, just like on Tuesday afternoon, the last time I'd ventured to John Richard's house. I took a deep breath and inhaled more smoke.

Just before we turned into the Aspen Meadow Country Club area, my tires chewed into a mound of dirt that had washed onto the highway from a house-construction site. I cursed and hit the brakes, then noticed a group of women ranged on a deck overlooking the club entrance. They were pointing first to Blackridge's police car, then to my van. They were talking excitedly. Neighborhood watch? Or neighborhood gossips, who'd be paid twenty-five dollars by the *Mountain Journal* for a news tip? In the absence of Cecelia, folks' desire for dirty laundry was still unquenchable. And the *last* thing I wanted was to face more reporters at John Richard's house.

No other vehicles awaited us in the Stoneberry cul-de-sac. Blackridge signaled for me to park. I pulled into another mound of shiny grit that had washed onto the street. I cut the engine and stared at the street, where glimmering pebbles speckled the drying mud. A fresh wave of dizziness assaulted me. Well, I was most assuredly not going to just sit in my vehicle getting anxious for Arch to arrive. I picked up the cell and dialed Tom.

"The team from the rental company is just starting on the tent," he informed me. "How are you doing?"

"I'm seeing spots in front of my eyes, so I'm not doing so hot. Speaking of which, have you heard anything about this new fire? I know it's up in the wildlife preserve."

"It's already covered a thousand acres, and they have zero containment." He yelled directions to somebody who'd called to him, then came back. "I heard something else, though." My heart plummeted as I imagined the gossips calling the newspaper, the newspaper calling the department, and everyone wanting to know what was going on at Dr. Korman's house. "It's about the bullets," Tom said, his voice terse. "The firearms examiner thought he recognized them from another homicide in Denver. They're doing the tests now."

I blinked. "*What?* A criminal who killed someone in Denver might have also shot John Richard? Have they solved the other homicide?" I looked up the driveway to John Richard's rental and wondered, *Who shot you? What were you doing? Would you not give them what they wanted?*

"They haven't solved the other case. But they're looking for connections. Look, I gotta go help these people, the wind is making their job tough."

The call waiting beeped, so I signed off. I hoped it would be Arch. To my dismay, the caller ID read "*Rainbow Men's Club.*" Just what I needed.

"Hello, Goldy? It's Sandee. Whatcha doin'?"

"Not much, Sandee. What are *you* doing?"

She giggled. "Gettin' ready to take my clothes off. Listen, your friend Marla called me. She wanted to give me a ride to, you know, John Richard's funeral tomorrow. My boyfriend's, like, jealous, and I'm afraid to just leave. If I tell him I'm going to a church meeting with a friend, that ought to work."

"Sandee." My voice faltered. I wanted to scream, *If you would just tell him the truth? Maybe ya'd get along better with him?* "Sandee . . . I know he's the jealous type. He beat up that bald guy who was paying attention to you in the club."

"Whoops!" Her voice sounded gleeful.

"And he was watching you and John Richard at Dr. Kerr's funeral lunch on Tuesday."

"He *wuz*? That prick!"

"So," I said with as much calm as I could muster, "what do you suppose the chances are that Bobby followed the two of you back to John Richard's house and then Bobby shot John Richard?"

"Gosh, I don't know!"

"Sandee! Does your boyfriend own a gun?"

"He used to. But he lost it."

Wait a minute. "What kind of gun did he lose, Sandee?"

"Ruger? Does that sound right?"

"What caliber was the Ruger?"

"Isn't Kaliber a beer?"

"When did he lose the gun?"

"I *don't know.*"

"When did he *say* he lost it?"

She sighed. "I mean it. I don't know. His elevator doesn't exactly go to the top floor, ya know?"

"Where is he now?"

"Now?"

I rubbed my forehead. Talking to an *actual* parrot would have been easier. What had John Richard seen in her? Not her brains, clearly. "Yes, Sandee," I replied. *"Now."*

"Practicing with the band? At the house? They're going on tour next week. Well, I keep telling him, this isn't really a tour, man—"

"Where's the house, Sandee?"

"What house?"

"The house where Bobby is practicing."

"Oh, 2468 Ponderosa Pass. He won't let me practice with them. If he's so jealous, I keep asking him, how come he won't take me with them? You know, Nashville Bobby and the Boys, Plus the Girl with the Boobs? But *he* says—"

Blackridge knocked on my window and I flinched.

"I have to go, Sandee."

"Wait a sec! So did they get to Dr. Korman's house? Tell those cops I want my stuff back!"

I signed off and rolled down the window.

Blackridge said, "We've got a team canvassing the neighbors, seeing if anyone caught a better look at the two guys who made the mess inside. Also, your son will be here shortly."

"Wait. You know Sandee Blue, the stripper? She just called me." Blackridge's face became impassive, so I rushed on: "She just told me her jealous boyfriend Bobby had a Ruger, and supposedly lost it."

"You and Sandee talk about weapons?" Blackridge asked.

I flushed. "Not really. I just thought I should pass on what she said." I gave him the address on Ponderosa Pass while he scribbled.

"Got it, Mrs. Schulz. This is *very* interesting. Thanks." Was that a *wee* crack in Blackridge's attitude toward me?

"What about the strip club Sandee works at?" I asked. I had to be careful, because I didn't want to press my luck with Blackridge, and I certainly didn't want to give away Marla's and my visit to the Rainbow. "Did you ever link that club to anything?"

"Not yet," he said. To my astonishment, Blackridge actually smiled at me before sauntering back to his vehicle.

I rolled the window back up and stared out at the gleaming gravel. Then I nabbed my cell and punched in the *Mountain Journal* office. It was past five, the sun was sliding toward the western mountains, and it was unlikely anyone would be there. But I was so used to Frances Markasian calling and demanding information that I thought it was time to give her—or her voice mail—a bit of her own medicine. And anyway, I couldn't bear to sit in this van and worry about Bobby Calhoun and his gun.

"Markasian," she answered.

I smiled in spite of myself. "Ask not what Goldy can do for you," I said. "Ask what you can do for—"

"Cut the crap, Goldy. I don't know what happened to Cecelia Brisbane."

"But you've got a theory, surely."

"Don't call me Shirley. Hold on a sec."

I sighed and looked out the window. The moon, a large, pale disk in the blue haze, was rising in the east. Birds still chirped in the trees, a sure sign we were a long way from the dark of night. I knew I shouldn't keep looking up at John Richard's house, but I did anyway. What did I feel? Nothing. Maybe that was denial. I knew guilt was hovering, waiting to pounce, but I wasn't feeling it at the moment. How many times had I wished him dead? Uncountable. But I was feeling neither guilt nor joy. Really, what I felt was numb. I shook my head in disbelief. *He's gone.*

And what had been going on with him, anyway? I didn't just mean with whatever crime or cruelty had gotten him whacked. I meant in general. So charming and yet so mean, he had been a conundrum. And now I was on the phone with a reporter—a sometime friend whose nutty intensity had driven me batty more than once—because I just couldn't understand John Richard, in life or in death. Worse, his murder had severely strained my relationship with my son. Maybe when this crime was solved, I'd be able to feel again. Maybe I'd be able to live again. Maybe.

"Goldy? You there? Sorry 'bout that. They've got a fire up in the preserve."

"I know, I heard. How big is it now?"

"Eleven hundred acres. They think it'll be contained by morning." She sighed. "I still don't know anything about Cecelia. Can you tell *me* something?"

"I wish I could. But she turned up dead just a couple of days after I found my dead ex-husband. Can't you give me some help? Any help? Please?"

"You think the two deaths are connected?"

"*I don't know.* It's just that having the two occur so close together is more than weird."

"Have you got anything to trade for it?"

I took a deep breath. Was it worth it? I had to take the risk. "I'll tell you, but you absolutely, positively cannot come over here now."

"Where's *here*?"

"Do we have a deal?"

"Yeah. Spill."

"John Richard's house was broken into this afternoon. Ransacked. The cops have got me over here now to go through it, see if anything is missing." I omitted any mention of Arch.

"Holy cow. When can I come over?"

"You can't. Just start bugging the cops in about two hours with your 'Do you confirm or deny' questions. If you're pressed, say a neighbor phoned you. Now tell me what you know."

"Okay, Goldy. Thanks for the tip. First of all, Cecelia Brisbane was extremely unhappy—"

"Do you think she committed suicide?"

Frances paused. "It's possible. But I wasn't picking up on her being depressed after the death of Walter. But lately, I couldn't say."

"Is this in code? What are you talking about?"

"What I tell you absolutely goes no further than this phone call." I grunted assent, and she went on: "Walter Brisbane was charming to everyone on the outside and a tyrannical boss, Goldy. I mean, the man was a nut. He yelled at Cecelia and treated her like dirt on the floor. After he committed suicide, she seemed to be okay for a while. Then lately she'd gone into a funk. I couldn't understand it, because everyone was complimenting her on that photo in the library, her daughter doing her patriotic duty in the armed services, that kind of thing. Cecelia would glow for a while, and then slump."

I said, "Do you know this daughter?"

"Alex? No. She's a naval officer. Cecelia said Alex's ship was doing exercises with the Greek navy off Piraeus." Frances inhaled. "You're going to tell me anything you learn about Korman, right? And you won't breathe a word of *this* until I've got it nailed down."

"Okay, okay. But I need to know if any of *this* involved John Richard."

"I don't know who it involves, yet. When I told you I didn't know what happened to *Cecelia,* I wasn't telling you the whole story. What do you think drove Walter to suicide?"

Brewster Motley's Mercedes pulled into the cul-de-sac. The sun winked off his windshield. I could just make out his blond head, nodding as he talked into a cell phone. Arch was supposed to be here five minutes ago.

"I need you to cut to the chase, Frances."

She lowered her voice. "I'm not sure about why, out of the blue, Walter packed it in. But my theory is that somebody threatened to expose him. You know that pay-phone call that preceded his death? They never figured out who it was from or what was said. Cecelia has been fine for all these years since he died, and then in May she started getting really, really depressed when she was at her desk. She'd put on a good face when she was in public, then come back here and go into a funk. I mean, as in, she'd learned who killed Kennedy and couldn't tell anybody and couldn't put it in the paper."

"And?"

"And I talked to her neighbor, Sherry Boone."

"Oh, God, Frances."

"Check this out, then. My theory was that old ghosts had suddenly come up in Cecelia's mind, and she was obsessed with whatever was bothering her." Frances paused. "In May, Cecelia broke down to Sherry Boone. Cecelia sobbed that her daughter, Alex, had claimed since age ten that her father had been having sex with her. Cecelia cried to Sherry that she hadn't believed a word of her daughter's story. But after Alex finished high school, when she left and wouldn't come back, Mother Cecelia began to wonder."

My hand gripping the phone went cold. "So you're saying Cecelia didn't know what was going on in her own house while Alex was growing up?"

Frances's voice was strained. "Do mothers ever know? Do mothers ever *not* know? You're the one with the degree in psychology."

I glanced at the clock. Brewster was still on the phone, and no cop was coming to fetch me. "So Cecelia was all happy because people were praising her for a daughter doing her patriotic duty. But this same daughter had been sexually violated by her father. And she was depressed because she was finally facing the truth. So . . . how and why did Cecelia die?"

"That's what I'm looking into now. When Cecelia did columns, she kept notes. Naturally, the cops took her computer and files. But when the news raced up here that it was Cecelia's body in the lake, I scooted over to her desk. By the time the sheriff's department arrived, I'd nabbed her disks. They weren't password protected, so I printed everything out."

"Frances—"

"How did you think I was going to get material for this story?" she protested. "After Cecelia got interested in something and did background research, she'd write up a bunch of questions that might get answered in a column. Like with your hubby and Courtney—"

"*Ex*-hubby."

"Yeah, well. Cecelia was poking into that tennis-and-golf tournament at the club, the one that's taking place today and tomorrow? She wanted to know who had paid for what in the sponsorship, and Korman's motive for putting up all that dough. Your *ex*-hubby was notoriously cheap with money, apparently."

"Tell me something I don't know. And his motive for the sponsorship was . . . ?"

"Dr. John Richard Korman was making his second debut into society," Frances announced dramatically. "On the tail of Courtney MacEwan. Or at least, on the tail of her tennis dress." Frances shuffled through some papers. "Here are the other things she was working on. 'A firing at the fire department.'" More shuffling. "'Teachers are starving and it has nothing to do with school cafeterias.' Here's something up your alley: 'Health inspector Roger Mannis—being paid off to create trouble?'"

"Did she have any research on that one?" I asked sharply. Behind me, a black-and-white was pulling up.

"Nope, sorry, or at least not on the disk I down-loaded. Here's her last note to herself. 'Hypocrisy? Look more closely at Vikarioses.'"

I drummed my fingers on the dashboard. "Is that about the money John Richard supposedly stole? You know, your theory on the down payment on our house? That he supposedly didn't repay?"

"No, no, no. I was wrong on that. Your ex got the money from his father, not the Vikarioses. I've got a source at the bank, and she looked up the old check."

I exhaled in relief. I *knew* Frances had been wrong. If John Richard stiffed somebody, he always crowed about it, then claimed he'd been justified. "So who called you with an anonymous tip with the claim about the fifty Gs coming from Ted Vikarios, and him demanding it back?"

"I don't know. It was just a woman's voice on my voice mail. Not only do I not know, it looks as if Cecelia didn't know anything about it, either."

The patrol car behind me flashed its lights. I was desperate to know if Cecelia had left any notes about the supposed rape. But I didn't want Frances looking into another allegation, especially since the cops were supposedly working on it. Beside the curb, Arch was looking around, his expression wary. "I need to hop," I told Frances.

"I want to know what's missing from Korman's house!"

"I *promise* I'll tell you later. The cops are here," I said, and hung up on her screeching protest.

I stashed the cell in my pocket and jumped out of my van. Arch's face looked so haggard, it was hard to believe he'd enjoyed his brief time at the water park and at Todd's. Probably his feelings—or lack of them—were fluctuating like mine. You can't feel grief all the time.

"Arch, honey," I began when I walked up to him, "you don't have to do this."

"Yes, I do." His words came out weary and resigned. His face set in bitterness, he glanced up at his father's rental Tudor. "You know the amazing thing? Say Dad hadn't saved that guard's life. Then the governor wouldn't have commuted Dad's sentence, and he'd still be alive."

I pressed my lips together and groaned sympathetically. Of course, I wanted to say, *If your father hadn't been engaged in something underhanded, he'd still be alive.* But I didn't.

"Mom?" Arch turned earnest eyes back at me. "The detective told me it wasn't bullets from your gun that killed Dad."

"I know."

Arch swallowed and adjusted his new wire-rimmed glasses. The splash of freckles across his nose, disappearing fast with adolescence, was suddenly visible in the late afternoon light. "I'm sorry I got mad at you. I know you didn't mean for your gun to get stolen. Oh, gee, Mom, I just feel so bad, and I didn't want to make it sound like I blamed you . . ."

I pulled him in for a hug. Oddly, I felt cheered. Arch was getting his conscience back; he was apologizing and meaning it. Maybe I hadn't done such a terrible job these last fifteen years. Then again, maybe he wasn't feeling hugely affectionate, as he wrenched himself away from my hug. After all, there were *people* around. I said, "It's okay."

"Mom, listen. I feel terrible." He looked down, then scraped the toe of his tennis shoe through the dirt deposited in the street from the recent rain. I remembered Tom's terse statement: *Your son has never played golf in his life.* Maybe now I was going to hear what he *had* been doing every Tuesday and Thursday afternoon. "Mom, there's something—"

"Come on, folks!" Blackridge called from the bottom of the driveway.

Arch whirled away and hustled to meet the detective.

Brewster Motley cantilevered himself out of his Mercedes and approached me with a spring in his step. I'd finally decided who Brewster most reminded me of: Tigger, in the Winnie-the-Pooh stories. Sure, Brewster had a client who was a suspect in a murder case, and sure, we were here at her murdered ex-husband's house to see who had trashed it. But hey! This is what Brewsters do best!

"Goldy! What's happening?" He wore khaki pants and a burgundy golf shirt, and I wondered what recreational activity the house inspection had interrupted. He stopped in front of me and pulled up on his belt—a grosgrain affair covered with little burgundy frogs— and eyed the cops at the front door. "You know what they're searching for?"

"Not a clue."

"Okay, look." He leaned toward me, but kept his gaze fixed on the cops. "Don't say anything unnecessary. Don't make any extraneous comments. If they ask you anything beyond, 'Do you see anything missing from this room,' say, 'I don't know.'"

"Fine. You heard about the ballistics test?"

He grinned. "You bet. But with a positive GSR on you, they may try to link you to that twenty-two."

I felt as if I'd been punched. "They would do that?"

He raised an eyebrow and gave me a grim smile.

"Listen, Brewster, you don't need to stay."

He ducked his chin, shaking the blond mop in an emphatic negative. "I'm here. I'm going in with you. The cops could try to trap you with questions. This whole *thing* could be an ambush."

"Even using Arch?"

"You bet."

I trudged up the driveway with my criminal lawyer at my side. At the front door, I gave formal permission for Arch to go in with Reilly and Blackridge, and agreed to accompany them. I felt an unaccountable dread, wondering if I really would detect John Richard's emotions before someone shot him in the heart and then the groin.

After crime-scene investigators had returned to the department, they'd given Blackridge the keys to the front door. To force their way through the windowed back door, the two vandals had shattered the glass. The kitchen floor was a mess. In addition to everything else, Blackridge added. Still, I was not prepared for what lay within.

It was as if a hurricane had blown through the house. Everything—and I do mean *everything*—had been pulled apart. The new leather sectional couch Arch had told me his father had bought had been disemboweled. Its stuffing lay in piles around the room. All of John Richard's CDs were scattered on top of the wood floor and the disheveled Oriental rug, which had been pulled up and moved halfway into the hall. The sound-system speakers Arch told me John Richard had paid ten thousand dollars for had been ripped open. Woofers, wires, and amplifiers lay strewn about like the guts of a giant robot. The vandals—or whatever they were—had even smashed the giant TV to smithereens. Why would someone who was searching for something do that? I began to wonder about these robbers' motives.

Arch stood, his mouth open, and took it all in. Under the detectives' gentle probing, he began an oral inventory of what he thought had been in the room. As Reilly scribbled, I stepped carefully into the slate-covered hallway. There, men's and women's clothing—Sandee's, presumably—had been unceremoniously chucked from the bedrooms. Athletic shoes, dress shoes, backless high heels with matching purses, John Richard's Italian loafers and high-end running shoes—all these lay heaped between the clothes. John Richard's beloved magazine articles about himself—

beautifully matted and framed—had been wrenched from the walls and smashed. Why?

Blackridge, who had followed me, saw my puzzled look. "Probably looking for a safe of some kind. Ditto with the television. You can buy them hollow, to conceal stuff."

"But ... why the mess?" I glimpsed John Richard's favorite *Mountain West* magazine article from twelve years before: "Korman Named One of Denver's Top Twenty Doctors." There was another: "Southwest Hospital Lauded for State-of-the-Art Obstetrics Program." What patients never knew is that those articles, even the magazines, were commonly paid for by the doctors themselves. They were like advertising supplements, even though John Richard (and others) often clipped off the teensy-weensy printed word *advertisement* before having them framed and hung in their offices.

Everything he did was a lie, I thought. *Everything. He never cared about other people, only himself.* Without warning, I remembered John Richard's strangely blank face when I hung up the phone and told him my grandfather had died. I'd slumped into one of our old kitchen chairs and started crying. He'd turned away and searched the refrigerator for a beer.

I gaped at the mess in the hall. Suddenly, I knew what he really was. I'd had all those courses in psychology, but I'd never seen it, not until he was dead. John Richard had been a psychopath. White collar, to be sure, but a psychopath nonetheless. Their main characteristic? They don't feel.

I swallowed, trying to remember what I'd learned. Psychopathy resulted from a genetic predisposition, not arising, researchers were now discovering, from environment. The serial rapists and killers had usually had an abusive childhood with all kinds of narcissistic injuries. But what about psychopaths born to loving, supportive environments? Yes, John Richard's mother had been an alcoholic, but he'd still been his parents' golden boy. And he'd gone on to use people and toss them, in an endless attempt to feel something. *To get a thrill.*

The male psychopath, I remembered, also was extremely adept at keeping a group of adoring women around him. The psychopath could look into their eyes and see what those women needed— affection, maybe, or flattery. Ordinarily, they were women with enormous dependency needs who....

None of this was making me feel really great. Still, I thought I'd known him. Understood him. But I hadn't.

I blinked. Blackridge was asking me a question, something about a weapon.

"Did Dr. Korman keep a firearm, Mrs. Schultz?"

"I don't know," I whispered. I didn't need Brewster's advice to answer truthfully. Even before the divorce, there were many things about John Richard Korman's life that eluded me. One thing stayed constant, though. Should I tell Blackridge?

The Jerk lied. About everything. He did what he wanted, when he wanted. *One of Denver's Top Twenty Doctors.* Pu-leeze.

"Nope," Arch piped up. "No gun. Dad tried to learn how to shoot, but he wasn't any good at, not like my mom—"

"Arch!" interrupted Brewster. He was standing by the hearth, arms crossed. He grinned widely at Arch and cocked his head. "You're a great kid. Just answer the detectives' questions with yes or no, okay?"

Arch's face darkened and he stared at the floor. Here

was at least one person who didn't react well to Brewster's charm. Still, I'd have wished that Arch's new foray into honesty could have stopped short of mentioning my prowess on the firing range.

I asked Blackridge, "What about the garage?"

Blackridge noiselessly pointed toward a door. "I'll take you."

I stepped around the pile of detritus that contained John Richard's trashed Wall of Fame articles, more women's shoes, and a slew of papers. Blackridge opened the garage door and gave me a wry smile. Reilly was now writing down Arch's recitation of what should have been in the guest room, also wrecked. Brewster clearly thought Arch needed more supervision than I did, so he'd followed them down the hall.

The vandals had wreaked particular havoc in the garage. The cops had hauled away the Audi in search of evidence, but this hadn't stopped the thugs. They'd dumped out two black plastic bags of garden waste, now a mishmashed heap of lawn clippings, dusty weeds, and small branches. From the suspended wall shelves, they'd pulled and dumped cans of paint, turpentine, weed killer, and fertilizer. As I surveyed the piles, I wondered how much of this stuff had been John Richard's, and how much of it had belonged to the house's owner. This was probably the last time *he'd* rent to a doctor.

"You have to ask yourself," Blackridge mused as he stared at the mess, "what were they looking for? And why didn't they get Dr. Korman to give it to them before they killed him?"

I recited my usual, "I don't know." When Blackridge gave me a wide-eyed look, I said, "I truly have *no idea* what was going on. But I'd like to stay here in the garage for a bit, if that's okay. I won't touch anything."

Ever wary, Blackridge circled the chaos. When he seemed satisfied that there was no evidence for me to tamper with, nor any valuables for me to steal, he said he was returning to the living room.

I made an effort to soften my tone. "Thanks."

When Blackridge had clomped away, I surveyed the garage, then sat on one of the cold concrete steps that led to the floor. When I took a deep breath, the mixed-up scent of spilled motor oil, mildewed grass clippings, and old paint assaulted my nose. I wasn't particularly enjoying being in there, especially since it inevitably brought back the memory of what I'd last seen in that space: John Richard's bloody, shot-up body.

I shuddered and closed my eyes, then allowed my mind to travel back. I didn't want to go to the memory of John Richard dead, I told myself. I wanted to see, or rather feel, what John Richard had been feeling, the moment before he was shot. Could a man who didn't seem to have feelings experience emotions right before he was killed?

Gooseflesh pimpled my arms. I didn't know if I was receiving an answer or just getting ridiculously chilled in this place. With my eyes still shut, I conjured up the garage door being opened by remote. I saw my ex-husband hasten the Audi forward. I imagined John Richard checking the car's rearview window before hitting the button to close the garage door. And then, what?

I swallowed. Because I did feel it. John Richard hadn't felt terror . . . or rage. What I was picking up in that garage was something entirely different.

Surprise.

Chapter 18

I walked back into the house and down the hall. While I was making my way around the piles on the way to the living room, my mind tossed up a joke we'd told in tenth-grade English. It begins with the wife of Dr. Samuel Johnson entering the library. There, she finds the great lexicographer making enthusiastic love to the parlor maid.

"Dr. Johnson!" Mrs. Johnson exclaims. "I am surprised!"

"Madame," replies Johnson (doing up his pants), "will you never attend to your diction? *You* are *astonished. I* am *surprised*!"

I amended my reaction to the garage. Someone had *surprised* the Jerk. And he'd been *astonished*.

Back in the living room, Brewster Motley and Detectives Reilly and Blackridge were talking in low tones as they headed for the front door. From their downcast expressions, it was clear that bringing Arch to the scene of the crime hadn't yielded the clues they'd hoped for. Brewster's cell chirped. He turned toward the hearth and began listening to the details of the next crisis. Amid this movement and chatter, Arch stood stock-still in the middle of the living-room mess.

"Honey?" I ventured.

"Yeah, Mom."

But he didn't move, and neither did I. Something was bothering him. At the front door, Blackridge twisted his head to see why no one was behind him. His wide, pasty face looked exhausted. Reilly cleared his throat and flipped to a new page on his clipboard.

Arch announced, "I think I know what the vandals were looking for."

Fifteen minutes later, he'd told us the whole story, and the cops' expressions had gone from downcast to gleeful. I, for one, was only glad that my son's rediscovered conscience had superseded his misguided loyalty to his father. What we all learned was this: Every Tuesday and Thursday, when John Richard and Arch had ostensibly been playing golf, they'd been trekking to a bank in nearby Spruce, Colorado. There, John Richard and Arch had opened a safety-deposit-box account. They'd each had keys. Since it was rare for John Richard to trust anyone, even his own son, this part struck me as odd.

"He said he couldn't trust a soul but me," Arch told us. "Plus, he swore me to secrecy, even though I have *no* idea what he was doing with the box. He made me promise not to try to get into it unless something happened to him. Anyway, I keep the key at home in my desk."

"How'd your dad work the bank visits?" Reilly again.

"Well, first he and Sandee and I went to the country club. Sandee went up to the golf shop while Dad and I went down to the basement. Dad would let me play pool while he went to the men's locker room to change out of his golf clothes. Then we'd go out the back door, walk around to the parking lot, and drive over to Spruce in the TT. My job was to wait in the car. After we'd done this a couple of times, I always took a book. Anyway, Dad would take the briefcase out of the trunk, and then he'd be gone for about half an hour. And I guess he didn't just go to the bank. Once I saw him come out of the collectors' shop."

"Collectors' shop?" Reilly asked.

"It's in the same strip mall," Arch replied. "The place used to be a movie theater, so it's huge. The owner buys and sells comics, dolls, key chains, silver, stamps, coins, china, stuff like that. It's a dump, but some of the kids at my new school like to go in and look around. I went with two of them last week. Didn't buy anything, though. And Dad wasn't there."

I was confused. "What in the world was Sandee doing in the golf shop while you and Dad did your bank run?"

Arch exhaled. "She was supposed to stay there and browse. If anybody asked where Dad was, her job was to say he'd gone to get his golf bag. Then when he went in to get her later, he'd be carrying the golf bag, in case anyone was asking questions."

So that was how Marla had gotten the idea that Sandee worked in the golf shop. With all that back-and-forth to Spruce twice a week, Sandee must have known the price of every golf shirt, jacket, and plus fours in the place.

"Did Sandee know what he was doing?"

Arch chewed the inside of his cheek. "I don't know. I don't think so. And Dad said I shouldn't tell Sandee where we were going. She never asked, anyway. She was always nice." He frowned. "I don't like keeping secrets. I guess that now that Dad's gone, it's okay to tell this one, though."

"You did the right thing," said Blackridge. Reilly nodded and snapped a rubber band around the thick wad of clipboard pages. Blackridge checked his watch. "Mrs. Schulz? The bank's closed. May we have permission to take your son over there tomorrow morning? We need to get into that box."

I looked at Brewster, who had closed his phone as soon as Arch made his announcement. Now he piped up: "As long as Mrs. Schulz and I are apprised of the contents of the box, then yes."

Blackridge and Reilly exchanged a look. Blackridge said, "If the material in the box tends to exculpate your client, then we'll tell you."

"No good, gentlemen."

"You drive a hard bargain, Counselor." Blackridge's tone was grudging as he and Reilly again headed toward the front door. "Sure. We'll tell you what's in there."

Arch said, "Cool!"

Brewster's smile was wide. Clearly, making cops do what he wanted was another thing Brewster loved best.

The cops agreed to pick up Arch at half-past eight the next morning, Friday. I stood by the van while Arch gathered the swim gear he'd stashed in the black-and-white. A breeze swished through the Alpine rosebushes girdling the rental house yard while I tried to think. Again, the scent of smoke made me shiver. Frances had said the fire would be contained by morning. Our town was almost nine miles from the preserve, but the smoke stinging my eyes made it seem as if the blaze was right down the street.

Okay, I reminded myself, *Think.* Boyd had told me the cops knew about the Smurfs John Richard was running to launder money. But if the Jerk was laundering what folks brought to *him,* why would he also need to visit a bank in Spruce?

Because he was skimming? Had that been why he'd been killed, and his house ransacked?

It *still* didn't make sense. I stared at the curb, where pearly rose petals now dappled the shiny ravines of dust. For a moment, I thought I saw some gold glittering in the gravel. But I reminded myself it was probably just pyrite, "fool's gold," of which we had an abundance in Colorado. And speaking of fools and their gold, I had another question. If someone was stealing from you, and you were going to kill him for it, wouldn't you try to find the money *first,* then shoot *later?*

The van door slammed. Arch called, "I'm ready, Mom," and slid into the front seat.

"How're you doing?" I asked, once we were zooming back home.

"Okay," he said, his voice weary. "You know who all this investigating makes me feel sorry for?" If he said his father, I was going to scream. But he didn't. "It makes me feel bad for Tom. You see how much goes into an investigation, and you think, here Tom caught somebody who drowned somebody else, and he lost in court. No wonder Tom's been down lately. You know, not his usual joking self."

A rock was forming in my chest. *No wonder,* indeed.

At home, though, Tom was whistling in the kitchen as he prepared dinner for the three of us: a giant submarine sandwich that was an elaborate affair put together with ingredients from his recent mammoth shopping trip. He'd scooped bread out of a large baguette, filled the center with a heavenly mixture of three Italian cheeses, sausages, salami, sliced garden tomatoes, and arugula, then topped the whole thing with his own garlic dressing. By the time we tumbled into the kitchen to see what he was up to, he was wrapping the sandwich before starting its weighting-down time in the refrigerator, which would help meld all the flavors. In a couple of hours, we would have a feast. No one eats dinner early in the summertime, anyway.

"How are you doing, Tom?" Arch asked, his voice full of concern.

Tom's head shot up at the unusual question from Arch. I could still see the pain in Tom's eyes, the heavy weight that seemed to have settled permanently on his shoulders. But I also could tell that he didn't want Arch to be worrying about him.

"I'm doing well, thank you, Arch." Tom pulled out two chilled soft drinks and placed them on the kitchen table for us. "You guys look whipped, though. How'd it go at your dad's house?"

Arch took a long swig of pop before recounting an abbreviated version of the trip to Stoneberry Lane.

"So," Tom mused, "a safety-deposit box, eh? What do you suppose is in there?"

"Bones," Arch said without irony, before announcing he was going upstairs to call Todd. At the kitchen door, he stopped and cast a long look at Tom. "I'm really sorry about your lost case, Tom."

Again startled by this sudden interest in his well-being, Tom gaped at Arch. Quickly recovering his composure, Tom replied, "Thanks for the concern, buddy. I'm sorry for your loss, too."

"I know." Arch spun slowly and retreated.

Tom's green eyes questioned me and I shrugged. He muttered something about wonders not ceasing as he placed the sandwich between cookie sheets, laid two stones on top, and put the whole thing in to chill.

"All right, Miss G. You still testing pies?"

"I am. So?"

"After you start on a new pie, I've got a story to tell you."

"Why not just tell me now?"

"Because I want it to be a *story* for you, not a call to action."

"Great." But I booted up the computer and printed out the recipes I'd been working on: crust made with butter and toasted filberts, crust made with butter-flavored shortening, crust made with lard, crust made with a combination of butter and lard.

"And for the filling?" Tom asked.

"I ordered many, many pounds of strawberries from Alicia. My dear supplier said they were the best she'd ever tasted. Plus, this time I'm going to omit the cream filling and just concentrate on the strawberries." I paused. "What are you doing?"

Tom chuckled as he foraged in the cupboard. "I think we need a chocolate treat." If I'd ever doubted my maxim that cooking was good therapy, Tom's first laugh in six weeks was proof enough.

"Are you going to tell me this story?" I asked, once I was rinsing fat, juicy strawberries.

Tom began, "You know how the rain washed out some dirt roads the other night?" I nodded. "It also washed things into the street— in this case, a dumped item that was found not far from Stoneberry. Our guys are thinking this thing rolled down Korman's driveway and into the street, or else our killer tossed it from the getaway car. So you have the dirt from the street, plus all that dust from Tuesday's big wind. After that, we had a hailstorm, and after *that*, a dog got hold of it, took it home, and chewed on it." I stopped slicing and stared at him. "But as it turned out, the dog's owner was giving a barbecue last night, and when he was picking up his yard, he found it and figured out some of the mess on it was from his dog's teeth and the rest was from . . . something else."

"What *are* you talking about?"

"The reason Korman's neighbors didn't hear the gun going *boom* was that it had a homemade silencer on it. A pink tennis ball." He stopped sifting ingredients and opened an envelope. He handed me a Polaroid of something smashed, dirty, and perhaps a bit pink.

"Where'd you get this?"

"Boyd. Our guys went out looking for Bobby Calhoun this afternoon, but he's up fighting the fire, and can't be reached. Then they got the call about the tennis ball. A judge signed a quick warrant to search Courtney's country-club locker. Didn't find anything. But in the tennis shop? Where the players keep their balls in cubbies with their names on them, sort of like kindergartners? Courtney's cubby had three cans of tennis balls. Two were closed and one was open. The open can had two tennis balls in it. Who opens a can and just takes out one ball? Our guys are talking to Courtney now."

I shook my head. Back to the Courtney theory. *Hell hath no fury like a woman scorned.* Means? Bobby Calhoun wasn't the only one who could own a Ruger. If Courtney had hired a professional hit man, then that guy might be the one who'd committed the murder in Denver all those months ago.

I measured the strawberries, then mixed together a judicious amount of flour, cornstarch, and sugar. I said, "So did you find out who was killed with the Ruger in Denver?"

From the envelope, Tom retrieved two more items. One was a poor-quality copy of what looked like an employee-of-the-month photo. The man, who couldn't have been more than twenty-five, had thick glasses and a thin, handsome face. The other photo was of even worse quality, and showed a couple. The woman was young and pretty, with lots of curly hair. They looked as if they were at a party. "The guy, Quentin Drake, was killed in broad daylight on a street in Denver. Quentin and his wife, Ruby, lived in a trailer in Golden."

"Ruby Drake?" That name was familiar. "Can you find out any more about them? About him?" I stared at the picture of the couple. "I've seen this woman somewhere."

"Preheat the oven to three-fifty for me, would you please, wife? You're not going hauling down to Golden to interview a widow."

I snapped the oven thermostat for him and slipped the pictures back in the envelope. Then I rolled out my newest dough experiment and fit it into a pie pan. "So, what do you know about this victim? Any points of comparison with the Jerk?"

"Quentin Drake was a computer geek for an engineering company before he got laid off. I don't know about her. You're not going after this guy's killer, Goldy."

I carefully stirred the strawberries into the sugar mixture and tried to sound nonchalant. "I know, I know. I'm just looking for a link."

We worked in companionable silence for a while. I carefully placed the pie in the oven, taking care not to jiggle Tom's brownie pan. He was washing the bespattered bowl and beaters and I was wiping the counters when Arch made one of his noiseless entries into the kitchen.

"I have something else to tell you," he began. When Arch had Tom's and my attention, he crossed his arms and looked at the floor. "I just don't want to get this guy into trouble. I mean, he's old. I can't imagine he would hurt anyone. I don't think he would want to hurt *me*."

Tom used his best interrogation technique when a suspect began to talk: *Say nothing*. Reluctantly, I followed his lead.

Arch let out a deep breath. "Todd and I figured out who's been following me. We tag-teamed our watch at Todd's house. The car was there, with the guy inside. I used Todd's telescope to see who it was." Arch's brow furrowed above his glasses. "Why would Ted Vikarios be stalking me?"

"Ted Vikarios?" I repeated. I pictured Ted standing, tall and charismatic, at the microphone in the Roundhouse.

"Ted Vikarios?" Tom repeated. "You mean the guy you said gave the long-winded speech at the lunch? Who had the argument with Korman? The one whose wife got ridiculed by the mean women? What's his background?"

"He's a former preacher. And a medical doctor." I recounted the history of Albert and Ted being co-department heads for ob-gyn at Southwest, and how they'd gotten religion. They'd gone their separate ways: the Kerrs to England for seminary and then Qatar for missionary work, the Vikarioses to fame, fortune, and, ultimately, ruin.

"Ruin?" Tom asked.

They'd . . . had a scandal, I said, with a meaningful look at Tom that said *sex*.

"Wait," interjected Arch. "Excuse me, didn't mean to interrupt. But I'm supposed to call Todd about this birthday party on Saturday. So . . . does something smell like *brownies*?"

Tom smiled. "If it looks like chocolate and smells like chocolate, then there's a pretty good chance that it *is* chocolate. Thirty minutes' cooking time. Two hours to cool, if we're being sticklers. Which we aren't."

"Great!" Arch headed toward the kitchen door, his conscience clear, his appetite set. "Call me if you figure out what's going on!"

"Tom," I said softly, after Arch was gone. "I may be beginning to see something." *If it looks like a payoff and smells like a payoff,* Nan had said, *maybe it* is *a payoff*. "Remember I was telling you about the Vikarioses' ruin?"

He nodded, and I gave him a brief account of the scandal concerning Talitha Vikarios and her out-of-wedlock child by Albert Kerr. The papers had gorged on the fact that Ted Vikarios, a man who made boxed tape sets called *Victory over Sin*, had a daughter who'd been living in a commune. And then Nan Watkins had told me Talitha was dead.

"If Ted Vikarios and John Richard weren't arguing about money after the funeral lunch, what *were* they arguing about?" I wondered aloud. "And most puzzling of all, why would Ted be stalking *Arch*?"

Tom's face was understanding as he reached for a squeegee and began scrubbing. "Sometimes if I just rejuggle all the pieces in a homicide, I come up with an answer."

But the words were not even out of his mouth before I knew. I said, "Albert Kerr had mumps when he was a teenager."

"And that's important because . . ."

I felt so low, all of a sudden. I couldn't even say the words. The kitchen spun around, and Tom's soapy hands grabbed me.

"Miss Goldy! What's wrong?" He eased me into a kitchen chair, then nabbed a cotton towel and filled it with ice. With great gentleness, he held it to my forehead. He whispered, "Don't try to talk."

"It's okay." In my mind's eye, I saw the photo of that dear, sweet candy striper as she hugged Arch and held him close. I remembered Talitha Vikarios even better than I had before. She'd been wonderfully attentive, she'd doted on the infant Arch. *You're so lucky, Mrs. Korman! I want to have a family someday, too! If I had a family, I wouldn't let anything destroy it!*

Talitha Vikarios had had one other person she'd adored, though. And she'd been weepy, too, as she held Arch. Inexplicably weepy.

I gazed into Tom's green eyes. "When a teenage male gets the mumps, it usually renders him sterile. Which explains why Albert and Holly Kerr didn't have any children. When Talitha Vikarios told her parents that Albert Kerr was the father of her child, she was lying."

"Whoa. Back up. So Talitha took off to have the child in some commune?"

"Yes. My bet is that when she was discovered by the media, she told what she thought was a white lie. Albert Kerr was far away, and couldn't be affected. Plus, while the Kerrs were overseas, there would be no way for Ted and Ginger to know that Albert had had the mumps when he was a kid. Holly told me about it when she was reminiscing."

Tom said, "So Albert Kerr had had the mumps and was sterile. But the Vikarioses, Talitha included, didn't know. Right? Why would she assign paternity to some guy who was sterile, and out of the country to boot?"

"Maybe I'm doing a quantum leap here, but *I* think she was protecting me. And Arch. Our family."

"So . . . are you saying you think the father of her child was John Richard Korman?"

"I am. I think he seduced her the way he did most pretty young nurses. I think she made the disastrous mistake of falling in love with him. They had an affair, and she got pregnant. She left to have the child, rather than abort."

"Oh, Miss G."

And then I moaned. Tom gave me a quizzical look. I said, "Before the Kerr memorial lunch, Ted Vikarios came into the kitchen looking for something. He yelled, 'Jesus God Almighty!' and startled us. But he wasn't calling on a supreme being, Tom. He was looking at Arch." I clutched the table. "Arch must look a lot like his grandson."

Tom groaned, but I held up my hand. I was thinking, trying to put it all together . . . or as much of it as I could guess at.

I went on. "Right then, when Ted saw Arch, I'll bet he figured it out. No doubt he and Ginger had been puzzling over this for a long time." I paused. "Let's say, after the discovery of Talitha's child, they believed Talitha's story that Albert was the father. The Kerrs, long gone, probably denied it from afar, in a flurry of correspondence. But let's say Talitha stuck to her story . . . and it looks as if she stayed in the Utah com-

mune, too. So the Vikarioses had no relationship with
their child or their grandchild, no money because their
tape empire had failed, and no more friendship with
the Kerrs."

Tom said, "I'm following you. But how do the Vikarioses end up in a country-club condo in Aspen
Meadow?"

I said, "Holly Kerr's husband was terminally ill with
cancer. She'd just inherited millions, but the money
couldn't help her husband. So maybe she *forgave* the
Vikarioses for suspecting Albert. She hated the stories
she heard from friends, about how the Vikarioses were
suffering. And she wanted to reconcile with them before her husband died. So she started sending them a
stipend. The Vikarioses were grateful, but they were
still left with the mystery of who had fathered their
grandchild and ruined their lives—"

Wait a minute. My kitchen shears had been stolen,
and John Richard's hair had been clipped after he was
dead. So Arch thought Ted Vikarios was an old man
who wouldn't harm anybody? Had Ted demanded the
truth from John Richard outside the Roundhouse? Had
he said, "Are you the man who impregnated my unmar-
ried daughter? Are you the man who ruined our lives?"

I said softly, "Ted Vikarios could have killed the Jerk
and then cut a swatch of hair for a paternity test."

"Now, Goldy, that is *reaching*—"

"I need to make a call." I tapped keys to pull up the
address book on my computer and scrolled to Priscilla
Throckbottom's number. What do you know, she had
given me both her home and cell-phone numbers. It
was only half-past eight, so with any luck . . .

"Priscilla?" I said breathlessly when she answered
her cell. "It's Goldy Schulz."

"I'm at the country club," Priscilla announced excitedly. "We're all still here, all still talking about Courtney MacEwan's *arrest*!"

"Courtney was *arrested*?"

"I saw the police come myself. We all did! They took her away!"

"In handcuffs, Priscilla? Did they read her her rights? Or did she just agree to go in for questioning—"

Priscilla's tone changed. "Is this why you're calling me when I'm entertaining friends at the country club?" Clearly, she wasn't going to allow someone, especially a caterer, to water down her story. "You called to ask questions about Courtney MacEwan? Or do you have something else on your mind?"

I took a deep breath, and smelled smoke. It was sweet, and it was . . . billowing out of our oven. "Just a sec, Priscilla!" I put down the phone and looked around wildly for pot holders. When I pulled out the pie, it was a steaming, gurgling mess. Hot strawberry goo dripped relentlessly from the pie-plate rim. A quart of red lava had already bubbled onto the bottom of the oven, where it was blackening into a smoking island. Tom grabbed his own pair of pot holders and helped me ease the pie onto a rack.

"Goldy?" Priscilla's voice called from the counter.

"Coming, coming!" I called. I'd made dozens of fruit pies. What had I done wrong?

"Goldy! I'm a busy woman, you know!"

Tom waved for me to return to the phone.

"Sorry about that, Priscilla. Ah . . . remember this morning, when you and the committee were talking about the Vikarioses?"

"I don't remember. Is this going to take long?"

"Priscilla," I stage-whispered, "I could keep you

posted on Courtney's status." Tom stopped wiping up the mess and rolled his eyes to the ceiling. "What the charges are, who her lawyer is, that kind of thing."

"Well, then." I could hear Priscilla salivating through the phone line. "All right, Goldy, so. What were you wondering about the Vikarioses?"

"Remember when the committee was discussing their daughter? The one with the child? I, uh, heard she died. The Vikarioses' daughter, that is."

"She did," Priscilla replied crisply. "Talitha. Last month, in Moab, Utah. A truck accident, was the story I got. Somebody cut off a pickup, which then swerved into the oncoming lane and hit Talitha."

"Do you . . . know what happened to the child? Talitha's child, that is?"

Priscilla snorted. "Ted and Ginger are taking care of the boy. He was hurt in the accident, and he doesn't have any other family, of course. I think it's a terrible idea. They're too old to have children." She inhaled. "Is that all, Goldy?"

"Um, yes. Thank you."

She lowered her voice. "When will you know about Courtney? One of the women here said Courtney precipitated her husband's heart attack by making sure he was having sex with that flight attendant before she stalked into their bedroom and surprised them. That's how she ended up inheriting all that money that she lavished on your worthless ex-husband."

I smiled in spite of myself. With Courtney, or with John Richard, nothing surprised me. "As soon as I know anything, I'll call you."

"By the way, I'm doing the flowers for your ex-husband's memorial service. That's one thing the garden club *can't* take away from me. That, and the planting we'll be doing up in the preserve, if they can ever manage to put out the fire! Did you hear they think some hikers are trapped back there?"

I told her that I had not heard that, then signed off. I asked Tom if he had picked up on a story about the blaze threatening some hikers in the preserve. He cocked a bushy eyebrow and replied that this sounded like more horse manure from Priscilla Throckbottom. Meanwhile, bless him, he had cleaned up the entire pie mess. His brownies had managed to bake alongside the strawberry volcano and were now cooling as he sliced his super-sub sandwich. Arch, sensing that a meal was imminent, had slipped back into the kitchen. To my astonishment, he washed his hands and began setting the table *without being asked.* The next time I got a big tip, it was going to Arch.

Arch pushed his glasses up his nose, peered around, and sniffed. "Did something burn?"

"It's okay, hon," I said.

"Good, 'cuz I'm starving."

But I wasn't. In fact, I was desperate to do something else altogether.

"Guys," I said to Tom and Arch, "I want to go over to the Vikarioses. Now."

It was the second time that evening that Tom laughed. "Forget it!"

"Mom," Arch pleaded, "I'm *so* hungry."

"Eat," Tom urged Arch. "Your mother's hallucinating and will snap out of it soon."

"Tom, I want to go and I want to go now. If you aren't going to come with me, then I'm going alone."

"What happened to your promise not to go into dangerous situations?"

"You can come. And bring a gun."

Tom put down the knife, then leaned forward on his knuckles. "I'd like to keep my job, thanks. You want, I'll call the department and Blackridge and Reilly can go over there tomorrow." When Arch shuffled into the walk-in in search of lemonade, Tom whispered to me, "And anyway, what would you say to Ted Vikarios once you got there?" He brought his voice up an octave to mimic mine. "Ted, did you kill my ex-husband? Could you please wait here while I call the cops?"

"No," I said calmly. "I'd say we were grieving and we needed pastoral care. We heard he was a pastor, and we'd like to come in and talk."

"Who is *we,* white woman?"

Arch had returned and was munching on a large wedge of sandwich. "If you guys go, ask Mr. Vikarios why he's been following me."

I chewed the inside of my cheek. I wouldn't feel comfortable leaving Arch home alone if Tom and I both went. But I truly had no idea what we might be encountering at the Vikarios condo. I wavered. Maybe this idea really *was* foolhardy.

"All right, all right," Tom said, his voice resigned. "Let me go call Boyd. I'll ask him to come here and stay with Arch."

Thirty minutes later, with Boyd and Arch scooping out vanilla ice cream to make enormous brownies à la mode, I followed Tom to his sedan. My husband was wearing a brown corduroy jacket, which I hoped concealed a shoulder holster, and he was holding a pair of high-powered binoculars. Once we were buckled in, Tom said, "We are *not* getting out of this car when we get there. I'm parking up on the road and then the two of us are going to see if we can spot anything suspicious. Then we'll make a decision." He held up his key chain. "We're not going anywhere until you promise not to go crazy on me."

"I promise." Sheesh! "Before you can say tiddly-winks, we'll be back home digging into your sandwich."

We chugged down toward Main Street. Tom said, "I'd rather be back home, thank you very much. On such a beautiful night, I'd rather be working with and devouring food—thank you very much. This very minute, you and Arch and I could be eating that sand-wich on our deck, by the light of the pearly moon, in-stead of traipsing around on a wild-goose chase—"

At the light on Main Street—there was only one, so locals just referred to it as "the light"—Tom eased the sedan to a stop. I turned to him.

"What did you say, Tom?"

"Goose chase. Eat outside. Deck. All of the above."

"Be serious for a second. Something about the pearly moon."

The light turned green; Tom accelerated. "All right then. How's *ghostly* moon?"

I was reaching for a memory. I'd seen something. Something as luminous as a ghost. Something that hadn't belonged where I'd seen it.

"The Vikarioses don't live far from John Richard's rental. Could you just swing by there?" I begged. "I think I dropped something. In the street, not at the house."

Tom shook his head. "It's a good thing I'm crazy about you, Miss G. Then again, maybe I'm just plain crazy."

The moonlight cast a pale light over the granite-and-moss rock pillars flanking the entryway to the country-club area. We passed a few cars—luckily, all the gapers had left their decks—and within moments were crunching over the gravel washout on Stoneberry. The evergreens, aspens, and Alpine roses ringing the cul-de-sac shrouded the pavement in darkness. When we stopped in front of the rental, Tom drew out a Maglite from the floor of the backseat. He held it in his lap for a moment, as if unsure if he should give it to me.

"What did you drop?" he wanted to know.

"A piece of jewelry. Several pieces of jewelry. They'll just take a sec to find, if they're still there."

"You don't wear jewelry, Miss G."

"Are you going to give me the light or not?"

When I slid out of the front seat, I snapped on the Maglite and tried to remember exactly where I'd seen what Tom is always telling his investigators to look for: *something out of place.* The smoke seemed to have dissipated, thank God, and the mountain breeze was sweet as sugar. Alpine roses by the curb bobbed to and fro. I trod gingerly over the asphalt and lustrous flood of gravel, sweeping the Mag as I went.

And then I saw them: a spill of pearls glowing in the moonlight, among a fall of creamy rose petals. I directed the flashlight's pool of light to where the wash of tiny, uneven stones had deposited the oyster's perfect nuggets. I reached down and picked them up, one by one. When they were securely in my pocket, I turned off the flashlight and returned to the sedan.

Maybe they were nothing. Maybe they were something. Should I bother Blackridge and Reilly again?

If the pearls were significant, there was a logical explanation as to why the crime-scene investigators hadn't found them. Everything—grass, trees, pavement—had been coated with dust when I'd discovered

John Richard on Tuesday. The pearls would have been easy to miss. But that night the hailstorm had bathed away the dust. Gravity and a stream of dirt had swept the pearls out of John Richard's yard and into the street, where anyone looking could have found them.

Chapter 19

"So they're not yours," Tom said. "What good will a handful of pearls do you? Scratch that. What good will pearls do the investigation?"

"It depends on what kind of pearls they are. Pearls from the Persian Gulf aren't cultured. Cultured pearls, which are the great majority of the pearls sold in this country, usually come from Japan."

"And you're going to tell me how you know this, right?"

I gave him a sheepish smile. "I grew up as a middle-class girl in New Jersey, and then went to a girls' boarding school. You don't think I know from pearls? On the way home, we can drop some of them at Front Range Jewelry, leave the owner a note."

"Humor me. Your theory is that if Courtney's the killer, they would be . . . what?"

"Cultured. But if we're looking at, say, Ginger Vikarios, it could be something else together. Holly Kerr and Ginger Vikarios are inseparable, now that they've reconciled. Ginger Vikarios's life was ruined by her daughter having a child out of wedlock. And if my theory, and Ted's theory, is that the Vikarioses just discovered that the *Jerk* impregnated their daughter, then that certainly would be a motive for murdering him."

"So . . . how do the pearls fit in?"

I sighed. "If the pearls are from the Persian Gulf, then Holly could have given them to Ginger! Holly has more pearls in her house than Tiffany's."

Tom chuckled and started the car. "Thin, Goldy. Wafer thin."

"I don't *know* from wafers."

"Clearly. But you're going to have to tell the detectives investigating the case about finding the pearls. You might not want to share these theories, though."

"You can tell Boyd tomorrow. I don't want the cops to know I was here. Now can we please make our other stop?"

He grunted assent and pulled out his spiral notebook. He looked up the address he'd jotted down and eased the sedan around the Stoneberry dead end. It was a good thing, too, because lights had begun to wink on in the houses rimming the cul-de-sac. Several faces appeared at windows.

I certainly didn't blame the Stoneberry residents for being nervous. Their neighbor had been murdered and his house had been vandalized. I just didn't want these folks to call the sheriff's department to come out and check on a car belonging to an investigator from . . . the sheriff's department.

When we had wound down one street and then another—the concept of *blocks* was foreign to Aspen Meadow—Tom drew to a stop under a streetlight. The wind rustled the aspens close by as Tom peered up at the sign for Club Drive. When he turned right, the smell of fire smoke drifted into the car. I exhaled, suddenly thankful that Boyd was staying with Arch.

The country-club condominiums had been built along an embankment that sloped down from Club Drive. Facing east, the condos could not boast the coveted view of the mountains, but some of them overlooked the golf course, and their clever design as multistoried duplexes gave them the look of large, mountain-style houses. Like the clubhouse itself, their beige exteriors—no change of color allowed—and cedar-shake-shingle roofs screamed Upscale Mountain-Resort Holiday Inn, but for retirees who wanted proximity to the clubhouse, they were perfect.

When Tom slowed to read mailbox numbers, I wondered how, exactly, the rift between the Vikarioses and the Kerrs, not to mention between the Vikarios parents and their daughter, Talitha, had been healed. Had Ginger written an angry letter to Holly, *Your husband impregnated our daughter out of wedlock, and now we're ruined?* Or had Ginger been so dumbfounded by Talitha's claim that she'd been embarrassed even to ask Holly if it could be true? Holly must have heard the story from *someone.* Knowing that Albert couldn't have fathered Talitha's child, Holly's forgiveness and *generosity* toward her old friends—a club condo alone cost half a mil—didn't look like a payoff at all, no matter what Nan Watkins said. It looked like true charity—all the more so because it wasn't widely known.

Tom pulled up to a dark driveway, turned off the lights, and cut the motor. My palms were damp. Tom lifted the binocs and focused. Then he moved them slowly until he stopped and refocused. He waited for what seemed like a very long time, but probably wasn't more than five minutes.

"Bingo."

"What?" I demanded. "Show me!"

He pointed to the northernmost of a set of three duplexes, then handed me the binoculars. "Condo on the left of the far one. Lower level. Looks like a family room. Shades are up, windows open, TV on."

As I'd learned on an ill-fated birding expedition, I wasn't too adept with binoculars. Still, after a few minutes I was able to make out Ginger, clad in a dark top and pants, sitting in a rocking chair. Ted was perched on a couch directly across from a brightly lit color television. On a coffee table in front of him, I could just make out . . . three glasses? My fingers began to hurt. I didn't even know what I was looking for.

"I'm not seeing," I said. "Oh God."

Just then, a young teenager—maybe fourteen—strode into the room. He was holding what looked like a bowl of popcorn. Ted and Ginger both said something to him, and the teenager laughed. He had toast-brown hair, glasses, and a thin face.

He was the boy I'd seen in town, of course. Once I'd seen him beside a herd of elk and the other time in front of Town Taffy. He looked just like Arch.

"That threesome doesn't look as if they harbor murder in their hearts," Tom observed. "Wouldn't you say? Pearls or no pearls? Victim's hair clipped or not? Of course, I've been fooled by criminals before. But if one of them was a killer, you'd think they'd at least close the shades."

I put down the binoculars. "Then why is Ted following Arch?"

"Because his daughter's dead and he wants to know

the piece of her history that's missing? Because he wants to fill in a piece of his grandson's history? Had enough?"

"So what's your theory on John Richard's murder?"

Tom tapped the dashboard. "I don't have one yet. We're missing something. Or some *things*. We don't have too few clues. We've got too damn *many*."

"Right." Suddenly, I felt dejected. As Tom turned on the car and reversed onto the shoulder, I asked, "So, now what? Do you think Reilly and Blackridge will want to talk to the Vikarioses?"

"Yeah, I do. Another job we can foist off on Boyd. He's going to be thrilled. So are Blackridge and Reilly. And if this gets out, it's going to be a mess, even if the *Mountain Journal* doesn't have a gossip columnist anymore. I can see the headline now: 'Who Killed Love Child's Father?' "

"Oh my God." My thoughts flew to Arch. How would he handle such a thing? The answer was that he wouldn't. Nor would Talitha's son. "Is there any way to investigate this secretly? There's got to be."

Tom took a deep breath. "I'll tell Boyd to tell the detectives what our suspicions are, but to keep it extra quiet. How's that?"

I didn't feel very reassured. Somehow I'd become mixed into this stew of folks with their secrets, their pain, and their rage, and I felt as if I was sinking. Or maybe that was my exhaustion. The day had been long, too long, and I was desperate for food and bed. Tom drove me to the jewelry store and handed me a paper evidence bag from his kit in the trunk. I wrote the jewelry-store owner a note, put it, along with the pearls, into the bag, and shoved the whole thing through his mail slot. I couldn't wait to get home.

But unwelcome news awaited us there. Arch was ensconced in the living room watching a TV show, but Boyd lowered his voice anyway. The medical examiner had completed his preliminary report, Boyd told us. It looked as if Cecelia Brisbane had been strangled.

The next morning, Friday, the tenth of June, dawned with a disconcerting gray haze hanging in the air. The smell of smoke was so strong that I made sure all the windows were closed. I even plugged in some fans to keep the air circulating. Like most mountain homes, we had no air-conditioning, which was probably just as well. The prospect of chilled, smoky air did not thrill me.

Scout and Jake went out with reluctance. They both seemed nervous, sniffing the air and darting tentatively around the backyard. After a few moments, both were pawing to come back in. Don't tell me animals are unaware of approaching fire.

And it *was* drawing near. What I'd thought was my own voice, wailing in my dreams as I confronted a dead ex-husband over and over, was actually sirens. According to the TV news, the fire in the westernmost, remotest section of the Aspen Meadow Wildlife Preserve had bloomed overnight from eleven hundred acres to two thousand. The fire was spreading faster than they could contain it. Aspen Meadow firefighters had called on Denver departments to send up volunteers. Worst of all, a pair of hikers was missing.

When I ventured outside to retrieve Jake's water dish, I was greeted by a loud roar from overhead. It was a huge cargo plane, bearing its load of orange fire retardant toward the thick evergreen forests of the preserve. I shuddered.

Blackridge and Reilly were due to pick up Arch at

half-past eight, to go to the bank in Spruce and check out the contents of the safety-deposit box. The only thing I had to look forward to was the memorial service for John Richard, which was set to start at one o'clock. And to tell the truth, I wasn't looking forward to that at all.

I took a deep breath but only smelled more smoke. I glanced around the kitchen, unsure of what to do with myself. The Furman County Sheriff's Department's new emergency reverse-calling mechanism had been widely touted as a foolproof mode of alerting residents to the need for evacuation. Our phones would ring if we were in danger, and we'd be given an hour to pack up our stuff and get out. How much of your life could you pack up in an hour? Your loved ones, your animals, maybe a few photographs. That was it.

The phone rang as I was making my usual double-shot espresso. The demitasse cup I'd been holding slipped away and shattered to smithereens. This was emphatically not because I'd had too much caffeine—in fact, I hadn't had any yet. I grabbed the phone, sure it was a recorded message telling us to get out.

"Goldy Schulz here," I said, my voice shaky.

"I know you're not using caller ID if you're answering like that," Marla said.

"You're up early, girlfriend. I thought you were the sheriff's department, telling me to round up our crew and get out."

"Listen up. I have two problems. One is that the smoky air makes it impossible for me to sleep. The other is that the Jerk's service is today. Remember you asked me to invite Sandee to come with us? Well, I did."

"I know. She called me."

"Well, anyway, I don't want to be alone right now."

I smiled. "Come on over."

"Are you making something yummy?"

"This instant, I am starting to prepare whatever you would like."

"Good. Because I never got a chance to taste what I'm looking at in the *Mountain Journal*."

My heart plummeted. I didn't remember submitting a recipe to the *Journal*, and anyway, this wasn't the day for their food page. "What is it?"

"Why it's *you*, naughty girlfriend, plastering a strawberry-cream pie onto the face of Roger Mannis, the district health inspector." I groaned. "You at least could have whacked him with lima bean soup or raw scallops. Why ruin a yummy pie?"

"I lost my head. Just come over, will you?"

She giggled and hung up.

Once I'd made myself a new espresso, I reached for butter-flavored shortening to try a new variation on my crust recipe. I was trying my pie again, but this time in a deep dish so we wouldn't have another eruption of Mount Saint Strawberry.

Half an hour later, I had placed the new pie on a cookie sheet and was just sliding it into the oven when the doorbell rang. Oh good, Marla. But it wasn't my friend. Reilly and Blackridge stood on our porch wearing wraparound sunglasses and dark suits. They looked like the Blues Brothers. Was their attire a joke? Knowing them, it wasn't.

My discomfort showed in my stiff voice as I invited the detectives into the living room. But they were acting very polite, even deferential. I wondered how they felt about the progress of the investigation. I was curious to know how the questioning of Courtney Mac-

Ewan had gone. And I was *very* curious to know if they'd found anything in Cecelia Brisbane's files, or if they'd come up with a theory as to who had strangled her, and why. But I refrained. I doubted the cops' new-found civility extended to coughing up answers to *my* questions.

"Big man upstairs?" Blackridge asked.

"Yes," I replied. The rushing sound of shower water was clearly audible. "Let me go roust my son. That's who you're here for, isn't it?" Blackridge nodded, and I reluctantly went on: "You've heard this rumor about him possibly having a half brother?" I got another assent . . . and was that a look of sympathy melting Blackridge's usually hard eyes? "I'd be very grateful," I said hesitantly, "if you wouldn't breathe a word of it to Arch."

Reilly exhaled. "We wouldn't, ma'am. We never would."

I thanked them and set off up the stairs, where I was surprised to see a freshly showered, tired-looking Arch sitting on his bed. He was neatly dressed in khaki pants and a white polo shirt. His right hand was closed in a fist, undoubtedly holding the key.

"You're all ready?" I couldn't hide my astonishment. "Did you set your alarm?"

He straightened his glasses with his free hand. "Yeah. I'm real curious about what Dad was doing."

I hugged my sides and made my voice low. "Remember we have the service today, hon?"

His look became guarded. "I know. One o'clock. I'll be ready at half-past twelve, if you want."

We agreed, and he took off with the detectives for Spruce. I checked on Tom, who was still sleeping. I was thankful that the sheriff's department had told my husband to take all the time he needed to help me during this bad time. The department wanted their premier investigator back in top form, not worried about his hapless wife.

An unaccountable uneasiness seized me as I made my way back to the kitchen. Something was bothering me, but what was it? This unsolved question, who had killed John Richard, hung like the smoky haze that now enveloped the evergreens and aspens outside. The investigation had produced plenty of suspects—the Vikarioses, Courtney MacEwan, Lana Della Robbia and Dannyboy, whom I was sure had been the suppliers of the cash to be laundered, even though the investigators had yet to prove it. I groaned.

Tom had said that when an investigation stalled, he went over every bit of information he'd already gathered. So I booted up my computer and reloaded the espresso machine. Five minutes later, I was sipping another double shot, this time mixed with half-and-half and poured over ice, as I scrolled through my notes.

When Marla ding-donged our bell and banged on the door—she always wanted you to *hurry up and let her in*—I hadn't come up with any new theories. Marla breezed through the door, clad in a pink pantsuit. She pointed to my iced drink.

"That stuff'll kill you. Fix me one, will you?"

I smiled and followed her to the kitchen.

"My doctor says I should drink herb tea. I told him if I chugged down herb tea first thing in the morning, I'd puke." Marla smiled when I handed her the latte. She sipped, nodded approvingly, and lifted her chin toward the computer. "What're you doing?"

"Reading through my file on John Richard. Trying

to see what I missed." I brought her up-to-date on the case, including the shot-up pink tennis ball, the pearls, and the possibility that the Jerk had fathered a child by the former candy striper Talitha Vikarios. Marla whistled.

"I heard about Courtney being picked up for questioning," she said. "I wonder what she'll tell the cops, if anything."

"Ah. While we're on the topic of wondering, I want to show you something." I put down my coffee and handed her the pictures from Tom's envelope. "Does someone look familiar here?"

"I've never seen the guy," she said immediately. "The woman. I know her. Who is she?"

"Ruby Drake."

"Ruby, ruby. Red hair." Marla tapped the photo. "Didn't recognize her right away. I mean, not with her clothes on. She was at the Rainbow when we went down there. Don't you remember, she was dancing near us, with a red light? It made her hair look almost purple. I thought she'd been one of the Jerk's girl-friends, remember?"

"And she sat with us and said she hated the Jerk. Now the firearms examiner says Ruby's husband, that guy you've never seen, was shot with the same gun that killed John Richard."

"Oh, dear, oh dear. Does Tom know about this?"

"No, but I'll tell him. He's asleep." I sighed and stared at my computer. "I just . . . feel as if I'm missing something else. Say John Richard was laundering money; say it was from the strip club. Even if you tortured him by shooting him in the genitals to tell you where the money was, and even if he wouldn't tell you, why shoot him right in his garage, instead of when he was strolling along a sidewalk somewhere? Why use a homemade silencer and then drop it in the street?"

I sipped my coffee and frowned. "Whoa." I put down my coffee and tapped keys, then I read the screen. "Here we go. The letter about the rape. It was sent to Cecelia Brisbane. Why? The day after the Jerk was killed, the note was delivered to me. And *then*, the day after that, Cecelia turned up dead."

"It's weird, all right." Marla drained her iced latte glass. "Who do you think could help us figure it out?"

"Who would know about the history of Southwest Hospital?" After a moment, I answered my own question. "Nan Watkins. While Tom alerts the department to check out the strip club again, maybe you and I could go visit her."

Marla strode to the sink and rinsed her glass. "Let's do it. I know she walks around the lake every morning. Maybe we can catch her."

"Hold on." Would Tom count this as a dangerous situation? "You don't suppose Nan could pull anything on us, do you?"

"Are you asking if a woman in her late sixties, who looks and walks like a large rodent, is going to karate-chop the two of us? The answer is no. Let's go."

Marla insisted on taking her Mercedes, as Nan might recognize my van and skedaddle before we could question her. Main Street looked strangely deserted, the stores swallowed in the murky cloud of fire smoke. The lake had turned an ominous, opaque gray, and I doubted we'd see any walkers.

But I was wrong. Marla and I had been huffing along the lake path for no more than ten minutes when we encountered Nan Watkins going in the opposite direction. She was striding along, pumping her arms vigorously.

She looked like a short, pear-shaped, gray-haired drum majorette.

"Stop!" Marla called, out of breath. "Nan! I'm dying. Cardiac arrest."

"Really?" Nan asked, all concern. She halted abruptly on the dirt path and backtracked to us. Her cheeks flamed from exertion, and she was even puffing a bit, which made me feel marginally better.

"No, not really," Marla retorted. "But our ex-husband is being buried today, and there's something we have to know before we put him to rest."

"Something you have to *know*?" she snapped. "I thought you needed me for a health problem!"

"No," Marla said, her hands on her hips, suddenly all business. "We need to know the name of the teenage girl he raped at Southwest Hospital."

"What?" Nan looked nonplussed. "I don't know what you're talking about!" She licked her lips and looked at the ground.

"Won't work, Nan," Marla replied. "The cops have a note the victim wrote to Cecelia Brisbane. If you don't tell us who it is, we're going to the sheriff's department and have them subpoena the information from you."

"You can't!" Nan sputtered. "They can't!"

Marla said, "Wanna bet?"

"Wait," I said. I looked straight into Nan's brown eyes. "Nan, my son needs closure on the death of his father. Please. If this woman or someone close to her shot John Richard, it would help us all put our lives back together if we could find that person and get them arrested. Please help us. Otherwise, this person could go over the edge and kill more people."

"She couldn't have done this," Nan whispered.

There was a bench nearby where fishermen sometimes sat as they tended their lines. Nan moved over to
it and sat down. She said, "I hate remembering this.
Talking about it. Nobody knows about it but me, and I
failed."

"You failed?" I asked gently.

"I failed *her,*" Nan said.

"Is the woman alive?" I asked.

"I think so." Nan fixed her eyes on the dark nimbus
hanging over the lake. "This all happened, oh, eight
years ago? Anyway, I heard she had left town to pursue
other endeavors, far away."

"She was from Aspen Meadow?" I asked. Nan nodded.

"What endeavors did she go pursue?" Marla demanded.

"It . . . doesn't matter. Anyway, she's far away from
here and unlikely to come back." Nan was quiet for so
long I thought she'd changed her mind about telling us.
Then she let out a resigned sigh. "She was fourteen."
Nan's voice was just above a whisper. "She was in the
hospital for a bacterial infection, which is extremely
unusual for a woman so young." Nan explained, "You
may not know that bacterial infections are often trans-
ferred from men to women. Anyway, she was very
pretty and voluptuous. Dr. Korman . . . was making
jokes about her, wondering aloud what she could have
been up to that would have brought on the infection."

I shook my head. So far, so typical.

"He . . . he came in one night when it wasn't his
shift. I thought he'd been drinking. He disappeared
into the young woman's room. She had a single because her family had money. A few minutes later, he
brought her out and took her into an exam room. I

asked him if he needed me to be with him, and he said no, absolutely not. Of course, back then nurses were always required to be in the room during a gynecological exam. So I . . . I figured he'd taken her in for a bandage or an injection . . . something. I never thought. . . ." Again Nan lapsed into silence.

"What happened?" I prodded, keeping my voice low.

Nan lifted her chin and closed her eyes. "He left the room about twenty minutes later. You know"—she opened her eyes and gave us an immensely sad look—"I thought I heard him laughing to himself. She, the patient, didn't come out. Then I heard her crying, so I raced down there. She *was* crying, and there was semen . . . oh God." Nan swallowed, and tears spilled out of her eyes. "He had raped her in the stirrups. And then he'd told her to go back to her room and keep her mouth shut."

"You didn't report him?" Marla asked.

Nan's expression and voice became bitter. "He was a *doctor*. He would have denied everything. And I can assure you, in those days, there would have been *no* punishment. I'm not even sure there would be any punishment today." She paused. "The only person who would have lost her job would have been me."

Marla and I exchanged a glance. I mumbled, "She's probably right."

"I know I'm right," Nan snapped. "Later, I kept wondering why our patient didn't scream when Dr. Korman first . . . started in on her." Nan swallowed. "I think I know now. The rumor is that . . . her father . . . had abused her, too. I heard this later. It would explain the infection, anyway."

"Oh my God," I whispered. "Who was it?"

Nan gave me a sour look. "Brisbane. As in Walter

Brisbane, the owner of the *Mountain Journal*. You know? Whose wife Cecelia could gossip about everything else because she couldn't face the truth. And now Cecelia is dead, too."

"Where is the Brisbane daughter now?"

"I don't know. Her name was Alex. Alex Brisbane." Nan took a deep breath. "Last I heard, she was in the navy, far away."

Chapter 20

We escorted Nan to her car. Spilling her guts had shaken her up, and she wasn't in the mood for walking anymore. I didn't blame her.

"Alex?" Marla repeated to me, incredulous. "That's what they called her. I don't have her in my database, that's for sure."

"It wouldn't be anything he'd brag about, I don't think. Not once he got sober."

We climbed into the Mercedes. Marla revved the engine and grunted. "So, did you ever know Alex Brisbane?"

I shook my head. "Still, it's a puzzle. Except for Cecelia, I don't know of anyone even related to Alex. Maybe Cecelia's remorse overtook her and she tried to hang herself. That would explain the ligature marks on her neck. When that failed, she drove into the lake."

"And this Alex?"

"I saw a picture of her at Cecelia's house. It's at the library, too. Alex was in Greece."

"In *Grease?*" Marla cried. "The Denver producers closed that show two years ago."

"Greece like the country, silly."

"Talking about grease makes me hungry for lunch," Marla countered. "We've got to eat before the Jerk's memorial service. Let's go."

At home, Tom and Arch were talking in the kitchen. Tom was in an unusually good mood, asking Arch questions while puttering around the kitchen. He had potatoes boiling on the stove—for potato salad, he said—and he was forming and seasoning large hamburgers from ground beef. Arch, sitting at a kitchen chair, looked shell-shocked. His mouth hung open and his glasses were skewed. What had they been talking about? And how was I going to tell Tom about Nan's confession when Arch was around?

"Uh-oh," Marla said, bustling up to Arch and giving him a kiss on the head. "Somebody doesn't look very good."

Arch took a deep breath and straightened his glasses. Tom stopped his food prep and flashed us a warning look.

"Here's what happened," Arch said, his voice dead. "The detectives found one hundred, eight thousand dollars in gold coins in the safety-deposit box. They took it down to the department." Arch rubbed his cheeks. "So. Do you think somebody shot Dad for that money?"

"Honey," I said softly, "I don't know. You did the right thing, though, helping those detectives."

Arch shook his head. "It didn't feel like the right thing. Especially since I promised Dad I'd never tell."

"Come on, Arch," Tom said jovially. "Lunch in half an hour."

"I can't," Arch said dismally. He raised his eyes to us. "I'm not mad at anybody. But I don't want anything to eat, and I don't want to . . . be with people. I just want to be by myself. Mom, I'm not trying to be rude. Could you just let me be alone until it's time to go to church?"

"Sweetheart—"

"Mom. *Please.*" I nodded. He quietly turned and left the kitchen.

While Marla, Tom, and I ate the hamburgers, we told him about our talk with Nan Watkins. He left the table to put in a call to the department. It looked as if Nan would have to talk to the cops, after all. When Tom returned, he served us his hot potato salad, along with a spinach salad that he had tossed with thick, crispy pieces of bacon and a fresh sweet-sour dressing. For dessert, he cut us slices of deep-dish strawberry pie and topped each piece with mammoth scoops of vanilla ice cream.

"Thanks for the feast," Marla declared, lifting a glass of water in salute, "celebrating the demise of one of the worst creeps who's ever lived!"

The woman was incorrigible.

At a quarter-past twelve, Arch came down the stairs. He still looked green around the gills. I was consumed with guilt for enjoying a prefuneral banquet. Marla, Tom, and I hadn't meant to rejoice over the Jerk's passing, it had just happened. And we'd been ultraquiet, in case Arch had decided to lie down. But I still felt bad.

Tom, looking devilishly handsome in a somber jacket and tie, drove Marla home (in her Mercedes!) so she could change into a black suit. We figured parking would be bad at St. Luke's, so we were taking as few vehicles as possible. But Marla had flatly refused to arrive at church in Tom's sedan, or, as she called it, "that disgusting old thing you call a vehicle."

I'd promised to pick up Sandee for Marla, so Arch

and I were taking the van. From the back of my closet, I pulled out a black silk dress that I'd bought to wear to a sheriff's department dinner, with my pearls . . . agh!

The jeweler! In all the hubbub of getting Arch off to the bank, making a pie, reading my notes, and intercepting Nan Watkins at the lake, I'd completely forgotten about the pearls I'd picked up on Stoneberry.

"I'll be waiting in the van," Arch said as he headed out.

"Two minutes. Just getting bottles of water." As soon as the door closed behind him, I tapped in the number for the jeweler. While I was put on hold, I scrambled with my free hand to find a canvas bag, into which I put two large bottles of artesian water. "Come on, come on," I said into the phone. The clock indicated it was 12:20. I was due at Sandee's at half-past twelve. Finally the jeweler clicked in.

"It's Goldy Schulz. I was wondering about those pearls I left you!"

"Fake." His voice was expressionless.

"Not real?" I cried, amazed. "Not genuine pearls?"

"Nope. Bye."

A man of few words, was our town jeweler. I lugged the water-bottle bag out to the van and revved the engine. Then I tried *not* to count up all the worthless leads this investigation had engendered. This case was more of a dead end than Stoneberry itself.

Sandee Blue had returned to the condo she'd previously shared with Bobby. It was in a townhouse area very similar to the one at Aspen Meadow Country Club, only this one bordered Interstate 70 and overlooked Denver. I wondered how Sandee's stripper dollars and Bobby's music could enable them to live in such a nice place. But maybe the band made more

money than one would suspect from listening to their
music.

"Thanks for picking me up!" Sandee burbled as she
teetered to the van in her black spike heels. Never one
for conservative dress, Sandee wore a tight, low-cut
black dress and sparkly jet jewelry. She'd teased her
platinum hair up in front and then loosely pinned that
section off her face. Two walls of long blond hair
swung by her ears. She looked very fetching. I wondered if she was trolling for a wealthy new underwriter.
No telling what Bobby's reaction to *that* would be.

"So Bobby's out of town?" I asked neutrally as I did
a seven-point turn in her steep driveway.

"Nope!" she cried gaily. "He's out fighting the fire. I
don't know why they call it the Aspen Meadow *Volunteer* Fire Department. If he didn't get paid for fighting
fires, he wouldn't be able to afford his house!" She put
her arm over the seat and turned to greet Arch. "Hey,
buddy! Still playing hockey?"

"Aha," I said quickly. "So you *knew* he wasn't playing golf twice a week."

"Uh-oh," came Arch's low voice from the back. I
opened my eyes wide at Sandee, who had turned
crimson.

"I wasn't supposed to talk about it," she mumbled.
"John Richard told me to keep my mouth shut."

"Really?" I said sourly. "How well did that work out?"

"Oh, Mom," Arch interjected. "Leave her alone."

"Sure," I said. "Fine."

Sandee turned back to Arch. "So! Did you get that
new stick you wanted? Have you used it?"

"I did get it!" Arch exclaimed. "I'm using it for the
first time tomorrow morning, at a hockey birthday
party."

"Cool! How's Todd?"

I really didn't begrudge Sandee's and Arch's friendship. In fact, I was glad for it. Before John Richard was incarcerated, he had largely ignored Arch during the weekly visits. Arch's visits to John Richard's house were often made more bearable by the presence of John Richard's chatty, immature girlfriends. And now here was Sandee blabbing almost flirtatiously with Arch. At least it was diverting his attention from the upcoming service. Sandee might not be terribly intelligent, I thought grimly, but at least she was good at lifting a mood.

When we arrived at the church, the parking lot was not even half full. Had John Richard really been so disliked? He'd treated hundreds of patients in Aspen Meadow over the years his practice had been here. Would so few come to remember him? Fewer even than Albert Kerr, who had practiced only at Southwest, and that had been fourteen years ago?

That's the problem with the arrogant, I thought as Arch, Sandee, and I scanned the small crowd for Marla and Tom. John Richard had *thought* he was much more powerful and popular than he actually was. Not to mention that over the past few years, he'd spent a good bit of his time behind bars. If his prison pals could have come, maybe the church would have filled up.

"You look very upset," Father Pete said, coming up beside me. He touched my arm. "Are you all right?"

I signaled for Arch and Sandee to go on up to the pew from which Marla was waving madly. "I'm fine," I said curtly. "It's Arch I'm worried about."

Father Pete let go of my arm. "I think your son is in better shape than you are. Goldy?"

"I'm here, aren't I? Thanks, Father Pete. I'm going to sit with my son now." And I scuttled away.

In the few minutes before the service started, I scanned the crowd. Courtney was there, giving everyone her cold gimlet eyes. So she hadn't been arrested after all. She wore a black dress that was somewhat more stylish than, but certainly as revealing as, Sandee's. Instead of pearls, she wore a gold necklace, a strand of what looked like miniature tennis balls. Why did I get the feeling that both she and Sandee were trolling for cute young doctors? Unfortunately for them, 99 percent of John Richard's doc buddies had abandoned him when he'd been convicted of assault. Not that they hadn't known what he was like. They knew, because I'd told their wives. But getting caught and sent to jail—that was taboo.

"Goldy!" Marla whispered. "Look in the back. Recognize anybody?"

I turned slowly. Well, well. Holly Kerr was sitting with Ginger Vikarios. I didn't know where Ted was. And it looked as if John Richard still had some loyal friends in the stripper community. Besides Sandee, there was Lana, who winked at me, Dannyboy the Lion-Maned, Ruby of the Dead Husband, and half a dozen other women whom I might have recognized if they'd taken off their clothes. Ruby Drake, I thought. Marla had thought Ruby and the Jerk were dating, and yet Ruby had told us she hated John Richard. Not only that, but the same gun had been used to kill her husband *and* the Jerk. Were the cops looking at her as a suspect? Should I?

Arch turned to see what we were looking at. His eyes bugged out at the sight of so many curvaceous women.

Tom stifled a laugh and said, "Hey, buddy, what are

you going to give your friend for his birthday tomorrow?"

And then, finally, the music and talking ceased. Father Pete, as imposing as ever, preceded the coffin. I did not know the four men who were pallbearers, probably that 1 percent who'd stayed loyal to the Jerk. Their procession down the nave was slow and deliberate. I checked Arch: His face was very pale.

"I am the resurrection and the life," Father Pete intoned. We all opened our service leaflets and began to read along with him. Arch dashed tears out of his eyes. Marla gave him a tissue and I put my arm around him.

" 'Blessed are they who observe justice, who do righteousness at all times,' " we read from Psalm 106. After that we recited Psalm 121, " 'I lift up my eyes to the hills, from whence does my help come?' "

I began to feel painfully, overpoweringly ill. How embarrassing would it be for Arch if I tried to slip out? Tom, sensing my discomfort, put his arm around me.

"I know what you're feeling," he said under his breath.

"What I'm feeling is *sick.*"

"Close your eyes, see if you can feel something."

Since Tom was about the least New Agey person I'd ever encountered, I did as bidden. After a moment, I got it. What I felt was a struggle. The more I focused on it, the clearer it was. I opened my mouth in surprise. "What is it?" I asked him.

"The presence of good and evil," he replied, his eyes fixed on the altar. "You're feeling the conflict. Unresolved."

Somehow, we got through it. In John Richard's will, he'd designated an old doctor friend to take care of the funeral arrangements. Payment for the funeral was supposed to come out of John Richard's estate—which I doubted was very large. But the doc had bought the coffin and made all the arrangements, so at least there was enough money for that. I'd have to leave worry about Arch's high school tuition to another day.

Arch had said he did not want to attend a graveside ceremony, which I honored. I didn't even know where John Richard would be laid to rest, nor did I care. The Jerk was most emphatically not my problem anymore.

When Marla asked if we were staying for the reception, Arch, Tom, and I declined. Sandee's Rainbow pals were taking her off to party, Marla said. When I ran outside to see if I could catch Ruby Drake, she was gone.

Arch, Tom, and I went home in my van. Yes, I was a passenger in my vehicle. But it felt as if I'd been run over by it. I asked Arch what he wanted to eat for dinner, and he said he'd been invited to Todd's for dinner and to spend the night, then Todd would take him to the party the next day. Didn't I remember him telling me all this?

I did not. But I told him it was fine. He clomped upstairs and began throwing clothes and hockey equipment into a bag. By the time Eileen Druckman showed up to take him, I had left a long message for Detective Blackridge, telling him about the fake pearls at the end of John Richard's driveway. I asked if he had questioned Ruby Drake. And had he gotten Tom's message about Nan's confession? Then I hung up.

I ran myself a hot bath and got in to soak. Tom insisted we get into pajamas—it was not yet five o'clock—and enjoy the ultimate comfort food: grilled-cheese sandwiches. He'd rented a lighthearted comedy set in Italy. I laughed and felt my spirits lift. By eight o'clock, we'd taken care of the dishes and the animals, and were snuggling in bed.

By quarter-past eight Tom was making slow, tender love to me. The gate to my soul swung open, and Tom's love flowed in. He kissed me over and over, saying, "You are the greatest gift I have ever received." He caressed my belly and thighs and said, "I will never cause you pain." When it was over, he held me tight and whispered, "I will love you forever and ever."

And then, finally, I began to sob.

Saturday morning we awoke to the sound of sirens. The smell of smoke was even thicker than it had been the day before. I coughed as I let the animals out. I revved up the fans, closed all the windows, and turned on the radio. The fire in the wildlife preserve had expanded to three thousand acres and was only 20 percent contained. They still hadn't found the missing hikers. More firefighters had been called up from Colorado Springs and Pueblo, and we would be hearing those trucks arriving all day.

In the kitchen, I felt at loose ends. I still had no idea as to what had happened to John Richard—who had killed him and why. Was money involved? I wasn't at all sure. And what about the clipping of the hair and all the other incongruous things found at the crime scene? Either the detectives weren't getting anywhere or they weren't keeping Boyd in the loop. I drank an espresso doused with cream. No Arch, no catering event, no amateur sleuthing? I couldn't think of what to do with myself.

Cook anyway, my inner voice commanded. And so I did.

I checked my file. There was one pie crust recipe I hadn't yet tried with the strawberry filling. An old standby, it featured unsalted butter and lard cut into flour and salt, then mixed with the smallest amount of ice water possible. Thank goodness for food processors, I thought as the blade cut the butter into the dry ingredients. When it was time for the lard, I scooped out the snowy white stuff and wondered, again, why it wasn't in more recipes. Okay, it was fat, but so was butter. And the addition of lard to baked goods made them incomparably flaky.

And then there was Beef Wellington, where the placement of lardons helped keep the tenderloin juicy and moist. Yes, lard could be—

Wait a minute. When we said a dish was larded with fat, it was because there was so much of it. The implication was that "larding" meant "putting in lots of layers."

But what else could you lard with layers? How about a crime scene? What if you planted Goldy Schulz's gun there, for example? Wouldn't that point to Goldy as the killer? And when the coroner found the victim's hair cut—could it be for a trophy, or could it be used for a DNA test? How about dropping fake pearls? Was that meant to point *to* someone, or was it meant to point *away* from someone else? If the cops also found a pink tennis-ball gun silencer, how would they know whether the killer dropped it by accident or on purpose?

Larding. That's what I was doing with the pie crust, whirling bits of fat that, when melted, would make the crust flaky and crisp. But if you larded a crime scene with lots of items, responsibility for the crime could point in any number of directions. If you were patient, gathering up your fake clues, then saw an opportunity to steal a gun or two, you could set up the whole thing, do the deed, and the puzzle would occupy the cops for weeks. Or months. Or maybe forever.

Tom came into the kitchen wearing navy slacks and a pale yellow polo shirt. He looked *hot*. Remembering the previous night, I got tingly all over.

"And where," I asked, "are *you* going, looking so spiffy?"

"Breakfast with Boyd. Then down to the department. Not too many folks there on Saturday. I want to see some of the guys. Clean up my desk. Get going again."

I smiled and gave him a tight hug. "Enjoy."

He took off. I sat on our back deck with my double shot of espresso, thinking. If you changed just one thing that had been presented as fact in this whole crime, everything would drop into place. What might that fact be? I had an idea of who could be behind all this planning and plotting, not to mention execution, in both senses of the word. But I had to be sure.

The Aspen Meadow Public Library opened at ten on Saturday mornings. Kids of all ages congregated outside the glass doors, some to do research for homework, some to use the library computers to get online, some to go to the weekly story hour with their mothers. We were all coughing and hacking in the smoky air. Discussion of the fire's progress dominated conversations. I waited with the kids and their mothers, not saying anything. I couldn't preoccupy myself with the fire, because I was focused on the one piece of information I needed. Then I would be sure.

We poured through the door on the dot of ten. I made a beeline for the "Locals in Armed Services" photo display. Then I studied the blown-up photograph. After a while, I went to the reference desk and asked for all their books on Greek architecture, and Aspen Meadow High School yearbooks from four and five years ago.

Within twenty-five minutes, I had my answer. She'd lost some weight, had some plastic surgery on her nose, maybe when she got her boob job. She'd changed her haircut and color. And she'd managed to fool all of us, even her own mother. She'd even hoodwinked the fellow who prided himself on being so smart: Dr. John Richard Korman, whom she'd set out to ensnare even while he was still in jail.

I raced back to the van and called Tom on his cell. No luck. Was he out of range? Had he left the phone in his sedan when he met Boyd at their breakfast eatery? I left a voice-mail message: *This time I'm sure. Call me back ASAP.* Just for good measure, I called Boyd. No answer there, either. I cursed the phone, banged it on the dashboard, then put in a call to the sheriff's department. Finally, *finally* I got Reilly.

"Listen, it's Goldy Schulz," I gasped. "I think I know who might have killed John Richard. Dr. Korman."

Detective Reilly had become cordial, if not exactly warm, since the cops had discovered that my gun had not killed John Richard, that I hadn't trashed his house, and that I'd known nothing about John Richard producing a love child with Talitha Vikarios. But Reilly did sigh when he heard my dramatic announcement about zeroing in on the killer. With forced patience, he said, "I'm listening, Mrs. Schulz. What did you find out?"

I summarized what I knew about Alexandra Brisbane, her terrible history, and what I believed was her motive for revenge. Then again, someone or someones close to her might have done the deed. I outlined how she, he, or they could have entrapped John Richard and gotten him into the money-laundering business, hoping he would start skimming . . . which was where the hundred and eight thou had come from. The murderer had hoped that John Richard would be killed for the skimming, as his predecessor, Quentin Drake, had been. And when John Richard escaped punishment, someone took matters into his or her own hands. Which is why the money launderers had shown up later and trashed John Richard's house. They wanted their cash back.

"Okay, Mrs. Schulz, slow down," Reilly said. "What data are you using to come to these conclusions?"

"The fact that the real Parthenon, its marble remains in ruins, is in Athens, Greece. And the Parthenon made from dun-colored stone is in Nashville, Tennessee."

"Run that by me again?"

"Alexandra Brisbane sent her mother, Cecelia Brisbane, a picture of herself in front of the Parthenon in Nashville. She said she was in the navy—never mind that no ships deploy out of Tennessee—because Alexandra didn't want her mother to know where she was. In addition, the photo was taken before Alexandra had shed fifteen or so pounds, had plastic surgery on her nose and boobs, and cut and curled her hair and dyed it platinum."

"I'm still not—"

"Alexandra Brisbane is Sandee Blue."

"What? Are you *sure*?" Reilly's voice was doubtful. "I mean, Cecelia was at that Kerr funeral lunch, and Sandee Blue was there with your ex. Don't you think Cecelia would have recognized her own daughter?"

"Not with her poor eyesight, and all those physical changes to her daughter."

"But . . . Alexandra was from Aspen Meadow. What about her high school friends who could have recognized her?"

I was ready for this. "At the library, I looked up Alexandra in the Aspen Meadow High yearbooks from four and five years ago. Besides her chubby-cheeked, mousy-haired class picture, there were photos of her in the Explorers' Club, beside Raccoon Creek, Cowboy Cliff, you name it. But she looked like a jock, not a stripper. Plus, she's now working at the Rainbow Men's Club. How many former back-country explorers do you suppose hang out there? I should add, Sandee has a very jealous boyfriend, Bobby Calhoun, otherwise known as Nashville Bobby. He has a Ruger that was supposedly stolen—"

"Okay, okay, we know that. Look, this is good information. Thanks. We've already radioed up to the fire chief that we want to question Calhoun as soon as they can spare him from the fire. The chief begged me not to take him off his line right now. And I'll consult with Blackridge to see about bringing Sandee in for questioning."

"But that's not enough—"

"Mrs. Schulz, please. I can't promise you anything. A lot of leads in this case have gone nowhere—"

"Like what?"

He exhaled. "Okay, how about Ted and Ginger Vikarios went straight from the Albert Kerr memorial lunch to a church meeting that lasted five hours? A handful of people claim the Vikarioses never left."

"Please believe me, Detective. I know I'm right this time."

"I *understand,* Mrs. Schulz. And we're going to follow up, I swear. But I'll tell you what we don't want. We don't want you questioning Sandee Blue. We don't want you going to the Rainbow Men's Club or anywhere else that could be dangerous. And by the way, your husband would say the same thing. Want me to go get him and put him on the phone with you? I think he just got back with Boyd."

"No, thanks. I just feel so . . . nervous, knowing that Sandee and Bobby are out there somewhere—"

"Please, Mrs. Schulz. You have concerns, call your lawyer. All right? I need to go now."

After I'd closed the phone, a cloud of worry descended on me. What if Sandee or Bobby tried to frame me further? They didn't know that the cops had picked up all the money from the safe-deposit box . . . what if they tried to get the key out of Arch?

I put the van in gear and started toward Lakewood. I'd tried to solve this crime, first because I was implicated, and second, for Arch. For closure. But would it be so good for Arch to know his father had been killed because he'd raped a teenage girl? I thought not. Especially since I believed that that woman or her cohort, or cohorts, had also killed her own mother, probably because Cecelia hadn't protected Alex from her own father. Was I crazy, or could all this be true? No matter what, we were talking about a very traumatized and disturbed individual or individuals. I certainly wasn't going to try to catch the killer. If the cops didn't want to follow up on my theories, then that was their problem.

But I'd promised not to go looking for trouble. And besides, I wanted to check on Arch. I'd never seen him skate for more than five minutes, anyway. He was such a good kid, and he'd been doing so much better since the school change, that he deserved some TLC . . . maybe a new outfit or lunch out after the game. Besides, I missed him.

* * *

The Lakewood rink was so mobbed with screaming kids that I thought my eardrums were going to pop. The lobby was teeming with boys in hockey gear and girls in figure-skating leotards and tights. Kids hollered at the desk attendant for locker keys and rental skates. Arch was nowhere in sight. I don't think I would have recognized him right off, not in a helmet and all those pads, anyway. I made my way to rink side and watched the skaters whizzing past. Finally I picked out a jersey that said "Druckman." The next time Todd shot by, I called to him to stop. This he did. He clomped, red-faced and sweaty, over the thick rubber padding to the spot where I stood.

"Where's Arch?" I asked. "I've been looking everywhere and I can't find him. I wanted to see him skate."

"He's gone!" Todd replied. "Somebody came to get him. The guy at the front desk might know who picked him up."

I shrieked all the way to the lobby.

Chapter 21

I unfolded the note with trembling hands. I cursed myself for not bringing Arch down here myself, for not figuring out the solution to John Richard's murder before that trip to the library. I tried to read, but the words swam.

> *Bring JRK's money to the Roundhouse at noon. Then you'll get your kid back. No cops. You screw this up, your son gets dumped in the preserve, right next to the fire.*

The note was unsigned. It was half-past eleven. I jumped into the van and headed back up the mountain. I put in a frantic call to Tom. One to Boyd. Another one to Reilly. Nobody was answering. I called the department dispatcher. My son had been kidnapped, I yelped, and I needed as many units as they could spare to hightail it to the Roundhouse, in Aspen Meadow. . . .

She told me to calm down, she'd see what she could do. Meanwhile, I pressed the pedal and hit I-70 going eighty miles per hour. Maybe if a state trooper picked me up on his radar, I could get him to follow me. I willed the cell to ring. Five minutes, ten minutes, fifteen minutes passed as I flew up the interstate, my horn blaring. The engine whined as I took the exit ramp at sixty miles per hour.

Oh, how I cursed myself for trusting her. That sweet act, anybody could be taken in. And had been. *When are you going to play hockey, Arch?* And my son so politely answering: *Tomorrow morning, in Lakewood.*

I flew through Aspen Meadow to the Roundhouse. No one there, either. It was five after noon.

I kept going up Upper Cottonwood Creek Road, toward the Aspen Meadow Wildlife Preserve. Toward the fire. *Please let Arch be all right,* I prayed.

The smoke became extremely thick halfway up the road. I was going to keep driving until a cop or fireman stopped me. Five miles up, I was flagged down. The road was covered with orange cones.

"You can't go in there, lady," a uniformed fireman informed me. He had a long, lined face and wavy gray hair matted to his egg-shaped head.

"Please help me," I begged. "Somebody has kidnapped my child and said they're going up to the fire. Maybe to meet someone, I don't know."

"Meet who?"

"Bobby Calhoun? Please, my son's life is in danger!"

The fireman consulted a clipboard. "Bobby Calhoun has been up with his line for the last forty-eight hours, lady. I would have known if he'd—"

"If you don't let me through," I screamed, "I'm going to drive right through these cones!"

"All right, all right. I'll lead you to the base camp for Calhoun's line. It's up by Cherokee Pass."

He strode purposefully to his fire-department pickup. A moment later I was following him along one of the dirt roads that led into the preserve. I began to cough from the smoke. My eyes smarted as I squinted to make out the pickup's rear lights. I closed all the van windows and pressed a button for the air to recirculate.

Was I right? Was Sandee driving Arch up to the fire? Had Arch told her the safety-deposit box was empty? Was she going to dump Arch, get Bobby, and then the two of them would take off together? How far did she think they'd get?

The fireman turned off onto a bumpy one-lane fire road lined with singed grass. I held my breath and prayed as the van groaned into the turn. Then I pressed the gas as gently as possible. The wheels lurched suddenly as I hit a small ditch. Somehow I managed to negotiate the ditch without vaulting the van onto the blackened grass.

Was the smoke turning orange, or was that my imagination? And was that snow falling or bits of ash?

Arch, Arch, I mouthed silently, my heart thudding. *Be safe. Let me find you.*

The fireman turned on his left signal and I followed. A ragtag row of pickup trucks were just visible through the heavy haze. The fireman parked and jumped out of his vehicle, with me close on his heels.

A group of firemen, their yellow outer garments zipped open, was sitting behind one of the trucks. As I came closer, I saw that their faces were blackened with ash. They were drinking water and talking in low tones to the fireman who'd led me up to them.

"Please help me," I burst out. "I can't find my son."

One of the men, his blackened face streaked with sweat, shook his head. "Ma'am, we've got at least two hikers who've been missing for a couple of days. We didn't see a kid anywhere, I promise. I saw Bobby Calhoun's truck come up from one of the fire roads a little while ago. He parked down there somewhere, but I haven't seen him—"

"Parked down there?" I cried, pointing along the row of parked trucks. "Somebody come with me, please!"

I turned and began trotting beside the trucks. The smoke made it hard to make out details of any of the vehicles. My coughing and hacking wasn't helping me think, either. I glanced back and saw, thank God, three firefighters jogging along behind me.

And then I saw the pickup. "Visit Nashville!" the bumper sticker screamed. I turned to the firefighters and waved them forward.

"This is it," I said, indicating the pickup. "I can't see if anyone's inside."

"Okay, ma'am. Stay put."

The firefighters exchanged a couple of words that I couldn't hear. Then a pair of them walked toward the truck, one on each side. With a quick nod, they simultaneously opened the driver's and passenger's doors.

Arch jumped out of the passenger side and coughed. I shrieked his name. He rushed toward me.

"Why are we here?" he demanded. "Sandee kept asking about Dad's safety-deposit box and saying we were waiting for you—" He began hacking and thumping his chest.

"Shh, it's okay now," I said. I tried to hug him, but as usual, he was not wanting an embrace, especially in front of tough-guy firefighters.

"Hey! Come back here!" the firefighter on the driver's side of the truck hollered. "Where do you think you're going?"

Through the smoke, I could just see Sandee Blue/Alexandra Brisbane, clad in some kind of black suit, running into the woods.

"Hey!" I hollered.

I took off after her. The firefighters, cursing, followed us.

The pine forest by the row of trucks ran up a steep hill. Panting, I began stomping through the underbrush, calling Sandee's name.

When she didn't answer, I shrieked, "You didn't have to kill John Richard, you know! You didn't have to kill him!"

Behind us, the firefighters, whose heavy boots were forcing them to a slower pace, were hollering that the two of us had better stop. Otherwise, their faint voices warned, we were *all* going to get killed.

Trying to listen to the sound of Sandee maneuvering through the underbrush, I ran blindly up the hill. Four minutes, five minutes, six. The smoke was becoming more and more dense, the air hotter.

Abruptly, the forest opened up at the edge of a wide cliff. There was nothing on the other side of the granite ridge but clouds of smoke. I halted, gasping.

Sandee was standing on top of a gray boulder at the very edge of the precipice. I blinked and squinted into the smoke. She was wearing what looked like a shiny black running suit and black tennis shoes. And . . . what was that hanging from her neck? A gold chain with a locket? What the hell was she up to now?

The firefighters' heavy boots crashing through the undergrowth, as well as their raised voices, became louder.

I coughed, tried to get my breath, and peered up at Sandee. "You didn't have to kill him." I panted, then said, "You could have had him charged and prosecuted."

Sandee's laugh was strident. "The statute of limitations on rape is eight years. Think I would have had a chance? How good a witness do you think a stripper would have been?"

The firefighters slashed through the last bit of undergrowth and arrived at my side. Two of them each took one of my arms. The third one addressed Sandee.

"You crazy bitch!" he shouted. "Get down from here! You want us all to get burned up?" In spite of myself, I shook my head. They didn't learn negotiating skills in firefighting school.

"No," she called blithely. "Just me. But you need to listen first. That woman you're holding, Goldy Schulz, did not kill her ex-husband, John Richard Korman. I did. I stole her gun and a couple more, and then shot him with one of them. My boyfriend, Bobby, wasn't in on it. I also strangled Cecelia Brisbane!"

Abruptly, she disappeared from the rockface. Had she jumped?

"What the—" I muttered.

"Oh, *dammit*," said one of the firefighters, the one who was holding my right arm. "What's off that cliff, John?"

"Nothing," John replied. "Raccoon Creek is a hundred yards down. She's a goner." He took a deep breath, his shoulders slumped. "We need to get back."

Three days later, when the fire was finally, *finally* out, four teams trekked back into the preserve to assess the damage . . . and look for the remains of Sandee and the hikers.

But they didn't find any human remains. The preserve is a very big place. So many people were evacuated, so many hikers and campers were forced out of the preserve, that the cops have yet to figure out who's missing and who's accounted for.

The team searching Raccoon Creek did make a discovery. On top of a boulder in the middle of the creek, they found a gold chain and locket. Bobby Calhoun, sobbing, identified it as the one he'd given Sandee.

I told Tom, and then Blackridge and Reilly, that it was possible—not probable, but possible—that Sandee had gotten away. She'd been a member of the Explorers' Club in high school and knew every inch of the preserve, including where the creeks and fire roads led. Besides, I said, who runs into a fire to commit suicide? Sandee had planned everything out—the murders, framing others with fake clues. Why wouldn't she have planned a getaway, too? Plus, she was a master of disguise, and . . .

My dear Tom, as well as Blackridge and Reilly, said there was simply no way. The detectives had interviewed the firefighters. They'd examined Cowboy Cliff, where Sandee had disappeared. Yes, there was a very narrow, rocky path down to the creek, but with all that smoke, nobody could have seen it or known its twists and curves. And given the size of the fire, no human could have made it out of the preserve alive.

"It's over," Tom assured me, pulling me in for a hug. "I never thought that I would be the one to say this, but we need to let go of this mess and move ahead. Okay, Miss G.?"

I groaned.

We had the memorial service for Sandee and Cecelia Brisbane the next week. Sandee had written up her story and mailed it to the *Post,* the *News,* and the *Mountain Journal.* So much sympathy was generated for her that Father Pete had to tell people to stop sending flowers to the church. Priscilla Throckbottom put an ad in the *Mountain Journal* saying that donations of pine seedlings could be made in Sandee's name, and the PosteriTREE committee would plant them in the forest when the skeletons were found. I don't know if she had any takers.

The church parking lot was filled to overflowing the day of the service. Everyone, it seemed, was trying to make sense out of these deaths. At the reception following the service, the words *tragic* and *pointless* kept coming up. Sandee had taken on evil to combat evil, and the whole thing had blown up in her face.

Blackridge and Reilly asked me to make a statement. I began by saying, *You think you know people.*

I thought I'd known Sandee. A stripper. A blonde. I knew she manipulated men to get what she wanted—first Bobby, then John Richard, then Bobby again. In her interactions with me, sometimes she'd acted ditzy, other times, self-centered. So I'd assumed that was exactly what she was. And all the time, she'd been watching me, watching Arch, asking questions, and taking notes. *Did you bring money?* she'd asked Marla and me. Planting the idea in our heads: Folks are dropping off money here, doesn't that seem strange? Only we'd been too dense to get the fact that John Richard was up to something shady.

Oh my, but Sandee was *good.*

Following the details from Sandee's letters, which told how she'd stolen both Bobby's *and* Dannyboy's Rugers, Blackridge and Reilly finally caught Lana and Dannyboy. Law enforcement was planning to bring murder charges against the two of them. The Denver PD was reopening the case of Quentin Drake, husband of stripper Ruby Drake. And then there was the incident of vandalizing John Richard's rental home, looking for the money he skimmed. The crime lab picked up some latents that matched Dannyboy's.

The Rainbow is closed now, and the archdiocese of Denver is negotiating to buy the place so it can set up a second soup kitchen. The church is hoping that, in time, people won't remember what kind of establishment it once was. I wish them well.

Blackridge and Reilly asked *why* I thought Sandee killed her mother. Because, I said, the mother had failed to protect her daughter. Cecilia Brisbane, who was observant when it came to the faults of those around her, was blind when it came to her husband. She was deaf to the needs of her own daughter, and now both Brisbane parents were dead. Walter had done the irreparable damage, which had been compounded by Cecelia's complicity.

And then, when Alexandra Brisbane was what—thirteen? fourteen?—John Richard Korman had raped her in a Southwest Hospital room. Nan Watkins had cleaned Sandee up and kept her own mouth shut. The detectives asked, Had Albert Kerr known what John Richard had done to Sandee? Had Ted Vikarios? I countered with, Would they have moved to punish John Richard if they had? I didn't know, but I doubted it. The only time John Richard's bad behavior had come home to roost for the Vikarioses was when the Jerk had impregnated their daughter, Talitha Vikarios. And she had left rather than abort the child or have our family embarrassed.

And so the reason for the double murder was—? Blackridge and Reilly asked.

I believed that Alexandra—Sandee with two *es*—had not been able to tell her mother directly what Dr. Korman had done. Why would she? Her mother had not believed her before.

So Sandee had gotten out. She'd changed her name, dyed her hair, become a stripper, and saved up enough money for plastic surgery. Sometime before her surgeries, she'd made a trip to Nashville. *Here I am, Mom!* As Arch would say, *Not*. And yet Sandee had been the same person inside, with the same pain. Maybe she'd tried confronting her father with that payphone call. Rather than face the truth, he had killed himself. What was left of the people who'd failed Sandee?

Well, there was that doctor who had raped her. She'd tried to get her own mother to talk about the Jerk's misdeeds in the *Mountain Journal*. But that hadn't worked. Cecelia had felt . . . what? Fear? Suspicion as to who had written her an anonymous letter alleging that a longtime Aspen Meadow doctor had raped a teenage patient? In any event, Cecelia had done nothing except mail the note to me.

So Sandee had put all her energy into planning the murder of John Richard Korman. According to Lana, who was working on a plea deal, Sandee had encouraged her to hire John Richard to run the Smurfs, who laundered all that cash that came in to the Rainbow. Sandee had known that John Richard would take advantage, that he wouldn't be able to resist skimming. As the cops say, "People don't change. They just get better camouflage."

You think you know people, and sometimes you do.

John Richard was unable to resist Sandee's seductiveness. Courtney MacEwan couldn't possibly compete with Sandee's years as a stripper. Sandee was good. Most important, she hadn't forgotten what had happened to her.

She'd had a month to put her plan into action. She'd

gathered the materials that would point to other people, acting ditzy the whole time, so we wouldn't suspect she was up to anything.

Does your mom protect herself? she'd asked Arch. *Ooh, a revolver? Where does she keep it?*

Where does that pretty Courtney MacEwan keep those pink tennis balls? she'd asked at the tennis shop, during one of her long waits at the golf shop. *Ooh, may I see one of those cans?*

At Albert Kerr's memorial lunch, when Ted Vikarios had seen Arch in the kitchen, he'd known immediately that the Jerk was the father of his grandson. The resemblance between the two boys was just too strong. Even I had thought Gus was Arch. So Ted had confronted John Richard in the parking lot, probably just as Sandee was coming back with my thirty-eight tucked in her bag. Aha, she'd thought, one more person to blame this on! She hadn't had anything of Ted's to plant at the scene, but she knew what the argument was about: a child whom John Richard had supposedly fathered. So at the last minute, she'd said something like, "Just a minute, honey," and run back to my van for one more thing: my kitchen shears to cut off a chunk of John Richard's hair, and make it look as if someone might do a postmortem DNA test.

Maybe it was that argument, the one between Ted and John Richard, that had made Sandee think, *Now I have enough suspects.* Ginger and Ted Vikarios seemed to be furious with John Richard. In addition to the clipped hair, Sandee could leave pearls that looked like Ginger's. And of course the very publicly jealous Courtney MacEwan was well known for those pink tennis balls.

And if all else failed, John Richard had a despised ex-wife who owned a gun, easily stolen.

And your theory on the death of Cecelia Brisbane? Reilly asked.

After all that, going over to Cecelia's house, strangling her, running her car into the creek, all these would have been easy, almost an afterthought. *Thanks for nothing, Mom.*

What none of this explained, I told them, was the attack on me at the conference center the morning this whole thing had started. I believed I could rule out the Jerk.

There was only one person left: Courtney MacEwan, whose life I had ruined, she claimed. But I hadn't been to blame for *that*. As usual, though, John Richard had been as unwilling as ever to take responsibility for his own desires. He'd wanted freedom to live on his own and do what he wanted. So he'd convinced Courtney, I firmly believed, that I was responsible for their breakup. And so she'd hired someone. Marla had even seen her paying him, although I couldn't prove anything.

Courtney had seen Roger Mannis stalking my events, yelling at me about infractions. It bothered me that I couldn't say without a doubt that Roger Mannis had messed up my food and attacked me. And yet he knew about the math of spoilage and how to turn off compressors that most people would just ignore. His skinny Uriah Heep body shape certainly matched the one of the person who'd shoved me out of the way and chopped the back of my neck.

What could I do about this? I couldn't get him fired on a hunch. With John Richard gone, would Roger Mannis become the new jerk in my life? Sort of like Moriarty, running through all of Sherlock Holmes's adventures as the impersonation of evil?

Courtney and Roger weren't talking, but that wasn't

the end of it. The next time I catered and Roger Mannis showed up to bother me, I was calling the cops. And I had a new gig coming up: A friend of Brewster Motley had tasted my food and wanted me to come into their law offices to prepare breakfast and lunch. I wasn't going to worry about Roger Mannis now; I was going to prepare for him. He wasn't going to hurt me again and get away with it.

And then, after all that, good began to happen.

The day after Sandee Brisbane ran into the fire, I called Ginger Vikarios and told her what I suspected about John Richard being the father of their grandson. *Let's get our boys together,* I'd said. Ginger had burst into tears. Fourteen-year-old Augustus Vikarios— Gus—would love to have a brother.

Along with her last will and testament, Talitha Vikarios had left her parents a separate set of instructions. It said that if Goldy Korman ever came into their lives and wanted to see Gus, it was okay, as long as she received the enclosed letter. When I visited Ginger Vikarios that same afternoon, she gave me it to me, along with heart-wrenching photos of Talitha with her little boy, who looked just like Arch, from infant to teenager.

Then, finally, I read Talitha's letter to me.

Dear Goldy,

If you ever do get this letter, it means that I died . . . not a pleasant thought! But you should know that my Gus and your Arch are half brothers. I don't imagine they look alike, but maybe they do. Anyway, I didn't tell anybody that Dr. Korman and I had an affair. I thought I was in love, but never mind. He wasn't. And the main thing is, I wanted you and Dr. Korman and Arch to be a happy family without me, and without Gus.

Oh, Goldy, please understand that I wanted my disappearance to be a gift to you. When I heard you were divorced, I wrote this letter and included it with my will, to be opened only if you somehow found out about Gus. I don't want him to be a burden to you. I just want him to have a family besides my parents, whose career in the church was ruined by his appearance.

I tried to do the right thing, a lot of right things, really, and I'm not sure any of them turned out right. But I have a great boy, and I hope you can find it in your heart to love him.

Talitha Vikarios

Acknowledgments

The author wishes to acknowledge the assistance of the following people: Jim, Jeff, J.Z., and Joey Davidson; Carolyn Marino and her brilliant team at Harper-Collins; Sandra Dijkstra and *her* fabulous team; Carole Kornreich, M.D.; Kathy Saideman; Dan Pruett, coroner investigator, and Triena Harper, chief deputy coroner, Jefferson County, Colorado; Lowell Fortune, Esq.; John Schenk, JKS Catering; Steve Langer, Panache Catering; Regina Carlyon; Meg Kendal, Denver-Evergreen ob-gyn; Julie Kaewert, Jasmine Cresswell, Lee Karr, Francine Mathews, and Shirley Carnahan, for friendship and enlightenment; Craig Aiken, R.N.; Johanna Gallers, Ph.D.; the Reverend Christopher Platt; and as ever, the most excellent Sergeant Richard Millsapps of the Jefferson County Sheriff's Department.

The Recipes

In-Your-Face Strawberry Pie (I)

Crust
1 cup chopped filberts
½ pound (2 sticks) unsalted butter, melted
2 cups all-purpose flour

In a wide, dry frying pan, toast the filberts over medium-low heat, stirring, until they emit a nutty scent and have turned a very light brown. Allow to cool on paper towels.

Preheat the oven to 350°. Butter a 9-by-13-inch or 10-by-14-inch glass pan.

Mix the nuts, melted butter, and flour until thoroughly combined, then press this mixture evenly onto the bottom of the pan.

Bake the crust for about 20 to 30 minutes, or until the crust is set and has turned a very light brown. Set aside on a rack to cool completely before filling.

Topping (see note, page 362)
1½ pounds fresh strawberries, trimmed and hulled
2 cups sugar
2 tablespoons cornstarch
1 cup water

Mash the strawberries with a potato masher until they are crushed. Measure them; you should have about 2 cups. Mix the sugar with the cornstarch. In a large saucepan, heat the strawberries, sugar mixture, and water over medium heat, stirring, until the sugar has dissolved. Stirring constantly with a wooden spoon or heatproof spatula, raise the heat to medium-high (low altitude) or high (high altitude), and heat to boiling. (The mixture will be *very* hot, so be careful of splatters.) Stirring constantly, boil the mixture for about one minute, or until the mixture is very thick and begins to clear. (It will not clear completely.) Remove from the heat and pour into a heatproof bowl. Allow to cool completely.

Filling
- 1 (8-ounce) package cream cheese, softened
- 1 cup confectioners' sugar, sifted twice
- 2 teaspoons vanilla extract
- 2½ cups chilled heavy whipping cream

Beat the softened cream cheese with the confectioners' sugar and vanilla until smooth. In a separate bowl, whip the cream until it holds soft peaks. (Do not overbeat.) Fold the whipped cream thoroughly into the cream cheese mixture.

To assemble the pie, spread the filling over the cooled crust. Carefully spoon the cooled strawberry topping over the filling until it is completely covered.

Chill the pie thoroughly, at least 4 hours, before serving. If you are chilling the pie overnight, cover it with plastic wrap, which you remove just before cutting.

MAKES 24 SERVINGS

Note: For the topping, it is best to start with about 2 pounds of strawberries before trimming and hulling. You will end up with about 1½ pounds of strawberries. Also, you should prepare the topping before starting on the filling, because it needs to cool completely before being spread on the filling. Finally, this recipe makes about a cup more topping than you need for the pie. Leftover topping must be refrigerated and used within 2 or 3 days. It is delicious on vanilla ice cream or toasted, buttered English muffins.

In-Your-Face Strawberry Pie (II)

Crust

    2½ cups all-purpose flour
    1 tablespoon confectioners' sugar
    1 teaspoon salt
    ½ pound (2 sticks) chilled unsalted butter, cut into
        1-tablespoon pieces and chilled
    ¼ cup chilled lard, cut into 1-tablespoon pieces
        and chilled
    ⅓ cup plus 1 to 3 tablespoons ice water
    1 egg white, lightly beaten
    Additional sugar

In a large bowl (or in the bowl of a food processor fitted with the metal blade), whisk together the flour, sugar, and salt for 10 seconds.

Drop the first four tablespoons of chilled butter on top of the flour mixture, and cut in with two sharp knives (or pulse in the food processor) *just* until the mixture looks like tiny crumbs. (In the food processor, this will take less than a minute.) Repeat with the rest of the butter and the lard, keeping each unused portion of each one well chilled until it is time to cut it into the flour. The mixture will look like large crumbs when you finish adding all the butter and lard.

Sprinkle the water over the top of the mixture, and either mix with a spoon or pulse until the mixture *just* begins to hold together in clumps. If the mixture

is too dry to hold together in clumps, add the additional water until it does. Place 12 ounces of this mixture into one 2-gallon zipped plastic bag. (This will be the top crust.) Put the remaining 15 ounces into another 2-gallon zipped plastic bag. (This will be the bottom crust.) If you do not have a scale, put a little bit more than half of the mixture into one bag, and a little bit less than half into the other. Pressing *very* lightly through the plastic, quickly gather each mixture into a rough circle *in the center of the bag*. Refrigerate the bags of dough until they are *thoroughly* chilled.

When you are ready to make the pie, preheat the oven to 425°. Have a rimmed cookie sheet ready to place underneath the pie.

Remove the bag of dough with the larger amount of dough from the refrigerator. Unzip the bag to ventilate it, then quickly roll out the larger crust (*still inside the zip bag*) to a circle approximately 10 inches in diameter. Using scissors, cut the plastic all the way around the bag and gently lift one side of the plastic. Place the bag, dough side down, in a 9-inch deep-dish pie plate. Gently remove the remaining piece of plastic so that the dough falls into the plate. Make the filling.

Filling
½ cup all-purpose flour
¼ cup cornstarch

1½ to 2 cups granulated sugar, depending on the
   sweetness of the strawberries
6 cups washed, hulled, and halved strawberries

In a small bowl, whisk together the flour, cornstarch,
and sugar. Place the strawberries in a large bowl and
sprinkle the flour mixture over it. Mix thoroughly.

Fill the pie with the strawberry mixture, then repeat the
rolling-out process with the other crust, and place it on
top of the filling. Seal the two crusts together around
the edges, and flute the crust. Using a sharp knife, cut
four or five 2-inch slits in the top crust, to ventilate the
pie. Using a pastry brush, brush the top of the pie with
just enough of the beaten egg white to cover it.
Sprinkle the top crust with a small amount of sugar.

Bake the pie in the lower third of the preheated oven
for 20 minutes, then slide the cookie sheet underneath
the pie and lower the heat to 350°. Continue to bake
the pie until *thick* juices bubble out of the slits, about
35 to 45 minutes.

Remove the cookie sheet and place the pie on a rack.
Allow it to cool *completely*. (Do not serve the pie hot
or warm.)

Serve with best-quality vanilla ice cream.

10–12 SERVINGS

Primavera Pasta Salad

8 ounces pasta
¾ cup chopped fresh scallions
¾ cup grated fresh daikon
2 cups halved best-quality fresh cherry tomatoes
¾ cup finely chopped cilantro
¼ cup (or more) vinaigrette (see below)
Salt and pepper to taste

Cook the pasta and drain it, but do not rinse it. Allow it to cool to room temperature, stirring gently from time to time to keep it from sticking. Mix the pasta with all the chopped vegetables in a large serving bowl. Add vinaigrette until every ingredient is lightly dressed (not slathered). Add more tomatoes, cilantro, or scallions to taste. Salt and pepper to taste. Chill. This salad is best served within 5 hours of being prepared.

4 SERVINGS

Vinaigrette
¼ cup best-quality red wine vinegar
1 tablespoon Dijon mustard
¾ to 1 teaspoon granulated sugar
½ teaspoon salt
½ teaspoon freshly ground black pepper
1 cup best-quality olive oil

Whisk together vinegar, mustard, sugar, salt, and pepper. Slowly whisk in the oil to make an emulsion. Whisk again before adding ¼ cup (or a bit more) to the salad. Refrigerate unused vinaigrette.

Party Pork Chops

4 1-inch-thick pork chops

Brine
  5 cups water
  ¼ cup kosher salt
  ¼ cup sugar

Marinade
  1 teaspoon dried thyme leaves, crumbled
  1 teaspoon dried rosemary, crushed
  2 garlic cloves, pressed
  2 tablespoons balsamic vinegar
  2 tablespoons olive oil

Rinse the pork chops with water and pat them dry with paper towels.

In a large bowl, whisk together the brine until the sugar and salt are dissolved. Place the pork chops in the brine, cover, and brine overnight in the refrigerator.

Drain the brine. Rinse chops in cold water and let stand in cold water 10 minutes. Pat dry.

Whisk together the marinade ingredients. Place pork chops in the marinade and allow them to marinate for 1 hour. (While the pork chops are marinating, you can make the apples; recipe follows.)

Preheat the oven to 375°. On the stove, heat a large sauté pan over medium-high heat, then pour in 2 table-

spoons oil and let it heat until it shimmers. Sear the chops for about 2 minutes on each side (until well caramelized), then flip and do the other sides for 2 minutes. You can either remove them from the pan and place them in a roasting pan, or, if your skillet can be placed in the oven, roast them directly in the pan.

Roast the chops until a thermometer indicates their interior temperature is 145°. While the chops are roasting, reheat the apples. Serve immediately.

4 SERVINGS

Party Apples

6 Granny Smith apples
¼ pound (1 stick) unsalted butter, divided
½ cup packed dark brown sugar
½ cup cognac

Core, peel, and slice the apples. In a wide frying pan or Dutch oven, melt 4 tablespoons of the butter and add the apple slices. Over medium-low heat, cook and stir the apples until they begin to soften, about 5 to 10 minutes. Remove them to a bowl. Melt the remaining butter in the pan and add the brown sugar. Over medium-low heat, stir until the sugar dissolves.

Remove the pan from the heat. Add the cognac to the butter mixture, stir it in, and heat this mixture over medium heat until it begins to boil. Boil for 4 minutes, stirring constantly.

Return the apples to the pan, place the pan over medium heat, and stir occasionally until the apples are hot. Either serve immediately or cool and briefly reheat at serving time.

4–6 SERVINGS

Got-a-Hunch Brunch Rolls

1 teaspoon sugar
¼ cup warm water
1 package active dry yeast
¼ pound (1 stick) unsalted butter, softened to room
    temperature
½ cup honey
1 tablespoon grated lemon zest, finely minced
1 tablespoon grated orange zest, finely minced
2 teaspoons orange extract
½ teaspoon salt
1 tablespoon lemon juice
6 large eggs (3 whole eggs and 3 eggs separated)
½ cup milk, warmed to 110°
1 tablespoon vital wheat gluten
5 to 6 cups bread flour
½ cup plus 2 tablespoons best-quality bittersweet
    orange marmalade

In a large bowl, stir together the sugar, water, and yeast. Allow to proof for ten minutes.

In another large bowl, beat the butter until creamy, about 5 minutes. Blend in the honey and beat until thoroughly combined. Add the zests, extract, salt, and juice. Beat until well combined. (Mixture will look curdled.)

Refrigerate the egg whites, covered, until you are ready to bake the rolls. Add the egg yolks and whole eggs one at a time to the butter mixture, and beat in thoroughly. Add the yeast mixture and the milk and beat on low speed until thoroughly combined. Set aside.

Mix the gluten into the flour. Add the flour mixture one cup at a time, beating thoroughly after each addition. Switch to a wooden spoon or dough hook when the dough becomes too stiff to beat. When the dough is pliable and only slightly sticky, turn it out onto a floured surface and knead vigorously for 10 minutes. (Alternatively, you can knead using the dough hook for 10 minutes.)

Place the dough into a large, oiled bowl, cover with a clean dish towel, and set it in a warm, draft-free place to rise until doubled in bulk, 1 to 1½ hours.

Punch the dough down, turn it out onto a board, and allow it to rest for 10 minutes. Divide it into 24 equal-size pieces. Butter two 12-cup muffin tins.

Keep the rolls you are not working with covered with a dish towel. Take each piece of dough, flatten it into a 4-inch circle, and spread with 1 teaspoon marmalade in the center, leaving ½ inch of space around the edge. Carefully roll the dough into a cylinder, pinch the ends, and pull the ends under to make a round roll. Carefully place each roll into a muffin cup. When you have filled all the rolls, cover them with a dish towel and allow them to rise until doubled, about one hour.

Preheat the oven to 350°.

Remove the egg whites from the refrigerator and whisk them until frothy. Using a pastry brush, paint the top of each roll. You will have egg white left over.

Bake a dozen at a time, until they are puffed and golden brown, and sound hollow when tapped, about 15 minutes. Cool on racks.

MAKES 2 DOZEN

The Whole Enchilada Pie

1 pound ground beef
1 medium-size onion, chopped
2 garlic cloves, pressed
⅓ cup bottled picante sauce
1 (16-ounce) can refried beans
1 (10-ounce) can enchilada sauce
1 cup sliced, pitted black California olives
1 teaspoon salt
6 cups crushed corn chips
3 cups grated cheddar cheese

Garnishes
Sour cream
Chopped fresh tomatoes
Sliced iceberg lettuce
Chopped green onions
Avocado slices

Preheat the oven to 375°. Grease a 9-by-13-inch glass pan.

In a wide frying pan set over medium heat, brown the ground beef with the onion and garlic until the beef is brown and the onion is soft.

Lower the heat and add the picante, beans, enchilada sauce, olives, and salt. Stir and cook until well combined and bubbly. Remove from the heat.

Place 1 cup of the chips in the bottom of the glass pan. Put half the beef mixture on top. Top with another cup of the chips and 1½ cups cheese (half the cheese). Put in the rest of the beef mixture, then the rest of the chips, then the rest of the cheese.

Bake the pie for 30 to 40 minutes, or until the center is hot and bubbly. (You can test the temperature by taking a small spoonful from the center.) Serve immediately with bowls filled with the garnishes.

8 SERVINGS

Goldy's Nuthouse Cookies

1½ cups blanched, slivered almonds, toasted and
   cooled
½ teaspoon baking soda
½ teaspoon salt
1¼ cups (4½ ounces) cake flour
1 cup (4½ ounces) all-purpose flour
½ pound (2 sticks) unsalted butter, softened to
   room temperature
2⅔ cups (10 ounces) sifted confectioners' sugar
1 large egg
1 teaspoon vanilla extract

Blend the almonds, baking soda, salt, and flours; set
aside.

In a large mixing bowl, beat the butter until creamy,
about 5 minutes. Add the sugar and beat on medium
low until very creamy, about 5 minutes. Reduce the
beater speed to low and add the egg and vanilla; continue to beat until well blended. Stir in the flour mixture just until well combined; do not overbeat.

Divide the batter into 3 equal pieces and equally dis-
tribute them in the bottom of zipped plastic freezer
bags. Roll each section of the dough into logs. Zip
the bags closed and place them in the freezer
overnight.

Preheat the oven to 350°.

Remove one log at a time from the freezer. While each log is still frozen, place it on a cutting board. Use a large, sharp knife to divide each log into 24 equal pieces. Place 12 of the cookies on an ungreased Silpat sheet on top of a cookie sheet. Flatten each cold cookie slightly with the palm of your hand. When the first two dozen cookies are baked and cooling, you may remove another roll from the freezer and start on it. (The cookies hold together better, cook more evenly, and develop a better texture if they are placed in the oven while they are still frozen.)

Bake one sheet at a time for about 10 minutes, or until the cookies have turned golden brown at the edges. Rotate the cookie sheets from front to back after 5 minutes. Cool completely on racks.

MAKES 6 DOZEN

Handcuff Croissants

4 croissants, split lengthwise
1 cup mayonnaise
1½-ounce jar marinated artichoke hearts, drained
    and chopped
1 cup crabmeat, flaked
⅓ cup Parmesan cheese, shredded
⅓ cup Gruyère cheese, shredded
4 green onions, chopped

Crumb crust
2 tablespoons unsalted butter, melted
1 garlic clove, crushed
1 cup soft bread crumbs
2 tablespoons finely chopped parsley
¼ teaspoon dried rosemary, crushed
¼ teaspoon dried thyme
¼ teaspoon dried oregano
¼ teaspoon dried marjoram

Preheat the oven to 350°.

Place the croissant halves on a Silpat sheet on a large rimmed cookie sheet. Mix the next six ingredients in a bowl, and spread this mixture on top of the croissant halves.

Melt the butter in a small frying pan and cook the garlic in it over low heat until translucent. Mix the rest of the ingredients for the crumb crust, then mix in the garlic and melted butter. Top each croissant with the crumb mixture.

Bake the croissants for 15 to 20 minutes, or until heated through.

8 SERVINGS

Trudy's Mediterranean Chicken

Sauce
  ½ cup olive oil, divided
  3 medium-size onions, thinly sliced
  6 garlic cloves, pressed
  2 cups tomato juice
  ½ cup sherry
  1 teaspoon salt, divided
  ¾ teaspoon paprika, divided

  4 boneless, skinless chicken breasts
  ½ cup all-purpose flour

Make the sauce first. In a large frying pan, heat ¼ cup olive oil over medium heat until it shimmers. Add the onions and immediately turn the heat to low. Stir and cook the onions for 1 minute, then add the garlic. Stir and cook over low heat until the onions are soft and translucent. Add the juice, sherry, ½ teaspoon salt, and ½ teaspoon paprika. Stir and cook until the mixture bubbles. Cover and keep over low heat while you prepare the chicken breasts.

Rinse the chicken breasts and dry them thoroughly with paper towels. Spread out a sheet of plastic wrap approximately 2 feet long and place the chicken breasts on it. Spread another sheet of plastic wrap over the chicken breasts. Using the flat side of a mallet, pound the chicken breasts between the plas-

tic to an even ½-inch thickness. Remove the plastic wrap.

Whisk the flour and the remaining salt and paprika together on a large plate. Dip the chicken breasts one at a time into the mixture, until they are completely dusted.

Preheat the oven to 350°. Grease a 9-by-13-inch glass pan.

In another large frying pan, heat the remaining ¼ cup olive oil over medium heat, just until it shimmers. Place the chicken in the pan and cook until seared on each side, approximately 3 minutes per side. Place the chicken in the glass pan. Pour the hot sauce over it. Place in the oven and cook *just* until the chicken is done, approximately 20 minutes. Serve immediately.

4 SERVINGS

Double-Shot Chocolate Cake

10 ounces unsalted butter
10 ounces bittersweet chocolate, broken into small
  pieces (recommended brand: Godiva dark)
¾ cup plus 3 tablespoons extra-fine granulated
  sugar
2 tablespoons Dutch-style cocoa (recommended
  brand: Hershey's Premium European-Style)
8 large eggs
1 teaspoon vanilla extract
Confectioners' sugar
Sweetened whipped cream or best-quality vanilla
  ice cream

Preheat the oven to 350°.

Butter a 10-by-1½-inch heavy-duty round cake pan.
Line the bottom with parchment cut to fit. Butter the
parchment. Set aside.

Fill a 16-by-11-inch roasting pan with 1 inch of hot
water, place the roasting pan on a baking sheet, and
put it into the oven.

In the top of a double boiler, melt the butter with the
chocolate. When the ingredients are melted, remove
the pan from the heat to cool slightly. Sift the sugar
with the cocoa twice, then whisk it into the melted
chocolate mixture.

In a large mixing bowl, beat the eggs until they are foamy. Add the vanilla and the chocolate mixture. Blend with a spatula until very well mixed.

Carefully pour the batter into the prepared cake pan. Gently place the cake pan in the water-filled roasting pan.

Bake about 40 to 50 minutes, or until the cake begins to shrink slightly from the sides and a toothpick inserted in the center comes out clean. Place on a rack to cool for 15 minutes, then invert carefully and peel off the paper. Allow to cool completely.

Just before serving time, carefully place a 9- or 10-inch cake stencil on top of the cake. Sift confectioners' sugar over the stencil, then remove the stencil.

Serve with sweetened whipped cream or best-quality vanilla ice cream.

16 SERVINGS

Brownie Points

12 tablespoons (1½ sticks) unsalted butter
6 ounces unsweetened chocolate, broken into small pieces
1 tablespoon unsweetened alkalinized cocoa (recommended brand: Hershey's Premium European-Style)
1¼ cups cake flour (high altitude: add 2 tablespoons)
¾ teaspoon baking powder
¼ teaspoon salt
4 large eggs
2¼ cups sugar (high altitude: subtract 2 tablespoons)
2 teaspoons vanilla extract
1½ cups chopped pecans, lightly toasted and cooled

Preheat the oven to 325°. Butter a 9-by-13-inch metal (not glass) baking pan.

Melt the butter with the chocolate in the top of a double boiler (over boiling water), stirring frequently. When the chocolate has melted, set the mixture aside to cool.

Sift together the cocoa, flour, baking powder, and salt. Sift again and set aside.

Beat the eggs until they are well combined, then gradually add the sugar, beating constantly. Add the vanilla and the cooled chocolate mixture, stirring until well combined. Sift the dry mixture over the egg mixture, and stir this mixture only until it is completely combined. Spread the batter in the prepared pan, and sprinkle the nuts on top.

Bake for 25 to 30 minutes, or until a toothpick inserted in the center comes out with only a crumb or two adhering to it. Remove to a rack and cool completely.

MAKES 16 LARGE OR 32 SMALL BROWNIES

Strip Show Steaks

4 ½-inch-thick, 8-ounce *prime-grade* boneless rib
  steaks (available through mail order or from a
  good butcher)
1 teaspoon salt, divided
1 teaspoon dried thyme, divided

Place the steaks in a large glass pan. Rub ¼ teaspoon
salt and ¼ teaspoon thyme into each steak.

Preheat the grill following the manufacturer's instructions. When the grill is ready, grill for 3 minutes per
side, or until done to your satisfaction. Do not over-
cook.

4 SERVINGS

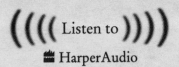

(((((Listen to)))))

HarperAudio

DIANE MOTT DAVIDSON DOUBLE SHOT

Unabridged CD
Performed by Barbara Rosenblat
10 Hours/9 CDs
0-06-073876-6 $39.95/$56.95 Can.

CD
Performed by Patricia Kalember
6 Hours/5 CDs
0-06-073875-8 $29.95/$42.50 Can.

Large Print
0-06-074243-7 $24.95/$34.95 Can.

www.dianemottdavidson.com

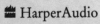

HarperAudio
An Imprint of HarperCollinsPublishers
www.harpercollins.com

ALSO AVAILABLE
Harper
LARGE
PRINT
Edition

AuthorTracker

Don't miss the next book by your
favorite author. Sign up now for
AuthorTracker bey visiting
www.AuthorTracker.com

10/07 sb

Carnival Pride℠
April 2 - 9, 2006.

7 Day Exotic Mexican Riviera Itinerary

DAY	PORT	ARRIVE	DEPART
Sun	Los Angeles/Long Beach, CA		4:00 P.M.
Mon	"Book Lover's" Day at Sea		
Tue	"Book Lover's" Day at Sea		
Wed	Puerto Vallarta, Mexico	8:00 A.M.	10:00 P.M.
Thu	Mazatlan, Mexico	9:00 A.M.	6:00 P.M.
Fri	Cabo San Lucas, Mexico	7:00 A.M.	4:00 P.M.
Sat	"Book Lover's" Day at Sea		
Sun	Los Angeles/Long Beach, CA	9:00 A.M.	

ports of call subject to weather conditions

TERMS AND CONDITIONS

PAYMENT SCHEDULE:
50% due upon booking
Full and final payment due by February 10, 2006

Acceptable forms of payment are Visa, MasterCard, American Express, Discover and checks. The cardholder must be one of the passengers traveling. A fee of $25 will apply for all returned checks. Check payments must be made payable to **Advantage International, LLC** and sent to: **Advantage International, LLC, 195 North Harbor Drive, Suite 4206, Chicago, IL 60601**

CHANGE/CANCELLATION:
Notice of change/cancellation must be made in writing to Advantage International, LLC.

Change:
Changes in cabin category may be requested and can result in increased rate and penalties. A name change is permitted 60 days or more prior to departure and will incur a penalty of $50 per name change. Deviation from the group schedule and package is a cancellation.

Cancellation:
181 days or more prior to departure	$250 per person
121 - 180 days or more prior to departure	50% of the package price
120 - 61 days prior to departure	75% of the package price
60 days or less prior to departure	100% of the package price (nonrefundable)

US and Canadian citizens are required to present a valid passport or the original birth certificate and state issued photo ID (drivers license). All other nationalities must contact the consulate of the various ports that are visited for verification of documentation.

<u>**We strongly recommend trip cancellation insurance!**</u>

For complete details call 1-877-ADV-NTGE or visit www.AuthorsAtSea.com

---

For booking form and complete information
go to **www.AuthorsAtSea.com** or call **1-877-ADV-NTGE**

Complete coupon and booking form and mail both to:
Advantage International, LLC,
195 North Harbor Drive, Suite 4206, Chicago, IL 60601